T0347345

White Fire

Adam Hamdy is a bestselling author and screenwriter. He lives elsewhere with his wife, Amy, and their three children, Maya, Elliot and Thomas.

By Adam Hamdy

Pendulum Trilogy
Pendulum
Freefall
Aftershock

The Scott Pearce Series
Black 13
Red Wolves
White Fire

Writing with James Patterson
Private Moscow
Private Rogue
Private Beijing

Standalone Novels
The Other Side of Night
The Girl Beyond Forever

ADAM HAMDY

White Fire

PAN BOOKS

First published 2023 by Pan Books
an imprint of Pan Macmillan
The Smithson, 6 Briset Street, London EC1M 5NR
EU representative: Macmillan Publishers Ireland Ltd, 1st Floor,
The Liffey Trust Centre, 117–126 Sheriff Street Upper,
Dublin 1, DO1 YC43
Associated companies throughout the world
www.panmacmillan.com

ISBN 978-1-5098-9928-9

9 8 7 6 5 4 3 2

A CIP catalogue record for this book is available from the British Library.

Typeset in Scala by Jouve (UK), Milton Keynes
Printed and bound by CPI Group (UK) Ltd, Croydon, CR0 4YY

MIX
Paper | Supporting
responsible forestry
FSC® C116313

Visit **www.panmacmillan.com** to read more about all our books
and to buy them. You will also find features, author interviews and
news of any author events, and you can sign up for e-newsletters
so that you're always first to hear about our new releases.

For those rising to meet the challenge of climate change.

Chapter 1

She was always free in her dreams. She was on the beach, surrounded by scores of people, her tiny fingers raking the hot sand. Her father was under the parasol, smoking a cigarette, telling her to come out of the sun. She burned easily, a consequence of her albinism, but she loved the warmth against her skin. She was seven years old, and she was happy and free. She looked down at her paper-white shoulder and saw nothing but skin. This was before the patch that had ruined her life. She longed to go back to those times. She looked at her father, who drew on his cigarette and smiled at her.

Brigitte Attali woke to the sound of her alarm. It had been two months since she'd become a captive to a toxin that was both capable of killing her and keeping her alive. She wore a black elastic armband over the XTX patch that had been stuck to her shoulder by Li Jun Xiao during the Red Wolves investigation. Ever since then, her morning routine had been the same; check she was still alive, then lift the elastic armband to make sure the patch was still stuck to her skin. She examined it now and found it firmly attached to her body like a parasite. She rolled out of bed and walked to the bathroom of her king-size suite in the Barbizon Hotel. The lights came on automatically, and she caught the reflection of her naked body in the large mirror over the basin. She'd lost weight these past few weeks, and her ribs were obvious, coiled around her like bony fingers, but she wasn't sure whether it was a consequence of the toxin or worry about the future. She'd faced death many times, but this was different. It wasn't a one-off event, an assault or incursion into hostile territory. This was an ever-present danger, looking over her like a brooding cloud. Sometimes she felt as if the grim reaper was lurking in the shadows of her life.

The patch on her shoulder delivered a mind-altering dose of fentanyl, and an engineered toxin called XTX that attacked and destroyed her parathyroid glands, shutting down her body's ability to synthesize oxygen. The patch's third ingredient was the hormone PTH, the very hormone the parathyroid glands produced. Without the patch's replacement supply of PTH, the XTX already in her system would kill her within moments, and she needed a new one every week.

The US National Institutes of Health had been working on a cure for all those affected by the patches – sold as containing fentanyl only – ever since she and Pearce had broken the Red Wolves and foiled their attack on America, but so far attempts to reverse the effects of the patch had proved fruitless. Brigitte had been forced to get used to a new and troubling existence and come to terms with the fact her life would likely be shortened by her condition. She'd spent weeks researching the XTX toxin and what it did to the parathyroid gland. In normal circumstances, the parathyroid gland could exhibit reduced activity or even be surgically removed if necessary, but in extreme cases it went into what was known as parathyroid crisis, which led to respiratory failure. XTX induced parathyroid crisis, and without the PTH hormone released by her patch, Brigitte would die in a matter of minutes. The stress of a death sentence had weighed heavily and it had taken her weeks to learn how to sleep again and get over the anxiety the patch would come off in the night. Eventually, after relying on sleeping pills to knock her out, she'd realized she wouldn't accidentally rip the armband or patch off in her sleep. The nightmares of waking for her last few gasped breaths didn't stop, though.

Brigitte opened her vanity case and unzipped the plastic pouch which contained her replacement patches. She had brought a dozen with her, enough for three months. She took one out, aware of how much she hated the infernal thing that was now keeping her alive. She peeled off the blister wrapper, removed the backing and placed the pouch face down on the counter. She pulled her armband down and peeled the used patch from her shoulder. Once it was off, she started to feel the effects of its absence. Her chest tightened and her heart rate jumped a notch. Her body was beginning to lose the ability to process oxygen. If she didn't apply the new patch, she would start to suffocate within three minutes. In four, she would pass out and after five she'd be dead.

She looked at herself in the mirror and wondered why she was fighting the inevitable. She'd thought about leaving it off many times before, but something had always stopped her. Maybe she was sentimental and had grown attached to her life, no matter how tortured and pathetic. But perhaps here, in this anonymous hotel room, she could—

She was interrupted by a knock at the door. She knew who it would be, and didn't want him to be the one who discovered her body. She applied the new patch, replaced the armband and threw on a robe. The fentanyl high hit as she tied the belt, but she was used to it now, and knew to relax into the rolling sensation that made the world seem as though it was melting around her.

She steadied herself, left the bathroom and pressed her eye to the spyhole to see Scott Pearce.

Chapter 2

Brigitte Attali had first been an enemy, then a colleague, and now a friend. She'd been a formidable adversary when they'd first encountered one another during the Black Thirteen investigation, but as he'd got to know her, Pearce had realized the hard-as-nails exterior concealed a vulnerable core. That vulnerability had become clear when she'd confided in him about the patch, revealing a weakness that might someday kill her. Ever since then, Pearce had wanted to protect her, and in a different life his feelings might have developed into something more, but their work was all-consuming and suffocated any personal relationships. Pearce had spent years giving all of himself to the job, first in the military, then in the intelligence service. When he'd been a green recruit, he'd had a vague ambition to start a family one day, but as the years ground on and he'd realized how difficult it was to meet someone and maintain a relationship, the ambition had faded. Like him, Brigitte had given herself to this life and their connection would never be anything more than professional. She was dedicated, even in the face of terrible adversity, and he admired her all the more for it.

Her eyes still shone with their customary defiance, but there was a frailty in them now. She was like a dragon made of glass, formidable at first glance, but delicate and fragile to those who took a closer look.

'I can do another hour if you like,' he said.

'I'm sorry,' she replied. 'I was just getting dressed.'

'It's no problem.'

They'd been alternating surveillance shifts, doing ten hours on and ten off, and it was time for their handover. Pearce was meant to stay in the lobby until she came down, but he'd been worried about her. He sometimes wondered how Brigitte managed to sleep with the patch that had ruined her life clinging to her. He'd have constantly been worried it would come off in the night.

'Give me two minutes to get dressed,' she said.

'It's really no problem,' he said.

'Scott,' she replied in her thick Parisienne accent, 'let me do my job. I don't want to sit in my room watching the clock. I want to do what we came here for.'

Pearce nodded. He might not understand how she could live with the patch, but he understood the need to throw herself into the job. He'd been doing the same for years. People let him down, hurt him, betrayed him, but the job was a constant. It had always been there, challenging him, pushing him, demanding his best.

'I'll relieve you at five,' he said.

Brigitte nodded and shut the door. Pearce lingered for a moment, before walking along the corridor to his own room. He used his key card to enter, kicked off his shoes and fell onto his freshly made bed. Within moments, he was asleep.

Chapter 3

Pearce managed to get his head down for ten minutes before Brigitte called him. Their target was on the move, and minutes later, Pearce had joined the pursuit on the streets of Amsterdam.

The canals were like veins, keeping the city alive. A testament to a bygone generation, they'd held the angry sea at bay and protected Amsterdam from being overrun. They shimmered a deep black and, here and there, in the darkest corners of the city, the moon and stars could be seen reflected in surfaces the colour of the slickest crude. Pearce hurried to stay within sight of their target, Nikos Kitsantonis, the Greek billionaire who was their only link to the man they knew as Elroy Lang.

Lang had been behind the Red Wolves' plot to take over the drug trade on the West Coast of America and had been responsible for countless deaths in Cairo and Seattle. He'd cursed Brigitte Attali with the XTX patch that both poisoned her and kept her alive. Pearce watched her now, on the other side of the canal, about a football pitch ahead of him. She was staying level with Nikos, doing an excellent job of tracking him without appearing to do so. Pearce knew she'd be sporting the scowl that had become her trademark ever since the fateful night in Qingdao when she'd been abducted and afflicted with the patch. It didn't take a psychic to know Brigitte burned with a single-minded desire for vengeance against Lang, and the fire hadn't subsided in the months since Seattle. Pearce was drawn to her anger and determination almost as much as her vulnerability.

'He's taking a left,' Pearce said quietly into his lapel microphone.

Up ahead, Brigitte crossed a bridge and joined Prinsengracht about fifty paces behind Nikos.

Pearce followed them and turned left onto a broad street. Prinsengracht was one of the city's widest canals, and four-and five-storey terrace buildings stood either side of the expanse of water. The surface glinted in the reflected light spilling through the uncovered windows. Dutch tradition discouraged blinds or curtains and many of the city's homes were open for Pearce to see as he passed, but etiquette required passers-by not to pry. Privacy by consensus rather than concealment.

Pearce wondered what secrets Nikos was concealing. The one photo Leila Nahum, Pearce's long-time friend and collaborator, had been able to find of Elroy Lang was from six years ago and showed Lang in the background of a picture taken at one of Nikos's business launches. The billionaire ran his own investment fund, NK Capital, and had interests in hundreds of companies around the world. Leila's image crawler had taken weeks to pull this one picture of Lang and match it to the drone footage they'd taken outside the Lightstar Arena in Seattle. Whoever had scrubbed Lang's likeness from the Internet had overlooked this one, tiny, partial image of him in the background.

When Leila had returned to Jordan to search for her

missing sister, Pearce and Brigitte had picked up Nikos's trail and followed him for weeks – from London to New York, then to Istanbul and finally to Amsterdam. He usually went everywhere with a sizeable security entourage, but tonight, when he'd left the Barbizon Hotel on the edge of the city's red-light district, he had been alone for the first time in weeks.

Pearce and Brigitte had been taking shifts in the lobby, working as a pair whenever Nikos and his men left the hotel. Ideally, Pearce would have liked another two people in the team, but Leila was looking for her sister, and Kyle Wollerton was spending time with his family. Pearce didn't know who else he could trust with this, so he and Brigitte carried the burden.

Nikos crossed the street and went over Museumburg, a short bridge that spanned the canal and led to the Rijks-museum, one of Amsterdam's most famous landmarks. The huge red-brick nineteenth-century building looked like the gothic palace of some goblin king, but any monsters inside tonight would be in human form. It was lit up with spotlights and banners celebrating Rembrandt's birthday. A crowd of people gathered outside the main entrance and a line of luxury cars deposited guests onto a broad red carpet. Most wore expensive cocktail dresses or black ties, and as he approached, Nikos looked out of place in his trademark suit and open-collared shirt. He joined the queue of people waiting to be checked by security.

Pearce caught up with Brigitte.

'We going in?' she asked.

Her distinctive white hair was concealed beneath a blonde wig, and she had brown contact lenses to hide her blazing blue eyes, but the fire was still there. It was always there, and

Pearce sympathized. He hated Elroy Lang for what he'd done to her. She was so vital and capable, and Lang had permanently damaged her.

Pearce nodded. A couple of security guards were checking the line for guest passes. Pearce and Brigitte waited until Nikos had reached the front of the line, and once he'd been allowed inside, they walked past the queuing glitterati, ignoring the grumbling, and presented themselves to the guard who'd admitted Nikos.

'AIVD,' Pearce said, showing a fake Dutch Intelligence and Security Service ID.

Brigitte did likewise.

'Problem?' the security guard asked.

'*Nee*,' Pearce replied in Dutch. '*Routine controle*.'

The guard nodded them through, and they climbed the concrete steps and went inside.

There were more security guards in the lobby, searching bags, but Pearce and Brigitte flashed their AIVD identification and were waved into the grand hall, which was buzzing with the sound of hundreds of people celebrating one of the Netherlands' most famous artists. The walls were lined with the old master's brooding artwork, and guests gathered in small clusters to admire the massive oil paintings. Banners hung from the ceilings and cocktail servers circulated, topping up drinks.

'I never liked Rembrandt,' Brigitte said. 'Too dark. One day I'll take you to see the Monet exhibition in Paris, and you'll see art that brims with life.'

'I'd like that,' Pearce replied.

He scanned the room and saw Nikos heading through an archway to their left.

Brigitte and Pearce followed and entered a long, broad gallery that took up nearly all of the south-east wing of the building. The room wasn't as crowded as the main hall and a couple of dozen guests drifted through the space in small groups, studying the works of Rembrandt and his students. Further on, Nikos joined two people who stood in front of a trio of portraits of Dutch aristocrats.

Pearce took a pair of glasses from his jacket pocket and activated the digital video capture system. He watched as the duo turned to greet Nikos. One of them was a glamorous woman who stood almost six feet tall in her needle-sharp heels. She had long silver hair that cascaded down her green evening dress. The woman was a stranger, but Pearce knew the man who was standing alongside her. It was Elroy Lang, the killer he and Brigitte had been hunting for two months. Pearce sensed Brigitte tense with furious energy, and he took her arm and moved behind a column to avoid being seen. Lang could lead him to Markus Kral, the man Pearce had seen in Seattle and Oxfordshire, the man who connected British far-right group Black Thirteen and the Red Wolves, an international criminal organization with roots in Chinese nationalism. Pearce hadn't expected to run into Lang tonight. They had to be careful.

'Don't do anything stupid,' Pearce said.

'I'm going to kill him,' Brigitte replied.

Pearce sensed movement and saw a man in a black suit peel away from the group he'd been standing with. He headed towards them with a look of purpose, and when Pearce glanced around the room, he realized three other men in suits were converging on them. Nikos might have come without his security detail, but Lang had brought muscle.

'We've been made,' Pearce warned Brigitte.

Chapter 4

Pearce glanced round the column to see Lang leading Nikos and the silver-haired woman along the gallery.

'You take Lang,' he told Brigitte. 'I'll deal with them.'

Brigitte nodded and hurried after Lang and the others. One of the four suited men tried to follow her, but Pearce rushed him, and delivered a rapid combination of punches that startled him and the gathered guests. His violence had disrupted the considered calm of the evening, and shocked eyes widened when Pearce punched the dazed man's windpipe. As the injured man doubled over, Pearce heard collective gasps from around the room. He sensed movement to his rear, and turned to see one of the other suited assailants produce a pistol.

Someone screamed at the sight of the gun, starting a rush of guests towards the main hall, and Pearce grabbed the collar of the man he'd punched in the throat and hauled him round to use as a shield, the instant before gunshots rang through the gallery. The man cried out and bucked as bullets struck his torso. Pearce drove his wounded captive towards the shooter and gained sufficient momentum to hurl the man at his horrified accomplice.

Pearce didn't give the shooter time to breathe and struck him on both ears with the heels of his palms. The shooter's hands went up instinctively, and he dropped his gun and tried to soothe the pain of ruptured eardrums, as the other two suited assailants bore down on him. Pearce caught the pistol before it hit the floor and wheeled round to shoot the men rushing towards him. He caught the first in the shoulder and the second in the leg and both men crumpled in pain.

The shooter made a vain attempt to recover his weapon, but Pearce clocked him in the face, knocking him cold. Pearce looked towards the main hall and saw museum security guards pressing through the gawking crowd. He turned the other way and sprinted along the gallery in pursuit of Brigitte.

'Where are you?' he said into his concealed mic.

'*South gallery,*' Brigitte replied through his earpiece. '*They're heading for a fire exit.*'

A moment later, fire alarms sounded throughout the building and Pearce glanced over his shoulder to see the crowd sweeping towards the main entrance. Two security guards broke through the herd and sprinted into the gallery, some distance behind him.

He ran right, into the south gallery, where custodians were helping guests to the nearest fire exit. Pearce joined the exodus and felt a breath of cool November air as he made it outside. Some of the finely dressed guests gathered in the museum grounds, while others made their way towards the gates. Pearce searched the area, but saw no sign of Brigitte.

'Where are you?' he asked again.

'*South-east corner,*' Brigitte replied breathlessly. '*Heading for Hobbemakade.*'

She was talking about the main road that ran to the east of the museum.

'I'm on my way,' Pearce told her, and he started running.

He sprinted past a long hedge, and across a semi-circular

patch of grass that was edged by a wide path where partygoers gathered, already talking excitedly about the evening's drama. As he made it to the far end of the hedge, Pearce caught sight of Brigitte near the edge of the grounds. Elroy Lang, Nikos Kitsantonis and the woman with grey hair ran ahead of her, but when they reached Hobbemakade, they split up. Nikos and the grey-haired woman went north, and Lang ran south. Brigitte didn't even hesitate. She sprinted after the man who'd cursed her with the XTX patch that had come to define her life.

Lang shot out of sight behind a building that stood at the very south-east corner of the museum grounds, and moments later Brigitte followed him. Pearce thought about going after Nikos and the unknown woman, but Lang was dangerous and he couldn't leave Brigitte to tackle him alone.

He gasped lungfuls like an air-hungry turbo and his legs pounded furiously as he chased them both down.

'*He's heading for the next bridge,*' Brigitte said.

'Copy that,' Pearce replied. 'I'm right behind you.'

Chapter 5

There was a special place in hell reserved for the man she was chasing, and Brigitte burned with the desire to cast him down. She'd felt depressed when Pearce had come to her room, but she'd come to life with rage and hatred for the man who had ruined her, and thoughts of her own death couldn't be further from her mind.

Pearce wanted to use Lang to lead him to Markus Kral, AKA Andel Novak, a shadowy figure who'd been photographed with Lang outside the Lightstar Arena the night of the Red Wolves' XTX attack. Pearce had also linked him to Black Thirteen, and was convinced Kral was a key player in whatever they were up against. Pearce wanted Lang to get to Kral, but Brigitte just wanted Lang dead. She redoubled her efforts and sprinted after Lang, who shot across the street and darted over Brandweer Bridge, a short crossing that connected the museum quarter with a residential neighbourhood. Brigitte raced over the bridge and followed Lang along a street that was flanked by low-rise apartment blocks. Brigitte caught a sudden sweet smell of marijuana as she ran through a cloud of smoke spilling from an open ground-floor window. Someone yelled something in Dutch, but she was moving too fast to make out the words. She was intent on revenge, and her burning lungs and aching legs hardly registered as she pictured the things she was going to do to Lang when she got her hands on him. Pearce wanted the man alive, but Pearce wasn't here.

She glanced over her shoulder and saw him running across the bridge. He was a good man, she'd come to appreciate that during the Red Wolves investigation, but the world was running out of need for good men. It needed people prepared to do dreadful things to send monsters like Lang back into the shadows.

Up ahead Lang disappeared into a tiny passageway between two apartment blocks. Brigitte followed, turning south and running into a narrow alleyway that was hardly wider than her shoulders. Five-storey brown brick blocks loomed over her, the edges of their rooftops almost meeting high above her head. She raced into darkness and felt her way in pitch-black for a few moments before she caught the faint outline of the walls at the end of the alleyway. She picked up speed as she made out leaves, branches and a tree in the distance. She was heading for a courtyard garden that connected the surrounding apartment buildings.

The blow came out of nowhere, a punch to the temple that sent Brigitte reeling as she burst out of the alleyway. Her determination to catch Lang had overwhelmed her caution and she'd paid the price. She staggered sideways and raised her arms to defend herself against a flurry of punches as Lang bore down on her. He was fast and strong. Her head was ringing and her vision blurring. She lashed out with a kick and felt it connect with his gut. He staggered back and she took the opportunity to move towards the centre of the courtyard, clearing her head with each step until she made it to the heart of a small residents' park. A few families were having evening picnics and in the distance a gaggle of teenagers gathered in a small playground.

Lang sprinted towards her and Brigitte braced as he tackled her. She drove an elbow into his back as they fell, and she heard cries from the gathered families as she hit the deck. Lang punched her and she covered her face as best she could. She cried out when he drove his fists into her ribcage. Then there was a groan and the blows stopped.

Brigitte looked up to see Lang being hauled back by two of the men who'd been sitting with their families.

'No!' she shouted, but she was too late.

Lang drove the heel of his palm into the first man's nose, sending shattered bone into his brain, and punched the second man's windpipe, collapsing it. As her two would-be rescuers fell to the ground, people all around the courtyard cried out and scattered, and Brigitte got to her feet. She was badly hurt, but pain meant nothing to her; adrenalin and fentanyl blunted its sharpest edge. She turned to face Lang defiantly. He had to die.

'Brigitte Attali,' Lang said. 'Real name Chloe Duval.'

How did he know her name? That information was buried deep within Mortier, the headquarters of the French Intelligence agency.

'Former DGSE agent and traitor to Black Thirteen. You are going to beg for me to kill you,' Lang said. 'But I won't. Not until you tell me who you and Pearce are working for.'

Lang launched himself at her with a combination of vicious punches and kicks that she did her best to block. She replied with a roundhouse and her heel caught his temple, knocking him back, dazed. She followed with a rapid flurry of punches, but he hit her with an uppercut that seemed to materialize on her chin. Her teeth clattered and her head swam with ringing pain, and he showed no mercy as he drove his fist into her solar plexus, winding her. Brigitte staggered back, and Lang sensed his advantage. He launched a savage attack, kicking and punching her until she was on her knees.

Brigitte gasped for air and coughed up blood. She spat a big gob on the grass and wiped tears from her eyes. She had never been beaten in single combat. The closest she'd come to defeat had been against Pearce, but Lang had demolished her.

'You and I will go somewhere private and you will tell me exactly what I want to know,' Lang said, looming over her. 'Then you will die.'

Brigitte tried to stand, but Lang knocked her back with a single punch, and she fell to her knees. She could hear sirens in the distance, but they would do her no good. Lang moved behind her, crouched, put his arm around her neck and hauled her to her feet.

'My people are on their way,' he said.

Brigitte felt the rough hand of unconsciousness clawing at her perception, and everything seemed to go distant. If this man took her, Huxley Blaine Carter, her employer, would be exposed, and Pearce and the others would die. Everything they'd worked for would be undone.

As she was dragged across the now deserted park, Brigitte realized there was only one way she could escape. She stopped her ineffectual struggling against Lang and reached her right hand into her top. Her fingernails caught the edge of the armband, and she pulled it down to expose the patch on her left shoulder. She said a silent prayer, asking for forgiveness for all her wrongs, and tore it off. She scrunched the patch into a sticky ball that would be impossible to undo, and as she felt her lungs tighten, she held it in front of Lang.

'You . . .' he said, trying to grab the patch.

She threw the ball into nearby bushes and staggered away from the man, gasping, trying to suck in air that was no longer of any use to her. She was losing the ability to process oxygen.

'Stupid,' Lang said. 'You have another one.'

He grabbed her and searched her pockets. He didn't notice her shaking her head weakly. She usually carried spares, but not tonight, not when they might go somewhere she could be searched. She didn't want to risk a security guard touching one of the cursed patches by accident.

When he didn't find another patch, Lang pushed her away in frustration. He hesitated. The sirens were close now, and she could see he knew it would be futile to stay much longer.

'Who are you working for?' he said, wrapping his fingers around her throat.

It was the last gambit of a desperate man. There was no air to squeeze from her. Brigitte laughed. Only the sound she made wasn't one of joy, it was the choking rattle of a dying animal.

Lang punched her in frustration, and she fell onto cool grass and watched him run south towards one of the apartment blocks.

Brigitte's lungs were on fire and her throat burned with the desire for another breath, but she'd taken her last. She was weeping and black tendrils tore her vision. She didn't have long. She forced herself up and sat cross-legged. She removed her wig and squeezed the contact lenses from her eyes. She would leave the world as she'd been born. As her body grew numb and her senses dimmed, she reflected on all the moments of her sad life. She hadn't been a good person, and she hoped that when she met her maker she would be forgiven for all her failings.

Chapter 6

Pearce heard sirens heading in his direction. He sprinted east along the residential street that led away from the short bridge, past apartment blocks, until he came to the narrow alley between two buildings.

'Brigitte?' he said into his concealed mic.

There was no reply. He'd picked up sounds of a scuffle but hadn't heard from Brigitte since he'd left the museum grounds. He saw a couple of people dart between the apartment blocks with an air of urgency, and followed them into the narrow alleyway. He ran through the darkness and emerged into a large courtyard flanked by apartment buildings. People were at their windows looking down, and the men Pearce had followed stopped in their tracks just beyond the mouth of the alleyway. A small group of people emerged from a doorway on the other side of the courtyard and Pearce saw some of them were crying. He hurried on, and as he moved beyond a tree that blocked his view, he saw a woman seated on the ground, her head bowed. Her white hair and alabaster skin shone in the evening light. It was Brigitte Attali.

He ran towards her, but knew she was dead before he even reached her. She was utterly still apart from a few wisps of platinum hair that fluttered on the breeze. Beyond her lay the bodies of two men, and as a group of distraught women and children approached, Pearce realized they weren't assailants, but family men, residents, yet more victims of Lang.

Pearce had seen a lot of death, but it never failed to touch him, and tonight was no exception. A lump filled his throat as he laid Attali on her back and straightened her legs. Her striking blue eyes were open, but blank, and the last of her tears rolled down her temples.

He checked her airway and breathed into her mouth before performing chest compressions. He lifted her collar to check her shoulder for the patch she'd revealed to him in Seattle. Her skin was bare, and Pearce knew Brigitte couldn't survive without the thing that had cursed her. She was gone. He sat on his heels and wiped his eyes. She looked at peace, but she was far too young to die, and unless Lang was already lying dead in some corner of this courtyard, her vengeance was unfulfilled.

Pearce sighed and his eyes filled with fresh tears, but he fought the storm of emotion and wiped them clear. He became aware of movement and got to his feet, tensed and ready for a fight, but instead of a threat, he saw fearful, hesitant residents crossing the courtyard to join the families mourning the fallen men. Some of them looked at Pearce uncertainly, but they said nothing and the only sounds that could be heard were the grief of children mourning their fathers and the laments of their widows.

'*Heb je de man gezien die dit deed?*' Pearce asked a grey-haired resident who drifted towards him in stunned silence. *Did you see the man who did this?*

'He ran away,' she replied in English, perhaps recognizing Pearce was stretching his Dutch.

Pearce nodded and watched the two families and their

neighbours grieving the loss of their men. He shared their grief, but unlike these people, Pearce knew he could strike the man who'd done this, delivering vengeance, if not justice.

He looked down at Brigitte and gently closed her eyes. She hadn't deserved what had happened to her, and she didn't deserve this death.

'I will find him,' Pearce promised quietly. 'I will find him and I will kill him.'

The sirens were close now.

He got to his feet and jogged towards the narrow alleyway, eager to put the sounds of grief behind him. Each cry was like a painful accusation, a reminder that he had failed. Brigitte was dead because he'd failed to protect her. He'd failed to stop Elroy Lang in Seattle, and now three more bodies were growing cold because Pearce hadn't been able to put the man down.

As he ran into the night, Pearce was lost to a swirling fog of shame and remorse. He wished he could reverse time, that he could tell Brigitte to stand down, that he could have been with her when she encountered Lang, that . . . He could have chosen any one of a number of alternate histories that wouldn't have ended in her death. There was even a version in which they gave up the job and the hard lives they'd chosen and escaped to some paradise together. Perhaps Railay, where he'd been happy for a while. But it was not to be and there was no way to undo the past. His only hope lay in the future, in a fierce resolve to see Elroy Lang answer for the suffering he'd caused.

Chapter 7

Freya and Luke ran ahead, jumping over pools of water left by the receding tide. It was one of those glorious autumn afternoons, sun beating down on golden sand, sea shining in the bright light, and for a while Kyle Wollerton could make himself believe his life was perfect. But reality gnawed at his fantasy and the constant pressure of the ticking clock reminded him that things were far from flawless.

He'd left Overlook, his home on the Moray Firth, and moved to Aberdyfi to be near his children. He was allowed to spend a few hours with them each week, and they were able to stay over once a fortnight. Esther, his ex-wife, had shown no mercy, and years of resentment at having been neglected while Kyle was away on jobs had spilled into their divorce settlement. Kyle hadn't fought her. He'd been too hurt by the double blow of realizing the years he'd planned to spend with his family would now be passed alone, and the woman he'd loved with all his heart had come to loathe him. He'd been wounded in action numerous times, but no one else had been able to injure him as badly as Esther. She had destroyed his sense of self and he'd spent a long time hiding in Overlook, maudlin and alone, drifting until Scott Pearce had come back into his life.

Luke kicked water at Freya, and she squealed, dodged the

spray and ran behind a woman walking her chocolate-brown Labrador. The dog walker smiled indulgently, and Wollerton responded in kind. The kids ran on, squealing and shouting at every washed-up jellyfish they passed, and Wollerton followed, glancing at the grey masses, feeling he had more in common with these stranded creatures than any of the people they passed. Families huddled in half tents to keep out of the wind, lovers shared flasks of tea, older couples paddled in the surf. Like the jellyfish, Wollerton had washed up in Aberdyfi, where he existed for the benefit of his children, and spent the rest of his time with no real purpose.

Pearce had asked him to help them tail Nikos Kitsantonis, but Wollerton was done working for Huxley Blaine Carter, the Silicon Valley billionaire who'd been less than entirely honest when he'd engaged them to take on the Red Wolves. Wollerton needed to come to terms with his divorce and be present in his children's lives. Besides, Pearce had Brigitte Attali, and Wollerton knew the formidable French spy was hell-bent on finding Elroy Lang. Wollerton owed Brigitte his life. She'd given him the means to escape the Red Wolves after they abducted him, and the life he had, however good or bad, was a testament to her bravery.

The beach grew more crowded as they approached the town centre, and all too soon Freya and Luke had arrived at the beachfront car park where Esther was waiting. She was in the same spot every Thursday, and Wollerton wondered whether spite motivated her to be so punctual.

Luke ran up the concrete steps to greet her.

'We'll see you a week on Sunday, Dad,' Freya said.

Luke waved. 'Love you, Dad.'

Esther offered nothing more than a disapproving scowl as

she gathered their children and led them to her car. A little over a month ago, they'd moved from the town centre and now lived three miles outside Aberdyfi on a smallholding, where Esther had indulged her fantasy of owning hens and goats in an attempt to become self-sufficient.

Wollerton climbed the big steps to the busy car park and watched his family drive away. The first few times, their departure had pained him, but now he was numbed by routine and felt little more than disappointment. When they were gone, Wollerton crossed the car park and walked along the seafront road past the fish and chip shops, ice cream parlours and souvenir stands to a narrow mews that ran north towards the hills that loomed behind the town. The two-bedroom fishing cottage he'd rented was the third building along the mews, which was shrouded in cooling shadow.

Wollerton saw someone sitting on his doorstep; Scott Pearce. He instantly knew something was wrong. His friend and former colleague looked deeply troubled, and he got to his feet as Wollerton approached.

'She's dead,' Pearce told him. 'Brigitte is dead. Elroy Lang killed her. There was nothing I could do to stop him.'

Wollerton felt his friend's pain and put a reassuring hand on Pearce's shoulder. He'd lost people in the field and he knew how hard it hit.

'It's OK,' he said.

'It isn't,' Pearce countered. 'It really isn't. He needs to pay for what he's done. And I need your help to get him.'

Chapter 8

Leila Nahum had been hunting her sister for months. A refugee from the Syrian civil war, Leila's entire family had been wiped out in the bloodshed, or so she'd thought. Huxley Blaine Carter had discovered Hannan, her older sister, had survived, and Leila had picked up her trail in Zaatari refugee camp in Jordan. Leila had interviewed aid workers and medics and discovered Hannan had tried to follow Leila to Europe. Leila knew from bitter experience how perilous that journey could be, and had been dismayed to learn Hannan had traded the last of their mother's gold to people traffickers in exchange for passage.

Leila pulled into the disabled space in the small car park directly in front of the Tasty Fine Foods warehouse, located on a soulless, labyrinthine industrial estate outside Braintree in Essex. Her legs were in terrible shape after the long drive, but she couldn't be bothered to get her wheelchair out of the boot of her Nissan X-Trail, and instead grabbed her cane, which was leaning against the passenger seat. Leila shifted and shuffled herself round until she could lower her painful feet onto the tarmac. Needles shot up her legs and scraped along her spine, and she grimaced as she shuffled forward and shut the car door. She leaned against her cane and walked the short distance to the aluminium-framed glass double doors that formed the humble entrance to Tasty Fine Foods. Every step was agony and made Leila regret her decision not to use her wheelchair, but she'd be inside soon, and would hopefully find somewhere to sit.

She pressed a doorbell and a moment later she was buzzed into a small lobby full of boxes of Jamaican jerk chicken sauce. There were a couple of tatty chairs beside the door and Leila lowered herself onto the nearest with a relieved groan.

'Can I help you?' A young blonde woman poked her head around an interior door.

'I'm looking for Richie Stewart,' Leila replied, fighting back a grimace.

'Do you have an appointment?'

'Tell him it's about Zaatari,' Leila said.

The woman nodded and withdrew, and Leila sat and focused on anything other than the pain in her back. She scanned the health and safety and product information posters without really absorbing their contents, listened to the sounds of activity coming from within the red-brick warehouse and smelled the aroma of sauces being cooked somewhere in the building. None of the distractions did any good, and the pain that had come to define her, a legacy of injuries sustained in childbirth, would not let her go. She was scowling when a short, stocky man with grey hair and a pockmarked face entered. He eyed Leila with the suspicion of someone who had something to hide.

'Yeah?'

'Richie Stewart?' Leila asked. She was in too much pain to stand and didn't even bother to make the effort.

'To my friends. Strangers call me Mr Stewart.' He took a step closer and leaned against a stack of cardboard boxes.

Leila ignored his alpha-dog reply. 'I have some questions about your business.'

'You interested in sauces?' he responded sarcastically. 'We do the best jerk this side of the Atlantic.'

Leila sighed. He was making the same mistake so many other men had made. He was underestimating her.

'You came rushing out here because your colleague said the word Zaatari, and you're trying to hide your concern that some stranger knows about your sideline,' Leila said.

Richie tensed and his suspicion deepened.

'What's your name?'

'That's not important,' Leila replied. 'I want to ask you about a woman one of your drivers collected from Zaatari.'

'I don't know what you're talking about. I make sauces.'

'This business is a front for your more lucrative operation. It gives you trucks and an excuse to send them all over Europe.'

'Who's been filling your head with nonsense?' Richie smiled, but the expression was devoid of joy.

'A mutual friend in Paris,' Leila replied. It wasn't a lie, but it wasn't quite the truth either. Her sister's trail had led from Zaatari all the way to the French capital, and a man called Adel Azzizi. This man, who Leila had tortured in his apartment in La Courneuve, had certainly not been a friend. He was another underworld sleazeball who profited from human misery, and he'd given up the identity of his English connection.

'Your friend is mistaken,' Richie replied, stepping forward. 'Come on. It's time to go.'

He grabbed Leila's shoulder and sent a jolt of pain down her back. She scowled when she looked at his stubby fingers.

'Why do some men feel they can maul women without

permission?' Leila remarked as she slid her hand into her jacket pocket.

'Oh will you behave, love?' Richie cautioned condescendingly. 'I don't want to have to teach you a lesson.'

Leila didn't bother responding. She pulled a syringe from her pocket, popped off the safety cover with her thumbnail and drove the needle into his neck. Richie's eyes widened as she pressed the plunger and filled him with a noxious cocktail of opioids and hallucinogens Pearce called the Evil.

Richie started clawing at his neck immediately and backed away from Leila with growing horror.

'I've just injected you with Evil. My colleague gave it that name because it causes intense pain and psychosis.'

Richie stumbled back and knocked over a stack of boxes.

Leila produced another syringe. 'This is the antidote. It will take away the horror that's beginning to consume you.'

Richie fell to the floor and reached towards Leila pleadingly, but he couldn't form words and just croaked pathetically.

'Tell me how I can find my sister. Her name is Hannan Nahum and she was transported from Zaatari six months ago.'

'I . . .' Richie struggled to get the words out, and his eyes widened at whatever living nightmare he was experiencing. 'I don't do that. Tonsi Aboud takes the shipments from Zaatari.'

Leila lashed out and hit his left thigh with the point of her cane.

'My sister is not a shipment. Where is this Aboud?'

'Brussels,' Richie groaned. 'Molenbeek. Aboud International Logistics.'

Leila stood up and turned for the exit.

'Please,' Richie said. 'The antidote.'

Leila threw him the other syringe, and he scrambled for it

desperately. She pressed through the doors, and as she neared her car she heard Richie scream. The Evil would really be kicking in, and the saline in the second syringe would do nothing to blunt its hideous edge. There was no antidote to the Evil, and Richie Stewart was about to spend several hours in a personal hell.

Leila's phone rang as she slid behind the wheel. She pressed the ignition button and took the call on Bluetooth.

'Hello?'

'*Lyly, it's me.*'

She recognized Pearce's voice.

'*B is gone,*' he said. He was being careful on an unsecured line, but the sorrow in his voice revealed more than words ever could. Brigitte Attali was dead.

'I'm sorry,' Leila replied. She hadn't like the French spy, but no one deserved an early death.

Leila sensed commotion and glanced over her shoulder to see the blonde woman who'd greeted her pointing at the X-Trail. A number of the woman's colleagues were gathered behind her and some pushed by her as they steamed through the warehouse entrance. Leila put the car in gear and sped away before they could reach her.

'Where can we meet?' she asked.

'*The mountains,*' Pearce replied, before hanging up.

Leila knew exactly where she needed to go.

Chapter 9

Pearce looked out of the huge window at the jagged peaks rising beneath a star field. The sky was clear, and the distant sun shimmered above the shadowed teeth. Pearce sat on a long corner sofa opposite Wollerton, who was in a large leather armchair. They were surrounded by paintings, sculptures and the trinkets of a rich man with space to fill. Pearce had been to Huxley Blaine Carter's mountain hideaway before, located high in the French Alps. The magnificent home was heavily fortified and built into the rock. Equipped with the latest surveillance and security systems, it was a home in which a person was never truly alone, and Pearce wondered whether he was being watched even now. Huxley had armed guards and dogs patrolling the perimeter and his physical security team seemed to have been stepped up since Pearce's last visit.

The sound of footsteps coming up the main stairs alerted Pearce and Wollerton to a new arrival, and Leila struggled up the last few steps, leaning against her cane. She was accompanied by one of Huxley's guards, who descended as soon as he'd shown her into the room.

'*Ya hayawaan*,' Leila said, calling Pearce an animal in Arabic.

She paused at the top of the stairs and Pearce saw her

suppress a grimace. He rose and hurried over, but she stopped him with a fierce look.

'If you're planning on doing anything gallant, get ready to feel the stick,' she said, brandishing her cane.

'Just a hug,' he lied. She was too proud for her own good. He wrapped his arms around her, and she patted his back. 'Good to see you, Lyly.'

'I'm sorry about Brigitte,' she replied, following him to the sofa, where she sat down with a loud sigh.

'Kyle,' she said. 'Good to see you.'

Pearce's mentor and former superior nodded sombrely.

Losing a member of any team was always difficult, but this loss had hit Pearce hard. He kept replaying the things he could have done differently, the ways in which he might have saved Brigitte.

A section of wall panelling retracted, and Huxley Blaine Carter emerged from a concealed passageway. His heavyset grey-haired adviser Robert Clifton, a former director of the National Security Agency, followed him out.

'Mr Pearce, Ms Nahum, Mr Wollerton, thank you all for coming,' Huxley said. 'I was very sorry to hear about Ms Attali. She was an excellent operative and a good person. Brave and loyal to the last.'

A lump rose in Pearce's throat. Huxley Blaine Carter had hired Brigitte after she'd been fired from the DGSE for blowing her cover during the Black Thirteen investigation. Huxley had known her as long as Pearce, and perhaps knew her better. He seemed genuinely moved by her death.

'We lost a good soul,' Clifton said, and they all took a moment to reflect on their colleague's passing.

'We identified the woman who was with Nikos Kitsantonis

and Elroy Lang,' Huxley said at last. 'Athena, run the footage from the Rijksmuseum.'

Huxley's home artificial intelligence system, Athena, turned part of the window opaque, before filling it with footage Pearce had shot from his surveillance glasses.

'Athena, bring up the identification file,' Huxley told the AI.

The video froze on the silver-haired woman, and the screen was inset with photos and background information.

'Mary Knight,' Clifton revealed. 'Thirty-four years old. Astrophysics PhD from Oxford. She was an academic, but became an environmental activist about ten years ago, and got drawn into Extinction Rebellion. She left after falling out with the leadership and went on to found a more radical group called White Fire. She's not on any security watch lists.'

'An environmental activist?' Wollerton remarked. 'What would Elroy Lang want with her?'

'That's what we need to know,' Clifton responded. 'Find out what they're doing, and use her to get to him.'

Pearce nodded. 'You got a location?'

'Knight was gifted an estate in South Wales by a wealthy benefactor. It's become White Fire's base of operations,' Huxley replied. 'Social media suggests they're wary of outsiders.'

'And we picked up Nikos's trail at Schiphol Airport,' Clifton said. 'Took a flight to New York.'

'And Lang?' Pearce asked.

'In the wind,' Clifton replied. 'No trace of him anywhere.'

'I want him,' Pearce said. 'He has to answer for Brigitte.'

'And if you kill him, how will you find Kral?' Huxley asked, referring to the strange bearded man who'd been on the periphery of the Black Thirteen and Red Wolves investigations.

'He'll tell me where to find Kral before . . .' Pearce trailed off. He didn't need to say any more.

'Nikos and Mary Knight are best bets,' Leila remarked.

'Agreed,' Wollerton said. 'So how do we do this?'

'I'll get inside White Fire,' Pearce replied. 'You and Leila go to New York. Find Nikos and see if he'll lead us to Lang again. But if he does, you're to observe. Do not engage.'

'Scott—' Wollerton began, but Pearce cut him off.

'You stay back, Kyle. He's dangerous. Really dangerous. If you find him, you call me. I'll make him pay for what he's done.'

Chapter 10

Pearce stared at the amber liquid in his tumbler and watched it catch the light as he gently rolled the glass around. Huxley and Clifton had left them a little over an hour ago, after agreeing how they would resource the operation. Leila had taken the billionaire at his word when he'd told them to make themselves at home, and had raided Huxley's impressive liquor collection, which was discreetly concealed in a cabinet behind another retractable wall panel. Each of them had their own bottle. Wollerton was drinking a twelve-year-old Strathisla single malt, Leila was losing herself in Greek ouzo, which she kept telling them reminded her of home, and Pearce was on Appleton aged rum on the rocks. None of them were in the mood for mixers.

'Is this a wake?' Wollerton asked, slurring his words.

Leila looked at Pearce uncertainly.

'Is this what we get?' Wollerton went on. 'A trio of sad folk, pretending they knew us?'

He stood up and crossed the huge room unsteadily until he reached the vast window that overlooked the mountains.

'What was her favourite colour? Did she like the Coen Brothers or Christopher Nolan? What food did she like?' he asked the peaks on the other side of the valley.

'Fattoush,' Leila replied. 'Her favourite meal was fattoush.'

'Really?' Wollerton asked with the naive belief only a drunk can muster.

'No,' Leila responded mockingly. 'I have no idea what her favourite food was, or which films she liked. What does it matter? Knowing such things only makes you feel better. She doesn't care. Wherever she is now, it doesn't matter to her what you think.'

Wollerton looked as though he was about to say something, but his mouth slowly closed.

'I didn't even really like her,' Leila confessed. 'I know we're not supposed to say such things when a person dies, but it's the truth, and it doesn't matter what I thought of her. She was brave and on the right side of whatever it is we've been doing, so she deserves to be honoured. And if we're the only people who can do that, so be it.'

She drained her glass and almost knocked the bottle over as she leaned forward to pour herself another.

'What does any of it matter?' Leila asked too loudly for a sober person. 'When you're gone you're gone.'

Pearce looked at the woman he'd probably describe as his closest friend and wondered how much he really knew her. Did she really believe the nihilism she was spouting? Or was it just a defence mechanism?

'I don't even know what I'm doing here,' Leila remarked. She was also slurring her words. 'I should be in Brussels, finding a man called Aboud. Not stuck here with you. Drinking to someone we've all realized we didn't know.'

'We knew her,' Pearce said quietly, and Leila scowled at him.

She was right to take his words as a rebuke. She of all people knew the pain of loss. She knew it wasn't just about grief, but a life ended, moments that would never come. Those moments didn't belong to him, Leila or Wollerton, they had been taken from Brigitte and that was what they should mourn – the loss of life, opportunity, a story ended far too soon.

'Brigitte Attali was taken before her time. She was a good woman and she was smart and strong. She did the right thing when it mattered,' Pearce said. 'What more is there to know? She saved my life and sacrificed herself for Kyle.'

Pearce noticed Leila's fierce look soften into puzzlement.

'The Red Wolves put one of the patches on her,' he revealed.

'What?' Leila exclaimed.

Wollerton shook his head.

'She didn't want anyone to know,' Pearce said. 'I think she believed it might make people see her as weak.'

Leila muttered something under her breath in Arabic. 'Poor woman,' she said. 'Poor, poor woman.'

'Exactly,' Pearce agreed. 'She was brave and selfless, and that's why we should remember her. That's why we should honour her.'

Pearce drained his glass, and Wollerton did likewise.

'To Brigitte,' he said.

'To Brigitte,' Leila echoed, and she emptied her glass.

Her eyes rolled a little and she looked woozy for a moment before she reached for the bottle. This time she knocked it over, but the cap held fast and she recovered it before it tumbled off the table. She poured herself another drink and Pearce did likewise.

'Just trying to reach the sweet spot,' Leila said. 'When it doesn't hurt anymore.'

Pearce sighed. Few spoke of the toll taken on the men and women who devoted themselves to this kind of work. Their sacrifice didn't end in the field. Their jobs exacted a price that could last a lifetime. Brigitte had made the ultimate sacrifice, but everyone in this room was carrying the scars left by lives given to service.

Leila groaned and passed out on the arm of the corner sofa.

'Lyly,' Pearce said softly.

She spent most of her days in pain, so the oblivion of alcohol was all too alluring for her.

'Kyle, give me a hand,' Pearce said.

They both staggered over to the unconscious Syrian, and Pearce checked her breathing before he and Wollerton lifted her by the arms and got her to her feet. She stirred and smiled, and her glassy eyes settled on Pearce momentarily.

'*Ya gedaa,*' she drawled, calling him smart for no apparent reason.

Her eyes rolled back and her lids closed, as Pearce and Wollerton walked her down the inner staircase and took her to her bedroom, located on the floor below.

They put her in her king-size bed, and Pearce shut the blinds, while Wollerton took off her shoes and arranged the covers.

'You think one of us should stay?' he slurred. 'In case she spews.'

He didn't even wait for an answer and slid to the floor. He curled up and passed out the moment his head touched the soft carpet.

Pearce smiled at the scene. Wollerton was like a faithful pet sleeping at the foot of Leila's bed. Pearce crept out of the room and carefully shut the door behind him. He started towards his room, which was further along the corridor.

'It's always tough, losing someone you care about,' Huxley said.

Pearce turned to see their host approaching from the other direction.

'Did she have any family?' Pearce asked.

Huxley shook his head. 'I think she was alone. Like you, Mr Pearce.'

The remark rankled. 'And what about you? Are you alone?'

'More than you can imagine. My money isolates me. My work, this work, makes other people a hazard.'

'Why do it then? Why are you after Lang? Why Black Thirteen and the Red Wolves?'

'I owe it to my father,' Huxley said.

Tate Blaine Carter had died in suspicious circumstances, and Pearce suspected Huxley blamed the people they were hunting – Lang, Kral and anyone else who was involved – for his death.

'Goodnight, Mr Pearce.'

Pearce nodded and watched Huxley walk away. One of the richest men in the world, but all his money could do him no good. He was just as broken as the rest of them.

Chapter 11

The drums sounded like the pounding hooves of distant cavalry, all out of time and thunderous. The chants rose above them, blending with singing that came from elsewhere. A group was blowing loud whistles and another was shouting. People held banners and eyed the police, who gathered in squads, surveying the enormous crowd. Pearce had no doubt there would be intelligence officers among the thousands who filled Trafalgar Square, and one of the many field trucks would be occupied by analysts who would be identifying known troublemakers.

Pearce picked his way through the crowd. He wore green combat trousers and a camouflage T-shirt and had let his stubble grow ever since the drunken wake at Huxley Blaine Carter's place in the mountains, three days earlier. He'd travelled to London, where he'd used the identity Robert Clifton had supplied him with to rent a room in a Paddington guest house.

He'd researched White Fire and found the group was going to be represented at the World's Byrning, a gathering of radical environmental groups in Central London. His legend wasn't far from the truth, and as he wandered through the throng, Pearce couldn't help but reflect on how different his life might have been if he'd never been recruited into MI6. He'd served with many who'd struggled to adapt to civilian life and drifted through the years searching for a sense of purpose. If he'd strayed from the right path, he might have fallen into crime or signed up with a radical group to give him a sense of purpose.

He passed through a group of hundreds of Extinction Rebellion protesters who were arranged around a procession of women with painted white faces, wearing striking red dresses. Finally, he saw the people he was looking for, their allegiance clear from the White Fire sign two of them carried. There were about thirty men and women between the ages of twenty and forty, young and angry. They were dressed much like Pearce, in khakis, combats and camo, and seemed to be at the rougher end of the spectrum of protestors. Pearce knew from his research that this group believed in direct action, which might explain why they'd settled near the edge of Trafalgar Square opposite a line of riot police. Three of their number, two men and a woman, were yelling abuse at the police line.

'You're not doing any good,' someone shouted.

The voice came from the much larger Extinction Rebellion group behind Pearce.

'Splitter!' shouted a young, shaven-haired black woman in the White Fire faction.

She was jostled by some men who were part of the Extinction Rebellion group, and the disorder spread until dozens of people in the competing factions were facing off and pushing one another.

Like a sudden storm sweeping in from a churning sea, Pearce sensed a change in the atmosphere. The air seemed to take on an electrostatic charge. The shouts for calm sounded increasingly desperate as troublemakers on both sides traded insults and jostled and shoved. There was a shift in the mood of the police, and they closed on the edge of the White Fire group. It was early in the day for the police to start kettling protestors, squeezing them into a small space, but the operational commander might view this as an opportunity to detain some of the worst troublemakers before they caused any real mischief. Pearce wondered whether police intelligence knew about the feud between White Fire and Extinction Rebellion and why more hadn't been done to keep them apart. It was too late now. A guy with a bull neck, shaved head and a hard, angry face threw a punch at one of the Extinction Rebellion protestors, and the rising energy of the scuffle crashed into a full-blown brawl.

Pearce was thrust to the epicentre by a rush of people moving to join their friends on both sides, and as the brawl spread, he went with the tide, eager to reach the black girl who'd kicked things off. A fight raged around her, but rather than shrink from the violence, she was throwing punches at every Extinction Rebellion member who came within range.

Someone grabbed Pearce's shoulder and he turned, instinctively ducked a wild punch and replied with a cross that decked his assailant. He was at the heart of the brawl now, and through the melee he saw the police mustering for a charge and heard shouted orders. The boys in blue did a good job of crowd control, but they weren't known for their subtlety. Once they got involved things would turn ugly and heads would get cracked and bloodied.

Pearce shoved brawlers out of the way and reached the shaven-haired woman. She turned to strike him and Pearce caught a glint of silver as he ducked the blow. She wore a pair of heavy chrome knuckles. He grabbed her arms and shook her.

'You need to leave,' he said, nodding at the police line.

The woman followed his gaze and had the sense to see what he saw; riot cops gathering for a charge.

'Splitting time,' she yelled to her crowd, but people were too caught up in the fight to register her words.

She nodded and followed Pearce as he pushed through the brawl towards St Martin in the Fields, the grand church that stood to the east of the square. He heard a roar and glanced round to see the police crash into the crowd, shields proud, batons flailing.

There was a surge the other way, and Pearce and his new companion got caught in a scrum of people rushing to engage the police. The air filled with screams and cries of shock and anger, and the protest degenerated into violent chaos as other police units rushed the scene.

Pearce shoved a man out of his way, and when the man was foolish enough to shove back, Pearce knocked him down with a punch that broke his nose. Those nearby cleared a path, and a few moments later Pearce broke the edge of the crowd followed by the woman with the shaved head. She didn't seem scared. On the contrary, she was smiling broadly with what appeared to be elation.

'Come on,' she said, grabbing Pearce's hand and leading him north towards the calm safety of Shaftesbury Avenue.

Chapter 12

Tonsi Aboud lived on the top floor of a five-storey nineteenth-century apartment building near the centre of Molenbeek-Saint-Jean, one of the oldest neighbourhoods in Brussels. Built in an ornate French imperial style, the block had seen better days. The high windows were edged with decades of grime and the white fascia had been turned a dirty grey. The entrance was formed by a pair of ornate wrought iron and frosted-glass doors and some of the panels were cracked or missing. Leila and Wollerton entered what once would have been a grand lobby, but now reeked of damp and neglect. The block had retained an old carriage elevator and a series of metal gates could be seen on every floor. The carriage itself was wood and glass and showed evidence of rot. Steel patches had been fitted here and there, and Leila didn't feel entirely safe as she and Wollerton rode up in silence. She could tell the former MI6 operative was annoyed by their stopover, but there was no way Leila was dropping her sister's trail.

'We have buildings like this in Syria,' she said. 'A legacy of the French.'

Wollerton replied with a noncommittal grunt.

'I could have come alone, you know.'

'I said I didn't mind,' he responded, but Leila could tell he did mind. Either that or something else was bothering him.

The elevator stopped and Wollerton pulled open the wooden doors and pushed the metal gate. Leila's cane tapped against the marble tiles as they crossed the landing to apartment twelve. The grand double doors had inbuilt frosted-glass windows behind an intricate pattern of ironwork that was far more attractive than steel bars. Leila pressed the doorbell and a chime sounded inside.

She heard footsteps, then a latch being turned, and the frosted-glass window opened to reveal a middle-aged woman. Leila guessed she was from Syria or Lebanon.

'*Oui?*' she said.

'We're looking for Tonsi Aboud,' Wollerton replied.

'I don't know him,' the woman replied.

Leila heard the sound of children playing inside.

'*Inti maratuh,*' she remarked, suggesting the woman was his wife. She saw from the woman's defeatist response that she'd guessed correctly, and that this was Mrs Aboud. She'd likely been given strict instructions on how to deal with any strangers and would face retribution if she didn't follow them.

'Who are you?'

'We're people who can make you and your children's lives very difficult,' Leila replied. '*Howa wahash auwi,*' she added, nodding at Wollerton. She'd just told the woman her companion was a very bad man. 'We just want to talk to him. I think he might have brought my sister out of Jordan.'

The woman shook her head.

'*Ochti, sa-idni,*' Leila addressed the woman as her sister and asked for her help.

There was a softness in the woman's eyes, but also fear. What price did she pay for the life she and her children had?

'He's not here,' she said. 'He's away on business.'

'Where?' Wollerton asked.

'I don't know. He never tells me where he goes.'

Leila was familiar with the air of sadness and resignation that accompanied the woman's words. She had spent time as the wife of two overbearing, abusive husbands.

'When will he be back?' Leila asked.

'Two weeks. Maybe three,' the woman replied. 'He never goes longer than a month.'

Leila nodded. '*Shukran*. Thank you.'

A faint smile flickered across the woman's face, before she shut the door.

'You believe her?' Wollerton asked as he followed Leila to the elevator.

'Yes. She's afraid of him, but she doesn't love him,' she replied. 'It's a combination that doesn't inspire loyalty. We'll go to New York and find Nikos and when it's finished, I will come back and talk to this man about my sister.'

'Talk?' Wollerton asked, pulling the elevator gate shut.

'I'll listen. He'll talk,' Leila assured him. 'One way or another.'

Chapter 13

The woman was buzzing with impish energy, and she and Pearce hurried along Shaftesbury Avenue, before cutting along Cecil Court. They ran past antique dealers and rare bookshops, and went south on St Martin's Lane. They had doubled back and now saw Trafalgar Square ahead of them, where the brawl had broken into a full-blown riot. The woman looked at Pearce with a mischievous smile and a sense of relief and led him across the road, down a side street to the Strand. She pushed him playfully and kept touching his arm as she recounted their escape from the protest.

'That was mad,' she said. 'The cops aren't holding back. And those XR idiots wading in like we're the bad guys. My name is Farida, by the way. Farida Amira.'

'Sam,' Pearce replied. 'Sammy Nour.'

He was using one of the aliases Robert Clifton had provided him with.

'I owe you a drink or something,' Farida said. 'You with people?'

'I came alone,' Pearce replied. 'Saw something about it on Twitter and thought I'd check it out.'

'Brave man. I'd offer you coffee, but I don't have any money,' Farida said.

'I can pay.'

'You could. Or we could go back to my place. I've probably got something to drink there.' She beamed and skipped ahead.

Pearce had targeted her because of the way she'd yelled at the Extinction Rebellion protester. There had been more recklessness than confidence in her demeanour and his assessment was being borne out by her behaviour. She was a thrill seeker, and clearly relished the violence and volatility of the situation they'd just escaped.

'You coming?' she asked.

She skipped on without waiting for a response, and Pearce followed.

They caught a train from Charing Cross to London Bridge and from there they took another almost empty train south into the suburbs. Farida studied Pearce as they rattled along the tracks past all the neat little gardens that lined the route.

'So you saw it on Twitter?' she asked. 'Your first happening?' She emphasized the last word in a mocking tone. 'That's what the hippies call them.'

Pearce nodded. 'A lot has changed for me recently. I'm looking for answers, I guess. Something different.'

'What questions are you asking?'

'Nothing big. Just what I should do with my life,' Pearce scoffed. 'I was discharged. Honourably decommissioned like an old aircraft carrier or something. After fifteen years. The army is all I've known since I was a kid, and now I'm out here with you lot.'

Farida smiled. 'Us lot?'

'Civilians. I've served all over the world. I've seen how it's changing. Something's happening to the planet,' Pearce said. 'Fires in Australia. Drought in Europe. Snow in Texas.'

'So you're a soldier looking for a new war?'

'Maybe. Doesn't seem like there's anything more important than the planet.'

Farida nodded and rubbed the stubble on the top of her head with her delicate fingers. He could see her mind working.

'What kind of soldier were you?'

'The fighting kind. Served with the SAS.'

He'd never refer to it like that in the company of another veteran, but this was a civilian and she needed to be sold. He kept his legend as close as possible to the truth to make his background easier to sell. Fewer lies left less scope to get caught out.

Farida pursed her lips. 'A proper soldier.'

'I was.'

She held his gaze with an intensity that might have unsettled others, but Pearce met her stare until she broke into a broad smile.

'Come on,' she said, getting to her feet. 'This is our stop.'

Pearce followed her and they left the train at Norwood Junction. She buzzed along the tunnel beneath the tracks and out of the station along a short street lined with a hardware shop, minicab office and supermarket. They turned right onto a busy main road and walked a few yards to a white door beside a fried chicken takeaway.

'My sanctuary,' Farida said as she unlocked the door and led Pearce inside.

He stepped into a narrow corridor that was full of pot plants and hanging baskets. Farida picked her way past them.

'My babies,' she said. 'Keep the smoke of the big bad city at bay.'

She climbed a steep flight of stairs and Pearce followed.

The grey carpet was worn, but the walls had been freshly painted; electric blue to his right, pink to his left.

Farida threw her keys on a sideboard and took Pearce's arm and pulled him into a living room that overlooked the main road. There were more plants in here, and books, lots of them, filling shelves and piled in disorderly stacks around the tatty furniture. The pastel-green walls were covered by framed photographs of striking natural scenes; mountains, the moon over a desert, a satellite image of the Earth with the sun cresting the edge of the globe.

'Do you ever wish we had more time?' Farida asked, turning to face Pearce.

He didn't know how to answer the question.

'I do,' she said, pulling him in for a kiss.

She was tall and slim and felt firm in his embrace, and Pearce couldn't help but be attracted to her wild spirit. It was good to feel something that wasn't anger.

'I might just have what you're looking for. A cause. Something worth fighting for. But we can talk about that later,' she said, before she kissed him again.

Chapter 14

Pearce listened to the rumble of traffic as he lay next to Farida. They were naked beneath a sheet, and she was smoking a joint. He'd cracked the window a touch to release the worst of the smoke and stuffiness, and could hear odd snatches of conversation above the sound of vehicles trundling along just outside.

Farida offered him the joint, and he shook his head. She shrugged and took another draw.

'At least I already know you're not a cop,' she remarked.

Pearce was puzzled.

'A few years back, police got in trouble for romancing members of activist groups,' Farida explained. 'A couple even had kids in secret. Led to some unsafe convictions and scandals, so policy was changed and cops were banned from screwing the people they were investigating.'

'So this was a test?' Pearce asked. He wasn't sure she was right about the change in policy, but he wasn't about to correct her.

'Partly,' Farida replied, edging closer. 'But mainly it was pleasure. That's what life should be, right? Fun. Uncomplicated pleasure. Why else are we here?'

Pearce didn't delve into her philosophy, which was at odds

with his own view of duty and service. 'Why are you worried about the law?'

'The government doesn't like us. We expose its failings. We tell the truth,' Farida replied, growing more animated as she spoke. 'We let people know we don't have long to save the planet, and we encourage them to take action against the greedy men who are pillaging nature to make themselves rich. Fat pigs for whom too much is never enough. And our children and our children's children will suffer to feed the system. If things get too bad, they may not have any future at all.'

She took a draw of the joint and exhaled a cloud of smoke.

'Sorry. I get worked up about people not being able to see what's coming. Anyway, that's why the government sends cops and spies against us to try to find out what we're up to. They want to stop us, but they can't do anything unless they catch us breaking the law. Which we never do, of course.'

She smiled darkly.

'Who's we?'

'White Fire,' Farida replied. 'We're a small group. Much smaller than XR, but we're effective.'

'Were those the people you were with?'

'Some of them. Our founder used to be part of XR.'

'XR?' Pearce asked.

'Extinction Rebellion. She fell out with them because she believes in more extreme forms of direct action. She says the time for education and protests is over. If we don't step up our activities, the world is lost.'

'What kind of activities?'

'If you want to know, you'll have to be initiated,' Farida replied. She leaned over and kissed Pearce. 'Don't worry, it doesn't hurt.'

'Do I have to go to a meeting?'

Farida chuckled. 'It's not Alcoholics Anonymous. Come to Sanctuary with me. It's a community in Wales. I'll introduce you. See if people take to you. You got wheels?'

Pearce nodded.

'Good. I need a couple of days to take care of a few things, but if you give me your number, I'll call you when I'm ready to shoot.'

Pearce nodded again. He had little doubt she would use the time to check him out, and, if they were sufficiently sophisticated, they'd also run his phone number. He wasn't worried. His legend was good and would hold up to any background checks.

'Sounds good,' Pearce said.

Farida smiled and kissed him again.

Chapter 15

Robert Clifton had given them an address in Brooklyn and they'd arrived the previous night to find a small two-storey house on Noble Street. A covered veranda ran the length of the white timber home, which stood in contrast to the three- and four-storey red-brick terraces lining the rest of the street. Cars were parked on both sides beneath high trees that were losing their leaves.

When Leila had first entered the house, they'd found food and clothes, and the casual visitor would have seen nothing but a couple of holidaymakers in an ordinary Airbnb rental. It was only later, when they located the vault where Robert Clifton had said it would be, in the basement behind a false wall, that the investment in the safe house became clear. The vault contained computer equipment, weapons, money and surveillance gear, everything they'd asked for and much, much more.

They'd spent the night watching TV and talking about the peculiarities of American society. Leila was always struck by the bizarre obsession with medicine and convenience food, and was certain the two were related, and Wollerton was more interested in the American fascination with guns and big cars.

Jet lag meant Leila hadn't been able to get to sleep until after two, and she woke a little before five and spent at least an hour counting the blemishes in the walls of her austere room at the front of the house. She finally fell asleep again after six, and was woken by Wollerton just after eight. He looked bright and well rested, while she felt like something that had crawled out of a grave.

Over breakfast, Leila accessed a little-known Five Eyes security programme that logged every hotel reservation in America and Europe, and she discovered Nikos Kitsantonis was staying at the Pierre, a grand hotel near Central Park.

They dressed, and Leila followed Wollerton out of the house, shuffling across the street, supporting herself on her cane, until she reached an old Jeep Cherokee that was one of two vehicles that came with the house.

'Never fails to take my breath away,' Wollerton said as they drove across the Queensboro Bridge.

The Manhattan skyline was an impressive feat of engineering, but Leila didn't share Wollerton's enthusiasm for it. Buildings represented gatherings of people, and the cruelty of others had given Leila a visceral dislike of human symbols. She much preferred the natural beauty of mountains or the desert. Danger was clear and could be easily understood. A mountain fall might kill, or a desert scorpion sting, but humans concealed the harm they might cause and much of their danger came in the form of hidden cruelties and twisted psychology.

They made slow progress through the rush hour traffic and finally reached 61st Street shortly after ten. Wollerton cruised past the hotel, turned left on 5th Avenue, and found a space on 59th Street. The lack of sleep had done little for Leila's chronic pain, and she had to bite back a wince with every step as they walked north towards the hotel. Fifth Avenue was quieter than it had been before the pandemic, but there were still enough pedestrians to make a nuisance and Leila had to weave her way around groups of tourists who'd stopped to admire the sights. The morning had the making of a cold day, which wouldn't improve Leila's mood as her legs and back always suffered in any chill.

Her cane tapped the black and white chessboard marble floor when they entered the busy lobby.

'What now?' Wollerton asked.

'Reconnaissance,' she replied, looking around the large room.

Ten people with bags and suitcases queued at a long wooden reception desk. Another two dozen or so people sat on benches and chairs in a seating area just off the lobby. There were quite a few men in suits standing around who could have been hotel security or Nikos's muscle. Pearce had briefed them on the Greek billionaire's security arrangements, and warned them he usually travelled with a well-trained crowd.

'Count them,' Leila said, and Wollerton nodded.

She dropped her cane, and the brass cap clattered against the floor. Almost everyone in the room looked in her direction, but when she saw one of the suited men standing by the lifts share a look with another who was seated in a chair near the windows, Leila reaped the rewards of her simple deception. She ignored the pain and crouched to pick up the cane.

'I've got one by the lifts, and another at the window,' she said.

'Got those,' Wollerton replied. 'There's another by the reception desk, and two by the lobby phones. Let me get pictures.'

He produced a pair of surveillance glasses and activated video capture. He scanned the room as Leila led him towards the lifts. They stepped inside an open car and Leila pressed the button for the twenty-third floor. The Five Eyes system had told them Nikos was in room 2305. After a short ride, they emerged into a small lobby. Another man in a suit leaned against a narrow console table, but he stood upright when he saw them, causing a large vase full of flowers on the table to wobble as his weight shifted. He eyed them with suspicion, but Wollerton nodded and said, 'Hello,' like a clueless tourist, as he captured the man's face on camera.

Leila shuffled along the corridor, which was lined with numbered doors, and when they reached a dog leg and turned the corner, they saw a longer corridor that was capped by a set of doors that led to room 2305; Nikos's penthouse suite.

Two large men in suits stood either side of the door and watched Leila and Wollerton with ill-disguised hostility.

Wollerton stopped by one of the doors and produced a credit card. He held it over the reader.

'The guy on reception told me not to keep it next to my phone,' he said loudly enough for the men to hear. 'We're going to have to get it reset.'

He walked back the way they'd come, and Leila followed. Nikos was guarded by professionals, and she and Wollerton would need to proceed with care.

Chapter 16

Pearce assumed his cover checked out, because Farida called him two days later and arranged a time and place to meet. He agreed to give her a lift to Sanctuary, the White Fire estate, on the black Honda CBR 1100 he'd bought to replace the silver one he'd lost during the Black Thirteen investigation. He figured as a would-be environmental activist, he should have a bike instead of a car, and guessed, rightly as it turned out, that the thrill-seeking Farida would approve of the lightning-fast ride.

Her face lit up when he stopped in the layby near Clapham Common. She stowed an overnight bag in one of the panniers, put on the spare helmet Pearce gave her, and jumped on.

They took the M4 out of London, and Pearce opened the bike up once they'd cleared the M25. The journey to Pelcomb Cross, a small village in Pembrokeshire, took four hours and they stopped a couple of times to refuel and stretch their legs.

They went to the end of the M4 and joined the A48, which took them through the rolling Welsh countryside. The landscape always reminded Pearce of St David's, the state-run Welsh boarding school he'd been sent to after being cast out of numerous foster homes, and the memory was a poignant mix of wistful nostalgia and sadness. He'd been abandoned by his parents, so Wales was always associated with that hurt, but it had been here that he'd been taken under the wing of Malcolm Jones, the headteacher at St David's, a kind and patient man who'd been responsible for shaping much of Pearce's young life.

It was late afternoon when they rode through Haverfordwest, the largest town in the area. They continued west for a few miles and, after more open countryside, came to a charming village that was set along the road. After another mile or so, Farida tapped Pearce's helmet and directed him to take a turn to their left. He signalled, banked the bike and took them down a narrow country lane. Another mile further on, Farida tapped his helmet again and pointed towards a set of wrought-iron gates set in a high stone wall. Pearce turned onto the driveway and slowed to a stop. There was a small cottage a short distance beyond the gates, and a stocky, grey-haired man emerged from the black and white building, his face curled in a scowl as though he had far better things to do.

'Yeah,' he said.

Farida opened her visor. 'Let us in, Martin.'

'Who's your friend?' the old man asked.

'Sam,' Farida replied. 'Like in *Green Eggs and Ham*. Sam I am. Well, Sam he is.'

Pearce lifted his visor and nodded at the man.

'I've cleared it with Hunter,' Farida revealed.

Martin shuffled forward, unlocked the gates and pulled one open.

'Thanks, you old canker,' Farida said.

'Bothermaker,' Martin countered with something like a smile. 'Well, go on then.'

Pearce kicked into first and followed the long driveway through woodland. He saw patches of meadow between the trees where birds flitted and insects fluttered. Pearce recalled something from his philosophy degree, Plato's theory of forms, and thought the perfect light cast by the warm sun on this natural paradise was as close to perfection as one could hope to get.

The trees petered out and gave way to a lawn that had been left to seed. Ahead stood a large three-storey manor house surrounded by smaller outbuildings. Beside them was a collection of tents, yurts and camper vans that made Pearce think of a summer music festival. There were peace and Earth symbols everywhere, along with other Celtic signs he wasn't familiar with, and rustic sculptures that represented the planet and the natural world. It was, as Farida had mockingly said, a happening.

The deep rumble of the bike's engine drew people from the various structures, and a small crowd had gathered by the time Pearce rolled to a halt outside the main house. He and Farida were surrounded by dozens of people. Some in shorts and T-shirts, others bare-chested, some in combats and camouflage, still others in kaftans and floral dresses. It was a motley group, but they all had one thing in common; they were pleased to see Farida. Pearce recognized some of the faces from Trafalgar Square, but they weren't twisted in hostility. Instead, they were smiling and once Farida introduced him, they welcomed Pearce like an old friend. They seemed warm and trusting, and for the briefest moment, Pearce felt guilty about the way he was planning to use them.

Chapter 17

Farida showed Pearce to an old VW Caravelle camper van that had been assigned to him. It was located behind a cluster of yurts in what had once been a paddock that lay to the east of the main house. His new digs stood beside three more vans and a bus that had been converted into a dormitory. He parked his bike beside the Caravelle, stowed his gear and followed Farida to the manor house, which was a grand but tatty stately home. She led him into a large catering kitchen at the back of the house, where she introduced him to Taz, a tiny woman whose straw-blonde hair whipped this way and that as she flitted around preparing a meal. Taz led a team of six volunteers, and, like it or not, Pearce became the seventh.

'I'll see you later,' Farida said. 'Be gentle with him, Taz.'

She gave Pearce a cheeky wink before leaving.

'We're making dinner,' Taz told him. 'Everyone has one night in the kitchen every week. We're feeding sixty. Tonight is fennel and lentil stew and mashed potato with coconut milk. You can chop the fennel.'

She led Pearce to his station, and he cleaned and quartered twenty fennel, which were then fried with orange peel by one of the other volunteers, before being put into the oven to roast with a green lentil stew.

When the meal was ready, Pearce helped carry the serving dishes to the makeshift canteen in the dining room of the manor house. He helped serve the stew and was greeted warmly by every member of the group as they came to collect their food. It didn't seem like a gathering of dangerous radicals. Most were aged between twenty and forty, and there were slightly more women than men. Their eyes shone with idealism for the most part, and the conversations seemed light and easy as people chatted in line.

When most had been served, Mary Knight, the woman Pearce had seen in the Rijksmuseum, entered, her striking silver hair tied in a tail that hung over her shoulder and fell a third of the way down her full-length brown linen dress. She was with Farida, who directed her towards Pearce.

'Mary Knight,' Farida said. 'This is Sam Nour. Mary founded White Fire.'

Mary bowed slightly. 'We embrace you to our heart and hold you true.' Her voice was light and soothing, the tone of a spiritual leader. She was thirty-four, but looked younger. Her eyes were a steel blue and sparkled with vitality. Her features were delicate and her limbs slender, and Pearce felt the pull of attraction, but couldn't tell whether the draw was her charisma or her physical attributes.

'Thanks for having me,' he responded.

'I see you've fulfilled your first turn in the kitchen,' Mary said. 'We each prepare one meal a week. A shared burden is a lighter one.'

'Is it always vegan?' Pearce asked.

Mary nodded. 'Meat does terrible harm to the planet. We live by example.'

'Would you like some?' Pearce picked up a plate.

'That would be very kind,' Mary replied, and she kept her eyes on Pearce as he served her food.

'Thank you,' she said, taking the plate. 'It was a pleasure meeting you.'

She went outside to join a group eating at a long picnic table. They made space and treated her with deference that bordered on reverence.

'Well, she likes you,' Farida said, pushing Pearce's shoulder playfully. 'Come on, get us a couple of plates and I'll introduce you to some of the others.'

'You do as she says,' Taz chimed in. 'You can all eat now,' she told the other volunteer cooks. 'But don't forget you're on washing-up duty.'

Pearce plated food for himself and Farida and followed her through a set of French doors into a well-kept garden. There was an assortment of picnic tables and benches and small groups of people were clustered at each. As Farida led Pearce past Mary Knight, he caught her eying him. She smiled when their eyes met.

'She really likes you,' Farida whispered as they walked on.

She took him to a table that was occupied by two men and two women.

'This is Sandy,' Farida said, signalling a woman with long blonde dreadlocks and piercings that glinted in the evening sun, 'Louis,' she indicated a muscular man with a bull neck, hard face, shaved head and stubble.

Pearce recognized him from Trafalgar Square.

'This is Cursor.' Farida nodded at a grey-haired, thin man in his fifties. 'And Tanya.'

Pearce sat next to the thirty-something, raven-haired, heavily tattooed Tanya.

'This is Sam Nour,' Farida told them.

'Another believer?' Cursor asked.

'I don't know,' Pearce replied. 'I'm looking for answers.'

'Don't expect them from Cursor,' Tanya advised. 'He wavers between believing the world is going to end, and that we'll all be saved by the men in suits.'

'Who wants to believe in the end of the world?' Cursor protested. 'I'm an optimist. I think we'll change our ways. At the eleventh hour, we'll fix this.'

'It's already the twelfth hour, but whatever,' Tanya responded.

'Where you from?' Louis asked with an accusatory scowl.

'London,' Pearce replied. 'You?'

'Never you mind.' Louis' broad Northern Irish accent answered the question. 'I don't want to know where you were born, lad. We all came from the mud. I want to know where you're from now. What you've been doing.'

'Let him enjoy his food,' Farida said.

'No one can enjoy this shit. It fills a hole is all,' Louis responded. 'Where you from, mate?'

'I spent the last fifteen years in the army, doing whatever they told me,' Pearce replied, holding Louis' stare.

'You ever serve in Ireland?' he asked, and the mood around the table chilled noticeably.

'Lou, come on, whatever people did before they came here isn't imp—' Farida tried, but he cut her off.

'Did you ever serve in Ireland?' he repeated.

The guy was clearing trying to establish himself as an alpha, and Pearce could either bow and present himself as subordinate, or rise to the challenge. He shook his head.

'No, I never served in Ireland. Is everyone there as friendly as you?'

Louis smiled and turned his head slowly, so everyone caught his grin. Pearce knew what was coming, and prepared for it. Sure enough, Louis' grin fell and he lunged across the table, upsetting plates and cutlery. Pearce stood, and slapped Louis down, so his chin hit the tabletop.

Pearce backed away, as Louis picked himself up.

'If you want to do this, let's not ruin everyone's meal,' Pearce said, and he took a couple of steps back onto an empty patch of long grass.

Louis nodded slowly and joined Pearce. They were about the same height, but Pearce's challenger had the weight advantage. Pearce glanced round to see Mary Knight and the others watching him. No one said anything. Was this a test? Or an initiation?

'Come on then, mate,' Louis snarled, adopting a boxer's stance. He held his hands high and tucked his head in like an experienced fighter.

Pearce chose a Muay Thai stance, more open, inviting an attack, and Louis took the bait. He stepped in and jabbed a couple of times. He was fast, but not quick enough to trouble Pearce, who dodged the blows. Louis came in again and jabbed twice, and followed them up with a cross. Pearce blocked them all and replied with a vicious flurry of jabs that were so quick they overwhelmed Louis. They were intended to disorientate rather than hurt and they had the desired effect. Louis staggered back, blinded by the storm, and Pearce punctuated the assault with a hook that caught Louis on the ear and knocked him down.

Pearce stood over the dazed man and watched him come to his senses. A smart fighter would know just how much he'd been outclassed.

'Jeez, mate,' Louis said. 'I was only playing.'

Smart, Pearce thought, *and cunning enough to try to heal some wounded pride.*

'I got lucky,' Pearce said, reaching out a hand and helping the brash man up.

Louis eyed him with a little more respect. 'You're handy, mate, no lying. But enough fooling about. Let's eat.'

Pearce sensed everyone around them relax and soon conversations filled the warm air. He and Louis returned to their seats at the table.

'Well that was a special welcome to White Fire,' Farida said, and she scowled at Louis playfully. 'I can assure you we're not all maniacs.'

'Proud Irishman, that's all,' Louis countered. 'Warrior spirit. He understands.'

Pearce nodded. Whether it was a test or an initiation, he'd passed.

Chapter 18

Pearce did his shift at the sink. No one mentioned the fight, but the other volunteers gave him plenty of space, and once the washing-up was done, Taz released him for some free time.

Most of White Fire gathered on the lawn or sat around tables, drinking. There were a couple of discreet smokers and a few circulating joints. The talk was far more serious than it had been over dinner, and people were trading thoughts on the imminent threat faced by the planet and how decades of trying to raise awareness had fundamentally failed.

'Makes me so angry,' Louis said. 'You try and explain runaway to people and they look at you like you're nuts.'

'Runaway?' Pearce asked, returning to the table where he'd eaten.

'It's the idea that once the planet passes a certain point, warming becomes self-sustaining. Eventually, all the water on the surface evaporates and then the atmosphere goes,' Farida said.

'See?' Louis remarked. 'He's here with us, and even he doesn't know what it is.'

Pearce was left reeling. They were talking about something that couldn't be true, could it? 'Is this a thing?'

Louis tutted.

'Yeah.' Farida took a draw on her joint. 'Some astrophysicists believe it's possible. Others think it isn't, but we'll get so close it might as well be runaway.'

Climate change had been background noise for years, but Pearce had never paid much attention to it. 'If it was this serious, someone would act.'

Louis cackled derisively and Farida released a cloud of smoke when she laughed. Cursor and Tanya exchanged disbelieving looks.

'Who?' Farida asked. 'The government? It's good for putting in bus lanes, awarding contracts to mates and starting wars so it can tell youngsters where to go and die. Educating the entire planet on an existential threat and getting them to do something about it isn't in the job description for any politician.'

The gathering took on a more serious significance. Pearce had dealt with Al Qaeda and ISIS, and knew the power of apocalyptic prophecies. A group that believed in the end of the world was vulnerable to manipulation and could be convinced to take desperate action. Was this what Elroy Lang wanted with White Fire?

'But if things were this serious, scientists—' Pearce began.

'Scientists would have warned us?' Farida interrupted. 'What do you think they've been doing for the past forty years? Some of them are still shouting. Others have given up and are getting ready for what comes next. What you see here is hope.' She gestured at the people around them. 'We're taking a stand, because we believe there's still time to do something.'

'What?' Pearce asked.

'Mary will tell you when you're ready,' Farida replied.

Pearce couldn't see the White Fire leader anywhere.

'It's getting cold,' Farida said. 'You want to go somewhere warmer?'

Louis shot Pearce a knowing look, but he ignored it. He was still reeling from the revelations and told himself they couldn't be true. True, he hadn't been paying much attention, but no one had ever suggested to him that climate change could result in something so catastrophic. Farida's devil-may-care thrill-seeking made far more sense in light of this. What was the point of worrying about danger today if there was to be no tomorrow? No government, no matter how inept, would allow such horror. If this was what was to come, it would change everything. It couldn't be real. These people and others like them had to be mistaken.

Farida slid her hand inside his, and stood. Pearce allowed himself to be led away, and followed the beautiful, intense woman into the night.

Chapter 19

Leila had her back against the balustrade and was slouched low to keep herself from being seen by anyone in the surrounding buildings. They'd chosen the roof of 800 5th Avenue, the tower opposite the Pierre, as the site of their stakeout of Nikos's hotel room. It was the tallest building in the neighbourhood, which not only meant it offered a good view of Nikos's suite, its height also made it difficult for anyone to spot them. The rooftops of 61st Street were all below them, and to their west was the broad expanse of Central Park. They'd been in position for a little over three hours. So much of their work was tedious monotony; watching a target for hours, listening to boring conversations, sifting through millions of lines of code.

Wollerton was next to her, operating the handheld console that controlled a trio of tiny drones, each little bigger than a house fly. The drones had enough battery life for four hours of service, and they had a bank of twenty-four in a flight case a few feet away, charged and ready to go. They had two drones in Nikos's suite and one in the corridor outside his room. A video screen on the console displayed live footage from the drones' on-board cameras. Leila was picking up their audio output on a pair of headphones, and could use a channel selector if she wanted to focus on a particular signal, but so far she hadn't heard anything of interest. Nikos had made a few phone calls and had spent the afternoon watching TV.

'Someone's coming,' Wollerton said, nudging Leila.

She looked at the console as he maximized the video footage coming from the drone outside the room so that it filled the screen. A housekeeper walked along the corridor as the door to the service area swung shut behind her. She had jet-black hair, paper-white skin, and eyes as dark as crude oil. She wore a grey and white uniform, sensible trainers and carried a set of towels. Leila switched to the audio outside the room and heard the housekeeper's gentle footsteps padding along the thick carpet.

'Turndown service,' she said, and the larger of Nikos's bodyguards produced a key card and pressed it against the reader.

He opened the door and, as he stood back to allow the housekeeper to enter, she drew a pistol fitted with a suppressor and shot both men. Leila was so shocked it took her a moment to register what had happened. Nikos's guards fell to the floor, and one of them blocked the image coming from the drone.

Wollerton handed Leila the remote console. 'Take this,' he said, getting to his feet.

He took his phone from his pocket, and as he ran towards the stairwell entrance, he made a call. Leila heard him say, 'Nine-one-one? I'd like to report a crime in progress. Double homicide at the Pierre on . . .'

The rest was lost when the stairwell door slammed shut behind him.

Leila turned her attention to the console and switched to one of the drones they had inside Nikos's suite. On screen, she saw the housekeeper moving quietly along the hallway, gun raised in the ready position. Leila wished the tiny device had some kind of weapon system, but it was purely built for surveillance. She realized they had packed something that might help, and leaned over to grab Wollerton's gear bag. She unzipped it and reached inside for the XAR Invicta folding rifle. She swung the barrel into place, locked it to the stock and leaned against the balustrade to get a good line on Nikos's hotel room. Leila made the mistake of peering over the edge and saw pedestrians and cars as tiny toys, hundreds of feet below. Her stomach churned, but she didn't have time for nausea. On screen, the housekeeper had crept into the sitting room.

Leila disengaged the safety, and ignored the pain in her legs as she sighted the rifle. It wasn't scoped, but if she couldn't hit her target, she could at least warn Nikos.

Experience had taught her she had a naturally dominant right eye, so she kept both open as she targeted the large window of Nikos's suite. She saw the Greek billionaire seated on a couch, watching TV, while two bodyguards sat in nearby chairs. The housekeeper was moving into position behind them.

Leila aimed directly at the murderous woman and curled her finger around the trigger. She tensed to fire, but there was a loud clatter behind her and she glanced over her shoulder to see three men in black clothes and ski masks burst through the stairwell door. All three held pistols, which they trained on her.

'Drop it!' the one closest to her yelled. 'Do it now!'

Chapter 20

Leila still had her hand on the rifle and she must have given some subconscious signal of her intent, because the nearest masked gunman stepped closer and gestured with his gun.

'Put it down.' His voice was gravelly and he spoke with a deep southern accent.

Leila had experienced so much pain and suffering in her life and wasn't afraid of death, but she wouldn't exchange the chance of seeing her sister for the life of a crooked billionaire. She glanced over her shoulder and saw the housekeeper move into the perfect firing position behind the three men.

Nikos's bodyguards were too slow to spot the danger, and the housekeeper shot them in quick succession, dropping each man with two bullets. Nikos tried to back away, and fell off the couch. When he righted himself, the housekeeper was standing over him.

He died on his knees, pleading.

The housekeeper glanced in Leila's direction. She knew she was being watched. She checked Nikos's body for a pulse, and, satisfied with her work, left the room.

'There's no point fighting. It's over,' the nearest masked gunman said as he pressed the muzzle of his pistol against Leila's temple. 'What's about to happen to you is inevitable.'

Chapter 21

Wollerton had called the police. He'd taken the elevator down to 5th Avenue, raced round the corner, dodged the traffic when he sprinted across 61st Street, and run into the Pierre.

He crossed the lobby briskly and went to one of the bodyguards he and Leila had spotted during their earlier reconnaissance. He chose the heavyset guy near the elevators.

'Your principal is in danger,' Wollerton said.

'Excuse me?' the man replied with instant suspicion.

'I think someone is here to kill Nikos Kitsantonis. He's in danger. Right now.'

The guy moved quickly. He grabbed Wollerton by the shoulders and pushed him against the cold marble wall beside the elevators.

Wollerton couldn't resist shaking his head.

Man, this guy is stupid, he thought.

'Do you really think I'd announce myself?' he asked. 'Is that the level of threat you're trained for? Lone nuts? Call your point men. Check your principal.'

'Shut up,' the guy said, and he started to frisk Wollerton, who glanced over his shoulder and saw the other lobby bodyguards heading in his direction. This wasn't going the way he'd hoped.

Wollerton twisted out of the big man's grasp, grabbed the man's head and slammed it against the wall. The guy staggered back, dazed, and his colleagues called out and started running, but Wollerton didn't hang around. He raced into an open elevator and found himself next to a nervous-looking woman and two children. They ran out.

'Sorry,' Wollerton called out after them as he pressed the close-doors button.

Nikos's bodyguards ran towards him, while their colleague staggered around, trying to come to his senses. The bawled commands and angry faces shrank in the gap between the closing doors, until they were gone.

As the elevator started climbing, Wollerton regretted leaving his ready bag and the Invicta rifle with Leila, and felt distinctly unprepared to tackle an armed assassin. All he had with him was a Trailblazer LifeCard, a tiny single-shot .22 folding pistol that was the same size as a credit card when collapsed, and only a little wider. He'd found it in the vault and had popped it in his wallet in case of emergency. He took the Trailblazer out and twisted it into pistol formation, before slipping it into his pocket. He stood with his back against the lift control panel and prepared himself mentally as the car slowed.

Would it matter if something happened to me? he thought suddenly. *Would I be mourned like Brigitte? Who would grieve? My kids?*

The doors opened and Wollerton suppressed his dark musings. He glanced round, and, seeing the corridor was empty, ran out. The doors slid shut behind him as he jogged to the dog leg where the corridor went right. He leaned against the wall and peered round the corner to see the housekeeper shutting the door to Nikos's suite and stepping over the two bodies that lay just in front of her. Whatever had happened was done, and he was too late, but she would be a useful source of information. She hurried along the corridor to the service area and used a key card to open the door marked 'employees only' before stepping inside.

Wollerton moved as the door swung shut, and reached it just in time to prevent it from locking. He pushed it open gingerly and peered round to see a service area full of supplies and housekeeping trolleys. There was no sign of the house-keeper, so he went inside. The service lift wasn't in use, but there was noise coming from beyond the stairwell door, so Wollerton crossed the room and pushed it open.

His heart skipped a beat when he found himself staring down the barrel of a gun.

The housekeeper, a woman in her mid-thirties with a cruel face and cold eyes, stood directly ahead of him. Behind her, two guys in ski masks lurked on the stairs. They must have been backup and Wollerton cursed his carelessness.

'Kyle Wollerton,' the housekeeper said, and Wollerton felt the bite of acid in his gut. People who knew his name were only ever dangerous. 'You're coming with me.'

He still had his fingers on the door handle, and the fact the assassin hadn't immediately shot him suggested she wanted him alive, which gave him a slight chance. He slid his other hand into his pocket and found the tiny trigger of the Trailblazer.

'Uh-uh,' the housekeeper said, gesturing at his concealed hand.

He pressed the safety, pointed the gun roughly in her dir-ection and pulled the trigger. There was a loud pop, and she stepped back as the bullet went wild. Wollerton whipped the door closed and slammed it shut.

He heard commotion on the other side and felt someone struggle to push the handle down, but he held fast. There was a pause and then three high gunshots through the door. They weren't aimed at him, but they had the desired effect. He let go of the handle and ran away, bursting through the service area door into the guest corridor, where he was immediately greeted with shouted commands from the three lobby bodyguards. Wollerton turned to see them at the other end of the corridor. They drew their weapons and started running towards him. Wollerton raced away from the service area as the door opened, and reached one of the two dead guards outside Nikos's suite. He reached inside the man's jacket to find a holstered pistol and pulled it free.

The housekeeper and her two masked accomplices ran into the corridor, surprising the lobby guards.

'Drop your weapons,' the guard Wollerton had escaped from said. 'Down. Now!'

'Identify yourself,' the housekeeper said.

'You identify yourself,' the guard countered.

'Mary Salchek,' the housekeeper replied. 'Federal Bureau of Intelligence.'

Wollerton experienced a terrible sinking feeling as the woman produced identification, which she flashed at the men.

'This man's name is Kyle Wollerton,' she said. 'He is a British mercenary and was sent here by persons unknown to assassinate your employer.'

Wollerton didn't need to hear any more. He opened fire on the housekeeper, forcing her and the masked men back into the service area.

'She's lying,' Wollerton tried shouting, but his voice was lost beneath gunfire from the lobby guards.

Bullets hit the doors behind him and the walls either side, and Wollerton reacted instinctively, firing off three rounds that caught the men in their legs. They went down yelping, but Wollerton had no time for compassion. He sprinted along the corridor and barged his way past the flailing men.

He glanced round and saw the housekeeper and her masked accomplices giving chase, and fired a couple of wild shots in their direction to slow them down.

He rounded the corridor and noticed one of the lifts was coming up. He slowed to a walk and concealed the pistol in his waistband as he approached the arriving car.

The doors opened to reveal four uniformed New York police officers.

'Please help. There's been a murder,' Wollerton said, allowing panic to rise in his voice. 'The killers are behind me. A woman and two men in masks.'

Wollerton looked round to see the housekeeper and two accomplices round the corner. They were immediately greeted by shouts from the newly arrived officers, who pushed past Wollerton as they drew their weapons.

He hurried into the waiting car and watched the housekeeper try to defuse the situation as the elevator doors closed.

Chapter 22

Wollerton knew what was coming next. He was going to be framed for the murders of Nikos Kitsantonis and his bodyguards.

The elevator sent Wollerton into a lobby full of agitated, concerned people. A couple of police officers were being led towards the elevators by a man in a grey hotel uniform, and more police were pulling up outside.

Wollerton played dumb and walked casually through the lobby. His body crackled with nervous energy as cops hurried past him, their radios squawking with chatter, but outwardly he was calm, like a man oblivious to the events around him. He expected the inevitable hand on his shoulder, but none came, and moments later he passed more police officers running in as he stepped onto the sidewalk. Another officer was yelling at a squad to establish a perimeter and start corralling guests in the hotel, but Wollerton was already beyond the officers as they formed a line. He dodged an ambulance pulling up, and pushed his way through a growing crowd that spilled onto 61st Street. He crossed the road, picking his way through the line of traffic backed up along the busy street. The drivers were focused on the commotion at the hotel and like many in the crowd, some had their phones out and were filming the unfolding action. He hurried round the corner, and ducked inside 800 5th Avenue. The lobby was deserted, and he took the elevator to the top floor. The drone footage would exonerate him and they were sure to have captured the housekeeper committing the murders.

When the lift reached the top floor, Wollerton ran along the corridor to a service stairwell. He ran a Codecracker, a hand-held device that was designed to overwhelm key-card systems, over the sensor, and a moment later the door buzzed open. He bounded up the steps two at a time until he was at the door to the roof. He immediately sensed something was wrong. The door was ajar, and when he stepped onto the flat roof, there was no sign of Leila or their gear anywhere.

Wollerton walked to the spot where they'd settled for their stakeout and saw scuffmarks in the gravel. He looked around, wondering what had happened to Leila. Had she gone to the Jeep parked on 60th Street?

He jogged back to the stairwell and returned the way he'd come. When he reached 5th Avenue, two more ambulances were pushing their way north, trying to turn the wrong way into 61st Street and force their way through an even larger crowd. Uniformed NYPD officers marshalled people onto the sidewalk, so the ambulances could reach the hotel.

Wollerton crossed 61st Street and headed south on 5th Avenue. He pulled his phone from his pocket and tried to call Leila, but there was no answer. He took a left onto 60th Street, and saw the Jeep Cherokee parked about a hundred feet from the intersection. It should have been his means of escape, but Wollerton's hackles rose as he drew near. There was a man reading a newspaper on the steps of Rotisserie Georgette, a small restaurant on the opposite side of the street. Growing anxious and paranoid, Wollerton eyed the faces of pedestrians around him. The housekeeper had known his real name. Leila was gone. His training kicked in, and the old discipline came flooding back. He had to assume everything had been burned. The car could be compromised and the house on Noble Street might be too.

Wollerton turned the way he'd come and made for the subway station on the corner of 5th Avenue. He jogged down the steps and lost himself in a crowd of travellers while he considered his next move.

Chapter 23

Pearce was lying in the dark. He shivered. His skin was pressed against a cold hard surface, but warm liquid pooled by his wrists. He tried to stretch his fingers to touch it, but they wouldn't move and when he looked down he saw his lower arms had been slit open laterally. He was rapidly bleeding out. From the darkness came a fox, its eyes blazing like red-hot coals in a furnace. It bared its teeth silently, and Pearce tried to scream, but nothing came.

'Are you OK?' a voice said from a different reality.

Pearce woke to find himself in the small double bed in his van. Farida was standing over him, naked.

'You were whimpering,' she said.

'Must have been dreaming,' he replied, grateful to have been rescued from his recurrent nightmare. He'd almost died in that alleyway in Oxford when Hector Drake, the operational head of Black Thirteen, had tried to kill him. Pearce would never forget the fox who had come for his blood and inadvertently saved him.

'Sorry if I woke you,' Pearce said.

'Woke me? Nah.' Farida slipped into her underwear. 'We're going on an outing.'

'An outing?' Pearce asked.

'Yeah. You're coming too. Get dressed.'

Pearce rubbed his face and checked his watch: 1.04 a.m. 'What kind of outing?'

'Mischief,' Farida replied. 'But it's all in a good cause.' She winked and flashed an impish smile.

Pearce had years of experience of early mornings and night-time operations, but he still didn't like them. He hauled himself out of bed and got dressed.

Farida led him through the grounds, past the vans, tents and yurts where others slept. She took him along the driveway in front of the house, and they went round the bend into the trees until they came to a white Ford Transit van. She opened the back doors to reveal the small group she'd introduced him to at dinner. They all wore black boiler suits.

'Put this on,' Louis said, handing him one.

'What are we doing?' Pearce asked, climbing into the van.

'What we always do,' Louis replied. 'Righting wrongs. That's what we're all about.'

Pearce sat next to Cursor, who shifted along the bench to give him more room.

'This is your chance to prove yourself,' Farida said, before shutting the back door.

Pearce heard her run to the cab, and moments later the engine started and a light came on in the cabin.

'It's alright to be afraid,' Cursor said. 'We all were on our first outing.'

'He's not afraid,' Louis remarked with a smile, as they started moving. 'You can always see it in the eyes. He's done this sort of thing before.'

He had no idea how right he was. Pearce had been living with danger for so long, it had become part of him.

Chapter 24

Leila was used to pain, but she hadn't ever felt anything like this. She was roused from unconsciousness by a sharp sting, and instinctively tried to raise her left hand – the source of her agony – but discovered it was bound. She was strapped to a metal chair. Dim light came through imperfections in a painted window.

Leila was in a gloomy room that was almost devoid of furniture. A woman – the housekeeper from the hotel – crouched over Leila's hand, and when she stood, Leila saw a needle had been thrust beneath the fingernail of her index finger. The sight of the thing sickened her and she bit her lip in renewed pain.

'Most people cry out,' a man said, and Leila heard footsteps behind her.

Elroy Lang came into view, looking as though he was ready for a hedge fund meeting. He wore a navy-blue suit and sky-blue shirt that was open at the collar, and seemed relaxed, unperturbed by the squalid conditions or the foul work being done by his associate. Leila burned with ferocious hatred, and renewed her struggle against her bonds.

'You really do have a high pain threshold,' Lang said. 'I deduced as much from your background. Your experiences in Syria must have been formative.'

The housekeeper turned to a small surgical table and picked up another needle. The tabletop was covered with gauze and on it rested more needles, PICC lines, and other surgical implements.

The housekeeper's hands felt warm as she clasped Leila's fingers. Leila had been unconscious for the first and wished she was for the second, as the needle was pushed into the flesh beneath her middle fingernail. Leila fought the urge to scream, but couldn't suppress a cry as the needle was pressed deeper. Tears came to her eyes and she started sweating.

'So, let me tell you what will happen,' Lang said.

Leila focused on his voice. He had a soft Californian accent, and she wondered whether it was real or affected. He was adept at the game, that much was clear.

'You will give us the name of the person you are working for and we will let you go.'

Leila knew they would never let her leave this place alive. The housekeeper was a professional, who obviously relished her work, and soon the pain would move beyond unbearable. Leila knew she had to do something to avoid untold suffering.

'I don't know his name,' she said. 'But I was given a way to contact him. Do you have my phone?'

'We've already been through it,' Lang replied.

'You think I'm that much of an amateur?' Leila countered.

The housekeeper reached beneath the tabletop and produced the phone Leila had taken from the vault in the house on Noble Street.

'*Mabrouk*,' Leila said, and time seemed to slow.

Lang realized something was wrong immediately and pushed the housekeeper away from him. She looked at Leila in horror as the explosive charge inside the device detonated. The blast sent a section of metal casing through the house-keeper's forehead, killing her instantly. Lang was thrown to the floor and cracked his head on hard concrete, and Leila was blown back and peppered by shrapnel.

She saw Lang groaning and knew she didn't have long. She hopped the chair over to the surgical table and leaned down to pick up a scalpel in her mouth. Lang was stirring.

She bowed as low as possible and dropped the scalpel into her right hand. Clasping it awkwardly, she cut at the cord that bound her. Lang was on his way back to this world, and Leila thought she heard distant noises, but she refused to be distracted and focused on her bond. She cut at the black cord until it frayed and snapped under pressure. The bonds around her left hand and feet were easier and she quickly cut them with a couple of swift incisions each. She winced as she pulled the needles from her fingers, and got to her feet, as Lang started to get up.

He roared, and Leila realized she was trapped in the room with a wounded beast. She staggered towards the door, and glanced back to see Lang fumbling with his jacket. Leila was a couple of feet from the door when a man entered. He was startled to see Leila almost upon him and reached for a pistol in a holster beneath his left arm. Leila rushed forward and stabbed him in the neck with the scalpel, moved past him as Lang fired a couple of wild shots in her direction. He'd managed to get his gun out, but was dazed and couldn't shoot straight. The bullets struck the wall beside the door as Leila stumbled into a corridor that was just as gloomy and grim as the room from which she'd escaped.

She heard footsteps coming from her right, and looked left

to see a rusty old fire door. She staggered towards it and pushed the bar, which gave at the first attempt. A blast of warm air hit her as she staggered into the night. She was in a railway freight yard near a highway.

They'll expect me to go for the road, Leila thought, and turned towards the freight yard, determined to confound her pursuers. Within moments she was out of sight of the fire door, concealed by stacks of shipping containers, and soon she lost herself in a twisting maze of the things. As she staggered away, she heard Lang yelling frantic commands. The pain in her legs and left hand was excruciating, but freedom had never felt so good.

Chapter 25

Wollerton walked Noble Street a couple of times to check the house wasn't under physical surveillance. He couldn't see any sign of operatives in the surrounding buildings or any of the vehicles parked along the street, but that didn't mean he was safe. The house could be subject to remote surveillance in any of a number of ways, but without some of the devices locked in the basement vault, he couldn't be sure. He needed some of the gear, weapons and money stored inside if he was to have any chance of finding Leila, so even though he couldn't be certain it was safe, he hurried into the house and went down to the basement. He assumed the place was compromised and that he'd be interrupted within minutes, so he worked quickly to put as much gear as he could into two large holdalls. He was halfway through filling the bags with weapons and ammunition when his phone rang.

'Hello?' he said.

'*It's me.*'

He recognized Leila's voice. She sounded as though she was outside near a road.

'*Are you at the place?*' she asked.

There was no way to be completely sure she hadn't been compromised, but she hadn't used the pre-agreed distress phrase. If she was being held under duress, she would work the words 'personal contact' into a sentence.

'Yes,' Wollerton replied. 'Where are you?'

'I ran into trouble. I'm OK now. Stay there. I'll be with you soon.'

The line went dead, and Wollerton put his phone away and finished packing the bags, before climbing the stairs and leaving the house. There was a pizzeria on the south-west corner of the street, and he headed for the dumpsters that dominated the sidewalk beside it. He pushed them apart, put the holdalls in the gap, and slid in backwards. He sat on a tiny patch of pavement and tried to ignore the foul smell coming from the dumpsters either side of him. Every now and then, he would crane out and check the street in both directions, but he had eyes on the house from his vantage point, and kept watch for Leila. A few people passed him, but no one paid him any mind. He was just another homeless person, bedding down for the night.

Some thirty minutes later, as night was truly starting to take hold, Leila came round the corner and walked by him on the opposite side of the street. She was moving strangely, and held her left hand with her right. Wollerton watched for a tail, but saw no sign of one. She walked to the house and retrieved the key from the tiny locker beside the front door. She peered through the windows before she returned to the door and opened it carefully. She moved inside slowly and Wollerton heard her say his name. She was probably paranoid about him having been compromised.

He got to his feet, grabbed the bags and hurried back to the house.

Leila started when she saw him enter. 'Being careful, huh?'

'I needed to be sure,' he replied. 'What happened?' He indicated her left hand, which was bloody. She also had cuts on her face.

'I was taken by Elroy Lang. The woman who killed Nikos Kitsantonis tried to interrogate me.'

'I'm sorry. I shouldn't have left you,' Wollerton said.

'You did what I would have done.'

'How did you get away?' he asked.

'I used the voice-activated charge in the phone. Killed her. Took Lang down just long enough for me to get out,' Leila replied.

Wollerton shook his head in awe. She made it sound so easy, but Wollerton knew from experience there was nothing easy about getting away from someone like Lang. Leila Nahum was as tough as they come, and he had no doubt she was underplaying the drama of her escape. He found new heights of respect for this formidable woman.

Chapter 26

Pearce thought about the number of times he'd been in the back of a helicopter, plane or troop carrier, preparing for a mission. He'd never been big on the banter some of the other lads had engaged in, and preferred to sit with his thoughts, running through his tasks, visualizing a successful mission, picturing every threat he could possibly imagine. He couldn't do any of that now, because he still had no idea where they were going or what they were supposed to do when they got there.

Louis eyed him from across the flatbed.

'What kind of action have you seen?'

Pearce didn't reply. Looking at the men and women in the back of the van, he saw only misfits and rogues, and couldn't imagine them tackling some of the things he'd had to do. Even after he was drummed out of MI6, he managed to get himself into the sort of trouble that would horrify these people. His recent history was stained with blood and suffering that was beyond this band of pranksters. Louis seemed the one most likely to get into real mischief, but even he came across like a puffed-out cockerel rather than a serious operator. Pearce suspected whatever they had planned would be well within his comfort zone.

They'd been on the road for almost three hours and had

stopped once near some anonymous woodland, so people could relieve themselves. The slight smell of diesel and the hum of the engine had become soothingly familiar, but it died away now as the van slowed to a halt. The engine fell silent and the front door opened. Footsteps, and then the rear doors popped open, letting grey light into the cabin.

'We're here,' Farida said.

Cursor, Louis, Tanya and Sandy grabbed small backpacks stowed under their benches and slung them over their shoulders as they climbed out. Farida handed each of them each a ski mask, and gave one to Pearce as he left the van.

He stepped onto caked mud, rutted by the massive tread of an agricultural vehicle, set hard by the hot sun. They were in a layby in a narrow country lane. Trees swayed overhead and clouds drifted across a pale sky as the last of the stars were dimmed by the approach of dawn.

Farida led them towards a gate beside the layby and took them into a large field of long grass. There was a steep slope up to some rough woodland and then beyond it, at the top of the hill, a huge house. It was only two storeys, but it occupied a vast patch of land, and made Pearce think of a slumbering, brooding giant.

'Hideous, isn't it?' Farida whispered. 'It was finished last year. This was all ancient woodland until that thing was built. It has the largest thatched roof in the world.'

Pearce realized the thick roof was what gave the building such a squat appearance, resting on the modern structure like a massive bushy toupee.

'Mask up,' Farida said.

They donned their ski masks and started up the hill. Pearce put his on and followed.

'What are we doing here?' Pearce asked.

'The house belongs to Tim Giles,' Farida replied quietly. 'He owns Invinza, one of Europe's largest hedge funds. Heavily invested in oil and big industry. We're going to give him a scare. Warn him off so he finds other places to put his money.'

Pearce looked at Sandy, Louis, Cursor and Tanya in a new light. This wasn't a prank or mischief. This was breaking and entering, assault and intimidation. He wondered just how much he'd underestimated them.

'Problem?' Farida asked.

Pearce shook his head. 'All good,' he replied, as they continued their climb towards the sleeping giant.

Chapter 27

They picked their way through the rough woodland and reached a high wire fence. Louis produced a pair of cutters and clipped an opening. Once they were through, the trees thinned and gave way to an immaculately landscaped Japanese garden. Stretches of perfectly manicured lawn were interspersed with ornate rock, gravel, and water features and beautifully arranged plants. Japanese forest grass fringed the borders and swayed gently in the warm breeze and the shadows of maple leaves cut striking patterns on the lawn as Pearce followed the others towards the house.

Motion-activated lights came on as they neared the grand home.

'He's alone,' Farida whispered. 'His wife and kids have gone on holiday.'

Pearce revised his impression of the group yet again. That information would have required surveillance and intelligence gathering, which suggested a degree of competence and preparation he hadn't anticipated. He followed Farida onto a terrace and they ran to a grey steel and glass back door.

'I'm here,' Louis said, catching up with them. He reached into his pocket, produced a small lock picking kit, and got to work on the door.

'Alarm?' Pearce asked.

'The nearest police station is fifteen minutes away,' Farida replied. 'Sometimes government cuts to police funding have unexpected benefits.' She nodded at the house. 'None of his kind will sleep so well. Nor should they.'

Cursor, Sandy and Tanya clustered round as Louis worked the cylinder lock. Pearce couldn't see anything through the glass panel, which was just as well, because Louis was taking an age to wrangle the mechanism.

'You want me to try?' Pearce asked.

'I've nearly got it,' Louis replied.

Pearce didn't like the delay or the fact the six of them were bunched so tightly around the back door. 'We should spread out.'

'There,' Louis said, and the lock clicked open.

As he stood, there was a deafening bang. The glass panel in the back door shattered and the frame around it exploded in a cloud of shrapnel. The shotgun blast caught Louis in the chest and knocked him onto his back.

He started crying immediately, which Pearce knew from experience was a good sign. Sandy howled and Tanya froze in shock. Pearce dropped to his knees and tore open Louis' boiler suit.

'The police are on their way,' a man said from inside the house. Pearce guessed it was Tim Giles. 'Take your friend and get off my property.'

Farida's eyes flashed. 'You motherfucker!'

She pulled what was left of the door open, and ran into the house. There was another gunshot, followed by the sounds of a struggle.

Pearce checked Louis' wounds. Although he'd taken a spray of shot, it looked like Giles had used cartridges filled with size 5 or 6 pellets, which might kill pheasant at a distance, but would only do serious damage if used on people at less than thirty feet. The injuries looked superficial, so Pearce grabbed Cursor's arm and pulled him down.

'Get him on his feet, and the three of you take him back to the van,' Pearce said. 'Go now.'

Cursor nodded and helped Louis to his feet. The wounded man was moaning and dazed, but he had the wherewithal to stand. Tanya helped the distraught Sandy away, and when he was sure the four of them were going, Pearce hurried into the house.

As he made his way along a short corridor, he could hear the sounds of a struggle; the crash of crockery, the smash of glass, the fierce grunts and groans of people engaged in a vicious fight. He passed through a large utility room and entered a vast kitchen.

The place was in disarray. There were pots and pans scattered everywhere, and pieces of broken glass, crockery and cutlery littered the slate floor. An over and under double-barrelled shotgun lay open on the floor with a couple of spent cartridge cases beside it. Tim Giles had Farida bent back over the marble countertop beside the sink. He had one hand around her neck and the other clasped a large kitchen knife. Farida held his wrist with both hands, but the life was being choked from her.

Pearce ran over to help, but before he reached the pair, Farida twisted free of Giles's grasp and released his arm. Suddenly freed of a countervailing force, the knife swept down and buried itself in Giles's gut.

Chapter 28

The financier wore a pair of blue boxer shorts and a white vest, but when he staggered round to face Pearce, both were drenched black. Giles made a terrible, guttural cry, like an animal being torn apart by a predator, and fell to his knees. The hilt of the knife protruded from his torso, and his fingers clutched at it weakly.

'Don't pull it out,' Pearce said, running over. 'Get the lights,' he told Farida, but when he looked round, she'd gone.

Pearce eased Giles onto his back and gently rested the man's head against the floor. The blood was coming fast, and when Giles coughed a cloud of bloody spittle filled the air. Pearce ran to a huge range cooker and grabbed the tea towels that hung on a rail beside it. He returned to Giles and applied pressure to the wound, but knew it wouldn't do any good. There was too much blood and even in the grey light, Pearce could see the man turning ashen.

Giles's eyes were full of tears and bewilderment and his breathing became increasingly shallow. Beads of sweat pricked his skin and his eyes sank back into his skull. His whole body trembled, and experience told Pearce this man didn't have long.

'I'm sorry this happened,' he said. 'Do you have a message for your family?'

Giles focused on Pearce, and his eyes blazed with hatred born of dark realization. He said something but his voice was too weak to carry. Pearce kept pressure on the wound and leaned down to hear better.

'Fuck you,' Giles rasped.

Pearce didn't blame the man. He would die in his own kitchen because a stranger had chosen to single him out and make an example of him for the cause. There must have been hundreds if not thousands of such investors around the world, millions if one included all the retail investors in oil stocks. Would White Fire target them all? No one had come here intent on death, but they had obviously been willing to commit violence. Even if the world was destined to burn, could something like this ever be justified? Giles would never have the opportunity to change. His death was a waste, and whoever inherited his wealth would likely never know why he'd died, making the entire episode pointless.

Pearce heard movement and turned to see Farida run into the kitchen from somewhere inside the house.

'Where have you been?' he asked. 'Find the light switch.'

'Why?' she responded. 'He's dead.'

Pearce looked down to see Giles's eyes had glazed over. He checked the man's neck and found no pulse.

'We should have left when Louis got shot,' Pearce said.

'I didn't kill him,' Farida replied. 'He was trying to kill me. He did it to himself. You saw – it was karma.'

'We shouldn't have come in.'

'You mean *I* shouldn't have come in. But I did, and now we're here,' Farida countered, an edge of anger creeping into her voice. 'You going to lecture me, Sam? Now? Eight billion people on the planet. I don't think this one's going to be missed. He was a bad 'un anyway.'

Farida was exhibiting the callous disregard for life that came with extreme belief. A chosen few who were indoctrinated to think they alone possessed true knowledge, a process of turning outsiders into 'the other', an unworthy enemy, and an apocalyptic prophecy about the end of the world that absolved one of guilt for any wrong because we're all doomed to die anyway. It was a dangerous belief system, and Pearce could see how it would warp the thinking of all but the strongest minds.

'He had a family,' he said in exasperation.

Farida paused and fixed him with a furious stare. 'You think I don't know that? You think I wanted him to die? I didn't want this. I don't want any of this.' She gestured at Giles's body and the spreading pool of blood on the floor. 'But we had to do this.'

'Why?' Pearce asked. What had she been doing in the house?

'Because,' she replied. 'We just had to.' She took a breath and composed herself. 'Come on. We don't want to be here when the police arrive.'

She hurried into the utility room, and Pearce wondered whether he'd misjudged her. She was clearly troubled by Giles's death, but was still devoted to the cause, which made her more than an adrenalin seeker or mischief maker. She was a believer, and one who was prepared to look beyond violence to the greater objective. She didn't think everything they did was good; she knew this was evil, but she was prepared to do it anyway. The ends justify the means; the most dangerous philosophy of all.

Pearce had seen his fair share of death, but he couldn't shake the feeling of futility at the way Giles's life had ended. He shut the man's eyes, got to his feet and followed Farida outside to find her waiting for him. She grabbed his arm and pulled him on.

'Come on,' she said. 'He's not worth crying over, and our tears won't bring him back. He's a casualty of war. Sad, but necessary.'

Pearce ran alongside her, and they moved towards the trees as the faint sound of sirens rose in the distance.

Chapter 29

It was a little before one when Leila finally came downstairs. She'd taken herself up to the bathroom in the house on Noble Street, and Wollerton had thought he'd heard her crying, but it had been difficult to be sure because of the sound of running bath taps. He hadn't known Leila Nahum as long as Pearce, but he knew her well enough to be sure she'd never admit to what she perceived as weakness. She was fiercely independent and strong, and Wollerton was in awe of her constant determination in the face of adversity. Even now, walking into the room, she faced a struggle without complaint. She leaned against her cane and supported herself against the back of a green corduroy armchair until she'd worked her way round to sit on the matching sofa, next to Wollerton. She'd cleaned the blood from her hands and face, but a few cuts and scratches were reminders of her ordeal. Her hair was still wet and the slick tresses that touched her shoulder left damp patches on her loose T-shirt.

Wollerton had found a YouTube video of a fireplace, complete with the authentic sound of crackling logs. It was soothing footage and reminded Wollerton of the fireplace at Overlook, where for a few brief months he'd been happy after retiring from the service.

Leila leaned forward and poured herself a bourbon from the bottle on the glass coffee table.

'You want some ice?' Wollerton asked.

'This is fine.' She knocked the contents of the glass back in one go.

'How are you feeling?'

'A little sore. Tired. Shaken.'

'Did they . . .' Wollerton trailed off.

It took Leila a moment to realize what he was referring to.

'Seriously?' she responded. 'What is it with men? Why do you always assume that's the worst that can happen to a woman?'

'I wasn't . . .' Wollerton tried. He felt like an idiot, but sexual assault was a known torture technique in some parts of the world.

'You were,' Leila cut him off angrily. 'I've had terrible things done to me in the past. It isn't what they do here,' she gestured at her torso, 'it's what they do up here,' she tapped her temple. 'They tortured me tonight, Kyle. The powerlessness I felt triggered far too many memories. It was traumatizing, but the overriding feeling I had was of anger. I killed my abuser tonight, for the second time in my life, and I made sure Elroy Lang will never underestimate me again.'

Wollerton nodded.

'Trust me, what they did tonight was plenty bad.' She stroked her left hand soothingly.

'I'm sorry,' Wollerton responded.

Leila nodded, and they sat in silence for a moment.

'Why would Lang kill Nikos? It looked as though they were working together,' Wollerton asked.

'I thought about it in the bath,' Leila responded. 'They obviously got wise to our surveillance. Maybe they killed him because he'd been blown. They can't be sure what we've learned or who we've told. Better to cauterize the wound. Kill him and get rid of us.'

'Ruthless,' Wollerton remarked.

'No doubt.' Leila touched her left hand again.

Wollerton could see blood blisters under two fingernails, and shuddered at the thought of the pain she'd endured. She caught him looking.

'I'll be fine. Let's focus on the job.' She took her soothing hand away and made a point of picking up the bourbon with her left.

'It's OK to be human,' Wollerton said.

'Really? Would you like me to sit here and cry? Would that help our cause?' Leila asked sourly. 'I've done all my crying, Kyle. I thought I'd cried a lifetime's worth of tears when I left Syria, but sometimes they still come. And that's OK. I don't need therapy and I don't need to be rescued from myself or anyone else.'

She stared at him pointedly.

'When was the last time you cried, Kyle?'

He thought back to all the self-pitying nights at Overlook. 'When my wife and kids left?' he admitted.

'Did it help bring them back?'

Wollerton wondered whether she was putting on a front. Was this a coping mechanism? Was she really this tough? Or was it a veneer? Had she been so close to hell, her soul had been cauterized?

'No, it did not bring them back,' Wollerton conceded.

'OK then. So let's focus on tasks and results and matters we can do something about,' Leila suggested. 'We should leave the past to resolve itself. Let's keep our minds on the job and find out why Elroy Lang had Nikos executed.'

Chapter 30

Louis lay on his back on the flatbed. Pearce lifted his T-shirt. The man was dazed and groggy, and moaned incessantly. Tanya held a torch over Pearce's shoulder to add to the illumination provided by the cabin light, and the beam rocked and swayed with the movement of the van. Pearce looked at the pattern of bloody wounds. They were well dispersed, suggesting Giles had been standing some distance away when he'd opened fire. It looked bad, but the small shot and distance meant it wasn't likely to be lethal. Pearce studied the holes in Louis' torso and was satisfied with his initial assessment. These were 5 or 6 shot, used for hunting game birds, but not much good against anything larger. However, there was an outside chance some shot might have penetrated Louis' heart or lungs, which could prove fatal, and the only way to be sure was an X-ray. Pearce banged on the partition that separated the cab from the cabin.

'He needs a hospital,' he said.

'Is he dying?' Farida's muffled voice came back immediately.

'Probably not,' Pearce conceded.

'Then keep him comfortable and do what you can for him.'

Sandy was the team's play-pretend field medic and she had a first aid kit in her tiny backpack. She knelt beside Pearce and looked utterly lost at the sight of the wounds.

'All we can do is disinfect them for now,' Pearce replied. 'Keep any infection at bay until we get back.'

Sandy nodded and got to work, wetting some gauze with antiseptic. Pearce sat on the bench next to Cursor, who smiled uncertainly as Louis kept moaning and crying. Sandy sobbed intermittently as she cleaned his wounds.

No one said anything else for the rest of the journey back to the White Fire Sanctuary. Their mission had been a disaster. A man was dead and another lay wounded, a living reminder of the shocking way they'd bungled their task. The others were embarrassed, shaken and ashamed. Apart from Farida, who'd seemed quite pleased with herself when they'd finally reached the van. Had Giles's death faded from her mind so quickly? Or was it a veneer to save face in front of her team? This was her mission, and she couldn't be happy with how badly it had gone.

Finally, after what felt like an age in the back of the windowless van, they slowed to a halt and Farida spoke.

'We're here.'

The van started moving again, and Pearce guessed they'd driven through the perimeter gates. They stopped a short distance later and the rear doors opened the moment the wheels were still. There was a crowd gathered outside, and three men jumped into the van and passed Louis to some of those clustered outside.

'Hunter Grey wants to see you,' one of the men told Pearce. 'The Blue Room in the main house.'

He jumped out and followed the noisy group of people who were carrying Louis off towards one of the tents.

Cursor nodded and he, Sandy and Tanya climbed out. The three of them were subdued. Pearce followed them into the

October sunshine. He squinted like a degenerate clubber whose night had dragged on way too long, as his eyes struggled to adjust to the light.

'You did good.' Farida was at his shoulder.

'No, I didn't,' he replied. 'If you'd let me know what we had planned, I could have helped scope out the mission.'

'It's the way we always do it,' Farida replied. 'Newcomers don't get told anything until they've proved themselves.'

Pearce wondered about the cost of such a rule. How many newcomers blundered into situations they were completely unprepared for?

'Want to come and help me shower?' Farida asked.

'Hunter Grey wants to see me.'

'Why? Who told you?' Her face fell instantly, as though she'd been stung.

'One of the guys who took Louis,' Pearce replied.

'You'd better go then,' Farida said at last. 'The queen mustn't be kept waiting.' There was more than a touch of bitterness in her remark.

'I don't understand. Who is Hunter Grey?'

'White Fire gives us all names to replace old ones given to us by the dying world,' Farida replied. 'You're to be initiated.' She looked hurt as she backed away and walked towards the camper vans. 'You have to go. You've been summoned.'

Pearce hesitated, and considered going after her, but he wasn't here to soothe Farida's feelings. He needed answers. He had to find out how Mary Knight and Elroy Lang were connected and whether she could lead him to the man who'd killed Brigitte. New names were often used by cults or radical groups to strip a person's identity and create a new sense of belonging. It was clear Pearce was about to take his next step in White Fire.

He went into the main house and in the entrance hall he found a woman with long red hair sitting on a battered sofa reading a book called *The Dare* by Lesley Kara. She was engrossed and seemed not to notice Pearce until he spoke.

'I'm looking for the Blue Room.'

'First floor,' the woman replied without looking up.

Pearce walked through the entrance hall and went into a massive lobby. The walls were covered with oil portraits of the long-dead members of some ancient family. The frames were tarnished and all around him Pearce saw evidence of decay. Curled wallpaper edges, cracked marble tiles, and damp patches on the walls suffused the place with neglect. This grand home had seen much better days.

Pearce climbed the sweeping staircase and went along the broad landing, which was covered by frayed red carpet. What would have once been regal was now tatty and tired. There were small ceramic plaques stuck to each of the wide doors. Pearce passed the Orange and Purple Rooms and came to the Blue Room. The plaque was decorated with intricate calligraphy and delicate paintings of posies. He knocked on the white door, which was roughly twice the width of one found in a normal home.

'Come,' a woman said.

Pearce went inside and found Mary Knight standing in front of a huge window. The sunlight was shining through her white linen dress and caught the contours of her body beneath the fabric.

'Thank you for coming,' she said, moving towards a seating area.

The room was thirty feet wide and forty long, and was obviously the master bedroom. A huge king-size bed stood against the east wall. There were three windows set in the south wall. Two armchairs and a sofa formed the seating area near the west wall. Just beyond that was an open doorway that led to a dressing room and marble bathroom. There were oil paintings, more portraits of the long dead, and further signs of dilapidation; damp patches on the cornicing and threadbare rugs and carpets.

'Hunter Grey?' Pearce said.

'Have a seat, Sam,' Mary replied. She eased herself into the armchair with its back to the window, so the glare of the sun caught the top of her head.

Pearce sat on the sofa.

'It's been a long journey,' Mary remarked. 'We are each given a new name to mark our commitment to White Fire. My name is Hunter Grey. A wise man gave it to me after a vision quest. He taught me the power of colours, and said my hair was a blessing from the universe. It marked me out for great things.'

Philosophy had given Pearce a respect for the mystical. Many of the earliest great thinkers, and even some of the more recent ones, had a fascination with the metaphysical, but while he respected mysticism as a rationalization of the unknown, he did not think it was the same as truth. The unexplained was simply a consequence of ignorance and he believed that, one day, even the most profound mystical experiences would be explained by science.

'I see you're a practical man,' Mary observed. 'Does this kind of talk bother you?'

'No,' Pearce replied. 'I'm just not used to it.'

'What do you think you are?' Mary asked. Her eyes were captivating and her voice was whisper soft. Pearce could see why people were drawn to her. 'Do you think you are a discrete being? An individual?'

She allowed Pearce to sit with the question for a moment before continuing. 'I don't. I believe we are expressions of the whole. Alan Watts said we're like waves, that people are part of an interconnected cosmos. You are the universe experiencing itself. As am I. Once one accepts this reality, one realizes one's purpose is not the gratification of the self, but rather to serve the whole. I am Hunter Grey because another expression of the whole named me so. It is a label for the energy we all share.'

'What energy?' Pearce asked.

'To save the world from those who would destroy it,' Mary answered. 'It seems we owe you our thanks. Farida sent me a Signal message saying the mission had gone badly. Apparently you performed well under pressure.'

'I did what I had to,' Pearce replied. 'If we'd planned it better, a man wouldn't have died, and Louis wouldn't be full of holes.'

'You'll understand if we don't trust you yet, Sam. When I was with Extinction Rebellion, we had problems with police attempts to infiltrate the organization.'

'I'm not police. And if I was, you'd all be in custody by now,' Pearce assured her.

Mary smiled. It was an indulgent, unsettling expression, as though she wanted Pearce to know she thought him her inferior.

'Why did you come here?' she asked.

'Why did you start this group?' Pearce was determined he wasn't going to let her direct proceedings.

She smiled again. 'I spoke with a wise scientist who told me how close we are to the end of all things and I asked the wise folk I know how best I could serve the whole. I went on many vision quests, searching for answers, and was rewarded with a truth. This group. These people. This place. They came to me in spirit before they came to me in the flesh. I had no choice. I started this group because it was necessary. But you haven't answered my question. Why did you come to White Fire?'

'For answers,' Pearce replied. 'I want to know how I can help make the world better. Safer.'

Mary stood and crossed the space between them. With the light behind her, Pearce could see her legs and hips through the linen dress.

'What makes you think it isn't already too late?' She put her hand under his chin and lifted it until he was facing her. 'If we'd acted twenty years ago, we might have been able to stop climate change, but now . . . well, we're just ghosts. Everything governments are doing is nothing more than theatre. They're going through the motions while we await the inevitable.'

'I can't believe that,' Pearce responded honestly. He didn't believe something this profoundly important could be a lost cause.

'After the way certain governments responded to the pandemic, do you really think they'd be effective at dealing with a problem like this?' Mary said. 'That man, Tim Giles, he was already dead. His demise was just brought forward in time.'

Here was that dangerous philosophy again: apocalyptic prophecy justifying wrongdoing. Pearce didn't like being handled, so he stood and looked her in the eye.

'If that's true, what's the point of all this? Isn't it just the-atre too?'

'Just because something is fated, doesn't mean we shouldn't fight to try to avoid it. Have you ever seen someone fall from a great height? Some people flap their arms, others run in the air. Their actions have no effect on the outcome, but perhaps they feel better trying in those last few moments. How would it be if we just accepted our doom? Isn't that the essence of the human condition? Fighting the inevitable?'

She leaned forward and kissed Pearce. His mind raced, wondering how this would complicate things with Farida. He didn't want to hurt her, but this was an opportunity to get close to the woman who could lead him to Elroy Lang.

'The belief we're already dead is liberating,' Mary said, gazing into his eyes. 'It frees us from the norms that confine us and lets us be who we really are. Show me your true self.'

She stepped back and lifted her dress over her head to reveal she was naked underneath.

'Death is freedom, Sam,' she said, taking his hand and leading him to the bed.

Chapter 31

Mary was confident, sensual and slow, and it was mid-afternoon by the time Pearce caught his breath. The two of them lay side by side, the sweat cooling on their bodies. The ceiling was covered by a fresco that depicted the sky and the painting moved from a light-blue cloud-covered sunny day by the dressing room door, to a black, star-speckled night over the bed. The plasterwork was cracked in places and there were some small pieces missing, but the overall effect was beautiful and as he looked up at the painted stars, Pearce wondered who'd commissioned such striking, ambitious work. Mary kissed him and leaned over to pour a glass of water from a jug on the bedside cabinet. She was about to take a drink when she hesitated and offered it to Pearce.

'I almost forgot the first rule of this place,' she said. 'Guests are paramount.'

Pearce sat up, took the glass and drank deeply. The water was flavoured with mint and the sweet infusion was refreshing. Mary kissed him again and pressed herself against him. He offered her a drink, but she waved it away, so he put the glass on the cabinet. She caressed and kissed him, and Pearce felt as though they could melt into one another. Her mouth became part of his and it was impossible to say where his body ended and hers began. He recalled her words about waves on an ocean, all connected, and certainly saw the sense of them now. Her hair seemed to come alive as it swirled around his face, and whenever it touched his skin there was a static charge.

Mary growled like a devil, and that's when Pearce realized something was wrong. He pulled away and saw her sighing contentedly, but what should have been a pleasurable sound was, to his ear, the savage roar of a beast. Their bond, her hair, the growl. He was hallucinating.

He backed out of bed, stumbled, fumbled for purchase, failed to find any and fell. As he lay splayed on his back, he looked at the glass of water, which seemed to shine, and tried to speak, but he was unable to form the words needed to convey the jumble of thoughts that cascaded through his mind. Above him, the portraits laughed and jeered, the old faces looking down at the naked, incoherent, incompetent man sprawled beneath them. Then came Mary, cresting the edge of the bed, leaning over him, her head looming, her eyes blazing, her hair alive like a knot of silver snakes, her skin shimmering alabaster white, glowing in the golden sunlight.

'Ibogaine,' Mary said, her voice taking on a deep slow quality.

Some distant part of Pearce cursed himself for his carelessness. Intimacy had made him vulnerable. It was one of the oldest moves in the game, and he'd fallen for it.

'Ibogaine is one of the most powerful hallucinogens in the world, Sam,' Mary said from somewhere high above him. The bed had become a cliff higher than El Capitan, and while her voice boomed like a god's, her head became a tiny pinprick in the far starry night. 'It's said those who take the journey find nothing but the truth. I know I did.'

Pearce tried to back away. He could feel his mind failing as the world became increasingly unreal. If he didn't get out now, there was a risk he'd blow his cover and give up not only himself, but the entire operation. No matter how hard he tried to move, his limbs remained fixed to the floor.

'You're going on that journey of truth, and I'll be with you every step of the way, watching and listening,' Mary told him. The world was almost black now, and Pearce felt himself drifting further into the void. 'You'll learn the truth about yourself, and I will learn the truth about you.'

Chapter 32

The bag swung like a pendulum as Leila crossed the lobby. There was no sign of the previous day's drama. It was just another lazy autumn afternoon in one of Manhattan's most exclusive hotels. The morning check-out rush was over and it would be a while before the evening check-in crowd arrived, so the place was reasonably empty and there was no one in line when Leila approached the reception desk.

'Good afternoon, ma'am,' the receptionist said. He was a well-groomed man in his mid-twenties. 'How can I help?'

Leila leaned her cane against the counter and supported herself against the cool marble as she hoisted the plastic bag so the man could see what was inside.

'I was here visiting a friend yesterday,' she said, and the receptionist's face fell.

'Such a tragedy,' he remarked.

'Yes. I found this phone in the lobby. I tried calling the number listed as home, but got no answer. It wasn't until this morning I realized it might have been dropped by one of the men who . . . well . . .' Leila left the implication hanging.

'You mean . . .' the receptionist said.

'Yes, one of the poor men,' Leila agreed. 'When I saw the news report, it suddenly occurred to me it might have belonged to one of the victims.'

The phone was a twenty-dollar burner Wollerton had bought from a store a few blocks from Noble Street.

'It might have some important evidence or something,' Leila suggested and the receptionist's expression turned sombre.

'Just one moment, please, ma'am.'

He went over to a heavyset man in a grey suit who stood in an alcove between the reception and concierge desks. The heavyset man listened to what the receptionist had to say and turned his hard face towards Leila, before moving towards her with the overconfident stride of a nightclub bouncer intent on intimidating people.

'Good afternoon, ma'am. My name is Josh Reidle,' he said. 'I'm security shift manager. My colleague tells me you have an item that might be of significance.'

'I think so,' Leila replied. 'I believe one of the men who was shot yesterday might have dropped this.'

She handed him the bag.

'Thank you. I'll make sure it goes to the police. Can I take your name?' He folded the bag around the phone and slipped it into his jacket pocket.

'Is that really necessary?' Leila asked.

'In case the police need to interview you, ma'am,' Josh said. 'You might have seen something important without even realizing.'

He leaned across the reception desk for a pen and paper.

'Isli Sultana,' Leila replied. 'Apartment twenty-six, one-five-six Park Avenue.'

She'd given the details of a real New York socialite who was of similar physical appearance.

'Thank you, ma'am,' Josh said.

'I hope they catch the people who did this,' Leila replied.

She picked up her cane and leaned against it as she left the hotel. She glanced up at the rooftop opposite and pushed the memories of her abduction from her mind. They'd tried and failed to break her, and she told herself that's the way it would always be. She'd endured hell in Syria, and nothing the world could throw at her would ever compare.

She walked along 61st Street to the corner of 5th Avenue, and, checking she wasn't being followed, went south along the busy road. It was a humid day, autumn reaching back to summer rather than yielding to winter, and Leila felt her clothes start to cling to her within moments. She turned east on 60th Street, and walked fifty yards until she reached a black Honda Odyssey minivan. She opened the back door and climbed in.

'I've got it in the lobby,' Wollerton said, indicating a flat panel display that showed a tracer signal overlaid on a digital map of the neighbourhood.

Leila slid into the captain's chair next to Wollerton's. The Odyssey was the second vehicle Robert Clifton had provided them with. A custom refit had converted it from a large family car into a travelling operations centre, complete with surveillance systems. Privacy glass obscured the computer systems, screens and state-of-the-art equipment that lined the sides of the interior.

'He's making the call,' Wollerton said, indicating the headphones in his ear.

Leila picked up a pair from the console and put them in. The phone she'd given the security guy contained a listening device as well as a tracker, and she heard Josh speaking now.

'*Detective Miller. This is Josh Reidle from the Pierre. A guest just dropped off a phone she found yesterday. She says it might have belonged to a member of Mr Kitsantonis's security detail.'*

Leila was disappointed she couldn't hear Detective Miller's side of the conversation, but they'd have to make do with what they had.

'Yes, sir,' Josh said. '*I'll keep it safe until then.*'

Leila turned to the computer terminal built into the console in front of her, and ran a search in the Property and Evidence Tracking System for invoices raised by Detective Miller. Leila had chosen the PETS system because it was the most vulnerable of the NYPD's databases, and if she could identify the evidence from the hotel, they'd be able to see which precinct it had been taken to. She got three hits, but only one Detective Miller was at a local precinct; the 19th.

'Detective Robert Miller,' Leila said, pointing to an on-screen list of evidence invoices, detailing submissions made the previous day. 'Works homicide out of the Nineteenth Precinct. Logged multiple evidence submissions yesterday.'

'Good stuff,' Wollerton replied. 'Let's go get what we need.'

Chapter 33

An hour later, Leila walked towards the 19th Precinct, a five-storey grey stone and red brick building on 67th Street. The Renaissance revival building was covered in intricate stonework, and dated back to a late nineteenth-century New York that hadn't been overrun by glass and steel towers. As Wollerton watched Leila climb the steps in front of the main entrance and go inside, he couldn't help but wonder how many criminals had been brought to justice there. He sat in the back of the minivan, which was parked a short way along the other side of the street, and registered the pain on Leila's face as she neared the doors. She had refused her wheelchair, which was folded in the back of the Odyssey. He'd only seen her in it a few times, and wondered at the level of discomfort that would lead her to use it, given she was clearly in pain now. Determined and relentless, she was an inspiration, and a salutary lesson for anyone who assumed disability equated to weakness. She was one of the strongest people Wollerton had ever known, and though he would never admit this publicly, despite her diminutive size, he found her quite intimidating.

He'd been mortified to have offended her during their conversation the previous night. He was a bit of a dinosaur and had missed the diversity and sensitivity training that had now become part of the job. He'd always assumed sexual violence was women's biggest fear, but perhaps that was a projection, because it's what men had historically prized in women; their virtue. Even in the assessment and perpetration of violence, men imposed their worldview and values. Wollerton didn't know if it could ever be changed, but he made a quiet promise to improve his own understanding.

Leila emerged from the precinct after five minutes and crossed the street. There was a blast of warm air when she opened the door and climbed into the Odyssey, and Wollerton caught the ripe smells of the city.

'OK, we should be in business,' she said, sitting in the captain's chair next to Wollerton. 'They use a Nexus Sentry key-card system.'

Leila rooted in one of the drawers under the console and produced a Codecracker, which she handed to him. 'This will work.'

He nodded. He'd used the Codecracker the day before. It generated thousands of signal combinations per second to overwhelm the card reader.

'Good luck,' she said. 'And whatever you do, don't get recognized.'

'I'll try my best,' he replied with a smile, as he put on a pair of dark sunglasses.

He climbed out of the minivan and crossed the street. As he approached the precinct building, he straightened the jacket of his dark blue suit and wished he'd chosen something lighter. The wool blazer started to feel oppressively close in the afternoon humidity. The sky above the canyon of buildings was gemstone blue, but the air was thick with moisture, and he quickly felt sweat pool in the small of his back. He sidestepped a couple coming down the precinct steps before hurrying inside.

The 19th Precinct was much cooler than the street, and Wollerton was relieved to feel the squall of perspiration sub-side as he made his way through the lobby to the security door by the main desk. There was a short queue of people waiting to be seen, and uniformed officers and civilian staff dotted the room. No one paid him any attention as he held the Codecracker over the key-card reader. After a couple of sec-onds, a light flashed green, and Wollerton pulled the door open.

'I'm in,' he said into his concealed lapel microphone.

'*Got you*,' Leila replied via his in-ear receiver. '*The tracer is located about thirty yards north-east of you.*'

Wollerton had a tracking device in his pocket and there was another in the phone Leila had given to hotel security. They'd tracked the device until it had fallen still, and identified the location of the evidence room in the building.

Wollerton walked along the corridor with the casual air of someone who belonged. He passed doorways that led to busy offices, a corridor that ran off towards processing and hold-ing, and lots of police officers, plain clothes detectives and civilian staff, but no one challenged him.

He reached a junction and when he turned right, he saw his destination; the precinct evidence room. A uniformed officer stood behind thick bulletproof glass. There was a coun-ter and two hatches, one large, one small, cut in the glass for signing evidence in or out. Behind the officer was a doorway that led to the storage facility where items were kept. Wollerton could see floor-to-ceiling shelves stacked with crates.

He stepped up to the counter, and was ignored by the

officer behind the glass, a sergeant in his mid-forties, balding and overweight, who had the air of someone who never did anything in a hurry. The guy didn't even look up from the form he was completing and he wrote with the slow deliberation of a toddler using their first crayon.

'Help you?' he said, glancing up at last.

'Yeah. I'm working on the Pierre shooting and have a phone to book into evidence,' Wollerton said.

'*That's a hell of an accent,*' Leila remarked.

Wollerton had spent years in the field and had perfected a convincing Bostonian accent.

'And you are?' the sergeant asked with as much ennui as he could slide into the words.

'Joe Allen,' Wollerton replied. 'Bureau.' He flashed a false FBI ID in the name of Special Agent Joseph Allen. 'We're assisting. Detective Miller asked me to run this down.'

Wollerton produced an evidence bag from his pocket. There was another pay as you go phone inside. He put it on the counter near the smaller hatch.

'Let me get the sheet,' the sergeant said, shifting off the tall stool that supported his weight. He went through the doorway and returned with a crate that had a folder clipped to its lid. He opened the hatch and handed Wollerton the folder before taking the evidence bag.

'Just fill in the basics. I'll add the SIM card and IMEI data number later when I update the PETS invoice,' the sergeant told him.

'Sure,' Wollerton said. He ran his finger over the touch-sensitive panel on the arm of his sunglasses.

'*I'm receiving you loud and clear,*' Leila said.

The glasses were transmitting everything he saw to the minivan.

Wollerton picked up a pen attached to a chain and opened the folder. The cover page identified the crate number and listed it as the fifth bundle of evidence in the Pierre homicides investigation. It detailed the investigating team and number and noted this was the crate for communications devices. Wollerton flicked through the folder page by page, capturing the details of every item taken from the hotel, including the SIM card and IMEI details of every phone recovered from the scene. When he reached the last page and a blank entry, Wollerton added his false name and fake details about where the phone had been found.

'Thanks,' Wollerton said when he was finished. He slid the folder back.

'No problem,' the sergeant replied, shutting the hatch.

Wollerton returned the way he'd come, and he'd only taken a few steps when Leila's voice filled his ear.

'*I've got the first phone. Verizon. I'm pulling up its location data now.*'

'You're something else,' he said quietly. 'At least let me get out first.'

'*No one's even going to know what I've done,*' Leila replied. '*Never hold back a star.*'

She was a star. He'd thought they'd have to steal the phones from the evidence room, which would have been a real challenge, but Leila had told him they only needed the SIM and IMEI numbers. Her technical skills would enable her to hack the cell phone carriers' location databases, which would tell them everywhere Nikos Kitsantonis and his associates had been since they'd arrived in New York.

Chapter 34

The smoke hit him first. It was sweet and pungent and reminded him of Bonfire Night at St David's. He and the other children had each been given two sparklers and got to stay up late to watch the fireworks. The air had been rich with the scent of gunpowder and smoke, and he longed to go back to those days, to be a child again and undo all his wrongs. If he could go back further, he could talk to his mother and promise to be the boy she needed, to be good and helpful. To be the person she wanted him to be, so she wouldn't abandon him. His mind tumbled through the past, sent on a journey by the smoke. There were other smells now, some even sweeter, others spiced, sandalwood and jasmine among them, and he was catapulted back to Cairo to the night he and the team had stayed in the apartment in Zamalek, when Brigitte had still been alive. She was so beautiful and vibrant. So strong. He missed her more than he thought possible.

Sound came next. Music. Notes dancing around him, lilting, spawning colours in the darkness. A violin, flute, table and accordion combined to play a jaunty tune, and his attention danced with it, moving through his life, picking out moments of failure, straining to change them, to undo what had been done.

He felt as though he was waking from a dream, but he

hadn't been asleep. He'd been out. Out of consciousness. Out of his mind, perhaps? He'd been on a journey to other realms and was returning to his body. The smells and sounds guided him there. And then came touch and vision. He felt tears on his cheeks, and wiped them away. He came back to his body and his eyes clicked on like a television, and he found himself standing in front of a blazing bonfire. He wore nothing and sweat glistened all over his body. People danced around him, and he saw faces he recognized coming close and dancing on. Some were also naked, others clothed. Their names escaped him at first, but they soon came back; Farida, Sandy, Cursor, Tanya, and others all laughing and capering as though he was at the heart of an important celebration.

Around them, others danced, some smoked and drank. Incense burned in pots, filling the air with rich exotic scents. A band played music and a choir of sorts chanted in a language Pearce didn't understand. It was incredibly lyrical. Celtic, perhaps?

He turned away from the fire and took a couple of faltering steps, but his legs ached with the deep weariness of a hundred-mile run, and he fell to his knees. What had happened to him?

He looked up to see Mary Knight emerge from the darkness. Hunter Grey. She was lit by the flickering flames and they danced across her face and flowing silver dress, making her look dangerous but more beautiful than ever. Her hem touched the cool grass, and the length of the dress made it look like a robe. Is that what she really was? A priestess?

As she neared, Pearce was assailed by a montage of distorted images. Memories? Hallucinations? He and Mary were having sex, then she was asking him questions about himself, his past, present and future. His purpose. He saw himself talking, but his words were lost to the effects of the ibogaine. Had he told her the truth? It was only now that he recalled he was a man with secrets to be kept, that he was here on a mission, with a purpose that made him an enemy of these people. Had he confessed that to her? Did she know who he really was?

Do you? he thought. *You've lived so many lies, do you know who you really are?*

Mary drew close and crouched down. She looked at Pearce and the fire caught her eyes and made him feel as though they were burning through him. He tried to look away, but she put her hands to his cheeks and forced him to focus on her.

'You're one of us now,' she said.

She smiled, and to his dismay, Pearce found himself crying tears of joy and relief. He'd been drugged before, but nothing had packed the punch of ibogaine. He was emotionally unstable, reeling in the aftermath of one of the world's most powerful narcotics.

'You're part of our family,' Mary went on. 'You have been reborn. Your new name will be Raptor Grey.'

She stood and raised her hands, and the noise of the band and celebration died away.

'We welcome a new child of the fire,' she said loudly. 'His name is Raptor Grey.'

A cheer went up, and Mary took Pearce's arm and helped him to his feet. He was overwhelmed and disorientated, and suddenly conscious of his nakedness. People he barely knew came to embrace him like family and his world became a blur of well-wishers. It was profound and emotional, but a small voice told him he was still very high and warned him not to get carried away by the effects of the drug.

Farida was last to present herself to him.

'Congratulations,' she said, but her tone was far from congratulatory. 'She gave you her name.' She pulled Pearce close and whispered bitterly, 'You're a grey. You're hers now.'

He thought he saw her eyes shimmer as she stepped away, but she was gone too quickly for him to be sure.

'You have done well, Sam,' Mary said. 'Your spirit is true. Come.'

Mary took his hand and led him towards the main house. Behind them, the festivities resumed with an enthusiasm that suggested the folk of White Fire were just getting started.

Chapter 35

Pearce woke to discover his brain being squeezed between the calloused hands of a strong and angry god. At least that's how it felt, and the residual hallucinogen in his system helped him picture an Olympian standing over him, crushing his skull, giving him the worst headache of his life. He squinted, and dimming the bright sunlight streaming through the three floor-to-ceiling windows seemed to dull the pain. He fumbled as he reached across the bed for a can of Coke on the beside cabinet. He cracked it open and gulped it down.

'The caffeine counteracts the worst of the hangover,' Mary said.

Pearce opened his eyes fully and looked for the woman who'd drugged him. She wasn't anywhere to be seen, so he got to his feet and staggered through the Blue Room to the dressing room. He heard running water and splashing and walked on to find Mary in a huge cast-iron bath at the heart of a grand bathroom.

'Good morning,' she said.

Was it morning? Pearce looked at the sunshine catching the tops of the trees beyond the two sash windows.

'How long have I been . . .' He trailed off. He was disorientated and wasn't sure whether to challenge her for what she'd done. Would a former soldier in search of answers be angry at having been drugged? Or grateful for the opportunity to find enlightenment? He wasn't sure what emotion would seem most convincing, so he stayed neutral.

'Two days,' she replied. 'Please don't be angry with me. I have a responsibility to keep everyone safe, and there is no better way to get to know a person.' She touched her palm to her solar plexus. 'Our connection is profound.'

Pearce wracked his memory, trying to recall what he'd told Mary, but he drew a blank. He obviously hadn't broken cover otherwise he'd have been cast out or killed by now, but he had no idea what he'd said or what truth or lies he now had to adhere to. It was a dangerous position to be in.

'Can you forgive me?' Mary asked. 'Join me. Let's baptize ourselves to mark a new dawn.'

Pearce wanted to be angry, but there was something so beguiling about this warm, charismatic woman. She was so direct and yet managed to retain an air of mystery. He lowered himself into the bath opposite her, and she moved to be next to him.

'We can't be long,' she said. 'There's someone I want you to meet.'

She kissed him, and whether it was a lingering after-effect of the drugs or his imagination, her touch felt electric against his skin.

An hour later, Pearce was in the passenger seat of a blue Mitsubishi Outlander hybrid as Mary steered it along deserted country lanes that burst with colour. The verges were dotted with late-blooming wildflowers and the trees by the roadside were rich in reds and yellows, their interlinked branches forming a canopy high above them. The mottled light breaking through took them from shade to dazzling sunshine every few yards.

Mary didn't speak much. Instead they listened to a RY X album, and she seemed to lose herself in the melancholy of the music.

'Isn't it beautiful?' she remarked, as they crested a rise.

The creased Welsh countryside was laid out before them, and stretched to distant mountains. The sunshine bled the most distant hills to pastel, but the nearest were a rich green.

'We've been terrible custodians of this planet,' Mary said. 'When I see it so empty and perfect, I wonder if it wouldn't be better off without us.'

She looked at Pearce as though hoping for a reassuring response, but he gave her none. What was there to say? Humans plundered the Earth for its natural resources and polluted its air and water with the by-products, but he wasn't about to apologize for his existence. Nor would he condemn others. Mary was engaging in dangerous talk. Someone who believed the world would be better off without people was capable of anything.

'That's where we're going,' she said, pointing towards a collection of modern buildings that shone in the valley below them.

It looked like a high-tech industrial park, but even at this distance, Pearce could see grass-covered roofs and large pipes fed by ground heating systems.

'We're going to see the man who convinced me we need to save the world,' Mary said as they started down the hill.

Chapter 36

It was the eyes that gave the man away. They were haunted by journeys to places no one was supposed to go, and flashed with an intensity that suggested he'd seen things that would have broken a weaker mind. An unstable anger and great sadness made it seem as though he was perpetually on the verge of tears. His mouth hid what his eyes couldn't, and as he showed Mary and Pearce into his office, Professor Jacob Silver made polite small talk about Wolf's Castle, the beautiful patch of Welsh countryside where his research facility was located. He'd named the facility after the neighbouring village; the Wolf's Castle Climate Science Research Centre.

The centre comprised five glass and steel buildings nestled in the folds of a valley. Each of the two-storey structures was the size of large supermarket and they were all equipped with the latest technology. The complex was set in grounds that had been landscaped with the environment in mind. A stream wound its way between the buildings, and meadows of wildflowers lay all around, sustaining the many beehives dotted around the property. The trees planted around the buildings were all slow-growing hardwood. A great deal of thought and investment had gone into the place, and Pearce wondered where an academic who was no longer affiliated with any university had managed to find the funds for such an operation.

'How many people have you got here?' Pearce asked.

'Eighty researchers and just over fifty support staff. It's the labs that take up the space. We're doing some real cutting-edge work here,' Silver said. 'Please have a seat.'

He indicated a large hessian sofa next to the corner window that overlooked the research complex. Pearce sat next to Mary, and Silver pulled up a stool and positioned himself opposite them.

The man was intense, and his skin was stretched tight over his cheekbones. He looked as though he hadn't eaten anything but angst for months. He stood about an inch taller than Pearce at six-three, but was probably twenty pounds lighter, which was notable given how carefully Pearce watched his weight for climbing.

Silver took Mary's hands and held them like holy relics.

'Blessings, Hunter Grey,' he said.

'And to you, Prophet,' Mary replied.

Pearce recognized the language and behaviours of a cult, and he knew from bitter experience that the devout were some of the most difficult and dangerous people to deal with. Indoctrination often made them immune to reason.

'This was Sam Nour,' Mary said. 'He is one of us now. His name is Raptor Grey.'

'A high honour, brother,' Silver responded. 'May your road be painless and your years long.'

Pearce couldn't have concealed his scepticism as well as he'd hoped, because Mary smiled and said, 'You find our ways strange. What better way to greet someone than to give blessings? And what kinder words could the Prophet wish upon you than a painless road and long years? Our behaviour is learned, and all our learned behaviour has brought us here, to the brink of planetary extinction. Perhaps it is time we learned new ways, ways that overtly recognize the value of life in all its forms.'

Pearce nodded. 'It's a lot to take in.'

'You will understand why we are the way we are, why we do the things we do,' Mary said. She turned to Silver. 'Tell him what's to come. Tell him how the world will end.'

The academic nodded and fixed Pearce with his intense, haunted eyes. 'Have you heard of "Deep Adaptation"?'

Pearce shook his head.

'It was a paper that was published in July 2018. Written by Professor Jem Bendell, it set out why the world is on course for total societal collapse in a matter of years. Climate change will make the way we live untenable.'

'He foretold our doom,' Mary remarked. 'But unlike prophets of the past, his work was backed by evidence.'

'It was a highly influential publication,' Silver continued. 'Disparaged and diminished by those who want to thwart change, but those of us who are interested in truth saw it for what it was; the klaxon. The alarm bell. The drumbeat of danger. "Deep Adaptation" informed some of the thinking of Extinction Rebellion, and pushed adaptation up the agenda at the UN. The idea that humans must adapt to the new reality, because the planet cannot adapt to us. More criticism came and, some say because of it, Jem backed away from his starker conclusions and tempered his message.'

Silver hesitated, and his eyes took on a dreamy, faraway look.

'But I believe his original message was right. That's what

we've been doing here. Building complex models, performing large-scale experiments to prove Jem's hypothesis. I'm working on my own paper.'

'Jake is one of the leading scientists in the field,' Mary interjected.

'I was. Until I spoke out. I was targeted by climate deniers, a rich network with deep pockets. They trashed my reputation and discredited me with my university. But I was fortunate enough to meet Mary and she found me the funding I needed to complete my work. My paper is called "Beyond Adaptation".'

Silver stood, walked to the window, and gestured at the world outside. 'Runaway is the theory the world reaches a point at which it enters a temperature feedback loop. The surface water and atmosphere evaporate, and the planet becomes a barren ball of dust like Mars. But such extreme forecasts miss the point. What happens if Africa loses ten per cent of its rainfall? Or Australia twenty per cent of its water? What if the water table drops in America? And Europe continues its process of desertification? How much does the climate have to change to make large parts of the world uninhabitable?'

He paused, and Pearce took in the significance of what he was saying. Climate change had been like static, a background presence, but increasing in volume. If even a fraction of what this man was saying was true, humanity was destined for a dystopian future.

Don't get sucked in, Pearce told himself. It was the first rule of working undercover.

'If things were that serious—'

'Governments would step in, right?' Silver cut him off. 'And how does any government tell people everything they value is not only at risk, but is putting them at risk?

International travel? Cars? Consumer products? The pleasures and luxuries we're conditioned to value will all have to change or go. How long do you think any government that told the truth would remain in power?'

Silver shook his head.

'No. They pretend and procrastinate, passing the problem to their successors, but we're running out of time. Pre-industrial living is coming for us through choice or necessity. The work we've done here suggests we have five years until the start of the collapse. The exodus of people from southern Europe and Africa to the north. The end of water in parts of Australia, South America and the Middle East. Unbreathable air in India and China and extreme weather events globally.' He gestured at their surroundings. 'Five years until everything is finished.'

'And you want to stop this?' Pearce asked Mary.

'I've already told you, I think we're past the breaking point,' she replied.

'This is about slowing it down,' Silver said.

'How?' Pearce asked.

Mary and Silver exchanged a troubled glance.

'What's the point of bringing me here and telling me all this if you don't trust me?' Pearce asked. 'I'm Raptor Grey. I'm one of you.'

Mary smiled indulgently. 'You are one of us. I brought you to see the Prophet so you could hear for yourself what we face. I want you to know what's at stake, so if you are ever asked to do a difficult thing, something that seems impossible, you remember why.'

'Who pays for all this?' Pearce asked.

'We have many friends,' Mary replied.

Friends with extremely deep pockets, Pearce thought. *Is one of them Elroy Lang? Or Nikos Kitsantonis?*

'Do you understand what the planet faces, brother?' Silver asked. 'Do you see why we must act?'

Pearce nodded, studying his companions closely. Whatever they had planned was sufficiently disturbing to trouble them, and what could trouble people who'd made their peace with the end of the world?

Chapter 37

When they left Wolf's Castle, a tiredness came over Pearce. He suspected it was an after-effect of the ibogaine, but couldn't rule out the possibility he'd been wrung out by what he'd heard in Silver's office. He didn't believe the world would end in five years, but he also didn't see how the modern way of life could continue without causing long-term damage, and he had to admit he felt doubt. What if these people were right? What if the crisis was far more urgent than he believed from his position of relative ignorance? Even if he ignored Silver as a fringe extremist who was connected to malevolent interests, what about all the thousands of scientists who'd signed countless letters and statements of warning? Why were people joining Extinction Rebellion and other environmental groups in record numbers? What did they know that he didn't?

They followed the road out of the valley, and when they crested the hill, Mary steered into a layby beneath a gigantic oak tree. She pulled to a halt, unbuckled her seatbelt and climbed out.

'Come on,' she said. 'You need restoration.'

Pearce's bones ached as he followed her. She led him over a stile built into a drystone wall, and took him onto a public footpath that crossed a field and disappeared into a copse of ancient trees.

'You came to us for answers,' Mary said. 'Have you found them?'

Pearce was noncommittal.

'What do you see?' she asked, gesturing around them.

'Sky, grass, trees, clouds,' Pearce replied.

Mary chuckled. 'Such a "man" answer. Look at the way the grass dances in the wind, the long roots of the trees that reach into the earth for nourishment, the clouds, the breath of man, beast and sea, gathered in the heavens waiting for the perfect moment to rain life on the earth. I see beauty. A beauty that is more perfect than anything humanity is capable of. This is our world. Our natural world, and we are encouraged to rebel against it at every turn. Worse than that, we have devised a way of living that rewards its destruction. From the plunder of land and ocean to the pollution of its waters and sky, we have been led down the wrong path, and the doom you've just heard is the price that must be paid.'

'And you say we can't stop it?' Pearce asked.

'If you want an easy falsehood, I could stand here and tell you the lie that everything will be fine. I could make promises about carbon targets, new technology and miracles that will enable us to continue living unsustainable lives,' Mary replied, passing into the shade of the first tree. 'I could lie, but the future is settled. I'm just its handmaiden. It is my job to deliver people into the new world as painlessly as possible.'

'Sounds like euthanasia,' Pearce tried.

Mary smiled and walked on ahead. 'Time comes for us all.'

The path narrowed as it wound through the trees. Pearce's mind raced as he followed the strange woman. How was she going to deliver people into the new world? Could someone who professed such a love of life be planning mass death?

She seemed kind and empathetic, but Pearce had encountered numerous psychopaths who could mimic such traits.

'Here,' she said when they reached a clearing.

The ground was covered by a bed of dry leaves and twigs, and it looked as though no one had been this way for an age. Shafts of sunlight fell through the boughs high above them. The air was cooler here, and still, as though it hadn't been disturbed for aeons.

'Raise your arms,' Mary instructed. 'And breathe. Breathe deeply.'

Pearce stretched his arms out and took deep breaths.

'Close your eyes,' she said. 'Be at one with the trees.'

Pearce did as instructed. Many philosophers believed in the power of nature to heal and inspire, and when he'd completed his distance-learning philosophy degree while serving, he'd shed many of his prejudices against what he'd once derided as New Age thinking, but being at one with the trees was too outlandish, even for him.

'Trees give off chemicals called phytoncides that have been proven to boost the immune system and promote regeneration of our bodies.' Mary's voice was quiet, almost hypnotic, and Pearce felt a pang of shame at having inwardly dismissed her thinking. 'It is just one of many examples of our symbiosis with nature. We were meant to live in harmony with it.'

Pearce didn't know whether it was the stillness, the moment of respite, or the natural chemicals Mary spoke of, but he began to feel a little better. He lowered his arms and took a deep breath, and when he opened his eyes he was surprised to find Mary only inches away from him. She moved slowly and silently as she put her arms around his waist.

'Better?'

Pearce nodded, and she leaned forward and kissed him.

'We should take comfort where we can. While we can,' she said. 'Your eyes look brighter. Is your soul clearer?'

Pearce didn't know how to answer such a question, so he kissed her. She was beautiful and strange and dangerous and he was starting to lose sight of whether he was playing a role, or developing genuine feelings for her and her cause.

He backed away, and Mary clearly sensed something was wrong. 'Something still troubles you. When you were speaking your truth, you told me of another soldier who tried to kill you,' she said, stepping forward to take his hands. 'You said he had ruined your life. A man called Scott Pearce.'

Pearce's heart pounded. So he had revealed something of the truth, but his life was so twisted and complex it was almost impossible to unpick truth from lie. Perhaps that convolution is what saved him from betraying himself and the others while under the influence of the drug. In a way, Scott Pearce had killed him. It wasn't his birth name. He'd taken it for himself many years ago, when he'd joined the army. A way to delineate who he was from who he would become. He'd chosen it from an obscure thriller novel he'd read. If he was honest, it was also a way to reject the parents who'd abandoned him all those years ago, to extinguish his father's name and erase the first name his mother had given him.

'Do you still carry the wounds of what he did in here?' Mary placed a hand against Pearce's chest.

'No,' Pearce said. 'I haven't seen him for years. And I rarely think about him.'

Mary didn't seem convinced. Did she know more than she was saying? Had Elroy Lang alerted her to the threat posed by Scott Pearce?

'We all have our demons,' Mary said, pulling him close.

'And you?' Pearce asked. 'What are your demons?'

She sighed. 'I'm haunted by things yet to come.'

The rustle of leaves and creak of branches filled the silence.

'But this isn't a place for demons,' Mary said at last. 'It is a place for angels.'

She stepped back and pulled off the straps of her dress so it dropped to the ground.

'It is a place for healing, comfort and the celebration of life, and we should honour it,' she said, pulling him to her.

Chapter 38

Wollerton was woken by the sound of a garbage truck rolling along Noble Street. There was beeping and mechanical grinding as it compacted the offerings made by a team of workers in heavy boots. Wollerton peered through the drapes to see them labouring beneath a clear blue sky. He wasn't surprised they were out so early and in a hurry to get the job done – the air in his bedroom was already hot and humid, and it was shaping up to be another unseasonably sweltering day. Any manual labour in the heat that would shortly hit would be unpleasant.

He pulled on a pair of light jeans and a green T-shirt and went downstairs to find Leila at the kitchen table, crouched over her laptop.

'Don't you ever sleep?' he asked.

'Not if I can help it,' she replied without looking up.

Wollerton knew something of Leila's painful past, but he wondered what horrors haunted her nightmares and whether they were they reason she rarely slept. Or was her insomnia a consequence of the chronic pain rarely acknowledged?

'Coffee?' he asked, moving towards the coffee maker on the countertop.

'No way,' she replied. 'I can't stand the American stuff. It's like rusty mudwater.'

'I'll take my caffeine fix however it comes.' Wollerton set about preparing a fresh filter and filled the machine with ground coffee. He preferred Italian stove-top percolators, but this would do.

'I've been able to track the phones since they arrived in New York last week,' Leila said, gesturing at her screen, which showed a map overlaid with numerous data points. 'They spent a lot of time at the hotel. One of the phones took visits to a massage parlour on Bowery, but I don't think that was Nikos. Probably one of the bodyguards.'

Leila zoomed in on a section of the financial district around Wall Street.

'All six phones went here three times in the past week.'

'What is it?' Wollerton asked.

'An office block. Home to sixty-four different investment and financial service businesses.'

Leila moved the map north, showing the area around Washington Square Park.

'Each time they went to Wall Street, they stopped at an address on 8th Street on the way back to the hotel. It's another office building.'

She brought up a Google Street View image of a seven-storey red-brick block.

'This one's interesting,' Leila said. 'It's home to the Rightway Patriots Network, a collection of media interests that promote conservative ideology. The biggest is a twenty-four-hour news channel called Rightway Twenty-Four.'

Leila opened a window that displayed a live feed from Rightway 24. The studio backdrop was almost entirely stars, stripes and eagles.

'*Liberals don't understand how they're hurting America,*' a perfectly coiffed presenter told his audience. A gaudy, patriotically styled chyron identified him as Kent Marsden. *'They've been steeped in decades of socialist propaganda that has brainwashed them away from core American values. Communism didn't build this country. Liberalism didn't make it great. Socialism doesn't keep it safe. America was forged by rugged individuals. Collectivism didn't give us the strongest economy in the world. It was built from the ground up by patriots and heroes willing to sacrifice and strive for success.'*

'Kind of glosses over the whole slavery thing,' Leila remarked.

'Switch it off,' Wollerton said. 'It's turning my stomach.'

Leila chuckled as she closed the window.

'There are visits to restaurants and a couple of bars,' she said, 'but these two are the most interesting targets.'

'OK then,' Wollerton said, pouring himself a coffee. 'Let's check them out.'

Chapter 39

Pearce spent half an hour lying in the glade with Mary, and most of the time passed in silence. He watched the leaves waving from swaying branches high above them and watched a few drift down and settle on the ground. He allowed his mind to wander. She was strange, but captivating, and Pearce found himself feeling guilty for misleading her. He assuaged his guilt by reminding himself that she'd drugged him, but should her dishonesty negate any qualms he might have about his? He hadn't made her any promises and had asked nothing of her. She'd taken what she wanted from him and seemed content with the free nature of their relationship. And part of him needed this. He wanted to be physically close to someone. He hadn't had any kind of intimate relationship since Railay Beach in Thailand, and although he'd felt something for Alexis Tippett-Jones, the woman who'd shot her father to save Pearce's life, and had slept with Farida, it had been a long time since he'd felt an emotional connection with anyone. So long, he'd almost given up hope of ever finding anyone.

He watched shreds of clouds drifting across a gap in the canopy and imagined a different life for himself. One where he was settled with a wife and children. He pictured himself living near Railay in Thailand, working as a rock-climbing instructor, guiding tourists to the expeditions of their dreams, coming home to his family and the simple pleasures of domestic life. But the fantasy vanished faster than the clouds. He was too damaged, too broken for such things. He'd experienced horrors that would be with him forever, and had perpetrated such things on others, acts that might haunt him in the afterlife. He'd be no more suited to a domestic existence than a mountain lion.

After a few more minutes, Mary leaned over and kissed him. 'Come on. We should go.'

They stood and dressed, and walked the footpath back through the trees and across the field to the car. The sun was hanging low, and as they drove back to Sanctuary, the Hunter Grey compound, the world was lit by a perfect golden light found only on the most glorious evenings.

They drove through Pelcomb Cross, the little village just east of the big house, and Pearce made a mental note of the petrol station and shop.

Mary turned into the driveway and Martin emerged from the gatehouse and let them in.

'Thanks, Martin,' Mary said, as they drove by.

They followed the long drive to the house, and Mary parked beside the east wing, near the motley collection of vans, yurts and tents. She and Pearce got out and when she headed inside, he walked towards the vans.

'Not coming?' Mary asked.

'I thought I would check on Louis,' he replied.

She nodded. 'Send him my love. Tell him I'm sending him nothing but healing.'

She entered the house through a side door, and when she was out of sight, Pearce checked his surroundings, and, certain no one was watching, he changed direction and walked towards the treeline. Once he'd crossed the lawn and was obscured by trees and undergrowth, he started running and made for the high perimeter wall that ringed the property about half a mile from the house.

It took him three minutes to get within sight of the wall, but his plan hit a snag when he saw a member of White Fire. The guy was smoking a joint, and Pearce assumed he was out for a private high until he noticed the worn stripe of grass where the man was walking. This was a perimeter patrol.

The guard was a couple of inches shorter than Pearce and a few pounds heavier and looked like an easy mark, but Pearce couldn't risk discovery, and trying to sneak up on him and knock him out carried too great a chance of failure. And besides, the moment he came to, he would tell the group he'd been attacked. Pearce cast around for inspiration and hit upon an idea.

He moved swiftly and silently to a sun-drenched clearing and gathered dry leaves and twigs into a pile. He took his Zippo from his pocket and set a small fire, before running to the edge of the clearing and concealing himself behind the bushes.

The smoke curled and rose in patchy clouds, until the flames really caught and sent a thick black plume into the sky. The lone smoker saw the fire and ran towards it, and as he reached the treeline, Pearce sprinted to the wall. He didn't skip a step, and used his momentum to throw himself into a running jump. He grabbed the lip of the wall and hauled himself up. When he looked round, Pearce could see the smoker furiously trying to trample the fire. Pearce left the man to it and lowered himself down the other side of the wall.

Chapter 40

Pearce covered the two miles to Pelcomb Cross in twelve minutes. He was sweaty and breathless by the time he reached the petrol station, but didn't care. He couldn't afford to be away from the White Fire compound for any longer than necessary and he had to be back before dinner, when his absence was almost certain to be discovered. A large red canopy hung over the petrol station, which stood to the north of the A487. The kiosk doubled as a convenience store and had been extended to provide space for a fish and chip shop. It was a popular place with holidaymakers and a line of cars was parked in the spaces outside the takeaway. Pearce headed for the convenience store and pulled open the glass door. A powerful smell of salt and vinegar hit him the moment he stepped inside, and he saw a queue of people waiting to be served in the chip shop section. He went to the deserted fuel counter, and as he approached, a wiry old man emerged from a back room.

'Evening,' he said, as he slid onto a high stool behind the counter. 'What can I do you for?'

'Do you have a phone I could use?' Pearce asked.

Pearce was being cautious. He had a burner in the van back at the compound, but he was almost certain his belongings had been searched and had to assume they would be again, and the call he was about to make had to remain confidential. Caution was the reason he hadn't brought a Ghostlink, the satellite communicator Leila had designed, or any other computer or comms gear. He was in deep cover and couldn't risk anything that might expose him.

'I lost mine,' Pearce lied.

'My sympathies,' the cashier said. 'There's an old payphone over by the motor oil. Takes cash or cards.'

'Thanks.'

'No car? You local?' the cashier asked.

'I'm visiting. Up at the hall.'

The change was instant. The cashier scowled and stiffened and his easy, friendly demeanour evaporated.

'I see.'

'Problem?' Pearce asked.

'This was a respectable village,' the cashier replied. Pearce could see him agonizing over whether to say more. 'Anne Chesholm was a fine woman. Most round here think she lost her mind falling in with those hippies. When she died, there was a right stink when her family found out she'd left them the hall. Shameful.'

He straightened, as though he'd suddenly remembered who he was talking to.

'No offence.'

'None taken,' Pearce assured him. 'I'm thinking of joining the group, but get a strange vibe.'

'You run back to wherever you came from, sir. They're no good.'

'Thanks for the advice,' Pearce said.

He walked along the aisles and when he reached the motor oils, he saw a payphone attached to the wall. He picked up the receiver, swiped his Sammy Nour credit card through the reader, and dialled a number he'd committed to memory a few days earlier.

'*Hello?*' Leila said after a couple of rings.

'It's me,' Pearce replied. 'I don't have long and this isn't a robust line. I need you to find out who funds a scientist called Jacob Silver. Runs a lab at Wolf's Castle, South Wales.'

'*On it,*' Leila said. '*We hit a complication our end. Our Greek friend ran out of road.*'

Nikos was dead.

'*We've found some invitations to some new friends though,*' she revealed.

They were following up new leads.

'Be careful,' Pearce advised.

'*Will do. How do I reach you with the information?*'

'I'll call you,' he said.

'*Good luck,*' Leila replied before she hung up.

Pearce replaced the receiver, buzzing with questions. Who would kill Nikos? And why? What would this mean for their chances of finding Elroy Lang and avenging Brigitte's death? With that avenue closed, Pearce had to be even more careful not to blow his side of the investigation.

He left the petrol station and sprinted back to the Hunter Grey compound, racing along the country lanes to bring him to the rear of the property. He skirted the high wall until he was directly south of the main house. He found a tree growing from a verge beside the wall and climbed it slowly until he could peer over the capstones. There was a run of open grass for fifty yards and then thick woodland. He couldn't see any sign of anyone, so he clambered onto the wall and dropped down the other side. He ran to the trees and picked his way through thick undergrowth until he reached the treeline near the house.

There was a lawn of rough grass between the trees and a paved area which abutted an extension that looked like a late addition to the country hall. Pearce recognized it as the laundry block, which was next to the kitchen. He checked the lawn in both directions, and, seeing it was clear, eased himself into the open. He was a few yards away from cover when he sensed he wasn't alone. He looked at the house and his eyes travelled to the second floor window directly opposite him. There, watching him with an unmistakeable air of suspicion, was Farida.

He nodded and smiled. She withdrew into the shadows without responding.

Chapter 41

Leila hated Kelly Dan the moment she saw her.

She'd spent the morning sitting in her wheelchair outside the Rightway Patriots Network building on 8th Street, watching people come and go, waiting for the founder of the alt-right media empire to arrive. Wollerton was parked further up the street in the Odyssey minivan, and they stayed in contact via concealed radio.

No one had paid Leila any attention as she sat on the sidewalk near the building, which was a block away from the Lao Ma Spicy restaurant. As the day went on, and the scent of Szechuan food filled the humid air, Leila finally gave in to her rumbling stomach and joined the lunchtime queue. She bought herself a lamb hot spicy stew and an iced tea, which she ate back at her spot on the sidewalk. She regretted her food choice, because it genuinely was a spicy meal, and made her sweat in the afternoon heat. She didn't care. Her dishevelled appearance meant people were more likely to ignore her. She guessed most of the Rightway staff and other passers-by thought she was homeless and she had done nothing to disabuse anyone of this notion. She wore a pair of torn jeans and a green camouflage T-shirt. Her hair was a mess and she hadn't bothered with any make-up. It was an all too easy role for a woman who often found herself tired of the conventions created by the expectations of others.

Her grungy look was in stark contrast to the polished perfection of Kelly Dan, who emerged from the back of an Escalade shortly after lunch. She was clearly a woman who paid meticulous attention to her appearance. Her sunshine-blonde hair shimmered, but didn't move in the gentle breeze. Her figure bordered on waiflike and her navy trouser suit hung from it so naturally a catwalk model would have been jealous. Kelly's face was a work of art, with mascara, foundation, lipstick and blusher applied with the care of an Old Master. Kelly was followed out of the huge SUV by a young female assistant who was clearly trying to emulate her boss in her wardrobe and styling choices, but who had a way to go before achieving the heady heights of perfection. If Leila had seen the two in a bar, she would have given them a wide berth. She preferred her lovers to have the rough edges of authenticity.

Both women glanced at Leila as they approached the building, and their expressions betrayed their disgust. Undeterred, Leila rolled her wheelchair towards them.

'Miss Dan, Miss Dan,' she said. 'My name is Iman Hosni. I'm a refugee from Syria.'

'We have an outreach programme,' the assistant cut in.

Leila noticed the driver of the Escalade and a man in the passenger seat get out of the vehicle and position themselves on the sidewalk, facing her. Both men were big and wore dark suits: bodyguards. But they weren't any good, because she was within striking distance of their principal.

'I'm not here for charity,' Leila said. 'I have a story for Miss Dan.'

'You can file tips through our website,' the assistant said, placing herself between Leila and Kelly.

'OK. Maybe I'll take it to Fox News,' Leila responded.

Forty-two-year-old Kelly Dan had been an anchor at Fox News, and had left under something of a cloud when she'd gone on a tirade against Covid-19 restrictions, declared the virus a hoax and made racist remarks about its origins. She regularly railed against Fox during her one-hour show, *The Dan Report*, and quite possibly hated her old network more than she despised socialism. Leila saw her threat hit home, and Kelly stopped walking and sized her up.

'What kind of story?' she asked.

'I was approached by someone who works for state senator Bob Mitchell. He offered me money to say I'd been assaulted by the East Coast Loyal Men,' Leila revealed.

The Loyal Men were a political group with chapters all over the country. Slightly left of the Ku Klux Klan and with more palatable branding, they were a group of far-right thugs who shouted about liberty and free speech, while intimidating immigrants and minorities. The East Coast chapter were linked to Bob Mitchell's Republican opponent Stuart Dawes. Leila had done her research and knew it was the kind of story Kelly couldn't resist; a liberal group offering her money to frame righteous patriots.

'Do you have proof?' Kelly asked.

Leila nodded. 'Audio and video.'

Kelly smiled. 'You'd better come inside.'

Chapter 42

Rightway Patriots Network was an outfit that was clearly trying to punch above its weight. Inside, the building was pretty tatty, and the lobby reminded Leila of a rundown public library that had tried to mask the blemishes of under-funding with motivational posters. Only in this instance, the motivational posters were of eagles and flags and quotes such as 'Rightway: the right way' and 'Right thinking for people who think right'.

She followed Kelly and her assistant, who was called Irene, into the elevator, and they took it up to the fifth floor, which had been converted into a giant open-plan office.

It was loud, chaotic and crowded. Desks were crammed into every available space and they were all occupied by preppy twenty-somethings who had the glint of zealotry in their eyes. There wasn't a non-white face in a room of sixty or so staffers, but Leila was sure Kelly would say that was luck of the draw rather than a deliberate hiring policy. No doubt these idealists felt they were doing good, patriotic work – the word 'patriot' was in the name of the network after all – but having watched some of Rightway's output, Leila recognized the shouty, biased journalism that was intended to sow division and discontent.

According to the Rightway website, the network attracted

an audience of over twenty million Americans and generated more than 100 million unique web users from all over the world. Leila pitied them. They had little idea how they were being manipulated by the use of emotive issues, and moved along a pathway of hate and radicalization. Viewers and web users wouldn't be aware of the objective of such manipulation. Even Leila didn't fully understand it. Was fear better for the economy? Did contentious editorial attract more advertisers? Or was there some more nefarious goal in mind? Leila suspected the latter, and if she was right, these young soldiers in the information war were unwitting fools in whatever campaign was really being waged.

Leila wheeled herself past the mass of desks and followed Kelly and Irene to an executive office located at the front of the building. Irene went to a vacant desk near the office, and Kelly led Leila inside and shut the door behind them.

'A lot of mouths to feed,' Leila observed as she wheeled herself near Kelly's desk. 'Business must be good.'

Kelly smiled as she sat in a plush executive chair. 'We do OK.'

Leila wondered who bankrolled the operation. The corporate structure was opaque and ultimate ownership obscure. She'd only been able to track it to Belize, where it disappeared into a blind trust. Offshore patriotism. National pride without national taxation.

'Can I hear your evidence?' Kelly asked.

Leila smiled. This was where it was going to get awkward.

'There is none,' Leila confessed. 'I needed some time alone, and you wouldn't agree if you knew the real reason.'

Kelly's smile wavered but didn't fall. It was as though she

was accustomed to being cheated. Perhaps a peril of operating in the world of fringe, toxic media?

'Which is?' she asked.

'Your relationship to Nikos Kitsantonis.'

Kelly's smile broadened but there was a darkness to it that overshadowed any sense of happiness. 'Never heard of him. It is a him, isn't it? It's always so hard to tell with these foreign names. What was your name again?'

Leila ignored her. 'He's been here twice in the past week.'

'Look around.' Kelly gestured at the gaggle of staffers beyond the glass partition. 'I employ hundreds of people. Dozens on this floor alone. Maybe this person was visiting a friend?'

'We have photographs of the two of you together,' Leila lied. There was no way Nikos Kitsantonis came here to meet a functionary.

'We? Just exactly who are you?' Kelly was finally rattled. 'I think you need to leave,' she said, getting to her feet.

She came round the desk and tried to grab Leila's RGK Octane, but the wheelchair didn't come with handles, making it difficult for others to control.

'You get out now,' Kelly said with rising frustration.

While she struggled to manoeuvre the chair, Leila slipped a tiny transmitter from beneath her thigh and stuck it to the underside of Kelly's desk.

'I can show myself out,' Leila said, taking control of her chair.

She hated people touching it without her permission, and reversed over Kelly's feet before rolling forward.

Kelly yelped and backed away.

'You know he's dead?' Leila remarked as she steered towards the door. 'Whatever he was up to is extremely dangerous.'

Irene must have heard things go sour, because she opened the door and stood beside it like a disapproving sentinel.

'Someone didn't like what he was doing,' Leila said. 'Better take care, Miss Dan. You don't want to end up like your friend.'

Leila felt Kelly glowering at her as she rolled through the bustling propaganda factory. She wheeled herself into the elevator backwards, and smiled at Kelly, who was on the phone as the doors closed.

Leila wasn't surprised to find the two suited heavies who'd been in the Escalade waiting for her when the doors opened on the ground floor.

'Ma'am, we're going to need you to come with us,' the shorter of the pair said. 'We need to ask you some questions.'

'There you are,' Wollerton boomed. He came rushing across the lobby. 'She wanders off sometimes. Especially when she forgets her meds,' he told the heavies, tapping the side of his head.

He pushed between them and cleared a path for her to wheel herself between the two suits. They eyed Wollerton, who smiled, but stared right back. Once Leila was clear, Wollerton joined her and they headed for the door.

'Meds?' Leila asked quietly.

'You're sufficiently unhinged to need them. That was quite a performance in there,' he replied. 'Did you have to upset her quite so much?'

'People make mistakes when they're angry. Besides, I really don't like her.'

They went outside and hurried along the street to the mini-van. Wollerton folded Leila's wheelchair and stowed it in the trunk, while she slid into one of the captain's chairs and listened to what the transmitter had already sent them from Kelly's office.

'Yes.' Kelly's voice came through the console speaker. '*Yes, I'm sure. They've linked me to Nikos. I don't know how. You were supposed to have taken care of this. That's the whole reason he was . . . yes. I am being careful. OK. We'll speak then.*'

Wollerton jumped in the driver's seat, fired up the Odyssey and started along 8th Street. Leila saw Kelly's bodyguards eye them as they drove past the building, but the privacy glass prevented them seeing inside.

'She made a call,' Leila said. 'Wasn't on any of the office lines. Must have been a mobile. She's definitely connected to Nikos Kitsantonis and from the sound of things, might be connected to whoever killed him.'

'We're going to need to take a closer look at her,' Wollerton remarked.

'Yes.' Leila nodded. 'A much closer look.'

Chapter 43

The people of the Sanctuary gathered around a fire that had been set in the paddock to the east of the grand house. Chairs and blankets had been brought over and everyone sat under the starry sky to drink, smoke and talk. Farida hadn't said anything to Pearce, but she'd eyed him with hostility throughout the evening meal. He couldn't tell whether she was suspicious or jealous he was now with Mary. Probably both. He didn't sit with Tanya, Cursor, Sandy and Farida, but had eaten with Mary and some of the more senior members of the group instead. Alan, a forty-something former police officer; Jenny, a management consultant who'd had a mid-life awakening; and Tolo, a Spaniard who gave nothing away about himself or his background. Pearce put the man in his late thirties and got the sense of someone intelligent and strong.

Farida was watching Pearce now. She sat alone, north of the fire, and her eyes took on a red glow whenever she looked directly at him. If Mary noticed, she gave no sign. She sat next to him on a blanket that had been laid out over the bone-dry, tufty grass, and chatted with Jenny.

Pearce got up and walked over to Farida.

'You OK?' he asked. He had to know if he was at risk of exposure.

'Don't flatter yourself,' she replied. 'Men come and go for

me. And for her.' She nodded at Mary, who smiled at them both. 'She's welcome to my scraps.'

'Scraps!' Pearce scoffed.

'I'm just trying to work out what you were doing in the woods,' Farida said, eying him unflinchingly.

Pearce had no doubt she'd been hurt by his relationship with Mary, and in normal circumstances, he would never have behaved in this way, but this wasn't about any of their feelings, not even his own. He was here for Brigitte Attali, to find the man who killed her, stop him from perpetrating whatever he had planned, and punish him for her death. Pearce was well acquainted with the dangers of utilitarianism and didn't feel good about his actions, but the question of whether the ends justified the means was a judgment call everyone made every single day of their lives, and in his opinion, in this instance he didn't have a choice. But did that make him any better than these people, who were also pursuing questionable ends because they believed in them? Pearce used to be able to put clear distance between himself and the morals of the people he was up against, but in this case he was getting confused. He sympathized with their cause, and he felt something genuine for Mary.

She trusted him because of their intimacy, not in spite of it. His problem wasn't faking an attraction – he was concerned he was warming to the sensuous, intelligent, unusual idealist, and found himself thinking more and more about her crusade. If the planet was in genuine peril, were these people villains or heroes?

'I was—' Pearce began, but his answer was cut short by a cheer.

He looked round to see Louis crossing the paddock. Sandy

and Tanya had risen and rushed across to help him. He leaned on the women for support and beamed broadly at the gathering, as the members of White Fire applauded, cheered and called his name. He passed through the group to a clamour of congratulations and back-patting.

'I hear I owe you,' Louis said, when he finally reached Pearce. 'Your quick thinking got me out of there.'

'It was a team effort,' Pearce replied, nodding at Sandy and Tanya. 'Good to see you up and about.'

'Couple of ounces of buckshot can't keep me down,' Louis said with a cheeky smile.

Mary came over. 'It's good to see you, Louis. Your strength inspires us all.'

'Thank you, Hunter Grey,' Louis replied, bowing slightly.

The gesture made Pearce think of a wild animal who'd been tamed by a druidess.

'Everyone,' Mary said to the group, which quickly fell silent, 'Red Fox is back with us, and I know we've keenly felt his absence. His sacrifice and bravery are a testament to the clarity of his soul. An inspiration to us all.'

There were murmurs of agreement.

'Raptor Grey met the Prophet today, and it reminded me of the darkness that lies ahead. We shall all need bravery and strength in the time to come.' Mary sighed. 'Our day is almost done. The Earth will shrug us off as it has so many species in its rich history. Most will perish, but a few, a wonderful chosen few, might survive for a time and if they're willing to strive and struggle, and they will be given the opportunity to build a new paradise. As I look around at the wonderful souls gazing back at me, I truly believe we will be among this fortunate number and I couldn't think of a more blessed group of folk

I'd rather be with. I want you to hold on to that knowledge during the hard days ahead.' She smiled. 'But for now, let us welcome back our brother.'

She clapped her hands, and applause and cheers broke out across the paddock. She hugged Louis, and as he watched them embrace, Pearce found himself questioning the morality of what these people were doing. Scientists around the world were warning about the catastrophic impacts of climate change. Only those with an agenda doubted it was real. The scientific community was united in its assessment of the severity of the threat. If the threat was real, was radical action justified? Did those who were informed have a moral duty to alert people who weren't? How far should they go in their attempts to avert a disaster that was almost beyond imagining? Was this eclectic group of misfits a microcosm of what was to come? Would the next wars be waged over the future of the planet?

Pearce had a tendency to get carried away with big ideas, and reminded himself of the job he was here to do. Mary's language and beliefs were the stuff of cult leaders throughout history. An exclusive group possessed of a secret not known by outsiders, chosen by destiny to live in a future paradise, but in order to earn their reward they had to endure some form of sacrifice. Pearce was being seduced by something his rational mind knew was a trick.

There was a climate emergency, but it didn't mean Mary and her tribe were right about how it was going to play out, nor did it legitimize their illegal actions. At least one man had died because of them, and Pearce reminded himself of Tim Giles taking his last breath in his arms. It was a memory he would hold onto the next time he felt himself losing his way.

That man's family would be devastated by his death, and his only crime had been to try to provide a good living for them. Pearce was here for Brigitte and for justice, nothing else.

'Shall we go?' Mary asked, stirring him from his reflection.

Pearce nodded.

'We should sleep while we can,' Mary went on. 'There's an action planned for tonight. I shall lead it myself, and I want you with me. We leave at two.'

'What action?' Pearce asked.

She took his hand. 'We're going to let the world know we exist,' she replied, leading him towards the house. 'We're going to spread the word.'

Chapter 44

'So, are we going to check out the address on Wall Street?' Wollerton asked above the sound of frying onions.

Leila sat at the kitchen table, hunched over her computer. They'd returned to the house on Noble Street after a quick shopping trip at the local Key Food supermarket.

'Don't let the onions burn,' Leila said without looking up. 'Now add the lamb.'

She was teaching Wollerton how to make *kebab hala*, one of her favourite childhood dishes, so he could impress his kids with a delicious meal. Her grandmother had innovated on the usual recipe and substituted lamb for beef, and Leila had continued the family tradition. Wollerton did as instructed and stirred in diced lamb, which sizzled as it hit the pan.

'Well?' he asked.

'You're doing fine,' Leila replied.

'Not this,' he objected. 'The other place Nikos visited. Shouldn't we check it? Find out exactly where he went?'

'I think I already know,' Leila replied, turning the laptop to face him.

The screen displayed the website of Western Atlantic Investments, a venture capital firm.

'I did some more digging into Rightway, and found some information on the Belize trust. Looks like it is controlled by Western Atlantic. And guess who sat on the board of advisors?'

'Nikos Kitsantonis,' Wollerton replied.

Leila nodded. 'And Miss Kelly Dan was added as a director of Western Atlantic last week. I think she replaced Nikos before anyone knew he needed to be replaced.'

'Succession?' Wollerton remarked.

'Why not? The timing seems too coincidental.'

'These people are cold.'

'That's not even the worst of it,' Leila said.

Wollerton waited expectantly, but Leila frowned.

'Don't be complacent,' she told him. 'Burned meat is a crime. Pay attention.'

Wollerton rolled his eyes, turned to the stove and stirred the contents of the pan.

'Now add the tomato paste, cumin and coriander powder, nutmeg and lamb stock,' she instructed.

Wollerton had all the ingredients in bowls, laid out on the counter. He was far too methodical to make an exceptional Middle Eastern cook, but Leila thought she could train him to be a good one. He added the ingredients to the pan.

'I've been digging into who finances Jacob Silver, the scientist Scott wants background on, and I discovered he gets his money from an outfit called the Overton Group. Overton is one of the principal investors in Western Atlantic.'

'So they're connected?' Wollerton asked.

'Yes, but it's who connects them that is of real interest,' Leila replied. 'The Overton Group is a private investment and research fund endowed by Bayard Madison Bank.'

'What? Lancelot Bayard Oxnard-Clarke?'

'Eighteenth Viscount Purbeck,' Leila confirmed, referring

to the corrupt, racist English baron who'd created Black Thirteen. 'He might have started it, but the current chairperson of the Overton Group is Alexis Tippett-Jones.'

'His daughter?' Wollerton asked in disbelief.

'Yes. It makes you wonder. Scott thought she shot her father to save his life, but what if she killed Oxnard-Clarke to cover up a bigger conspiracy? What if she was involved?'

Wollerton feigned being hit by a brick and staggered back a couple of steps. 'My mind is blown.'

They both took a moment to absorb the significance of Leila's hypothesis.

'And a cup of water,' Leila said, when she could no longer stand the sound of dry frying. 'Stir it in, and put the pan in the oven.'

Wollerton nodded and did as instructed.

'Patricide? That's a bad place to go,' he observed.

'Yes, but if these people are zealots, her father would have expected no less, and would likely have done the same to her if the tables had been turned. I encountered people like this in Syria. Members of ISIS. Nothing is above the cause.'

Leila paused, reflecting on the evil she'd seen and suffered herself.

'I'm sorry,' Wollerton said. 'For what happened to you.'

'Thanks, but it wasn't your fault and it's not your place to apologize any more than it would be right for me to say sorry your wife left you.'

Wollerton nodded and they were silent for a moment. He was a good man. Not perfect. No one was, but he was good, with a kind heart. If she didn't prefer the company of women, Leila might have been interested in him.

'You think that's what they did to Nikos?' he asked.

'They knew we were watching him. Maybe that's their policy. Eliminate threats. Cut off anyone who's compromised,' Leila replied.

Wollerton whistled as he put the pan into the hot oven. 'Pearce is going to freak.'

Leila sighed. If she was right, and Alexis Tippett-Jones hadn't been an innocent victim, Pearce was unlikely to take the news well. One thing she could say with certainty about the stubborn, determined, dangerous man; he hated being played for a fool.

Chapter 45

Mary wasn't like Farida. She ran her operation professionally and briefed everyone in advance. She, Alan, Jenny and Tolo sat with Pearce in the back of the van. They all wore black boiler suits. Farida was driving, and they could hear the steady growl of the engine as the van chewed the miles between Pelcomb Cross and London.

'We should arrive at Heston Technology Park a little after four,' Mary told them. 'Our target is Zyberian Network Solutions.'

She held an iPad and flipped between Google Maps and images of their intended target as she briefed them. Zyberian was an Internet backbone provider and managed many of London's high-capacity online businesses and websites. It was responsible for routing twenty per cent of the capital's Internet traffic. The firm was located in a technology park not far from Heathrow.

'We'll stop at the adjacent industrial estate, by this logistics firm, and cross the grounds here,' Mary said, indicating a stretch of open land on the satellite image. 'Once we reach this point, Alan and Jenny will disable Zyberian's exterior cameras by cutting the CCTV power supply located in a junction box here.'

She tapped a small outbuilding on the screen. 'Sam, Tolo

and I will infiltrate Zyberian's data centre and head for the main server room.'

'What are we going to do when we get there?' Pearce asked.

Mary smiled, but didn't reply.

'Once we've done what we need to do, we'll go back the way we came, and get out of Dodge,' she said.

'Any physical security?' Pearce asked.

'Three guards. Two in the control room, one on patrol,' Mary replied. 'When the cameras go down, I expect someone will be sent to check them, so knocking them out should double as a distraction, but we won't have long.'

She took them through the plan a couple more times, and gave everyone the opportunity to ask questions. When the van finally slowed to a halt, the group was well briefed, but tense and silent. Farida jumped out of the cab and opened the rear doors. Everyone put on their ski masks, and stepped into the warm night.

They were parked at the edge of an industrial estate, beside a grass bank. Pearce could see the technology park over the rise and it looked as it had in the images on Mary's iPad. Bright new buildings stood beside landscaped grounds and huge car parks. Abstract sculptures dotted the open spaces, illuminated by atmospheric spotlights.

'Come on,' Mary said, and she led them across the grassy bank.

Pearce glanced over his shoulder to see Farida begin changing the false licence plate on the van. They crested the rise and ran down a long grassy slope on the other side. Up ahead was the junction box that housed the CCTV power supply.

Alan and Jenny stopped beside it, and Pearce, Mary and Tolo ran on.

The Zyberian building was the size of a football pitch. Three storeys high, the walls were predominantly constructed of silver metal hexagons, which made Pearce think of a bee hive. The few windows were black in the gloom, and the place was silent and still.

Mary signalled them to stop, and pulled a radio from her pocket. 'Are we ready?' she asked.

This was one of the more mundane operations Pearce had ever been involved in, but his heart was still racing and he felt the charge of excitement as he sucked in lungfuls of cool air.

'*You're good,*' Jenny replied. '*The circuit is down.*'

Mary nodded and the trio started running again. They sprinted across a car park and went to a fire exit in the middle of the building. Tolo produced a tiny compressor attached to a couple of metal plates. He wedged the plates between the frame and door, and switched on the compressor. A small pneumatic jack separated the plates and drove them further and further apart, until the lock popped and the door swung open. There was no alarm, just the sound of buckled metal settling.

They were in.

Chapter 46

They ran along a concrete corridor until they reached an interior door, where Tolo worked his magic with the compressor again.

'*We've got a guard en route to the junction box,*' Jenny said over the radio.

'Got it,' Mary said, as they hurried further into the building. 'Fall back.'

Pearce followed Mary and Tolo past empty offices, down a long corridor, through a number of doors until they came to the secure section of the building. Pearce saw a huge server room through a strip window of reinforced glass. Racks and racks of servers stretched into the depths of the vast chamber. At the end of the corridor stood a heavy vault door set flush in the wall. Tolo's tiny pneumatic jack wouldn't be much good against something like that.

'Stay here and keep watch,' Mary told Pearce.

She strode towards the vault door, pulled a key card from her pocket and ran it over the reader. The locking mechanism came to life, and massive pressurized bolts retracted into the door before it swung open automatically.

'A gift from Tim Giles,' Mary explained, flashing the card. She and Tolo went into the super-cooled chamber and the heavy door closed behind them.

Pearce kicked himself for underestimating these people. Farida hadn't panicked after Giles's death. She'd gone into his house to obtain the key to this door. He must have been an investor in the company or on the Zyberian board. White Fire wasn't on a wild tour of mischief. These people were working methodically, moving towards some objective that was as yet unclear. Pearce peered through the strip window, but couldn't see any sign of Mary and Tolo. He was desperate to know what they were doing, but left on the outside there was no way of knowing. Did Mary really trust him? Or had he been told to keep guard because she still had suspicions?

Whatever they were doing wasn't interrupted and a few minutes later the vault door opened and Mary and Tolo stepped out of the server room.

'Let's go,' she said, and led Tolo and Pearce back the way they'd come.

They retraced their steps and made it to the concrete corridor that was capped by the exterior fire door.

'We're clear,' Mary said into her handheld radio. 'Are we good to go?'

There was no reply.

'Do you copy?'

Again, nothing.

'Let me go first,' Pearce whispered, and he pushed past Mary and crept to the fire door.

He eased it open and when he stepped outside, he felt gloved hands on him immediately. He looked round to see a uniformed police officer trying to pull him out of the doorway.

'You're under arrest—' the big man began, but Pearce cut him off with a kick to the shin.

Three other police officers rushed past their colleague and grabbed Pearce's arms and shoulders. He knew the drill well; they would try to get him on the ground, so he bucked and brawled, resisting like a wild animal.

'Spray him!' one yelled.

A heel stamp would do no good against steel toecaps, so Pearce scraped the side of his shoe along the shin of one of the officers, and the man winced and backed off, clutching his leg. His retreat freed Pearce's left arm and he brought it round to grab the hand that was trying to douse him with pepper spray. He pushed it aside and the jet of liquid hit one of his assailants, who cried out and released his hold. Pearce drove a fist into a third officer's face and knocked him down, and he slipped free of the final cop and started running.

'Tase him!' someone yelled, but Pearce had already opened up too much ground.

He sprinted away from the grassy slope, and saw an opportunity in leading the police away from the other White Fire members. If they hadn't already found Farida, his diversion might give Mary and Tolo a chance to escape and it would offer him the time he needed to contact Leila.

He ran along the building with the four officers in pursuit, moving a little awkwardly in their body armour. There was no sign of other cops and, as Pearce glanced back, he was glad to see Mary and Tolo slip out of the fire exit and run across the car park towards the grassy slope.

Pearce reached the end of the building, and, as he rounded the corner, he saw three police cars and two motorcycles in the car park, and another four officers mustering around one of the cars.

Pearce seized the element of surprise and ran towards

them. He launched himself across the bonnet of the nearest car and slid out of reach of the assembled officers. He jumped on one of the police BMW R1200s and started the ignition. One of the motorbike officers raced over and tried to grab him, but Pearce kicked him away, stamped on the gear pedal and shot forward. A car might have seemed the safer option, but Pearce knew most British police forces had standing orders not to pursue a motorcyclist, particularly not one without a helmet, in case they caused an accident. Pearce glanced in his mirror and saw commotion, but no sign of pursuit. He gave quiet thanks to health and safety regulations as the bike roared and spirited him away.

Chapter 47

Pearce ditched the motorbike on a side street near Northolt tube station. He removed his ski mask and laid the bike on its side between two parked cars, so it would be harder to spot. He hurried along the residential street, past a parade of shops, and across a dual carriageway that was almost deserted. It was too early for rush hour, too late for ravers. He caught a dawn train into Central London and got off at Greenford to take another train going west, back the way he'd come. He changed trains and directions a couple of times until he ended up in Shepherd's Bush.

He emerged from the modern station beside the Westfield Centre as rush hour was starting, and took comfort in the number of people who were around. He left the station and went to one of the payphones on the broad promenade that led to the huge mall.

He used his credit card to place a call, and it was answered after a couple of rings.

'It's me,' he said.

'*We found the scientist's financier,*' Leila replied. '*An old friend of ours.*'

Leila paused.

'*Alexis Tippett-Jones,*' she said at last.

Pearce was stunned. Alexis Tippett-Jones, the woman who had shot and killed her own father to save Pearce's life.

'*She's connected to the Greek and whatever's happening over here,*' Leila went on. '*Through an outfit called the Overton Group.*'

Pearce churned the events of the Black Thirteen investigation through his mind. Had Alexis murdered her father to protect a wider operation? She'd played the victim to perfection, but was she the one really pulling the strings? He thought back to that night after he'd faced down Hector Drake, and recalled the look of recognition on her father's face. Was there acceptance? Had he known he needed to die? And the Overton Group was a sick joke. The Overton Window was a well-known theory that described the acceptable limits of political policy. Shift the Overton Window and you could make previously unimaginable policies palatable.

'Thanks,' Pearce replied. 'I'll be in touch.'

'*Be careful,*' Leila said.

'You too,' he responded before hanging up.

He leaned against the phone, feeling like a fool. Had his pity for Alexis blinded him to the truth? He cursed his poor judgment and turned away from the phone only to be shocked by the face that was inches away from his.

It was Louis.

'Hello, Sam. If that is your real name. Who were you on the phone to?'

Pearce tried his best to dissemble, 'Jeez, mate. You gave me a fright. What the heck are you doing here?'

He tried to move away from the phone.

'Easy, fella,' Louis cautioned, drawing Pearce's attention to a pistol he held in the pocket of his hoodie. 'I asked you a question. Who were you on the phone to?'

Pearce didn't answer.

'Farida told me she'd seen you out by the woods. Asked me to follow you.' Louis held up his phone, which displayed a locator beacon. 'She put a tracking device in your boiler suit.'

Pearce couldn't believe it. He'd been tagged and tracked by amateurs.

'Who were you talking to? Law? Security services?'

'I was calling Farida. We got split up,' Pearce replied.

'Calling Farida?' Louis sneered. 'Good idea. Why don't we do that now?'

He looked down at his phone, and Pearce surprised him with a punch. Louis stumbled and the gun went off. The bullet flew high and wide, and people around them screamed and scattered. Pearce drove his shoulder into Louis' gut, but the Irishman cracked his pistol into the back of Pearce's skull.

The world swam as they fell onto the pavement. Pearce rolled off Louis and staggered to his feet. He kicked the gun from Louis' hand and it clattered towards the tube station. Louis went after it, and Pearce started running.

He sprinted towards the busy main road. When he glanced round, he saw Louis on his feet, trying to get a clear shot, but people were scattering left and right. He pocketed the pistol and gave chase. Somewhere nearby, a siren sounded and it was joined by others.

Pearce sensed the situation could spiral out of control, and knew he had to get away as quickly as possible. He leapt a metal railing and jumped into the main road that linked Shepherd's Bush roundabout with the green. He ran across three busy lanes of traffic to the median, earning himself screeching tyres, horn blasts and angry shouts, but he made it to the concrete carriageway divider. When he looked round, he saw Louis jump the barrier and land on both feet.

There was a loud horn blast, a screech of tyres, and suddenly Louis wasn't there. He'd been hit by a motorbike that had been speeding along the bus lane. His broken and twisted body flew through the air and hit the road some ten feet away. The bike dropped onto its side and scraped to a halt inches away from him, as the rider tumbled along the tarmac. People screamed and cried at the horror, and Pearce caught a glimpse of Louis through the lines of traffic, which had suddenly stopped. His eyes were vacant, and blood oozed from a mortal wound in his temple.

He was dead.

Some people raced towards the accident to help, others got their phones out and started filming. Pearce turned away and hurried across the three lanes on the other side of the median. He jumped the metal barrier and headed for Addison Road, a residential side street that would take him towards Olympia.

He intended to get well and truly lost.

Chapter 48

'How did he take it?' Wollerton asked.

'Hard to say,' Leila replied. 'But if I know Scott Pearce, it won't have gone down well.'

'To shoot your own father . . .'

'Evil, but I've seen people do worse,' Leila remarked.

She slipped her phone into her pocket and did one last check of the gear in her backpack. She and Wollerton were both in black and he had a matching pack full of tools and equipment.

'Ready?' he asked.

Leila nodded and picked up her cane. She slung the bag over her shoulders and started for the door.

'I can carry it . . .'

She cut Wollerton off with a scowl. There were days when she felt broken by the strain of her disability, and nights when she wanted to cry for mercy, but to accept help from him would be an admission to herself that she was less than she once was, that she was somehow not as capable as those around her, that the men who'd abused her had succeeded in taking something from her, and she couldn't let them have even the smallest victory. So instead of letting Wollerton carry her bag, she bit her lip in an attempt to force back the pain, walked faster and led him outside.

Leila could hear light traffic in the distance, but Noble Street was as still and silent as a morgue. They hurried to the minivan and Wollerton got behind the wheel. She climbed in beside him, and moments later they were on their way to Manhattan.

It was shortly after three in the morning when they arrived on 8th Street. They parked near the Rightway building, and Leila's body coursed with adrenalin as she climbed out of the car. They walked past the shuttered stores and lingered beside an archway while they waited for a couple of cars to make a turn at the intersection. Leila was alert and alive with the nervous energy of an operation, and for a short while the pain in her legs and back receded. Danger was good for her. Satisfied there was no one around, they ducked into the archway and went down an alleyway beside the block.

Wollerton used a chisel to force open a mesh gate that restricted access a few yards along the alley, and he and Leila pulled on ski masks as they walked into the shadow between the high buildings either side. Wollerton shut the gate behind them, and they went on until they reached the service entrance of the Rightway building. He produced a lock-picking kit and had the folding door open in under a minute.

Leila rushed inside to the alarm terminal they'd studied on the schematic she'd hacked from the building security company, but she discovered the system wasn't armed.

'Odd,' she remarked.

'Lucky,' Wollerton responded.

Leila didn't believe in luck and tended to assume the unexpected was bad news. Their plan had involved her disabling an active alarm system, but it wasn't on, so as they moved through the service area, Leila was even more alert than usual.

They walked along a corridor and reached the main lobby without incident, and Leila breathed a little easier when they got into the elevator.

Leila had left an audio bug in Kelly Dan's office, but she also wanted a line into the company's network, so she could pull data and comms from any phone or computer in the building. She was also going to install video surveillance in Kelly's office.

The elevator door opened when they reached the fifth floor, and Wollerton was about to step out when he stopped dead and pulled Leila to the side of the car as he took a step back.

'Hey,' she said.

'I know why the alarm wasn't on,' Wollerton whispered.

'Hello?'

Leila recognized Kelly Dan's voice. She craned her neck to peer out of the lift, and saw Kelly standing in the doorway of her office, looking in their direction. Leila stepped back.

'Hello?' Dan said again, this time with an unmistakeable edge of fear in her voice.

'What do you want to do?' Wollerton whispered.

Leila wasn't sure. What the heck was Kelly doing in the building at this time of night? Was she alone? They certainly couldn't do the work they'd come here for – Kelly might object to the installation of cameras and a shadow surveillance network on her servers.

'We could take her,' Wollerton suggested.

Leila looked at him in disbelief, and he shrugged.

'There's no one else around,' he added.

Kelly would probably have a lot of valuable information, and interrogation might shortcut a lot of surveillance. Leila nodded and Wollerton stepped out of the elevator. Leila followed and saw Kelly retreating into her office. She slammed the door shut, locked it, ran to her desk and picked up the phone.

Wollerton sprinted across the large space, dodging between some of the desks, jumping over others. Kelly spoke some hurried words, and reached into her desk drawer for something, and when she turned, Leila saw she had a gun in her hand.

Kelly opened fire on Wollerton, shattering the glass divider that separated her office from the open-plan space. Wollerton ducked behind a desk, and Leila did likewise. The thunderous cracks of gunfire echoed off the walls as bullets chewed into the desk in front of Wollerton, but Kelly made the terrible mistake of emptying her clip, and as soon as the barrage stopped, the man was on his feet. He sprinted across the office as she hurriedly tried to reload. Wollerton smashed through the remnants of the shattered partition, and barrelled into her room as she brought the gun up for a shot. Kelly managed to get a single wild bullet off before Wollerton smacked the gun from her hand and knocked her out.

Leila heard commotion coming from the stairwell, and moved to the fire door that was halfway along the east wall. Two men burst through the door, and she recognized them as the guys who'd emerged from the Escalade and tried to intimidate her when she'd first encountered Kelly. They reached for their weapons when they saw Wollerton, but didn't notice Leila flip her cane so she could wield the heavy metal head as a club. She cracked the larger of the two on the back of the head, and caught his surprised comrade square on the nose as he turned in stunned disbelief. Both men went down instantly, out cold.

Leila nodded at Wollerton, and he replied in kind. She wasn't a big fan of improvisation – it relied too much on luck. But sometimes it paid off.

Chapter 49

Pearce wished he could go back to the phone booth, to the moments before Louis died, and do things differently. Regret gnawed at him, hollowing him out. He hadn't liked the guy, but that didn't mean he wanted him dead. Pearce couldn't shake the memory of Louis being tossed in the air and hitting the road, tumbling until he came to a halt, broken and lifeless. Remorse sent waves of angry frustration surging through him, and his body seemed to almost burn with fury at himself for having been so careless. He raged against his inability to undo what had been done. Louis' death wasn't just a personal blow, it significantly complicated his investigation into White Fire. Louis had revealed Farida had been the one to put him under surveillance, but did Mary know? And had Farida been in contact with Louis during the tail, or had he been working alone? Had he called Farida before challenging Pearce at the phone box? Pearce puzzled over the possibilities as he walked to Bayswater. The questions added to his feeling a failure. Everything he'd worked so hard for was at risk, and he couldn't help but be angry at himself.

He'd taken a circuitous route to Olympia and shed his boiler suit in a public toilet, before travelling across West London, through Hyde Park to an Internet cafe he knew on Queensway. Situated between an off licence and a Russian deli, the

Queensway Computer Market was a mishmash bazaar of clothes, Brazilian food and computer supplies, and, located in the back of the shop were half a dozen old desktops that passed for an Internet cafe. Pearce paid cash and took a terminal that allowed him to watch the comings and goings in the shop. He researched Alexis Tippett-Jones and discovered she'd assumed her father's roles as a patron of the arts, philanthropist and businesswoman. A recent *Evening Standard* profile revealed she prided herself on doing a full working day at Bayard Madison, the bank once owned by her father. Armed with a better picture of what Alexis had become, Pearce used the payphone at the back of the shop to call the bank.

'*Good morning,*' a voice said. '*Bayard Madison.*'

'Alexis Tippett-Jones,' Pearce replied.

'*May I ask who's calling?*'

'Scott Pearce,' he replied.

There was a long pause.

'*Scott.*'

It had been months since he'd heard Alexis's voice, but he still remembered it, and felt his anger rise as he recalled the sob stories she'd told about her life at the hands of her father and the men around him.

'Ms Tippett-Jones,' Pearce replied. 'I'm in London and wondered if you might have—'

'*How about coffee?*' she cut in. '*Eleven thirty any good?*'

'Only if it doesn't put you out.'

'*I always have time for old friends,*' she replied. '*Come by the bank.*'

Pearce hung up, wondering what she knew. It was one of the most challenging aspects of the game, not knowing whether you were walking into a room with someone who had reason to kill you. If she was connected to Elroy Lang, it seemed likely she would know about the Red Wolves. She was financing Jacob Silver, which meant she might have a hand in whatever White Fire was up to. Was she eager to see him because he was a source of intelligence she thought she could mine? Or did she see it as an opportunity to neutralize a threat? If she really had murdered her father to protect a wider objective, she would almost certainly harbour terrible resentment towards Pearce for putting her in that position.

Whatever her motives, Pearce knew his. He had to find out what White Fire had planned, stop them, and use them to get to Elroy Lang. If Alexis was involved, he had a good idea how he could exploit her to his advantage.

He left the Internet cafe and walked down to Bayswater Road, where he hailed a cab to take him to Liverpool Street. He went to a shirtmaker behind the railway station and bought a suit, shirt, and shoes. Looking every inch the city worker, Pearce crossed Bishopsgate and walked along Great St Helen's, the shortcut that led to 1 Undershaft, the glass and steel tower that was the home of Bayard Madison Bank.

Chapter 50

As tall as it was, number 1 Undershaft was dwarfed by its high-rise neighbour, the Leadenhall Building. Artem Vasylyk, a Ukrainian billionaire who'd been embroiled in the Black Thirteen conspiracy, had once kept an office in the Leadenhall Building, until he'd been shot there. It was only during the Red Wolves investigation that Pearce learned Leila had been the one who'd killed him, and her deception had taken him a while to get over.

Pearce crossed the broad plaza, heading south towards the entrance to 1 Undershaft. The huge buildings towering over him were monuments to a time when companies wanted centralized command and control to be reinforced by physical presence. The Covid-19 pandemic had changed all of that. Office blocks had lower occupancy, some had been converted into apartments, and the City of London was a much quieter place than when Pearce had first staked out the building where his old friend Nathan Foster had been murdered.

There weren't many people around when Pearce reached the main entrance. He looked down at the slabs beneath his feet and tried not to picture Nathan dying on these stones, hurled from the building by a man Pearce had hunted. Pearce said a silent prayer of remembrance to honour his lost friend and went through the large double doors into a huge vaulted lobby, where Alexis's father, Lancelot Oxnard-Clarke, had once threatened him. Pearce thought back to the night the eighteenth Viscount Purbeck had been shot by his daughter, and tried to recall the look on her face, but his memory was fallible, and each time her expression was different. One moment, she was the reluctant executioner saving an innocent from her deranged father. Then she was the cold, calculating killer putting him in the grave to protect some wider conspiracy. Pearce could not rely on his recollection for answers; he had to find out the truth from her.

He went to the reception desk and said he was here to see Alexis. The receptionist waved him through security to an elevator with a smoked mirror interior, and he took it to the twenty-seventh floor.

Alexis greeted him warmly the moment the elevator doors slid open. No anonymous receptionist or prolonged wait in the opulent lobby for him. She was there in person in an elegant black trouser suit and red blouse. Her wavy hair was gone, and her blonde locks had been cut short and straightened. She looked as though she'd lost weight, and her blue eyes shone from her gaunt face like tiny stars.

'Scott,' she said, stepping forward to embrace him.

Covid-19 had changed the way people viewed physical contact. Handshakes and hugs had ceased to be ubiquitous, even after the advent of vaccines. She smelled good, though.

Perhaps she wants to make a point, lull me into a false sense of security, Pearce thought.

'Ms Tippett-Jones,' Pearce replied.

'It's Lady Purbeck now, if you plan on being so formal,' she replied. 'Or you could just call me Alexis. After what we've been through together, I'd think that more appropriate.' She flashed a disarming smile.

She's dangerous, Pearce told himself. *Much more dangerous than her father.*

'Come on,' she said. 'We can have coffee in my office.'

She led him out of reception through a set of glass doors into some of London's most exclusive real estate with magnificent views looking south over the City.

'What brings you to this part of town?' she asked.

'I'm looking in on some old friends,' Pearce replied. 'I thought I'd check on you, since I was nearby.'

Alexis smiled. 'As you can see, I'm doing fine.'

They stepped into a huge, vaulted antechamber where three assistants sat at well-spaced desks. Alexis nodded at them and took Pearce through a set of walnut doors into a vast office. London rose from the paved streets, stretching its great steel fingers to the sky. In the distance lay the dome of St Paul's Cathedral and beyond it the shining river.

Alexis's desk was the size of a large bed and was covered in screens that displayed financial market information. She took him to a four-sofa seating area near the corner window. A silver coffee set had been laid on a table that stood between the cream couches, and Pearce saw a curl of steam rise from the pot. Money could buy invisible service and perfect timing.

'Cream? Sugar? Milk?' Alexis asked as they sat across from one another.

'Cream, two sugars,' Pearce replied.

'That's a pudding,' Alexis scoffed.

'It's my one vice.'

She smiled, made his drink, and handed Pearce a china mug so fine it was almost translucent. She took hers black.

'What do people like us talk about?' she asked. 'You've more experience of the extraordinary than me.'

'I don't think that's true,' he replied. 'Look around. None of this is ordinary.' He took a sip of coffee. 'This is perfect by the way. Thanks.'

'All this is just the product of money. I'm talking about life and death and all the terrible things we've seen. That's extraordinary, and that's where you have more experience than me.'

'Again, I'm not sure that's true.'

Alexis hesitated.

'Have you ever heard of a scientist called Jacob Silver?' Pearce asked.

She smiled again, but this one wasn't meant to be disarming. It was canny. 'So now we get to it. The real reason you're here.'

'No reason,' Pearce countered. 'I just heard he'd been making some bold claims about climate change, and when I looked him up I saw he has one of your father's foundations listed as a funder.'

'Really? I've never heard of him, but then I try not to get into the weeds too much.'

Pearce was almost certain she was lying, but she seemed so earnest.

'Is it possible your father had a partner, someone who might have been working with him?' he asked.

'This is starting to feel less and less like a friendly visit.' Alexis's tone was light, but her eyes betrayed irritation.

Good, Pearce thought. *Is all this talk about your father touching a nerve?*

'Sorry. The Black Thirteen thing still plays on my mind. I

just have so many unanswered questions,' he remarked. 'You know what it's like when you have an itch you can't scratch.'

'I hire someone to scratch it for me,' Alexis replied. 'My father had no partners.'

'Artem Vasylyk?' Pearce countered.

'He was never a partner. He was a criminal.'

'Do you think about your father much?' Pearce pressed, and he was rewarded with even more irritation. If she had killed Lancelot Oxnard-Clarke to protect some bigger conspiracy, she would likely hate Pearce for having put her in that position.

'No, Mr Pearce, I do not.'

'Whoa. Mr Pearce. I thought we were friends, Alexis.'

'We are,' she replied, taking some of the bitter edge out of her voice. 'But some friendships are rooted in an unhealthy connection, and it is perhaps best they are left to rot in the soil near the bitter tree from which they sprang.'

'So I'm a rotten apple?'

Alexis didn't smile, and her eyes blazed with hatred. She put down her coffee cup, while Pearce took another slow and deliberate sip.

'How long have you been working with Elroy Lang?'

The name was like a flamethrower that incinerated any vestiges of a civil veneer.

'So we come to it,' she snarled. 'I don't know this man, but it doesn't sound like the kind of name that should be bandied around. You're a liar, Mr Pearce. You came here on the hunt and you will leave empty-handed.'

Pearce put down his cup and stood.

'Why did you kill you father?' She looked as though she might murder him on the spot, so he pressed on. 'Does his ghost haunt your nightmares? What secret was worth the price of his death?'

He saw the truth the instant he'd asked the question. Alexis's face flushed and her chin quivered. It didn't matter how adept she was at acting; patricide was too great a horror to remain concealed behind a mask. Even a psychopath would experience visceral anger at being shamed, perhaps not at the crime itself, but certainly at being exposed, and it was clear Alexis felt exposed.

'Get out!' she yelled. 'Get out!'

Pearce had his truth. She hadn't killed her father to save him. She'd acted to protect something or someone else. His death had sealed the Black Thirteen investigation and stopped everyone, including Pearce, from looking any further. But his eyes had now been opened, and he had to find out what would make a woman murder her own father.

Chapter 51

Pearce rode the lift down from Bayard Madison, feeling angry and frustrated. Leila hadn't trusted Alexis, but he'd been taken in by her hard-luck tale, and she'd played the role of victim to perfection. Leila had not linked her to Elroy Lang, and if Pearce found out she had anything to do with Brigitte's death . . . well, she'd have a greater debt to be settled. As things stood, she was already in the frame for the murder of her father, a role in Black Thirteen and all the deaths the group had caused, and whatever White Fire had planned.

Pearce was only mildly surprised when the lift didn't stop at the ground floor. He'd expected to pay a price for his visit, but hadn't thought it would come so soon.

He stood by the elevator control panel so he would be concealed when the doors opened. As the lift slowed, he crouched so his head was at waist height. The car stopped and the doors slid back.

Pearce held his breath in the silence.

Then came the sound of movement. Feet gently scuffing on concrete. Pearce saw a shadow reflected in the smoked glass interior, and then a gun pushed hesitantly into the lift.

A large man with long, greasy black hair crept inside with his pistol in the ready position. Pearce punched him in the groin, throwing all his weight into the blow. The man groaned and doubled over, and Pearce grabbed the pistol, twisted it against his assailant's stomach and pulled the trigger. The gunshot reverberated around the tiny space, masking the man's cry. A second gunman, blond, with a scarred face, stepped into the lift, but he was too slow with his weapon, and Pearce shot him in the chin, blowing off the top of his head. He toppled backwards through the open doors.

There were shouts and commotion outside, and Pearce guessed from the noise he was facing at least half a dozen men. He pushed the gun into the open doorway and fired blindly, and was rewarded with more shouts and the sounds of multiple people scattering.

Pearce worked quickly. He pressed the 'close doors' button and sealed himself in the car with the first gunman, who was mortally wounded and groaning. Pearce pressed the button for the lobby, and when nothing happened, he tried them all, but the lift didn't move. He rifled through the man's pockets and found two magazines, a wallet and a phone.

He reloaded the pistol and pocketed everything else. He heard movement outside, and the doors started to open.

'Come on,' Pearce said, grabbing the wounded man, hauling him to his feet, and spinning him round just in time.

Two gunmen concealed behind the bonnet of a BMW 5 Series twenty feet away opened fire as soon as the doors opened. Bullets thudded into the man Pearce was using as a shield, and he started to go heavy as his life ebbed away. Pearce knew he didn't have long. He drove the dying man forward with one hand, while shooting at the gunmen with the other. They took cover behind the car, and Pearce let go of his mortally wounded captive as the man's feet struck the legs of the blond who'd fallen outside the lift. His captive went down, and Pearce went with him, falling on his side, twisting, so he could see to the right of the elevator, where another gunman lay in wait. Pearce was dimly aware there was another shooter to the left of the lift, but he focused on this one target and brought his pistol round as the man opened fire. Two of Pearce's shots went wide, but the third struck the man in the head and he went down.

Pearce landed behind the mortally wounded man, who'd fallen on the blond, and their gruesome stack provided him with some cover from the shooter on the left. Their bodies shuddered with the impact of each bullet. Lying flat on his back, pressed close to the bodies, Pearce lifted his arm and fired a couple of rounds in the direction of the BMW to keep the gunmen down. The barrage from his left stopped, and he heard a reload, so he sat up and hit the shooter with a couple of slugs in the chest.

As the man fell, Pearce grabbed the blond gunman's pistol, which had fallen inches away from the man's hand, got to his feet and sprinted to a pillar to his right. Gunshots echoed around the underground parking garage, and chunks of concrete flew everywhere as bullets hit the ground at his feet, but the two gunmen by the BMW missed their mark, and Pearce took cover behind the narrow concrete support.

Bullets bit into the pillar and dust swirled in a violent cloud. Pearce heard a screech of tyres and looked over the tops of the nearby parked cars to see a trio of vehicles – a Mercedes E-Class, Lexus ES and Tesla Model X – steaming down a ramp. They raced along the lane and pulled up by the BMW.

'He's over there,' one of the gunmen said to the others who emerged from the newly arrived cars.

There were four men in each, and it didn't matter how

good he was, the odds of him making it out alive would only fall the longer he stayed pinned down. He searched the underground car park for inspiration. There was a bank of four elevators to his left, then a fire door that led to a stairwell. To his right, about ten feet away, was a row of parked cars, twenty or so, well spaced out before the ramp that led to the exit. Pearce rated his chances of making it to either the stairwell or ramp as poor. Sometimes with the odds against you, madness was the only option. He reloaded the pistol he'd taken off the first man in the lift and held it in his right hand. He grasped the other gun he'd taken off the blond shooter with his left and ran round the column directly towards the BMW.

He opened fire the moment he broke cover, sweeping wildly with his left hand, targeting with his right. He shot the two gunmen by the BMW, and a third next to a black Mercedes E-Class. The wild shooting and the sight of their comrades falling had the desired effect and the other gunmen took cover.

Pearce reached the BMW, opened the driver's door while shooting, slid behind the wheel, hit the ignition button and threw the car into gear. The BMW roared towards the ramp as bullets thudded into the chassis and shattered the rear window. Pearce swung the car round, shot up the ramp, crashed through the barrier, and raced into the street.

Chapter 52

Pearce sped along Undershaft and glanced in the rear-view mirror to see his attackers' cars burst from the underground car park behind him. He raced past St Helen's Church and pulled a sharp right turn onto St Mary Axe, a narrow street that ran towards the Lloyd's Building. A police car screeched to a halt ahead of him, sirens blaring, lights flashing, blocking the mouth of the street.

Pearce cursed the City of London's rapid response units. He turned the wheel, and the engine growled as he jumped the kerb and mounted the pavement to cut between a lamp post and a run of concrete blocks and bollards. He clipped a bright red postbox and the back of the BMW shimmied as it joined Leadenhall Street heading west. The Lloyd's Building went by in a blur, and behind him the Mercedes, Lexus and Tesla bounced off the pavement and shot onto the street. The Tesla was viciously fast, and sped forward at incredible pace until it was level with Pearce. The passenger held an MP5 and opened fire, shattering Pearce's window and sending bullets zipping through the air around him.

He stepped on the brakes and the BMW's rear bumper collided with the front of the Lexus. More gunshots came from the passenger in the Lexus, and bullets whipped through the shattered rear window. Further behind him, there were more sirens, but Pearce wondered what good police would be against such heavily armed gunmen. The audacity of his attackers suggested they weren't the slightest bit concerned by the authorities.

He swung the wheel right and collided with the Mercedes, which spun out and crashed into a run of bollards in front of the Leadenhall Building. The driver of the Lexus slowed, and his passenger showered the BMW's bonnet with bullets. Smoke and steam rose from the engine, and through the clouds Pearce saw more police cars pull up and block the junction with Bishopsgate. Armed response officers jumped out, guns drawn.

The Tesla swiped the BMW and the car veered left. It collided with the kerb and one of the tyres burst, but Pearce didn't fight the drag and allowed the car to mount the pavement. He pulled the wheel hard left, applied the handbrake and the car went into a violent spin until it came to a crashing halt against the building that stood on the corner of Whittington Avenue, the road to Leadenhall Market.

Pearce leaped from the car and sprinted along the narrow street, as the Tesla and Lexus screeched to a halt. Surrounded by grand buildings, Pearce could see the intricate grey stone relief and glass roof of Leadenhall Market ahead of him. He raced past a Waterstones and on beyond the Brokers Wine Bar as a barrage of gunfire began. He returned wild fire, and glanced back to see his assailants break for cover.

He ran round the corner and entered the market proper. There weren't many people inside, but the few who saw him scattered as Pearce approached, guns in hand. He heard more sirens and the roar of engines and realized he would get cornered and killed in this place if he wasn't quicker.

His footsteps echoed off the glass roof and artisan shop-fronts as he raced on. He made it to Gracechurch Street, and darted to the other side as a hail of bullets started coming from the market behind him. Pearce heard the shouts of police to his north, but didn't miss a step as he barged past a couple of pedestrians, along the front of an office block, before taking a sharp right into Corbet Court, a tiny alleyway between the grey stone building and the hotel next to it.

The area east of Gracechurch Street was a maze of old alleyways and passages, and Pearce knew them well. He ran along Corbet Court, passing into a tunnel that cut through the ground floor of an office block, until he reached St Michael's Alley. He slowed to a walk when he passed through an arch-way into George Yard, a landscaped area between office buildings that featured circular flower beds ringed by stone benches. Pearce concealed the pistols in his jacket pockets and hurried across the cobbled yard. He skipped across Lombard Street and down Clements Lane, a narrow cut-through that would take him out of the maze. Checking he wasn't being followed, Pearce jogged the last few yards to the end of the road and hailed a cab on the corner of King William Street. He jumped in and told the driver to take him south towards the river, before sinking back in his seat and catching his breath.

Chapter 53

Taking Kelly Dan was one of those ideas that seemed to make sense in the blind heat of the moment, but in the cold dawn light, abducting the newswoman and bringing her back to the house on Noble Street wasn't the best move Leila had ever made.

They'd tied her to a metal structural support in the garage and gagged and blindfolded her. Leila had run a scanner over Kelly to check for any tracking devices. They'd been caught out before when Black Thirteen had used embedded tracking devices to tag MI6 turncoat Dominic McClusky and Alexis Tippett-Jones. Finding nothing, they'd left Kelly to stew for a while.

Wollerton had finally gone down to her at 6 a.m., and Leila had stayed in the kitchen where she could hear the muffled sound of him asking Kelly questions. He'd come up after thirty minutes, frustrated, shaking his head.

'She won't talk.'

'Let's try together,' Leila suggested.

She went down first and didn't bother with a ski mask because Kelly would recognize her voice. Wollerton followed with a mask over his face.

'You know he's going to kill you if you don't give him what

you want,' she said, as she shuffled off the bottom step. 'It will be a painful death.'

Leila leaned against her cane and walked over to Kelly to remove her gag.

'I need the toilet,' she said the moment the fabric had cleared her mouth. 'It's been hours and I can't hold it anymore.'

Wollerton looked at Leila and shrugged, but before either of them could respond, there was a loud bang that shook the building, followed by the sound of the front and back doors flying open, and heavy footsteps running into the house.

'How?' Leila asked in complete disbelief. She'd been so careful to scan the woman thoroughly, and they'd gone to great lengths to ensure they hadn't been followed from Manhattan.

Kelly raised her left hand and pressed her thumb and forefinger together. 'Off,' she said. 'On.' She separated the digits and smiled darkly. 'You messed with the wrong woman, honey.'

Leila was in awe of the simplicity. An embedded transmitter buried in Kelly's flesh would broadcast a signal unless she applied pressure, at which point it would cut out. All Kelly had to do was press her thumb and forefinger together while she was being scanned and she would prevent the signal from being detected. Leila could have kicked herself, but now wasn't the time.

Wollerton was already at the vault. He had the door open and was arming himself. The footsteps on the ground floor got closer and closer, and, as the first of them started down the basement stairs, Wollerton used a Heckler & Koch HK416 assault rifle to spray a volley of bullets at the first set of feet. There was a scream, and shouts of, 'Get him up,' and, 'Get him out of there,' followed by a sudden retreat.

'Let's go,' Wollerton said, slinging a backpack onto his shoulders.

He handed Leila a loaded Heckler & Koch MP7 compact sub-machine gun, and she checked the safety and switched it off.

'We leave her,' Wollerton said, making a point of showing Kelly the C4 charge he was setting near her feet.

Kelly struggled against her bonds. 'Down here!' she yelled. 'Help me!'

'Come up unarmed and you won't be hurt,' a voice shouted down.

'They want us alive,' Leila whispered to Wollerton. 'Lang wants to know who we're working for.'

'Come and get us,' Wollerton responded.

A smoke grenade came tumbling down the stairs, trailing a thick plume in its wake. Wollerton took off his ski mask as he ran into the vault to grab two respirators from a shelf. He handed one to Leila, and she pulled on the full-face protection. She fired a burst at the top of the stairs to let their assailants know the smoke hadn't had the desired effect.

Wollerton set the timer on the explosive for ninety seconds and activated the countdown. 'There's enough C4 here to take out the entire building. You want to live, you tell us what we want to know.'

Coughing and spluttering, Kelly looked at the countdown, which went through eighty seconds.

'No.'

'Fine. Good luck in the next life,' Wollerton said, moving away. 'Let's go,' he said to Leila, who had her sights trained on the stairs.

'OK, OK,' Kelly responded, hacking another lungful of thick smoke.

Leila kept one eye on the stairs, as she and Wollerton moved back towards the bound newswoman.

'I was recruited by Elroy Lang,' she said. 'He claims to represent powerful conservative interests. Said they needed my help.'

'To do what?' Wollerton pressed.

'I was to—' Kelly began, but she was cut off by a bullet hitting her in the chest.

Leila looked round, and peered through the smoke to see a masked shooter at the small letterbox window at the side of the house. She opened fire and Wollerton joined her, and the gunman bucked as bullets hit him. He fell away from the shattered window, and Leila turned to Kelly, who was slumped in the chair. She crouched and saw Kelly's eyes rolling in and out of consciousness. A wet stain of blood was spreading across her chest, and her breathing was rapid and shallow.

'This wasn't a rescue mission,' Leila said to Wollerton. 'They came to silence her. No loose ends. Dominic McClusky, Nikos Kitsantonis. These people are ruthless.'

'Whit,' Kelly said so faintly Leila almost didn't hear.

Leila held her breath, removed her respirator, and turned her head so her ear was near Kelly's mouth.

'What was that? What are you trying to say?' asked Wollerton.

'They used me,' Kelly groaned. 'Whitman. Look at Whitman.' She moaned and fell still.

Leila replaced her respirator, and searched for Kelly's pulse. 'She's gone.'

Wollerton nodded gravely. 'We need to leave.'

He ran to the back of the basement and pulled a metal

shelving unit towards him. The shelves were on casters and came away with a section of false wall. Leila went into the narrow tunnel beyond, and Wollerton joined her and pulled the secret door shut behind him.

'We don't have long,' he said, removing his respirator.

Leila did likewise and switched on the torch on her phone. She led Wollerton along the passageway until they came to a short wooden ladder. Robert Clifton or whoever had designed the safe house had prepared it well. The escape tunnel would take them into the alleyway that ran behind the gardens of the houses on Noble Street. Leila climbed the ladder and opened the manhole cover at the top. She scanned the alleyway, which was clear, and clambered out. Wollerton followed, and checked his watch.

'Cover your ears,' he said.

Leila took his advice and turned away from the house, just as an almighty explosion shook the neighbourhood. The shockwave tore chunks out of the garden fence, and Wollerton and Leila shielded themselves as best they could.

When the blast died away, Leila peered through a gap in the fence to see that the Noble Street safe house had been levelled, and flames were licking the sky.

'Subtle,' she said.

'Effective,' Wollerton replied.

He started along the passageway, but Leila lingered for a moment, staring at the devastation and wondering what kind of organization they were up against. Kelly Dan had joined many others who'd been murdered by their own people. Her last words were stuck in Leila's mind, and as she set off after Wollerton, she wondered who or what Whitman was.

Chapter 54

It was shortly before eight in the evening when Pearce arrived at Sanctuary, the White Fire compound. He'd caught the express train from Paddington to Cardiff and had then taken the local connection to Haverfordwest, where he'd hired a taxi to take him the rest of the way.

He'd spent the journey puzzling over his situation. Louis was dead, but before he'd been killed he'd admitted he'd been sent to spy on Pearce by Farida, so at least one person in White Fire was suspicious of him. There was no way of knowing if she and Louis had been in communication before his death, or whether she'd spoken to Mary or anyone else about her suspicions. White Fire had a connection to Elroy Lang through Mary, and to Alexis Tippett-Jones through their scientific 'prophet' Jacob Silver. Those connections weren't chance. The fact Alexis had set her heavies on him so quickly told Pearce two things. The first was that she was definitely continuing her father's work. Those men might not have worn the paramilitary uniforms of Black Thirteen, but they were cut from the same cloth. The second was that she must have high-level protection to be so unconcerned with making a mess on her own doorstep. The men chasing him had been unfazed by the appearance of the police, which suggested they were confident of avoiding any blowback. Lancelot Oxnard-Clarke had managed to get Pearce's old boss at MI6, Dominic McClusky, on the payroll, and there was no reason Alexis couldn't have done the same in the security services or police.

Pearce had considered placing Alexis under surveillance, and with the extensive resources of MI6 at his disposal he would have done so, but he was working alone and White Fire was the softer target. If Mary still trusted him, he could use her to get to Alexis and Elroy Lang. But it was a big if. There was a chance Louis and Farida had marked him as a traitor and his life would be forfeit the moment he returned.

There was no sign of danger when the taxi driver dropped him off and Martin opened the gate to let him in, wearing his usual taciturn expression.

'Thanks,' Pearce said, as he walked into the compound.

'No bother,' Martin replied.

He didn't give Pearce a second glance as he returned to his gatehouse, but for all Pearce knew he was in there phoning the main house to warn them the traitor was back. Pearce remained alert and on guard as he walked the long drive.

He heard shouts and laughter drifting through the wood, and when he neared the treeline and had a better view of the paddock beside the house, he saw a celebration in full swing. The people of White Fire were dancing, the band was playing and there was a long table set with two kegs and platters of food. People were having a great time, chatting and laughing, and it certainly didn't seem like a wake for Louis or a trap set for a traitor.

Mary was sitting on a blanket with Alan, Jenny and Tolo, and she beamed broadly when she saw Pearce emerge from the trees.

'Sam,' she said, hurrying towards him. 'You made it.'

She embraced him and then looked him up and down.

'I couldn't move around London dressed as I was,' Pearce said, explaining the suit, which made him feel like even more of an outsider.

'Wise,' Mary remarked. 'Come. Tell us what happened.'

She took Pearce by the hand and led him through the celebration to the blanket, where they sat next to Jenny.

'You made it out OK?' he asked.

'Thanks to your diversion,' Mary replied. 'And no doubt you've seen our success?'

Pearce shook his head. 'I've spent the day making sure I wasn't being followed.'

'Oh,' Mary exclaimed. 'Then you don't even know why we're celebrating. Show him,' she instructed Alan.

He handed his phone to Pearce, who looked at the screen and saw a message that said:

The world faces a climate emergency. If we don't act now, humanity will become extinct in less than fifty years. The White Fire is burning.

'Look at the address,' Mary said, peering over his shoulder.

Pearce opened the web address bar to see he was looking at the *Daily Telegraph* homepage.

'We hacked Zyberian's servers to take over their clients' websites. Our message is the only thing visible on hundreds of news and business websites,' Mary revealed, bubbling with enthusiasm. 'This is what you helped us achieve, Raptor Grey.'

She leaned over and kissed him.

No worries about being branded a traitor, Pearce thought. *These people believe I'm a hero.*

'What did you do to him?' Farida's angry voice carried above the surrounding din.

Pearce looked round to see her striding towards him.

'Farida?' Mary asked, getting to her feet. 'What's happened?'

Farida ignored her, and focused her anger on Pearce. 'What did you do to Louis?'

The tears in her eyes and palpable rage were like a storm that muted the celebrations as she swept towards them.

'What's she talking about?' Mary asked Pearce.

'I don't know,' he replied.

'He's dead,' Farida said, thrusting her phone in Mary's face.

Her screen showed a BBC London story covering a fatal motorcycle accident in Shepherd's Bush.

'Was this you?' Farida demanded of Pearce. 'Did you do this?'

Pearce guessed Louis hadn't been in contact with her during his pursuit, otherwise her accusations would have been more definite.

'Do what? What are you talking about?' he responded. 'Why would this have anything to do with me?'

'He . . .' Farida began, but she didn't go any further, and Pearce knew then that the surveillance hadn't been approved by Mary.

'He what?' Mary asked.

'I thought . . .' Farida said, but she couldn't come up with a convincing response.

'What was Louis doing in London?' Mary pressed. 'I didn't give him permission. He should not have left Sanctuary while we were on mission. Did you know he'd gone?'

Farida glared at Pearce and shook her head. 'No. I had no idea.'

Mary put a consoling arm around Farida's shoulder. 'It's natural to feel anger when we lose a loved one,' she said sympathetically. 'But Sam has been through his own ordeal and we should be grateful for his return while we mourn one who was not so lucky.'

Pearce sensed Farida had many things she wanted to say, but they all remained unspoken. She looked at him with ill-disguised contempt before turning and storming back to the house.

Mary rolled her eyes and shook her head in pity. She turned to address the gathering, which was about to become a wake for their fallen friend.

Pearce kept his eyes on Farida and wondered how much she knew, and just what kind of problem she would become.

Chapter 55

Leila's legs were killing her. They hadn't dared risk going to the Odyssey because the minivan would almost certainly have been identified by Kelly's tracking device as the vehicle that had transported her. So Leila and Wollerton had travelled on foot, walking Brooklyn's busy streets as the rush-hour traffic thickened. Wollerton had insisted they take great care to ensure they weren't being tailed by man or machine, and their journey had involved stretches under bridges and in pedestrian tunnels to confound potential satellite or drone surveillance. Finally, when he was satisfied they weren't at risk, they walked four miles to a used car lot on Fulton Street in Queens. The place had one of the lowest customer review ratings on Google, and Wollerton had chosen it because it looked like the kind of yard that did 'ask no questions' business.

Leila forced herself along Fulton Street, past graffiti-covered buildings that stood mere feet away from a rusting and mottled section of elevated train track. The track's high steel girders and wooden sleepers cast bone-like shadows on the cars that travelled along the road directly beneath it. Leila tried to lose herself in the rattle of trains, hum of traffic and growing heat of the day; anything to distract her from the pain rising from her legs and shooting up into her spine.

Wollerton had been on edge, and hadn't wanted to talk about the investigation until they were safe.

'Car, call, crash,' he kept repeating, whenever she raised questions about the who or what of Whitman.

The car dealership was on the corner of Fulton Street and New Jersey Avenue, and the salesman who emerged from the shipping container that had been converted into an office was a fast-talking, jovial, engaging guy in his early forties. The most dangerous type of salesman because he immediately created the impression you'd known each other for years. He showed Leila and Wollerton a selection of vehicles on the packed forecourt, and they opted for a 2009 Honda CRV in sky blue. Wollerton haggled just enough to pass for a genuine customer, and paid for the car on the credit card Robert Clifton had given him. They drove out twenty minutes later, and Leila groaned as the seat took the weight off her legs. She switched the air conditioning onto full and groaned with relief again.

Wollerton drove them through the hustle and bustle of Queens to Highland Park, a large forested stretch of parkland centred around a reservoir. They turned off Vermont Place, an access road, and pulled to a halt in a quiet parking lot at the edge of woodland. Wollerton grabbed his bag from the back seat, and took out a cell phone.

'You want to make the call?' he asked.

Leila nodded, took the phone and dialled.

'*Yes?*' a woman answered.

'Our location was compromised,' Leila said.

'*Casualties?*'

'Not on our side.'

'*One moment,*' the woman said, and the line went quiet.

Was she conferring with Clifton? Or Huxley Blaine Carter? Leila wondered.

'*Find a safe location*,' the woman told her. '*Keep this line open. Wait until we contact you.*'

'I lost my gear. I need you to run a search,' Leila responded.

'*Go ahead.*'

'Whitman,' Leila revealed.

'*Anything else?*'

'No. That's all we got. Look into Whitman.'

'*OK*,' the woman replied, before hanging up.

'Well?' Wollerton asked as Leila took the phone away from her ear.

'We need to find a safe place to lie low,' she replied.

'See. I told you; car, call, crash,' he said, before putting the CRV in gear and driving them out of the parking lot.

Chapter 56

Pearce woke suddenly. He was in the large bed in the Blue Room, but Mary was nowhere to be seen. Moonlight framed the edges of the long drapes and shone into the dressing room and empty bathroom beyond. Pearce couldn't pinpoint what had roused him, so he got to his feet and went to the nearest window. He pulled back the drape and peered into the driveway to see the Lexus and Tesla that had pursued him from Alexis's office. He recognized the cruel faces of the men emerging from the vehicles as those who'd attacked him in the underground car park. A battleship-grey Range Rover pulled up alongside the other cars, and Elroy Lang climbed out and issued instructions to the men, who sprinted into the building.

Pearce grabbed his clothes from the foot of the bed, and pulled on his jeans as he crossed the room. He opened the door to find Mary on the landing. She was in her favourite white linen dress, and looked directly at him with unflinching, cold eyes.

'Did you think we wouldn't talk?' she asked.

She brought her arm up from behind her, and Pearce saw an old revolver in her hand.

'These people aren't on your side, Mary,' he said. 'They're

using you. Whatever they want from you will further their aims, not yours.'

Pearce heard hurried commands and footsteps rising from the floors below.

'Our interests are aligned,' Mary assured him. 'You think I'm some naive puppet? You should know what I am by now, Scott Pearce.' She paused, and Pearce tried not to show his surprise. 'Yes, they told me your real name. They told me you were a spy once. Now you're just a gun for hire. A traitor. Betraying us. Betraying humankind. You should know I'm a priestess. I'm handmaiden to Mother Earth, and I serve her above all.'

Pearce was even more surprised to feel a pang of disappointment. It seemed he had developed genuine feelings for her.

'Please, Mary—'

'He's here,' she shouted, cutting him off.

She was beyond saving, so Pearce crossed the space between them.

'Stay back,' she said, waving the gun at him uncertainly. 'Back.'

He deflected the pistol as she brought it up towards his face, grabbed it and disarmed her. She tried to hold him, but he pulled away.

'I'm sorry,' he said, and he sprinted upstairs.

'Help!' Mary yelled. 'He's escaping!'

The second floor of the house would once have been the servants' quarters. The ceiling was lower and there were a lot more doors, packing the corridor with smaller rooms. A couple of doors opened, and bleary-eyed members of White Fire appeared, looking at Pearce in bewilderment.

'Stop him!' yelled a voice from downstairs.

Pearce sprinted west to the end of the corridor, and barged past Alan, who stood in his doorway.

'What are you doing?' he asked.

Pearce ignored him and ran to the window in the corner of the room. He heard footsteps thundering along the corridor as he lifted the sash window.

Alan approached, but Pearce brandished the pistol at him, and he backed off. He hovered uncertainly as Pearce swung his legs over the sill.

'Have you lost your mind?' Alan asked.

Pearce found purchase on a stone lip a couple of feet below the window. He slipped the revolver into his waistband and edged his way along until he was able to reach the cast-iron drainpipe that ran down the corner of the building. It seemed sufficiently solid for Pearce to gamble.

'He went in there,' a voice said.

'He's here,' Alan called out.

Pearce grabbed the drainpipe with both hands and started a rapid descent as Alan's room filled with men. He used the iron tube like a fast rope and controlled his fall down the side of the building just enough to avoid serious injury. He dropped the sixty feet in three seconds, hit the ground with a heavy thud, and rolled clear. He glanced up to see faces appear at Alan's window, before sprinting towards his van.

He danced between tents and other campers until he saw his bike parked outside the Caravelle. He could see the key in the ignition and raced towards it, but just as he passed the neighbouring camper, Farida stepped out from behind the Caravelle and levelled a shotgun at him.

He stopped dead and held up his hands.

'Back up,' Farida said.

'These people aren't your friends,' Pearce responded. 'They're using you. They're using all of you.'

'Who are you?' she asked.

'My real name is Scott Pearce. I'm here because one of those men killed my friend. She died trying to do good,' he replied. 'These people were behind Black Thirteen.'

'The far-right group?' Farida frowned.

'Yes, and they've been involved in other plots to destabilize government, and commit mass murder,' Pearce revealed. 'They're not your friends. Come with me, Farida.'

She wavered.

'Please. I'll tell you everything. And I'll tell you what happened to Louis. I didn't kill him.'

She hesitated, and there were shouts from the house. His pursuers were outside now, trawling the grounds.

Farida nodded, and Pearce grabbed the helmets from inside the Caravelle.

'Thank you,' he said as they pulled them on.

She propped the shotgun against the van and mounted the bike behind Pearce. He pressed the ignition and the engine roared to life. He kicked into gear and accelerated across the field towards the drive. He cut over grass and wove between trees and when the wheels bit tarmac, he turned. They were almost at a bend in the driveway when two gunshots rang out, and Pearce felt Farida shudder. He heard her cry out in pain, and raced to the cover provided by the curve of the drive. He stopped, and she slumped, stumbled off the bike and fell to the ground. He dropped the kickstand, dismounted and kneeled beside her.

'Farida?' he said, removing her helmet.

He saw the pain and horror on her face. Blood pooled around her, and it was clear she wasn't going to survive. Her breathing was shallow and her eyes drifted in and out of focus. She said something Pearce couldn't hear.

'Save your strength,' he said. He reached into her pocket for a phone and made an emergency call.

'The Alchemist,' Farida said. 'Find the Alchemist. Leonardo Vincenza. Find him.'

'*Hello, nine-nine-nine emergency,*' the operator said, but it was too late. Farida was dead.

Pearce hung up, and saw spotlights shining along the driveway. There were shadows running through the trees, and he heard the sound of car engines coming to life. He touched Farida's motionless lips and fought a rising tide of grief and anger. He got to his feet, mounted his bike and roared towards the gate, where he found the old man, Martin, blocking his path.

He produced the revolver he'd taken from Mary and waved it at the man.

'Open it,' he said, before firing a warning shot.

Martin's resolve crumbled, and he hurriedly opened one of the gates. Pearce sped through the gap and shot onto the road to freedom.

Chapter 57

Pearce raced along the A487 away from the White Fire compound. The Blackbird was too quick for Lang's men to pursue him, and once he hit the A40 on the other side of Haverfordwest, he opened up the throttle and devoured the miles. No matter how fast he went, he couldn't shake the memory of Farida dying in his arms. He was troubled by how he'd treated her. His work with MI6 and the special forces Black Ops unit the Increment had conditioned him to always put the mission first, but here was a beautiful, vibrant woman who he'd first cast aside and then led to her death. He pictured her at the protest, so full of the energy of change, then at her flat in the throes of passion, so alive and vibrant, then still and lifeless, dead on the ground, killed shielding him, drawn into a battle that wasn't of her making.

Pearce thought of the others he'd lost along the way. Nathan Foster, the first to die at the hands of Black Thirteen, then Wayne Nelson, killed protecting him, and Brigitte Attali, dead because he was too slow to save her. There was Essi Salamov and all the innocents who'd died or had their lives irreparably changed in Seattle. So much human suffering, and for what purpose?

Pearce twisted the throttle and pushed the bike faster and faster along the A40, a winding country road in this corner of

Wales. Hedges and trees flashed by in a blur and the scattered clouds overhead passed as though blown by a hurricane. Pearce felt the bike start to lose contact with the road and glanced at the speedometer to see he was doing over 130. He throttled back and slowed down.

Never ride high or angry, he thought, recalling the advice his vegan, countercultural motorcycle instructor had given him.

He saw a green and white canopy ahead, and kicked down through the gears to pull into a petrol station that lay to the south of the road. He stopped beside a phone box at the edge of the forecourt, removed his helmet, hung it on the handlebars and killed the engine. The petrol station was an independent, with a small shop and a cage that housed propane canisters. Pearce nodded at the cashier who eyed him from within the kiosk. He went into the phone box and used his fake credit card to pay for a call to a number Robert Clifton had made him memorize.

'*Yes?*' a woman answered.

'I need a meeting,' Pearce responded.

'*I can put you through.*'

'No. It needs to be face to face.'

'*Where?*'

'London.'

There was a moment's hesitation.

'*If he agrees,*' the woman said, '*a time and place will be sent to the secure drop.*'

The line went dead, and Pearce hung up and dialled another number.

'*Go ahead,*' Leila said when she answered.

He was relieved to hear her voice. 'I've hit a wall. Our friend from Seattle showed up with some of his pals.'

'*Sorry to hear that. You OK?*'

'Yes, but I lost another friend,' Pearce replied, trying not to think about Farida lying on the driveway.

Leila hesitated. '*We had a similar party here.*'

'Let's meet in Madrid,' Pearce said, using their pre-agreed proxy for London.

'*Sounds good,*' Leila replied. '*On our way.*'

Pearce hung up, wondering what sort of trouble Leila and Wollerton had encountered. He'd wanted to tell her about the Alchemist, Leonardo Vincenza, but he couldn't risk revealing information on an unsecured line. The Five Eyes intelligence services shared a system that monitored all phone calls in and out of Europe for certain keywords. The Russians had their own version. It was possible the word 'alchemist' and the name 'Leonardo Vincenza' had been flagged.

Puzzling over the identity of the man Farida had named with her dying breath, Pearce got back on his bike, fired up the engine and continued his journey east.

Chapter 58

Leila and Wollerton had taken a couple of rooms in the Five Towns Inn on the Rockaway Turnpike, just east of John F. Kennedy Airport. The two-star motel was opposite a drive-thru Burger King and across the six-lane highway from a massive storage facility. They used the fake IDs Robert Clifton had given them and paid for the rooms in cash. Leila didn't care about luxury, all she'd wanted was working air-conditioning, and the simple three-storey motel delivered with a giant, humming unit that super-chilled the room.

She and Wollerton had been chewing over the callousness of Kelly Dan's murder and discussing their next move when Pearce called. Leila had been expecting one of Huxley Blaine Carter's minions, and had been glad to hear from her friend, but he sounded wrung out. Whatever he'd been through had obviously taken a toll, and she couldn't wait to be reunited with him.

'We're moving out,' she said to Wollerton after she hung up.

'Really?' he said.

'That was Scott. He wants us in London.'

They didn't have any belongings they could take on a plane, just the bag of weapons and gear Wollerton had grabbed from the vault, which wouldn't clear customs. Leila called an aircraft charter firm and arranged a Gulfstream G650 using the account Clifton had provided them with. While she was on the phone, Wollerton hid the guns and gear in an air vent in the bathroom.

Twenty minutes later, they parked the CRV outside the Sheltair private terminal at JFK, and moved slowly through passport control while their aircraft was being prepared. When they finally walked out to the stand, thirty minutes later, night had truly fallen, and the last of the sunset was a thin line of light visible on the horizon. The pilot and co-pilot welcomed them on board, went through the safety briefing and had them airborne in fifteen minutes.

Wollerton settled into a plush chair and was asleep within moments, but Leila couldn't relax. She replayed Kelly Dan's last moments and kept seeing the woman's shock and horror that her people had turned on her. Leila wondered why she'd given them the name Whitman. Were they involved in whatever Lang had planned?

Two hours into the flight, when they were into the dark skies above the Atlantic and Leila had spent what felt like an eternity shifting uncomfortably in her seat, she nudged Wollerton with her foot. She felt like a petulant child, but the ease with which he'd fallen into a deep sleep irritated her, and her misery needed company. He stirred, but didn't wake, which was even more annoying. How could he be so relaxed?

Leila kicked him again, and this time his eyes snapped open and he sat up suddenly. She looked out of the window and pretended not to notice him rub his face and stretch.

'Did we hit some turbulence?' he asked.

'Oh, you're awake,' she replied. 'No, it's been a smooth ride.'

'You OK? Did I wake you?' he said, and Leila felt a pang of guilt.

'No. I haven't been able to sleep. Just keep replaying everything in my mind. These guys are rough, whoever they are.'

'Tell me about it. They wasted two of their own assets, rather than risk exposure,' Wollerton agreed.

'We saw the same when we were up against Black Thirteen,' Leila responded.

'Ruthless. Wolves devouring the wounded to keep the pack moving.'

'I keep thinking back to Black Thirteen. I didn't trust Alexis, but I was taken in,' Leila admitted. 'It seems we missed a huge piece of the puzzle.'

'Yeah. It makes me wonder what else we've missed.'

'And why we're the ones missing it?' Leila asked, and she saw from Wollerton's puzzled expression that he hadn't understood her. 'Where are the security services? We have a far-right terror attack in Britain connected to a plot to subjugate America, now linked to whatever Lang is planning next. This should be on people's radar.'

'We know they've been able to infiltrate intelligence agencies,' Wollerton suggested.

'That would only get them so far. Intelligence is one piece on the board. Oxnard-Clarke owned one of the world's most prestigious private banks. Finance is another piece. What are the missing pieces for something this big? Think beyond the operational elements.'

'Political?' he suggested.

Leila nodded. 'Political. And?'

'Military?' Wollerton said.

'Military,' she agreed. 'I'd add media and technology.'

'And we're the ones taking it on?' he scoffed.

'Exactly. A washed-up has-been, no offence—'

'Don't be so hard on yourself,' Wollerton cut in.

'An obsessive, disgraced operative, and me, a brilliant but often misunderstood genius.'

Wollerton smiled. 'And our mysterious billionaire financier.'

'Yes, Huxley Blaine Carter. He says his father was killed by these people, but why? I meant to do some digging into Tate Blaine Carter, but I got sucked into the search for Hannan.'

Leila pondered the situation.

'I feel like a lab rat stuck in a maze,' Wollerton remarked. 'I can see what's directly ahead of me, but only the scientist knows the full extent of the maze.'

'The question is, who's the scientist? Who knows what's really going on?' Leila replied. 'If I'd known what Pearce was getting me into—'

'You'd still be here,' Wollerton cut her off.

'And you?' she asked.

He hesitated. 'I was lost. If I'm honest, I was depressed. Spending my nights listening to sad songs, drifting without any sense of place in the world. Esther and the kids gone. I think part of me wanted to leave this world.'

Leila pitied the man. She'd faced more adversity than most, but everyone was fighting some kind of battle. 'I'm sorry to hear that.'

Wollerton nodded. 'Pearce gave me a sense of purpose. Something bigger than myself. I see my kids a few days a month, and I'm not even sure how much of a connection I have with them. I don't know if anyone would even notice if I was gone.'

Leila's heart broke for the grizzled veteran opposite and

she could see him choking back a lump in his throat. 'I'd notice. Who else could I have such cheerful conversations with?'

Wollerton smiled. 'And where else would I get to spend time with a misunderstood genius?'

Leila chuckled. 'Why don't you go back to sleep?' she suggested, suddenly feeling very guilty for having woken him.

He settled into his seat and closed his eyes. Leila did likewise. She had to try to get some rest. They would be in London in a few hours and she suspected she would need every scrap of energy her battered body had to offer.

Chapter 59

They arrived at Heathrow shortly before midday and took a cab from the airport into Central London. Leila was glad to be back on familiar ground. Everything seemed so much smaller than the grand buildings of Manhattan, but there was something comforting in the more human sense of scale. The trees and open spaces were rich with autumn hues, and as they drove through Hyde Park, Leila lingered over the crowds of people enjoying the warm day. She wondered whether she would ever live a life of such normal pleasures, but immediately felt guilty. How could she be thinking of such things when her sister was still out there?

Hannan could be suffering, and I'm pining for people-watching, Leila chided herself. *You won't have anything approaching a normal life until you've found your sister.*

Leila and Wollerton left the taxi on Edgware Road and walked west along Connaught Street. They went south on Albion Street, and doubled back on themselves to make sure they weren't being followed. Wollerton was obsessive about security, and when he was finally satisfied, they returned to Connaught Street, turned left and walked a little further until they reached a tiny access road that ran between a four-storey mansion and an eight-storey apartment block. They walked between the two high buildings and soon emerged on

Connaught Close, a short, narrow cobbled mews lined with quaint two-storey terraced houses. Leila saw immediately why Robert Clifton had selected the property. It stood in the centre of a row of similar homes, and had large green-framed windows that gave good visibility of the only way into the mews. The surrounding rooftops were flat, which offered a variety of escape routes into neighbouring streets, and Leila had no doubt there would be a back door and another exit route.

One of the green double doors opened, and Pearce stepped out.

'Good to see you, Lyly,' he said, as he embraced Leila.

She always felt better seeing her old friend, even if he looked harried and exhausted as he did now. 'You too.'

He shook Wollerton's hand and pulled him into an embrace.

'You look knackered,' Wollerton remarked.

'It's been rough,' Pearce replied.

He was thinner than the last time Leila had seen him, his face was drawn and his eyes ringed by dark shadows.

He led them inside the house, closed the door and locked it with a steel bar. The living room was decorated like a contemporary hotel lobby. All style and no soul, but it was comfortable and Leila was grateful when she slid into a wide armchair by the window. She kept an eye on the mews entrance and massaged her aching legs.

Pearce and Wollerton sat on opposing blue corduroy sofas and traded accounts of what had happened. Leila chimed in with details when Wollerton's sketch needed filling out, and soon they were all up to speed.

'They killed Kelly Dan because you took her?' Pearce asked.

'Looks that way,' Wollerton replied.

'Same thing happened to Dominic McClusky,' Leila noted, referring to Pearce's former boss who'd been murdered by Black Thirteen operatives when Pearce had taken him captive.

'Yeah,' Pearce agreed. 'And look what they were trying to protect; the Black Thirteen attack. So what are they trying to protect now?'

'I've been wondering about that,' Leila said. 'Maybe it's not about any one mission. Maybe they're protecting something bigger.'

'So what do we do?' Wollerton asked.

'Find the Alchemist. Whoever this Leonardo Vincenza is, Farida thought he was important,' Pearce replied.

'And Whitman,' Leila said. 'We need to know who Whitman is.'

'I'm going to meet our financier,' Pearce told them. 'He sent me details of a time and location this morning, using the secure drop.'

The secure drop was an encrypted digital mailing service Leila had established to enable them to safely communicate with Huxley Blaine Carter and Robert Clifton.

'You think he can help?' Wollerton asked.

'I'm tired of being kept in the dark,' Pearce said. 'Huxley Blaine Carter suspects these people had a hand in his father's murder. He's been tracking them longer than any of us. I can't believe a man of his talent and resources hasn't got more to go on. I'm going to get him to tell me everything he knows about these people. I want the whole story. I want to know exactly what we're up against.'

Chapter 60

Pearce had ditched his CBR 1100 Super Blackbird on the outskirts of London, and had felt a stab of regret leaving another beautiful machine, but he couldn't take the chance it had been reported stolen or otherwise flagged in connection with an offence by Lang or one of his associates. Pearce had reached the safe house near dawn, after a couple of cab journeys. Thankfully the house came with two cars, which were parked in a secure garage on the corner of Portsea Place, a short walk from Connaught Close. There was a gun-metal grey Range Rover Vogue and a silver Toyota Landcruiser. Pearce took the Range Rover and drove the powerful car through the streets of West London until he reached the A40 flyover. He took the ramp out of Gloucester Terrace and joined the overpass that cut its way through the high-rise estates of Ladbroke Grove and Acton. He continued west out past Hanger Lane and Northolt, following directions that would lead him to a set of GPS coordinates and his meeting with Huxley Blaine Carter.

His destination was a field in the middle of the Chiltern Hills, near a village called Maidensgrove. The satellite image on the car's GPS system showed the field was surrounded by thick woodland on three sides, and was set well back from the nearest road. The closest house was at least a quarter of a mile away, and the meeting point was accessed by a winding mud track that connected it to a narrow B-road. It was isolated, that was for sure, but it wasn't until Pearce reached the spot, shortly before 3 p.m., that he truly understood why Huxley had selected it for their meeting.

The satellite image failed to convey the topography of the area. The field was actually the summit of a hill that was ringed by forest on three sides. There was clear visibility to the treeline in every direction, and a helipad had been marked out on the grass near the southern edge of the forest. A black Bell 429 GlobalRanger stood in the long grass, rotors idle. Beside the aircraft was an open-sided structure with a fibre-glass roof. About the size of a large hotel room, the canopy did nothing to obscure the view, but would prevent satellites from photographing whatever was beneath it.

The Range Rover made light work of the badly rutted track, which had been baked hard in the recent autumn heat. Pearce parked beside the chopper and saw Huxley and Robert Clifton seated beneath the canopy. The chopper pilot was in the cock-pit, keeping a watchful eye on the track, and four of Huxley's bodyguards stood at each corner of the canopy, facing outwards.

Pearce got out of the Range Rover and approached the two seated men.

'Mr Pearce,' Robert Clifton said, getting to his feet.

'I'm not used to being summoned,' Huxley remarked as he stood. 'And I wouldn't have come for anyone else.'

'Tell Ms Nahum we're looking for any Whitmans connected to Kelly Dan, as she asked,' Clifton said. 'We've got nothing so far.'

'Alexis Tippett-Jones is financing White Fire,' Pearce said.

Huxley and Clifton exchanged surprised looks.

'Nikos Kitsantonis is dead, so is the woman who very briefly took over his interests. Killed by Elroy Lang's people. Most likely because we were on to them.'

Huxley and Clifton said nothing, and their silence frustrated Pearce.

'A woman died in my arms last night because she made the mistake of trying to help me,' he said.

'I'm not sure what point you're trying to make,' Huxley responded. 'I'm sorry for the poor woman, but we didn't kill her.'

'No,' Pearce countered. 'You didn't do anything.'

He had fought for everything. His entire existence had been defined by struggle, the triumph of will over a system that had decided people like him shouldn't succeed. Mixed-race, abandoned, in and out of foster homes, troubled and troubling, the odds had been stacked against him from the start, and here was this rich, tanned, entitled billionaire in his designer T-shirt, pressed slacks, deck shoes and thousand-dollar sunglasses, shrugging off the death of yet another unfortunate who'd happened to cross their path.

'You never do anything. You send others to do it for you,' Pearce said. 'Well, you can count me out. I don't work for people I can't trust.'

'And why do you think you can't trust me?'

'You never explained how you came to know about Black Thirteen,' Pearce replied. He pointed at Clifton. 'He said you have algorithms searching the ether, but no algorithm picks up the kind of human intelligence that leads to something like Black Thirteen. Just what is your interest in all this?'

'I told you; my father—' Huxley protested, but Pearce cut him off.

'Your father died and you suspected he was killed by these people, but that's not the whole story, is it?'

Huxley looked at Clifton, who sighed. Neither man responded.

'OK,' Pearce said. 'I'm out.'

He started walking towards the Range Rover, and when he left the shade of the canopy, he felt the afternoon sun on his face. He squinted up at the sky, relishing the idea of a clear horizon for himself, devoid of dark clouds.

'Wait,' Huxley called out.

Pearce looked back to see the billionaire's shiny confidence had gone. He seemed smaller, hesitant, maybe even broken.

'What is it? What do you know? Why did Alexis kill her own father? What was she protecting?' Pearce asked.

He closed on the two men, and Clifton stiffened. The man had picked up on Pearce's anger.

'Really?' Pearce scoffed. 'You think you could stop me?' He indicated the bodyguards. 'You think they could? If I wanted to hurt him, he'd already be on the ground, suffering. Tell me what you know, or I walk.'

'Have you heard of Apostoli?' Huxley asked.

Pearce shook his head. The word meant nothing to him.

'It is the Greek word for mission. It comes from the same root word as apostle. The Apostoli is a secret organization. My father was a member, but he turned against them. That's why I think they killed him,' Huxley revealed.

'Your father was a member?' Pearce asked in disbelief.

'He was going to expose them,' Huxley said.

'Expose?' Pearce felt his anger rising. 'Your father was a member of this group and you didn't think to tell us?'

'Would it have made a difference?' Huxley snapped back. This was clearly a difficult admission. His father had been one of the bad guys. 'You don't know if you can trust me, I don't know if I can trust you. Outside of the Apostoli, three people know my father was a member, and we're all standing right here. This isn't something I share lightly,' his voice lost its edge as he calmed down. 'I hope you appreciate that, Mr Pearce.'

'Who are they? Russian Intelligence?'

Huxley shook his head. 'This isn't about nation states. After you foiled the Red Wolves, you called what they and Black Thirteen had done "street espionage". I said that was a good description. This is about ideology, and you don't need a nation to spread ideology, you just need to take it to the streets.'

'What ideology?' Pearce asked.

'Some of them are religious fanatics. They want a return to religious orthodoxy. Others are political conservatives drawn to the group by its right-wing ideologues. Markus Kral, the man you saw with Lang outside the Lightstar Arena, is a believer in chaos and conflict. He thinks the world is fated to experience an apocalyptic war, and he will do everything in his power to bring it about. What the Russians did and are still doing in Ukraine is part of Kral's plan. And there are still others who are members of Apostoli because of the money that is to be made from the chaos.'

'And which ideology motivated your father?'

Huxley looked stung by the question. 'Religion. He saw America descending into godlessness. Silicon Valley in particular is a haven for whatever vice takes your fancy, and he said some of the excesses he saw made him sick. Physically and spiritually. He believed Apostoli was a way to redeem America. Over time he discovered the true nature of the group and some of the other people he had involved himself with. Once that happened, he wanted to bring it down.'

'And that's when they . . .' Pearce left the implication hanging.

Huxley nodded.

'Does that mean Alexis Tippett-Jones is a member?' Pearce asked.

'So it would seem,' Huxley replied.

'What do they want?'

'Ask ten members and they will give you ten answers. Some want war, chaos, destruction. Others want to crush liberal ideology, put women back in the kitchen, and minorities at the back of the bus. It is a coalition of ideologies that threaten the bedrock of what we've come to know as modern society. It's perhaps easier to say what they stand against; liberty, equality, fraternity, justice, opportunity. They sow distrust and undermine those principles at every opportunity.'

'Who leads it?' Pearce asked. 'Cut off the head . . .'

'No one knows,' Clifton replied. 'Huxley's father, Tate, turned to me to help him take precautions against the group and to identify the leaders.' He paused. 'I failed him.'

'You did what you could,' Huxley assured him.

'And you didn't think we needed to know this?' Pearce asked, his anger rising. He'd studied the workings of Propaganda Due, an extremely influential Italian secret society established in the aftermath of the Second World War, and knew just how dangerous these groups could be. One that had international reach and membership drawn from the intelligence, financial, political and business communities would be formidable. 'You put us into situations where the odds were stacked against us.'

'You put yourself there, tracking Chatri Angsakul from Pakistan to Thailand,' Huxley said, referring to the Thai man Pearce had killed in Islamabad whose involvement in the terror attack had convinced him other co-conspirators had escaped justice. 'Islamabad was an Apostoli operation. You were on the trail of these people long before you ever met me, Mr Pearce. You just didn't realize it. It's one of the reasons I hired you.'

'Nathan Foster, Wayne Nelson, Brigitte Attali might all still be alive if they'd known what they were up against,' Pearce objected, but his heart wasn't in his words. He'd blundered into this without any assistance from Huxley Blaine Carter. His friends' deaths were on him.

'Do you really think so, Mr Pearce? My father knew what he was up against and it didn't do him any good. Apostoli reaches into almost every country in the world. It has members in the corridors of power. If I'd told you the scale of the thing, would you have believed me?'

Pearce hesitated. Propaganda Due, the post-war network, had over a thousand members drawn from the upper echelons of Italian society. If Pearce hadn't seen the FBI files and extensive documentation that supported the existence of the group, he wouldn't have believed such a conspiracy could exist. Apostoli was bigger, more ambitious and, based on his experiences, far more dangerous. Huxley was right; he probably wouldn't have believed in it if he'd been told. He had to see it for himself.

'And how could I be sure you weren't a double agent sent

to lure me into the open?' Huxley went on. 'They've been trying to find out who you work for, haven't they?'

Pearce nodded.

'I couldn't tell you before, but I'm telling you now. The threat is real and it's bigger than you can possibly imagine. These people will exploit every weakness, widen every division and sow chaos and conflict at every turn. They've funded and amplified everything from the far right to the far left, from pandemic deniers to environmental extremists. The end isn't important – the only outcome that interests them is destruction.'

Huxley's words hit home. Alexis Tippett-Jones was a case study in the zealotry membership required. Pearce couldn't even begin to imagine how warped a person had to be to murder their own father.

'Are you still going to walk?' Huxley asked.

Pearce didn't reply. He studied the billionaire and his security adviser.

'You should have told me,' Pearce said at last. 'We would have approached this differently. I'm not going to walk, but when I've dealt with Lang, you and I are going to have a talk.'

Pearce walked back to the Range Rover, more determined than ever to avenge Brigitte and bring down Lang and his foul organization.

Chapter 61

Pearce pushed the Range Rover along the M40, and the powerful car chewed the miles between Oxfordshire and London. Huxley had kept them in the dark, but as the vestiges of his anger ebbed away, Pearce conceded the man had a point. An operation of this scale would normally be the preserve of nation states, and even then there were only a handful that could execute multiple operations on different continents. Pearce had seen things through eyes that had been trained for post-Cold War espionage, a world of terror groups backed by nation states, of asymmetrical warfare, but this was a different game entirely. People started with belief, and from that shared belief came the ability to acquire resources and personnel. The nation state was redundant, made obsolete by corporations and individuals with sufficient resources to reshape the world. People like Huxley Blaine Carter. Wollerton had been right when he'd told Pearce he'd need to tear up the espionage rulebook.

Wollerton had been talking about Black Thirteen. What would he have said if he'd known Black Thirteen was only a tiny piece of the puzzle? If he'd been aware of the much larger game at play? Huxley Blaine Carter had been wrong to suggest it wouldn't have made any difference to their engagement. If Pearce had been aware of Apostoli, he wouldn't have been so reactive, and instead of focusing on thwarting the tactical plays, he'd have tried to have strategic impact on the organization. But Huxley had been right in a way; Pearce would have struggled to believe in a network of this scale if he hadn't put the pieces together himself.

Pearce had told Huxley they needed to talk once he'd dealt with White Fire, but he wasn't sure what he would say to the man. Did he want to take on something like this? Revenge against Elroy Lang was driving him, and he wanted to find Markus Kral, but if he dealt with those men, what then? Prove the Apostoli network exists and use the information to clear his name and get reinstated at MI6? Work for Huxley, ripping the network apart? Or quit and live an easy life as a climbing guide, shepherding tourists around Railay Beach, a paradise with clear warm water, cloudless skies and some of the world's most beautiful routes? The place regularly called to him, but he wasn't sure he was ready to retire from the game, despite the questions he had about his motivation. He was yesterday's man as far as the service was concerned. And even if he could get himself reinstated, he wasn't sure he wanted his old job back, so why keep going?

He reached London as the afternoon was coming to an end. Rush-hour traffic was heading west, so he had a reasonably clear run into Paddington. He took the Bayswater Road, along the edge of Hyde Park, which was crowded with people enjoying the evening. When he arrived at the house on Connaught Close, he found Leila and Wollerton at the kitchen table, both hunched over laptops.

'Where did you get those?' Pearce asked.

'There's a gear vault behind the wardrobe in the upstairs bedroom,' Leila replied. 'He found it.'

'I think there's one in every safe house these guys have,' Wollerton added. 'Good job too. You should have heard her complaining. She was like a drug addict jonesing for a fix.'

'Ha!' Leila scoffed. 'How did it go?'

'His dad was one of them,' Pearce replied, registering the surprise on their faces. 'Turns out Huxley knows a lot more about what we're up against. It's a group called Apostoli. International. Long reach, lots of resources. Leadership is unclear, but the group is tapped into government, law enforcement, military, security and intelligence, you name it. He says they killed his dad because he turned against them.'

Wollerton whistled. 'And when was he going to tell us this?'

'He says we wouldn't have believed him if he'd told us. We had to see it for ourselves,' Pearce revealed.

'Like the bloody Matrix.' Wollerton laughed bleakly.

'Yeah, I don't buy it either,' Pearce said. 'I think there's more he isn't telling us, but I'll get to him in time. We need to deal with Lang first.'

'I haven't had any luck with Whitman,' Leila responded.

'Huxley says his people are still working on it.'

She nodded. 'But we've identified the Alchemist.' She turned her screen so Pearce could see it. 'Strange character. MIT graduate.' She flipped through windows that showed Lorenzo Vincenza's academic record and media clippings. He was a tall, gaunt man with long blond hair and eyes that looked sharp enough to pierce into other dimensions. 'He's a software engineer who moved into genetic medicine.'

Pearce was surprised. 'Not the sort of things that strike me as interchangeable.'

'They are,' Leila told him. 'A lot of genetic medicine involves computer modelling and structuring artificial protein sequences. Architecture and engineering on a nano scale.'

Leila opened a window that showed a profile in *Silicon Entrepreneur*, a Silicon Valley start-up magazine. The article covered the launch of Vitenza, Lorenzo's genetic medicine company, and featured a photograph of the founder. He wore a black T-shirt emblazoned with a large sequinned skull, and the expression on his face was one of pure contempt. Pearce wasn't sure whether he was angry at an individual or the world or just the photographer, but the rage seemed to radiate off the screen.

'He started Vitenza five years ago, but has struggled to get any products to market,' Leila said. 'Investors started whispering about his prospects, and it affected him. He took to social media. Went on a Twitter rampage.'

Leila brought up a Twitter page for an anonymous account called The Alchemist. The profile picture was of a faceless shadow in a hoodie.

'The Alchemist posts incendiary stuff about politics, the economy, the pandemic,' Leila observed.

'How do you know it's him?' Pearce asked.

'I don't. Not for sure,' Leila conceded. 'But it's one of those open secrets people talk about. He never confirmed or denied it, but social media pins the account on him.'

'And your source used both names, right?' Wollerton suggested.

Pearce nodded. 'So where is he?'

'No one knows,' Leila replied. 'His friends reported increasingly erratic behaviour a few weeks ago, and then he disappeared. Someone filed a missing persons report, but no one has seen him since.'

Leila opened another file window. This one showed a specific thread of the Alchemist's tweets.

Pearce read the first one aloud. '*The world has been vaccinated with spike protein. Could someone design a pathogen that triggers an immune cascade?*'

The thread went on to give details of how a hostile actor could target such a specific vaccine antigen to create what would in effect be a contagious toxin that would turn people's immune systems against them.

'I don't follow,' Pearce confessed.

'When you're vaccinated against something like a coronavirus, you develop a very narrow immune response,' Leila explained. 'If someone released a genetically engineered virus that was slightly different to the one you'd been vaccinated against, your immune system could go into overdrive trying to defeat it, all the time delivering an off-target response that only made things worse.'

'Is that really possible?' Pearce asked.

'You can see from the comments opinion is split,' Wollerton replied.

'When did he write this?' Pearce asked.

'Two months ago,' Leila replied. 'And look who liked the last tweet.'

She drew Pearce's attention to a user called 'Huntergirl'. The name meant nothing, but Pearce recognized the profile picture immediately.

It was Farida.

Chapter 62

'You think she introduced this guy to White Fire?' Leila asked.

'Maybe,' Pearce replied. 'If he's working on a biological agent . . .' He hesitated. 'We need to inform the authorities.'

'We've got to expect Apostoli to have people on the inside,' Wollerton remarked.

'It doesn't matter. This is too big. Let's alert the Joint Biosecurity Centre, the Box and Vauxhall Cross,' Pearce said, referring to the UK government's biosecurity group, MI5 and MI6. 'It doesn't mean we have to sit back. We need to keep at this in case one or more of them has been compromised.'

'What do you have in mind?' Wollerton asked.

'We go for Alexis. If she killed her father to protect the Apostoli network, then she must be influential within the organization. And she's been financing Jacob Silver and White Fire, so it's reasonable to assume she knows what they're planning.'

Wollerton nodded.

'When you say go for her . . .' Leila said.

'Take her. Make her answer questions,' Pearce responded.

'You don't think it would be better to go for a softer target?' Leila pressed. 'Mary Knight?'

Pearce could see where Leila was heading. 'This isn't personal, if that's what you're thinking. Mary is a pawn in all this.

She might not even know what White Fire is being used for, and she's expendable to Apostoli.'

'And Jacob Silver?' Leila asked.

'A recruitment and radicalization tool. He's the hawker who stands outside the circus and gets people into the tent. He won't know anything.'

Leila nodded. 'Just want to make sure your reasoning is clear. A lesser man would be tempted to go after Tippett-Jones for getting the better of him.'

'I'm not a lesser man.' Pearce smiled. 'Don't get me wrong, I have a personal interest in her, but not because she fooled me. I want anyone who might have been responsible for Brigitte's death.'

'I'm with you,' Leila conceded.

'How do we do this?' Wollerton asked. 'If this Alchemist guy is for real and they're planning some sort of biological attack, we've got to assume time is of the essence.'

'We go tonight,' Pearce replied. 'You have Alexis's London home address?' he asked Leila.

'She has a house in St John's Wood.' She opened Google Maps and brought up a satellite image of a home on Cavendish Avenue, a street of mansions and bling palaces.

'We check it out,' Pearce told them. 'If it looks good, we take her tonight. If not, we grab her en route to the office in the morning. Same way we took McClusky.'

'That didn't end well for him,' Wollerton remarked.

'I know how to disable their upgraded tracking devices now,' Leila said. 'They won't find her.'

'Let's do it then,' Pearce said. 'By this time tomorrow, I want us to have Alexis Tippett-Jones, and I want to know how we stop the Alchemist.'

Chapter 63

Leila piloted a micro drone along an alleyway beside a grand block of flats on Elm Tree Road. The flats stood directly west of Alexis's home and the two gardens abutted each other. The drone fed infra-red video footage back to the screen on Leila's remote control, and it showed the alleyway widen into a small landscaped garden behind the block. The tiny aircraft flew over patios, rockeries and beds packed with flowers and mature shrubs, and then rose over a high bright wall to reveal Alexis's home. The satellite images didn't do the four-storey, cream-coloured mansion justice. Constructed in a classical imperial style with columns, archways and Romanesque stonework, the house must have had at least ten thousand square feet of living space. It was set at the end of a long garden, most of which had been laid to lawn. The place would have been worth tens of millions at the height of London's property boom. Slightly less after the pandemic, but still highly sought after.

Leila piloted the drone over a small waterfall that fed into a pond packed with koi. Pearce and Wollerton watched her make tiny adjustments to the flightpath using the remote control. Thankfully there wasn't much of a breeze to throw the aircraft off course, but Leila still gave it her complete attention because she didn't want to let her friends down.

They were both dressed for a night operation and wore black combat gear, body armour, heavy boots and ski masks, which were currently rolled up as hats. The information captured using the drone would tell them whether to abduct Alexis from her home, so it was crucial Leila got things right.

They'd spent a couple of hours analysing the property and discussing plans, while Pearce and Wollerton readied their gear and weapons. Pearce had collected the Range Rover from the secure parking garage and brought it to Connaught Close to be loaded before they'd driven to Elm Tree Road.

'I see a camera,' Pearce said, indicating a CCTV unit located high on the back wall of the house.

A single-storey extension protruded from the right-hand side of the building, and its flat roof offered access to the first-floor window just above it. They'd discussed the extension when they'd seen it on the satellite image.

'Looks like a good way in,' Wollerton noted.

'We can disable the cameras,' Leila advised. 'A micro-EMP will take out everything within a fifty-metre radius. The drone is shielded with a Faraday cage.'

Pearce nodded. 'Open window,' he noted, pointing to the screen.

'Doable,' Wollerton said.

Leila piloted the drone towards a window that was three feet to the north of the edge of the flat roof and roughly three feet above it.

'Quite a jump,' Pearce responded.

'Don't go soft on me, Scott.' Wollerton smiled.

Leila flew the drone through the open first-floor window, grateful for the warm autumn night. They would never have found such easy access in winter. The drone went inside a large bathroom with a double tub and twin washbasins, and flew through an open doorway into a large, opulently decorated bedroom.

'That's her,' Pearce said, indicating Alexis Tippett-Jones, who was asleep in the king-size bed.

There were two more windows on the right of the room, both of which were open.

'Looks like we've got our pick,' Pearce said. 'You go in through the back? I'll use one of the side windows?'

Wollerton nodded.

Leila piloted the drone through a gap between the bedroom door and frame and took the aircraft over a balcony landing that opened onto a large hallway.

'No sign of physical security,' she noted.

'We should assume there's some in the building,' Pearce said. 'We grab her, take her down the stairs, and out through the front door to the street where Lyly will be waiting.'

'Works for me,' Wollerton responded. 'What's our policy on collateral damage? What do we do if we run into trouble?'

'Neutralize it,' Pearce replied.

Chapter 64

Pearce and Wollerton pulled down their ski masks before they left the van. They ran across the street into the alleyway beside the block of flats. A few feet into the passageway, their path was blocked by a locked full-height metal gate. Wollerton went first, and found a foothold in the metalwork, boosted himself against the wall of the apartment building and clambered over. Pearce followed and jumped down onto the paved passageway that led into the garden.

He and Wollerton sprinted across the open space, their body armour and gear bouncing with every stride. They both had MP7 sub-machine guns slung over their shoulders and Heckler & Koch HK45 pistols at their hips. Wollerton used an apple tree at the back of the garden to lift himself onto the high wall that separated the two properties, and Pearce went after him.

Alexis's garden was just as they'd seen it on screen. They raced across the manicured lawn, past the waterfall and pond, until they were near the terrace. Pearce signalled Wollerton to halt, and they both crouched down. Pearce produced a small device from a compartment on his gear belt. It was the size and shape of a grenade, but instead of a pin, there was a plastic cover that protected a red button. Pearce lifted the cover, pressed the button, which started flashing, and tossed the device. It landed on the grass not far from the terrace, and there was a prolonged burst of light from the red button the instant before the lights went out in the neighbouring houses. The EMP device had disabled whatever surveillance and security systems Alexis had installed.

Pearce signalled Wollerton to move and they ran onto the terrace. Wollerton went left to a column that rose up the rear of the building next to the extension, and Pearce went right, the other side of the low structure. There was sixteen feet of paving slabs before a narrow lawn that stretched to the boundary wall with the neighbouring property. Pearce ran to a drainpipe that descended from the roof guttering, and started climbing. He leveraged his weight against his feet and walked up the wall, hand over hand, applying pressure every step of the way. When he reached the first floor, he jumped and grabbed the sill of the open window to his right, the one closest to Alexis's bed. He pulled himself onto the sill and squatted on the broad piece of stone to push the sash window wide. Moving silently, he lowered himself into the room.

He pushed through a gap in the heavy drapes and looked to his left to see Wollerton moving through the en suite bathroom.

'This is becoming a habit, Mr Pearce,' Alexis said, sitting up. 'I'm assuming that is you.'

Pearce had stumbled in on her once before, or at least he thought he had, but hers had been the only open window the night he'd broken into Purbeck House, her father's stately home. Had he been meant to find her window? Had it been a trap?

Is this a trap? he wondered darkly.

Alexis seemed unperturbed by the two men in her

bedroom, and stretched as she got to her feet. There was just enough light to see she wore a black vest and matching leggings.

'What do you want? To take me?' she asked. 'Question me? Hurt me?' She said the last words sarcastically and flashed a mischievous grin.

'You're coming with us.' Wollerton gestured with his MP7.

'I'm not going to fight the inevitable,' she responded.

'We take her out of the window,' Pearce said.

'It *is* Scott Pearce,' she remarked with something close to glee.

Pearce didn't like the Reaper's chill, the cold feeling of death's hand shivering down his spine. It usually signalled something was wrong and he felt it scrape his vertebrae now. 'We lower her onto the flat roof and into the garden.'

Pearce grabbed Alexis, and he and Wollerton marched her into the bathroom.

'We could just take the stairs,' Alexis remarked.

Pearce climbed out of the open window and dropped onto the roof.

'Send her,' he said.

Alexis eased herself out and followed Pearce down. He steadied her when she stumbled.

'Very gentle,' she remarked mockingly.

Wollerton climbed out of the window, and they moved along the roof to the end of the extension. Pearce jumped onto the lawn, Alexis climbed down and Wollerton leaped after her.

As they started across the lawn towards the back wall, the folding patio doors drew back and silhouetted figures flooded out of the house onto the terrace, weapons drawn. There were over twenty men, all armed, and Pearce recognized some of them from the gunfight at the Bayard Madison offices.

Alexis grinned.

'Game over, Mr Pearce.'

Chapter 65

Alexis backed away confidently.

'I had thought you might go for Mary Knight or the scientist, but the better part of me knew you wouldn't be able to resist the queen,' she said. 'As you can see, I've inherited my father's taste for enhanced security.'

'Drop your weapons,' one of the men said.

Pearce hesitated.

The odds were against him and Wollerton. They'd blundered into a trap.

'There's a panic room,' Alexis revealed. 'It's not on any plans and it's impervious to standard surveillance techniques. I've turned it into my security team's barracks. Keeps them very much off the radar.' She walked over to Pearce. 'You're out of your league. You always were.'

He thought about grabbing her, but suspected they'd execute Wollerton. She only needed one of them alive to tell her who they were working for, which Pearce guessed was the reason they were both still breathing.

'Now, we're going to take you,' Alexis said. 'Question you. Hurt you.' She was so close her breath caressed Pearce's face.

He pictured himself putting a bullet between her eyes. How different from when they'd first met in the private members' club on Golden Square. He had been attracted to her, but now her beauty was tainted by her corrupt soul. She was sour in every possible way, but she was no use to them dead, and the price of seeing her fall would be his own demise.

'Get away from them!'

Leila's voice boomed across the garden and she emerged from the passage beside the extension, carrying an M4 Commando, a powerful machine gun that was equipped with an underslung grenade launcher. She didn't flinch as the men on the terrace turned their guns on her. They backed away from her as she approached, because they became aware she was holding a block of C4 against the barrel of the gun, and had her thumb over the detonator.

'I never liked you,' Leila said to Alexis. 'And you've more than lived down to my expectations.'

Alexis studied the Syrian closely.

'You're wondering if I'll do it. Make your quick calculations carefully, your ladyship. Figure out this and figure out that, but don't let your bias get you killed,' Leila cautioned. 'We both know they're dead if I let you take them. And you know me, you know what I've been through. Death would be a welcome relief. So if that's what it takes to ensure you don't have them . . .'

She stroked the detonator with her thumb, and Pearce smiled at the sheer audacity of what she was doing. He had no doubt she would make good on her threat, and saw Alexis believed her too.

Leila walked towards her two friends. Pearce saw her wince with every step, but someone who didn't know her might not register the pain she was in. Some of the men around her were clearly weighing their chances of disarming her before she detonated enough C4 to kill everyone in the garden and take out half the house. None of them mustered the courage and soon she was standing between Pearce and Wollerton.

'Here,' she said, handing Pearce the large M4 and taking the MP7 in exchange.

It felt good to have one of the world's most powerful hand-held weapons in his grasp.

'Come on,' Leila said to him and Wollerton. 'You too.'

She signalled Alexis, who scoffed.

'I mean it,' Leila said.

Alexis had made the mistake of staying close, and Wollerton grabbed her arm, pulled his HK45 from its holster and pressed it against her head.

'Funny how quickly things can change,' Wollerton said.

'Back off!' Leila yelled at Alexis's men.

She walked towards the passage and Wollerton followed, pulling Alexis. Pearce brought up the rear, and swept the squad of men with the M4.

'Back!' he commanded one of them, who was edging closer.

Leila led them to a side gate with a broken lock and took them through the front garden to the street, where the Range Rover was parked across the driveway.

Wollerton pulled Alexis towards the SUV, while Pearce walked backwards keeping his gun on the gang of men, who followed them like a pack of hungry wolves.

Pearce sensed movement and looked up to see a sniper targeting Leila from one of the second-floor windows. He swung the M4 round and opened fire. The glass shattered and the sniper vanished.

When he looked round, he saw Alexis dig her nails into Wollerton's face and try to run, but Leila grabbed her round the neck and squeezed hard. Alexis let out a choked scream and Pearce hurried over. The tense energy had shifted to imminent danger, and Pearce had little doubt someone else was going to try something stupid.

Alexis fought against Leila, and stamped on her foot. She managed to break free and ran for the house before Pearce could stop her. Gunfire erupted from another upstairs window and Pearce targeted the muzzle flash. The shooter fell silent as lights went on in the houses opposite.

Emboldened, the gang of men tried to rush Pearce, but he shot one of them in the leg to keep the others at bay. The man went down, howling.

Alexis made it to the front door, and another gunman appeared and ushered her inside. Pearce cursed their misfortune, but the tide was turning and they'd be lucky to escape with their lives. They couldn't risk trying to go after her.

'Let's roll,' Pearce said.

He, Leila and Wollerton jumped into the Range Rover. Pearce kept the rear passenger door open and his M4 stayed on the men as Wollerton stepped on the accelerator and the Range Rover raced away.

Chapter 66

Pearce woke to find muted sunlight filling his bed-room. He still felt the burning shame of failure. He, Wollerton and Leila had taken a long and circuitous route back to the safe house on Connaught Close and he had hardly spoken a word. He had been furious with himself for underestimating Alexis yet again. If it hadn't been for Leila monitoring them via the drone, and her quick thinking . . . well, he couldn't bring himself to think about where he and Wollerton might be.

He hauled himself out of bed and tilted the blind that covered the only window in his small room. The mews beyond was like a well, but there was enough sunlight to penetrate its cobbled corners. The sky above was a perfect blue and in no way reflected the grey storm that gripped Pearce. He wasn't accustomed to failure. He pulled on a pair of grey combats and a black T-shirt and went downstairs.

Leila and Wollerton were in the kitchen nursing hot drinks, and eyed him sheepishly when he entered.

'Tell me about it,' Wollerton remarked. 'Did we screw up royally or what?'

'We made the news,' Leila said, turning her laptop towards Pearce.

There was a small piece on BBC London about a shoot-out in St John's Wood.

'Any record?' Pearce asked.

'No mention of video or photo evidence,' Leila said. 'And nothing's shown up on social media. Police are saying it was a burglary gone wrong.'

Pearce shook his head and sat down.

'Coffee?' Wollerton asked.

'No thanks.' Pearce sighed. 'We made a right mess.'

'It happens,' Leila said, but her attempt to console him only made Pearce feel worse.

She and Wollerton exchanged a shifty look.

'I don't want to drag the mood down further,' she said, 'but you're not going to like this.'

She opened a window on her laptop to show a Rightway Patriots Network news article that was headlined, 'Former Soldier Wanted in Connection with Murder at British Country House'.

Pearce saw his old service photograph staring back at him, alongside a larger image of Farida caught smiling on a summer's day. He couldn't bear to think of her taking her last breaths in his arms, and the fact his face was public and being tied to her death only deepened his despondency.

'I'm sorry, Scott,' Leila said. 'They've set you up to flush you out.'

'I . . .' Pearce hesitated.

'Don't worry about the story,' Leila advised him. 'I'm running a denial of service attack that's preventing anyone else from accessing it, and I'll soon have hacked their server to take it down permanently.'

'Thanks,' Pearce responded quietly. 'Her death was my fault. She was no angel, but none of us are. She was so full of life.'

A lump came to his throat.

'Sorry, man,' Wollerton said.

'Thanks,' Pearce replied. 'I don't know where we go from here.'

'I'm working on something,' Leila said, but Pearce's phone rang before she could reveal more.

'Unknown number,' he remarked.

'If they'd traced its location, they wouldn't be ringing, they'd be knocking,' Wollerton said, and Leila nodded.

'*Sam, or whatever your name is, it's me.*'

Pearce recognized Mary Knight's voice.

'*The police have just released me from questioning. I need to see you. I have to make amends.*'

She sounded as though she was crying.

'Where?' Pearce asked.

'*The wood where we stopped after going to see the Prophet,*' Mary replied. '*Six o'clock.*'

Pearce checked the time. He could make it. 'OK.'

He hung up, and Leila and Wollerton looked at him expectantly.

'That was Mary Knight. She wants to meet.'

'It's a trap,' Leila said.

'I agree,' Wollerton added.

'Possibly, but I have to take the risk,' Pearce replied. 'She just lost one of her own. Grief changes people. We all know that. I've got to chance it.'

Leila and Wollerton didn't look convinced.

'I want you to do whatever you can to find the Alchemist or Alexis. I'm going to Wales.'

'You'll be careful,' Leila said.

'Always.'

Chapter 67

The Range Rover was hot, so Pearce had taken the Land Cruiser from the garage on Portsea Place and he pushed it to its limits as he sped along the winding country lanes. Wollerton had tried to come with him, but Pearce had refused. He had taken the equipment he needed to keep himself safe, and he wanted Wollerton in London in case Leila got a lead on Alexis or the Alchemist. Pearce was careful filling up with fuel, and chose self-service pumps to avoid interacting with any petrol station staff who might recognize his face. The Rightway story framing him for Farida's murder hadn't been picked up by any other news outlets, but Pearce couldn't be sure he wasn't a genuine suspect in the police investigation into her death.

His service record was supposed to be sealed, and the speed and ease with which Rightway had obtained his photo suggested Lang or Alexis or whoever was behind the disinformation still had connections within the UK government or intelligence services.

Pearce had grown up studying Cold War history, and when he'd joined the service, the game was geared around neutralizing threats posed by foreign states, but increasingly countries were becoming irrelevant, or, worse, they were being hijacked to serve the agenda of powerful interest groups. The Internet had made it possible for ideologically sympathetic people to find each other across national borders, meaning a religious, right- or left-wing extremist could connect with a like-minded zealot halfway around the world, and influence politics in another country without leaving the comfort of their own house. The rise in division and social conflict meant there was an increasing number of people primed to be radicalized, their frustration and anger at some perceived wrong making them vulnerable to manipulation. An organization like Apostoli could exploit these feelings to finance groups that fostered division and extremism and use people without them realizing the role they were playing in the wider game.

White Fire was a perfect example of such a group. Protecting the environment or saving the world was a noble cause that would attract well-intentioned activists, and the science provided by Jacob Silver would underpin a belief system that justified radical action. The science might be real, or it might be hyperbole – Apostoli didn't care, as long as it looked plausible to the people who were being radicalized. Pearce wondered whether Mary had realized she was being manipulated. If it wasn't a trap and she'd truly had a change of heart, had Farida's death been the catalyst? Pearce thought about the two women he'd used to try to reach Lang, and felt intense shame. One had been killed trying to help him, despite the fact he had cast her aside to further his mission. The other had obviously developed feelings for him, but he'd just used her as a means to an end, even though part of him was drawn to her. But he was a professional and professionals weren't allowed to explore such feelings. He had to do the job and the mission took precedence at all costs.

But, in truth, he wasn't an operative anymore. Not in the

strict sense. He was a private citizen, a contractor. Some might say a mercenary. And yet he still didn't cut himself any slack and operated by the same code that had guided his army and MI6 careers. Mission first. Success at all costs. Had his training and resolve robbed him of his humanity? It was hard to conclude otherwise, and with each mission, each death, each betrayal chipping away at his sense of right and wrong, Pearce wondered whether the day would come when he would cease to be the good guy. Was it already here? Had he ever really been one? Was he any better than his enemies?

He was feeling low and disgusted with himself as the Land Cruiser climbed the hill towards the spot where he and Mary had stopped. He pulled over about a mile away from the layby and got out. He took a flight case from the boot of the Land Cruiser, placed it by the side of the road, and opened it to reveal a small drone and remote control.

Seconds later, the drone was airborne, flying over a field of long grass towards the wood, sending footage from its camera back to the remote's video screen. The evening sun was slipping behind the trees and the Welsh countryside was bathed in golden light. He rotated the camera to see a single vehicle parked in the layby; Mary's Outlander. As the aircraft approached the wood, Pearce piloted it higher and got a clear line of sight for miles in every direction. He saw no living creatures, save for a few sheep grazing in neighbouring fields.

Pearce took the drone down low over the trees, and flew over Mary, who stood in the glade where they'd had sex. There was no sign of anyone else.

He brought the aircraft back, packed it away, grabbed an HK45 pistol from beneath the spare wheel, and pocketed it, along with a couple of magazines. He jumped in the car and drove the last mile to the layby, where he parked in front of Mary's car.

Pearce hurried along the footpath into the wood and found Mary in the glade. She approached him hesitantly, and as she neared, Pearce registered tears in her eyes. He could tell she wanted to embrace him, but suspicion held her back, and it was probably better that way. He was not to be trusted, because he didn't have her best interests at heart. She was a means to an end for him, nothing more, but she deserved so much better. The realization that he saw this sensitive, intelligent, charismatic, beautiful, distressed woman as a mission objective disgusted him. How was he any better than Lang, who had similarly manipulated and exploited her?

'They say your real name is Scott Pearce,' Mary said. 'They're looking for you.'

Pearce didn't respond.

'You were right. I didn't realize who I was dealing with. I know you didn't kill Farida,' she choked on the name, 'but they made me tell the police . . .' She broke down. 'Elroy Lang made it clear what my choices were. They would do the same thing to me.'

So he was a suspect in the police investigation.

She gazed at Pearce with nothing but pain in her eyes.

'Was any of it real?' she asked. 'You and me. Did it mean anything?'

'I wish I could take all this away,' Pearce said.

'So do I.'

She staggered forwards and embraced him. He put his arms around her and she shuddered as she wept.

'I don't know what I'm doing anymore,' she said. 'I told myself Tim Giles, Louis, these were necessary sacrifices, but

Farida? She was killed by one of our own. At least I thought they were our own. I told myself it didn't matter if outsiders died because they're part of the evil destroying the world, but there will be people mourning them just as we mourn those who matter to us.'

Pearce nodded.

'And what are we trying to save? What is the point of saving the world if we lose the things that make us human? If we dehumanize people?' Mary asked. 'They killed Farida like she was nothing. I suppose that's when I realized we're all outsiders to someone. You were right. They're using us.'

'Can you help me stop them?'

Mary looked up, her eyes glistening. 'What do I mean to you?'

'I'm not who you think I am,' Pearce replied. 'This was . . .' he trailed off.

'A job?' Mary stepped away. 'Don't feel bad, Raptor Grey. I know what it's like to have a cause.'

She wiped her eyes and smiled. 'Look at me. Leaders don't cry. Mystics don't ask questions. Visionaries don't pander to uncertainty. Am I any of those things?'

Pearce didn't know what to say. Mary was distressed and he wanted to take her pain away, but he didn't know how.

'I'm not your problem anymore,' she told him. 'Farida found a man, the Alchemist, online and introduced him to me. Lang and his people have been financing us for three years. I gave them the Alchemist. He's quite brilliant.'

'What is he planning?' Pearce asked.

Mary shrugged. 'They never told me. They just needed me to do certain things. Tim Giles, the Zyberian data centre. I had to help Tolo extract something.'

'What?'

'I don't know. He had a specific machine identifier. He took something from it,' she replied.

'What would they need from Zyberian?' Pearce asked, puzzling over the question. 'So all your activism was cover for whatever they've got planned?'

'Not all of it, but recently, yes,' Mary admitted.

'And Alexis Tippett-Jones?' Pearce asked.

'I met her once. She's been funding Jacob's work. The Wolf's Castle Centre wouldn't exist without her.'

'Do you know where I can find the Alchemist?' he asked.

She shook her head. 'They would never tell me his location, but I heard Lang say they're on track to launch tomorrow night.'

'Launch what?' Pearce suspected he already knew. Lang must have been talking about the Alchemist's synthetic pathogen.

'I don't know, but whatever they've got planned is happening at midnight tomorrow.'

Thirty hours, Pearce thought. *Thirty hours to find the Alchemist and stop him.*

Chapter 68

'I suppose this is goodbye,' Mary said. She hesitated. 'Was any of it real?'

'I think your cause is good,' he told her. 'I don't agree with how you've chosen to fight it.'

'I meant you and me.'

Pearce knew exactly what she'd meant. He felt sorry for her. Hunter Grey was considered an almost mystical figure by her group, but in truth she was just as vulnerable as anyone he'd ever met. He didn't want to hurt her.

'I wish it could be,' he replied.

'That's an elegant answer. Thank you for not lying to me.'

'What will you do?'

'What can I do?' she asked with a degree of exasperation. 'Go back. See if I can disentangle White Fire from these people. They have what they wanted from us, so hopefully they'll let us go.'

'Be careful,' Pearce cautioned. 'They don't leave loose ends.'

Mary sighed. She stepped forward and kissed Pearce.

'Wouldn't it be nice to make your wish come true?' she suggested. 'To go somewhere far away, just you and me and make what we had real. Leave all this behind and give ourselves time and space to live. To find one another. To learn to love one another.'

Pearce was impassive, and Mary stepped away with an air of defeat.

'Goodbye, Scott Pearce,' she said, before starting through the glade towards the footpath.

He didn't respond. He couldn't say anything in case he gave away how tempted he was by her suggestion. A normal life of simple pleasures.

Instead, he waited and watched her go. He'd feared a trap, but had encountered a woman who'd tested his resolve in ways he hadn't expected. Would he ever feel entitled to a happy existence surrounded by those he loved?

Now isn't the time for wistful dreams, he told himself.

Mary had confirmed his worst suspicions about the Alchemist and what Lang and Alexis had planned. If she'd been telling the truth, she'd been used like so many others who'd had the misfortune to encounter Apostoli.

He stayed in the glade a while longer, listening to the evening birdsong, watching insects dance in the shafts of sunlight that penetrated the rich canopy. Finally, when he was sure he wouldn't catch up with Mary, Pearce headed for the layby.

He stayed alert for signs of trouble, but none came, and Mary's car had gone by the time he reached the Land Cruiser. He stowed the pistol and ammunition beneath the spare wheel, and used an electromagnetic signal detector to make sure the car hadn't been bugged. When he was certain the vehicle was clear, he jumped in the driver's seat and headed back to London.

As he reached the Hammersmith Flyover, the city was coloured by dozens of shades of artificial light, flickering electronic billboards drawing the eye. Pearce made it back to the parking garage a little after eleven, Central London as dark as it ever got.

He checked he hadn't been followed and once he was sure he didn't have a tail, he hurried to the house on Connaught Close.

The smile on Leila's face told him she had good news. Wollerton emerged from the kitchen sharing her air of satisfaction. He sat on the arm of the sofa next to Leila, and Pearce took the chair opposite.

'Good to see you didn't get yourself killed,' Wollerton joked.

Pearce smiled. 'She confirmed Alexis has been funding White Fire and Jacob Silver, and she said they're planning something with the Alchemist. It's happening tomorrow at midnight.'

'What?' Leila asked.

'She claimed not to know, and I believe her. She's a pawn, like Ziad Malek,' Pearce said, referring to the guy who'd been manipulated into joining the Red Wolves and doing their dirty work in Seattle. 'What have you found?'

'Something,' Wollerton confessed.

'You said you'd let me tell him,' Leila objected, leaning across to rap Wollerton on the legs with a replacement cane she'd picked up from somewhere.

'What have you got?' Pearce asked.

'The Alchemist,' Leila replied, opening her new laptop, which was on the coffee table in front of them. 'I didn't want to get your hopes up, but during last night's entertainment, when I got physical with the villainess, I stuck a micro-tracker in her neck. Like this one.'

Leila showed Pearce a tiny fragment of metal. 'It was developed by one of Huxley's companies for the CIA. Prototype, so

I wasn't sure it would work when I found it in the vault, but it does. We tracked Alexis to a building in Canary Wharf, so Kyle and I took a drive out there. Sent in a drone. We got this.'

Leila played a video file, and her laptop screen showed the interior of an office in a high-rise block. Alexis and a number of her security detail stood around a man who sat at a desk and worked on a large laptop. Pearce recognized Lorenzo Vincenza from his profile photograph. He wore a pair of large headphones and a black hoodie.

'We found him,' Leila said.

'Good,' Pearce replied. 'So let's go get him.'

Chapter 69

It was a little after 4 a.m. when Pearce and Wollerton approached the north service entrance of Tower Four, one of the skyscrapers in Canary Wharf. The opaque glass door was set in the north-east corner of the building, beneath a covered walkway, opposite a row of shops and restaurants that were still and shuttered. The service entrance had a CCTV camera covering it.

'Are we clear?' Pearce spoke into a tiny microphone concealed in the cuff of his dark grey boiler suit.

'Deactivating camera now,' Leila replied. She was in the Land Cruiser, which had been converted into an improvised mobile operations centre and was parked in the Canada Square car park, a block away. 'You're clear.'

Pearce and Wollerton, who was in a matching boiler suit and had a holdall slung over his shoulder, stepped up to the door. They'd disguised themselves as a couple of cleaners, part of the army of night workers who kept the massive financial district ticking over. Pearce ran the Codecracker over the key-card reader, and after a few moments, a light beside the door flashed green and the lock clicked open. The automatic door swung wide, and Pearce and Wollerton entered the building.

They walked quickly through a small lobby into a narrow

corridor, and stepped inside a men's changing room filled with cheap metal lockers, clothes and towels belonging to service staff. They walked through the otherwise deserted room to a door on the other side and stepped into a broad, plush front-of-house corridor.

'We're coming up to the lifts,' Pearce said.

'I'll have one waiting,' Leila told him.

She'd hacked the building control system and could operate most functions from the Land Cruiser.

'Eyes,' Wollerton said, as they entered the huge lobby on the south side of the building.

A security guard sat behind the long reception desk, and Pearce nodded at the man when he glanced over. He wasn't interested in them, and, after nodding back, returned his attention to something he was watching on an iPad.

Pearce and Wollerton stepped into an open elevator.

'We're in the lift,' Pearce told Leila.

'Got it.'

The doors closed, and the key card-operated control panel was overridden and the car started to rise.

Wollerton slung the holdall off his shoulder and crouched to open it.

'Still get a rush,' he remarked as he handed Pearce an MP7 and four magazines. 'I thought I'd have been blunted to it by now, but the old ticker is thumping and my mouth is as dry as the Sahara.'

'Yeah,' Pearce replied. 'Never changes. I'll take the two on the left. You take the ones on the right.'

They'd flown a drone around the building to take a count and get positions. There were four men in the lobby by the elevators on the twenty-seventh floor, and another eight with Alexis and the Alchemist in what Pearce guessed was a lab.

Wollerton loaded another MP7, and he and Pearce fitted suppressors to their barrels.

The liquid crystal display counted up to their destination; 24 . . . 25 . . . 26 . . .

There was a quiet chime and Pearce and Wollerton exchanged silent nods as the doors started to open.

Pearce went first and saw the four men roughly where they'd been during the drone flyby; two on seats by the window to the left of the lift, and two by a reception desk to the right. One of the seated men was rising and reaching into his jacket. Pearce shot him twice in the chest, and rapidly turned his gun on the man's companion, who had managed to get his gun out. Two more cracks from his MP7 and the second man went down.

Wollerton had moved to follow immediately, and Pearce had been aware of four shots behind him. When he looked round he saw two bodies by the reception desk. He nodded at his old friend, who returned to the lift and grabbed the holdall.

'First stage complete,' Pearce whispered into the mic.

'I've got movement inside,' Leila replied. She had the drone outside the building and was keeping eyes on the Alchemist. 'Looks like they're moving him.'

Pearce cursed inwardly and wondered how they knew. He and Wollerton hadn't made a lot of noise and none of their targets had got a shot off. He cast around the lobby and spotted the faint red glow of an infra-red light.

'They've got a camera. Independent of the building security system,' Pearce said. 'They know we're here.'

Chapter 70

The double doors leading out of the lobby erupted, showering the room with splinters as bullets tore through the hardwood. Pearce barged Wollerton into the open lift as the air filled with machine-gun fire. The smell of powder and smoke, the thunderous rattle and whip and zing of bullets slicing the air sent Pearce's heart into overdrive and adrenalin flooded his body.

Pearce dropped to his belly, leaned out of the lift and replied with a sustained burst from his MP7, and the barrage subsided.

'They're moving him. Fire exit on the south side,' Leila said.

Pearce aimed at the remote camera and opened fire. The tiny device shattered, blinding their assailants.

'Give me two green ones,' Pearce said, and Wollerton reached into the holdall and handed him two M67 grenades. 'We clear it,' he said, and Wollerton nodded.

Pearce took the safety clip off one of the grenades, pulled the pin, leaned out of the lift and tossed it towards the double doors. He ducked inside the car, and covered his head as the device exploded. The sprinklers activated, showering the space.

He heard the sound of pained groans coming from beyond

the wrecked doors as he sprinted from the lift. Wollerton followed and the two of them split for the walls either side of the doors. Bullets burst through the ragged remains of wood still hanging from the frame, and filled the lobby with another barrage, but the attack was brief and the moment it stopped, Pearce readied the second grenade and tossed it through one of the large holes in the door next to him.

'Grenade!' someone on the other side yelled, and Pearce and Wollerton ducked and covered their heads as an explosion rocked the corridor.

'Let's go,' Pearce said.

He opened the door and peered into the corridor beyond to see four badly disfigured bodies.

'I think you've got a clear run to the fire escape,' Leila said. 'I'm trying to shut down the sprinklers.'

Pearce and Wollerton swept the blast-damaged corridor. Offices lay either side and they made cursory checks through the open doorways as they ran south towards a sign pointing in the direction of the fire exit.

They came to another pair of doors, and Pearce opened them cautiously. They led into an open-place office which was empty apart from a long table and a couple of dozen chairs. There were sweet wrappers, Coke cans and other detritus by an upended chair near the head of the table, which is where they'd seen the Alchemist sitting during the drone flyby. Pearce was surprised to see the space was otherwise empty. He'd expected a lab or at least some kind of biological storage facility.

Pearce ran across the room towards the fire door, which was hanging open. He was about twenty feet away when a gunman stepped into the frame and opened fire. Pearce dropped to the floor to dodge the spray of bullets, but Wollerton wasn't so quick and caught a volley in the chest. He went down with a groan, as Pearce rolled and replied with his MP7. He hit the shooter in the shoulder and head, and the man collapsed.

Pearce got to his feet and ran to Wollerton, who was moaning.

'Damn,' he said through gritted teeth. 'I used to be faster. That hurt.'

Pearce opened Wollerton's boiler suit and checked his body armour had stopped all the slugs.

'You're OK,' he told his mentor.

'Don't feel like it,' Wollerton remarked, getting to his feet. 'Go on then.'

Pearce smiled and nodded. He sprinted to the door, stepped over the dead gunman, and started down the fire stairs, taking them three or four at a time, jumping from one landing to another. He heard people moving below him, and when he glanced over the railing, into the well, he saw flashes of clothing a few floors down. Wollerton was a couple of flights above, moving more slowly. The impact of the bullets had knocked the wind out of him.

Pearce ran on, teetering on the edge of falling, as he jumped, bounced and careened his way down the stairs.

He passed a fire door on the twentieth floor, and, to his dismay, it opened behind him. He turned to see another gunman with a direct line on him. A gunshot split the silence, and a hole opened up in the gunman's skull. Pearce looked up to see Wollerton on the landing above, gun raised.

'I've got your back,' he said, and Pearce ran on.

If their surveillance was correct, the Alchemist would now only have Alexis and two men with him, and when Pearce glanced down the well, he didn't see any evidence of a big entourage, just glimpses of a handful of people fleeing.

He pressed on, and by the time he reached the tenth floor, he was a couple of landings above them. The Alchemist was in his black hooded top, but when he looked up, Pearce recognized his face from his photo. He had a satchel slung over his shoulder, and had two bodyguards with him. One of them pointed a pistol at Pearce and opened fire. The man didn't stop to take the shot, which went wild. Pearce stepped away from the edge of the well to avoid the follow-ups.

When the shooting stopped, Pearce moved to the handrail, and aimed his MP7 at the stairs below. He heard the trio's footsteps echo off the bare concrete walls, as his finger curled around the trigger. The moment the man who'd shot at him came into view, Pearce pulled the trigger. Two rounds caught him in the neck and he collided with the handrail, lost his balance and fell eight storeys, hitting the concrete on the ground floor with a terrible thud.

Wollerton overtook Pearce.

'Come on. No hanging around.'

The two of them sprinted down the remaining flights.

Pearce's legs ached and his heart pounded and his lungs burned, but he was used to pushing his body, and raced on. He and Wollerton had made it to the first floor when they heard the fire door slam open. They cleared the last couple of flights and raced through the open door into the street.

Pearce saw the Alchemist running for a Mercedes G-Wagen waiting about fifty feet away. He shot him in the thigh, and the man tumbled and hit the pavement with an ugly crack.

Pearce heard a gunshot behind him, and turned to see

Wollerton spray his MP7 at the last bodyguard, who'd been lying in wait behind the fire door.

'Come on!'

Pearce recognized the voice and looked ahead to see Alexis urging the Alchemist up from the back seat of the G-Wagen. He sprinted towards the wounded man, who dropped his satchel as he got to his feet. The Alchemist staggered towards the car, not registering the loss.

'Your machine!' Alexis shouted, stepping back out of the car.

The Alchemist looked back in dismay to see Pearce was only a few feet away. Any courage he might have had failed him, and he hobbled to the car, pushed Alexis aside and hauled himself in.

Pearce raised his MP7 and took aim at the man's back, but Alexis stepped across him as he climbed in, and her face filled Pearce's vision. She glared at him before climbing in and shutting the car door as it raced away.

Wollerton took a few shots at the tyres, but missed, and a moment later the Mercedes veered around the corner onto Upper Bank Street and disappeared from sight.

'You're not going soft, are you?' Wollerton asked.

'She can't talk if she's dead,' Pearce replied, hoping that was the real reason he hadn't taken the shot.

He walked over to the Alchemist's satchel and picked it up. He opened it to find a large laptop.

'Now we have something she wants. Something that's clearly important to her. His machine.'

Alexis was seething. Scott Pearce had once been nothing more than an inconvenience, but she'd hated him ever since the night at Purbeck House when she'd been forced to shoot her father. She hadn't been particularly close to Viscount Purbeck. He'd been a lying, cheating, villainous swine to Alexis's mother, Willow Tippett-Jones, but once Alexis had recruited him into Apostoli, he'd been a loyal servant to the cause, and father and daughter had established a new relationship. She'd been his recruiter, handler and superior within the organization, an arrangement that never even occurred to most people.

Like many others, Pearce had been unable to see beyond the damsel in distress cover Alexis had created for herself, and she'd played the role of victim well, but she wasn't one. Her stepfather, Philippe Durand, had educated her in the philosophy of traditional thinkers when she was fifteen, and she'd quickly come to realize the dangers posed by liberal ideology and its aim of destroying all the old social institutions. Durand had introduced her to Markus Kral when she was twenty-one, and he'd recruited her into Apostoli. Kral was an amazing man, and widely revered even by those who weren't members of Apostoli. His name was whispered in reverent tones in the homes of many of the oldest European families, in the hallowed chambers of the Church of St Peter, and in corridors of power in governments around the Western world. His published works on the essence of social cohesion were widely read, but less well known were his books on civilizational decline and the impending race war that would reset international relations for centuries to come. There was an even deeper knowledge he shared with only a handful within Apostoli's inner circle. Alexis had not been admitted to this exclusive group yet, but Kral had tantalized her with the promise of admission if the White Fire mission succeeded. It had been his idea to name their operational groups after colours, and Elroy Lang had come up with Black Thirteen, Red Wolves and White Fire.

'How the hell did they find us?' the Alchemist asked, righting himself as the Mercedes sped away. 'I'm bleeding,' he added, clutching his leg.

'You'll live,' Alexis told him. The bloodstain was growing too slowly to be coming from an artery.

Her more pressing concern was the answer to the Alchemist's question. She had a suspicion she'd been used by Pearce and his band of misfits. She thought back to the previous night when they'd invaded her home.

'Do we have a scanner?' she asked Tyler, her driver.

He was an imposing former US Secret Service agent.

'Yes, ma'am,' he said, reaching for the glove compartment.

He handed Alexis an electronic scanner device, not much bigger than a mobile phone, and she switched it on. Beside her, the Alchemist was tying his belt around his leg to try to stop the bleeding. She ran the scanner over her body, starting at her feet and working up. When she reached her neck, an alarm sounded. She shook her head, annoyed at her carelessness. Kral had taught her to be meticulous in her approach. Kyle Wollerton or the Syrian had tagged her during their failed attempt to abduct her. The device must have been so tiny. She suspected it had been the Syrian and recalled the rough way Leila Nahum had grabbed her by the neck.

'What is it?' the Alchemist asked.

'They bugged me,' Alexis replied.

She felt her neck and found a tiny lump beneath her skin, just beneath her ear.

'Tyler, do you have a knife?'

He raised his eyebrows and glanced in the rear-view mirror, but didn't say a word as he handed her a four-inch tactical blade he kept in a pouch on his belt.

'I need you to cut it out,' Alexis told the Alchemist.

'What? No!' He shrank against the car door as Alexis offered him the knife. 'Can't *he* do it?' He indicated Tyler.

'He's driving,' Alexis said. 'Getting us away from the people who would ruin everything you've worked towards. Do it.'

He took the knife grudgingly, and Alexis turned her back on him and lifted her hair so he could get at her neck.

Tyler slowed and pulled over.

'What are you doing?' Alexis asked. 'We can't risk him being captured. It's bad enough we lost his machine. Just hold the car as steady as possible.'

Tyler nodded and accelerated.

'Get it out,' Alexis told the Alchemist. 'Every second you waste is a chance for them to find us.'

She felt the man's cold hands on her neck. They were sticky with his own blood.

'Hold still,' he said, trying to steady her.

Alexis winced when the blade penetrated her skin, and she

bit her lip as he widened the incision. His fingers pressed into the wound, and a moment later she felt a slight release of pressure.

'Got it,' he said.

Alexis wanted to cry out, but Kral had trained her never to show weakness around subordinates. She took a couple of tissues from a dispenser in the centre console and pressed them to her neck.

'Will you look at that,' the Alchemist remarked, holding a tiny shard of metal. 'I wonder how it's powered?'

'Get rid of it,' Alexis said.

He lowered the window and tossed the device into the street. He looked at Alexis expectantly.

'Thank you?' he suggested.

'Can you proceed?' she replied coldly.

He nodded. 'Get me to my backup machine.'

'And the one they stole?' Alexis asked.

'The moment they switch it on, it will tell me its location.'

'Will they be able to detect the signal?'

'No. My tech is beyond them,' he said. 'What will you do when you know where they are?'

'Kill his associates. Take Pearce. Learn his secrets and then make him pay for my father's life,' Alexis replied, relishing the prospect of what was to come.

Chapter 72

Leila was struggling. She sat in the kitchen of the house on Connaught Close, working on the Alchemist's laptop, desperately wishing she could be rid of the pain coursing up the back of her legs into her spine. The slightest move made her wince and it was reaching the point at which she might have taken some Paramol and Valium if she'd had any, but the combination would have sent her to sleep, and it was a release she couldn't afford right now. She needed to know what the Alchemist was doing with Alexis Tippett-Jones and Elroy Lang, and his machine was the key.

Pearce and Wollerton had said they'd stay with her, but she forced them to rest. They were the tip of the spear and needed to be strong. She could hear Pearce's deep breathing drifting from the living room. Wollerton had gone to his bed, but Pearce had crashed on the sofa in his gear, ready for trouble at a moment's notice.

Leila checked her watch. It was approaching 7 a.m. and she'd been working on the Alchemist's computer for more than an hour. She'd checked it for booby traps and tracking devices before carefully booting it up in safe mode to avoid any traces. She'd discovered and neutralized a sophisticated auto-corrupt program designed to destroy all data on the machine, and was now digging around recent applications for clues that would reveal what he had planned. The machine was full of junk; videos, memes and conspiracy theories about all sorts of outlandish topics. There was nothing on genetics, pathogens or biology, which Leila thought was odd, given the man's background.

She couldn't find anything to point to why this machine was so important, nor any sign of what the Alchemist had been working on. She sat back and groaned as her back lit up in agony. It felt as though her hips were firing shards of glass up her spine. She grimaced and tried to reason out the pain. She focused on the computer, its inbuilt webcam staring at her like an unblinking eye. It was the one piece of software she hadn't examined.

Sloppy, Leila thought.

She leaned forward and opened the webcam application folder and did some digging to find a whole collection of concealed files. She came alive with the thrill of a lead and her pain shrank into the background as she searched through the folder. There was a programming sandbox that had been used recently to work on some intricate code that looked like it was a plugin for a web server.

Leila studied the code carefully and after a while her excitement at finding the folder gave way to dread, and she sat back and stared at the screen, open-mouthed. The Alchemist was indeed a genius, and his talent had enabled him to create a beautifully simple horror.

Chapter 73

Pearce was roused from oblivion. Even his dreams could sense his exhaustion and had left him alone. He'd promised himself a short lie down, but had fallen into the dark netherworld between life and death, and returned to the world feeling neither restored nor revitalized. He opened his eyes to see Leila standing over him, shaking him gently.

'I know about Whitman,' she said.

A fringe of sunlight trimmed the curtains.

'What time is it?'

'Seven twenty,' she replied. 'You need to see this.'

He stretched and got to his feet. He could hear the sounds of the city, and the room was already developing a stuffy feel, London feeling airless even as the temperature cooled.

Leila led him into the kitchen and called up to Wollerton as they passed the stairs. She took Pearce to the Alchemist's oversized laptop, which was on the kitchen table.

'God it's early,' Wollerton said, stumbling into the room in a T-shirt and a pair of boxer shorts.

Pearce was still in his tactical gear, minus the boiler suit, and looked forward to showering off the night's grime once he'd seen whatever Leila had to show him.

'Some of us haven't slept at all,' Leila said.

'Well, yeah, if you want to get all boastful and make a thing about it,' Wollerton countered, and she scoffed.

'Boastful,' she muttered. 'If only I had something to boast about. I assumed Whitman was a person. It's a place.'

She opened Google Maps and pinpointed Whitman, nestled in the thickly forested hills of upstate New York.

'It's a tiny hamlet. Nothing extraordinary about it,' Leila revealed. 'Except two months ago the local authorities did a deal with a subsidiary of Rightway Patriots Network to test a new form of satellite Internet. Participants were paid a thousand dollars per household, and if successful the plan was to roll the service out to remote communities across the state. Rightway put routers in sixty homes. A week after they were installed, all sixty routers failed.'

Leila opened a text-heavy document.

'The state conducted an investigation, but was prevented from making any details public because of the confidentiality agreement it had signed with Rightway. I hacked the state Office of Information Technology Services to get a copy of the report. It wasn't just the routers that failed. Every single device with a chip that was connected to the network failed. This included fuse boxes, power supply units, refrigerators, cars, just about anything with a power supply. When they opened up the devices, they found their processors had burned out. Rightway compensated all the families and the state in a secret settlement, and their satellite Internet arm was shuttered.'

'But . . .' Pearce suggested.

'But I don't think this was ever meant to be a viable business,' Leila said. 'I'm pretty sure this was a test.' She opened the folder of concealed files on the Alchemist's computer. 'I found an old file with coding designed for the Whitman network on the Alchemist's machine.'

She picked up Wollerton's laptop from the seat next to her and put it on the table.

'What have you done?' Wollerton asked.

His machine had been stripped of its housing so the processor and motherboard were visible.

'I've installed the Alchemist's file on this machine,' Leila revealed. 'Watch what happens when I run it.'

She opened the DOS prompt, typed a run command and hit enter. Nothing happened for a moment, then a tiny curl of smoke appeared from the processor and the screen went dead.

'Before the Alchemist got into biotech, he specialized in computer engineering. We were wrong – he's not creating a biological agent, he's designed a digital one. He's built a virus that sends computer chips into overdrive, causing them to run so many calculations they are overwhelmed. They burn out.'

Leila winced as she tried to pull the processor from the board. It was extremely hot and Pearce noticed the plastic around it had curled, and the plume of smoke had thickened.

'I think the Whitman network was a test so he could prove his virus works. He's created a virus that gets microprocessors to fry themselves. This isn't a simple reboot or anti-virus job. This is an entirely new processor.'

Pearce began to understand the significance of what Leila had discovered.

'If this virus spreads, it will destroy any machine it comes into contact with,' she said. 'There are processors in every modern car, truck, bus, train, fridge, power plant, reactor, and they're all connected and talking to each other. If enough processors are destroyed it could cripple an advanced economy. If it disables the electricity supply, this virus could take us back to the Middle Ages. Everything from food distribution to medicine storage requires power. This could wipe it all out, and it would take weeks, if not months to repair.'

'The social unrest,' Wollerton remarked. 'The loss of life. Wow.'

'Why haven't they released it?' Pearce asked.

'Viruses normally work by tricking someone into opening an infected file,' Leila replied. 'This one spreads on a host network, automatically infecting processors once it's been implanted on the network . . .'

'Zyberian,' Pearce interrupted. 'The Internet service provider I infiltrated with White Fire.'

Leila nodded. 'They have a system upgrade scheduled for midnight tonight. My guess is White Fire stole a copy of the upgrade so the Alchemist could tailor his virus to spread using the Zyberian network. As it spreads, it will propagate to other providers, so if he's successful, I'd expect the virus to knock out somewhere in the region of sixty per cent of the processors in the country. Close to ninety in London. Once it reaches that many machines, who knows what will happen? How do you restore power when the machines needed to manufacture or transport equipment have been disabled?'

'We gamed this when I was at Six,' Wollerton said. 'An electromagnetic pulse from a nuclear device is supposed to have a similar effect. When power and transportation go down, everything is hit. Food shortages start after seven days, medicines after twenty-eight. Operations and emergency medical interventions stop immediately. Everyone on life support is at risk. Workplaces are shuttered. Communications and entertainment cease. When the Americans modelled it, their congressional inquiry estimated an electromagnetic attack could wipe out ninety per cent of the population within twelve months.'

'I don't think it would be that bad,' Leila responded. 'But it would be bad enough.'

'We need to—' Pearce began, but he was cut off by an explosion that shook the building.

Chapter 74

Pearce was accustomed to combat, but no amount of experience ever blunted the adrenalin rush that hit during an attack. His heart started racing instantly, and his senses went into overdrive. He grabbed an MP7 from the holdall beside the kitchen table, and tossed it to Wollerton, who ran to the door.

The sound of footsteps echoed along the hallway, and then came the thud of something hard hitting the ground.

Pearce closed his eyes. 'Flashbang!' he yelled.

And sure enough a loud, disorientating boom set his ears ringing, and a flash of light shone against his eyelids.

When he opened his eyes, he saw Wollerton firing the MP7 along the corridor. Pearce glanced round to see Leila reeling in her seat, blinded and deafened by the blast.

He kneeled down, grabbed another MP7 from the holdall, and flipped the safety as he ran to the window.

He stuck his fingers between the slats to push them apart, and peered through the blinds to see a group of masked men in black tactical gear crouched beside an unmarked van. Two other vans blocked the mews entrance. Pearce recognized the shielding posture the men had adopted; they were expecting another explosion.

'Take cover,' Pearce shouted as he backed away from the window.

He didn't move quickly enough, and a daisy chain of demolition charges blew out the front wall of the kitchen, knocking Pearce flat. When he rolled onto his back, heart thundering to bursting, he saw the mass of bricks tumbling towards him.

Chapter 75

Leila saw black. She heard nothing but the shrill ringing inside her head. Her ears burned, her eyes stung, her
body was riven by pain and her mind was charged with fear.

Then things came into focus.

The table.

The laptops.

A blur that looked like Wollerton spitting fire through the
doorway.

She sensed another shockwave and turned to see a shape
that looked like Pearce running away from the window. His
horrified face sharpened out of the blur. He was caught by the
shockwave, which lifted Leila out of her chair and sent her
crashing to the floor. The same blast knocked Pearce off his
feet, and when he tumbled to the floor, Leila watched with
horror as the outer kitchen wall collapsed on him, burying
him entirely.

'Kyle,' she yelled, but she could not hear her own voice, and
feared she might have been rendered mute.

She glanced round and saw him acknowledge her, but in
that brief moment of recognition she sensed sadness. She
could feel it too.

Their luck had run out. They were defeated.

Leila cursed herself for her failure, because they could only have found the safe house by tracing the Alchemist's machine. She'd overlooked something or failed to detect a creation that was so advanced she wasn't even aware of it. And that stung bitterly; the thought her friends would die because she wasn't good enough. She wasn't concerned about herself. She'd lived many lives beyond the one she was due. She'd expected to die in Syria, so every day since then had been a bonus.

She fought through the pain and rolled towards the holdall, and a blue hand grenade she saw nestled near the opening. She reached for the explosive and glanced at Wollerton, who shook his head when he saw what was in her hand.

He fired a volley of shots along the corridor and then his eyes went wide with dismay at the sight of something behind Leila. She turned to see four masked men climb through the hole in the kitchen wall and stride over the bricks that covered Pearce's body.

One of the men levelled a gun at her and pulled the trigger. Leila looked down and immediately felt cheated. Instead of a hole in her ribs, she saw a dart.

Tranquilizer, she thought, as the world went distant.

She glanced round to see Wollerton had also been hit. A tranquilizer dart was stuck in his neck.

Leila had always wanted a swift and painless death, but she doubted she would get one. As she spiralled into unconsciousness, she mourned Pearce, and wondered what darkness lay ahead.

Chapter 76

Alexis stepped through the wreckage of the kitchen wall and removed her ski mask. The air was thick with smoke and dust, and the only sound came from the rubble settling. Four of her men ran into the kitchen and hauled Leila Nahum and Kyle Wollerton outside to the waiting van.

Alexis picked up the Alchemist's laptop. He had a backup, but without this machine no one would be able to prove what he'd done. She looked around for Pearce, but saw no sign of him in the ruined kitchen.

'Where's Pearce?' she asked.

'Here,' Tyler said.

Her driver and primary bodyguard was crouching in the rubble that she'd walked over. He'd removed a few bricks to reveal Pearce's dust-covered face. Alexis walked over the uneven wreckage and crouched beside the motionless man who'd caused her so much trouble. She removed her right glove, and pressed two fingers to his neck, searching for a pulse. She found none.

'Knife,' she said.

Tyler reached to his belt and produced the four-inch knife again. She unfolded the blade, studied Pearce's face for a moment, and drove the knife into his shoulder with all the force she could muster. The blade sank to the hilt and there was no response from the dead man.

'He's gone,' she said with more than a hint of disappointment.

Scott Pearce, the man she'd dreamed of tormenting, had eluded her one last time. She pulled the knife from his body and returned it to Tyler. He pocketed it and checked his watch.

'Four minutes. We've already pushed our luck with the police response,' he said.

As if on cue, Alexis heard the first sirens and got to her feet. 'We'll just have to get what we need from the other two. Come on.'

Alexis followed Tyler into the corridor. Her men had already returned to the vans, which had their engines running. Alexis pulled on her ski mask and stepped into the mews, where neighbours were at their windows, gawking at the carnage, desperately trying not to be seen. Some had phones out, and the footage would make sensational viewing on YouTube, but it would offer law enforcement nothing. The vans had never existed and she and her people were anonymous assailants in black.

There wouldn't be a problem, even if we were caught, she thought. *Our friends would never allow the law to take its course.*

Alexis followed Tyler across the cobbled mews and climbed into the waiting van.

Tyler gunned the engine and followed the two vans that were by the mews entrance.

As they all sped away, Alexis glanced back to see the ruined safe house was a still as a grave.

Chapter 77

Jules Swain steered the ambulance down the narrow entrance to Connaught Close, and when it entered the short mews, she was greeted with a scene of devastation. It was immediately clear why they'd been called. The third house on the left had been partially demolished.

Jules and her partner, Dave Leigh, were first on the scene, and she pulled up in front of the wreckage as neighbours began to emerge from their properties. Some were in their pyjamas; others were dressed and ready for work.

Jules got out, wondering how long it would take someone to clear the property for entry. It looked borderline, and they weren't supposed to go inside anywhere at risk of collapse.

'In here!'

Jules heard a voice coming from inside the building, and as she moved round the ambulance she saw a man in a suit waving to her from beyond the gaping hole where the front wall had once stood.

'There's someone in here,' the man said. 'I think he's dead.'

'What do you think?' Dave asked.

Jules shrugged. She was trained to help people and save lives, but a paramedic trapped inside a collapsed building was no use to anyone.

'It looks pretty safe to me,' Dave suggested.

Jules eyeballed the damaged home. She did the job to help people and save lives, not score points with the health and safety bods.

'I'll get the defib,' Jules said. 'You grab the bags.'

They retrieved the kit and clambered through the hole in the wall, walking unsteadily over rubble until they reached the man in the suit. Jules smelled the acrid stench of high explosives through air that was a soup of dust and smoke. The man in the suit shuffled aside as she crouched next to another younger man who was buried under rubble. Bricks had been cleared from his head and chest, and Jules checked for a pulse but found nothing.

'Get pounding,' she told Dave, who reached into the kit bag for a pair of scissors, while she prepped the defibrillator.

Dave unzipped the man's vest, which looked like body armour, and cut through the T-shirt underneath. With the man's chest exposed, he started compressions.

'How long has he been out?' Jules asked the man in the suit.

He gave her a bemused look. Was he in shock?

'How long?'

'Maybe a couple of minutes since the explosion,' he replied.

She attached the defib pads to the patient's chest and took a reading. Some hearts couldn't be restarted. Others could be brought back to rhythm with minimal damage.

'V-fib,' she said. 'He's shockable.'

This man could be saved. He'd probably been unlucky with shock or impact trauma.

Dave kept going with the compressions, while Jules reached into the resus bag for a shot of adrenalin. She administered it quickly and calmly. She'd attended enough calls to know patients weren't served well by hurried panic.

'Adrenalin,' she confirmed to Dave. 'I'm going to shock him.'

Dave stopped compressions and leaned away.

'Please stay clear,' she told the man in the suit.

She checked the patient one last time, and was momentarily distracted by more sirens and flashing lights as a couple of police cars pulled up outside.

'Clear,' she said, shocking the patient.

She checked the defibrillator, but there was no pulse.

'He's going to need another one,' she said. 'Clear.'

She shocked him a second time, and checked the defib.

Nothing.

'Again,' she said. 'Clear!'

She shocked him a third time.

Nothing.

'He's gone,' Dave said sadly.

'No,' Jules replied. She reached into the resus bag for another shot of adrenalin, and picked out a second of amiodarone.

'Adrenalin and amiodarone,' she confirmed to Dave as she administered both.

She could tell from his pitying expression he considered her the queen of lost causes. There were more sirens nearby, but she paid them no mind and focused on the patient.

'Clear,' she said, shocking him a fourth time.

Chapter 78

Pearce came round with a start.

There was a woman.

Two men.

She had long blonde hair.

A warm face.

Smiling.

Relief.

Had he been asleep?

He felt alive. More alive than ever, as though his veins were charged with electricity. He looked down to see his body armour and T-shirt had been cut open and there were medical pads stuck to his chest.

Were they taking readings?

He followed the wires to a defibrillator.

Had he been dead?

His mind raced and his body was on fire with energy.

'Please don't move, sir,' the woman said.

She wore a green uniform, like one of the men.

Paramedics.

It all came flooding back. The attack on the house, the explosion.

'Where are Leila and Kyle?' he tried to say, but his words came out as a rasped jumble.

'Please, sir,' the woman repeated. 'We'll get you out of here soon.'

Leila and Kyle, Pearce thought, and their faces strobed through his mind.

'My name's Jules and I'm here to help. You're confused. You might be concussed or have other injuries. We've given you adrenalin to help restart your heart, so you might feel as though you have more energy than usual,' the female paramedic revealed. 'You also appear to have been stabbed in your shoulder. Just take it easy.'

But Pearce didn't feel like taking it easy. He felt alive and vital and he had a mission. He shrugged against the bricks that covered him.

'Sir,' the male paramedic said.

Pearce paid the man no attention and wrenched himself free. Jules gasped when she registered the MP7 that was still in his right hand.

'Gun,' the man in the suit said quietly, and the trio backed away fearfully as Pearce got to his feet.

'Sir,' Jules said again, this time much more hesitantly.

'You! Get down!' a voice boomed.

Pearce looked through the hole in the front wall to see two police officers approaching the building.

'Drop the gun and get down,' one of them commanded.

He was holding a Taser.

Pearce fired a volley of shots into the air, inches above the officer's head, and he and his colleague scattered, shouting warnings to a small crowd of onlookers who were peering round the ambulance.

Pearce staggered over the rubble, and with each step the electricity filling his veins seemed to grow more intense. He could feel the power of life itself coursing through his body and by the time he reached the cobbled street, he felt unstoppable.

He heard chatter from the radios of the officers to his left, and saw more uniformed cops to his right, standing near police cars that had been parked across the mews entrance. He shot another burst into the air as he ran towards them, and they ducked for cover. Pearce got into one of the cars parked across the passageway, a BMW X5 in the livery of the Metropolitan Police. He hit the ignition button, turned the gear selector and stepped on the accelerator. The modified X5 shot forward, and he swerved around a crowd of police officers and onlookers, some of whom were trying to stop him. Once he was clear, Pearce picked up speed, raced across the next junction and along Hyde Park Square. Black railings flew by on one side and multi-million-pound terraced properties on the other.

He had no idea how long he'd been out, but had to assume Leila and Wollerton had been abducted. He hit the horn to warn an oncoming taxi, and it quickly pulled to the side. His heart thundered erratically as he turned on the lights and siren. He shot down Strathearn Place and saw cars ahead of him pull over. The X5's tyres screeched as he turned left. He sped round a sweeping bend and joined Brook Street. Traffic parted, giving him a clear view of the gates across Bayswater Road. The lights were against him, but the siren was doing its work and vehicles had stopped on the already busy road. He raced through the gates into Hyde Park.

As he accelerated around the long curve that marked the start of West Carriage Drive, the road that bisected the grand park, he took his phone from his pocket and pressed and held the 'home' button.

'Call "Seven",' he said, and the phone's digital assistant rang the number Robert Clifton had given him.

A moment later a woman answered.

'*Hello?*'

He couldn't tell whether it was the same person he'd spoken to from the petrol station in Pelcomb Cross.

'I need to find three vehicles,' Pearce said.

'*This isn't—*' she began.

'I don't care,' he cut her off. 'My friends are in danger and I have to find them. Three dark blue Transit vans.'

He gave their licence numbers using the NATO phonetic alphabet.

'I don't care what our mutual employer has to do. Find them. Find them and call me back.'

Pearce hung up and put the phone on the passenger seat next to him. He heard sirens in the distance, and had no doubt a manhunt was underway. He was wanted in connection with Farida's murder, and his escape from the mews would only make the situation worse.

He was approaching the Serpentine, the large lake at the heart of the park, and forked left, down a public parking area. He pulled into an empty space and killed the lights and sirens. A couple of passers-by looked at him uncertainly, but he smiled and nodded in response.

His heart raced, fluttering in and out of rhythm, and he hoped he wasn't doing himself any long-term harm by pushing himself so soon after resuscitation. He swept the parking area and road beyond it in both directions and kept glancing at his phone, willing it to ring. Finally, after what seemed like an age but must have been under a minute, the phone rang. Pearce answered it instantly.

'*All three vehicles are on Knightsbridge near Hyde Park Corner. They're heading west,*' the anonymous woman said.

'Thanks,' Pearce said, before hanging up.

He started the engine, reversed out of the space and raced along the parking area towards the lake. When he reached the shoreline, he followed the road to the right, and switched on the siren and lights as he re-joined West Carriage Drive.

If he was fast and his luck held, he might just be able to catch them.

Chapter 79

Pearce shot over the bridge that spanned the western edge of the Serpentine, jumping the speed bumps and weaving between his lane and the oncoming traffic which gave way to the loud police car. He raced on with the Albert Memorial gleaming gold to his right, jumped the lights, sped across Kensington Gore, and accelerated until the grand museums of Exhibition Road went by in a blur. The X5 bounced with every bump and contour as it gobbled the yards to the Cromwell Road, but it was a heavy car with a commanding presence, and hugged the tarmac as Pearce swerved to avoid a couple of slow pedestrians who hadn't seen him coming. There were two cars at the traffic lights at the south end of Exhibition Road, and Pearce slowed, wondering whether to turn left towards Knightsbridge, or . . .

When he looked right, Pearce saw the convoy slowly pulling away from the pedestrian crossing in front of the Natural History Museum. He stepped on the accelerator and turned the wheel hard right as he roared across the Cromwell Road. Horns sounded and tyres screeched as he flew over the junction, and the engine growled as he pushed the car to its limits. The back end swung out as he straightened up, and the X5 lurched forward when the rear tyres found their grip. He was gaining on the trio of vans, which had just gone through the next set of traffic lights at the junction with Queen's Gate, on the south-west corner of the Natural History Museum. Pearce's erratic heart skipped a full beat when he saw the trailing van stop suddenly. The back doors flew open to reveal two masked gunmen wielding Heckler & Koch M27 light machine guns.

Pearce didn't know where Alexis had recruited these men, whether they were the same mix of ex-military and Special Forces that had made up Black Thirteen. Whoever they were, they'd been poorly trained. Stopping during a pursuit and presenting a stationary target was a mistake, no matter how much firepower you had.

And they had a lot.

The two gunmen opened fire, and a hail of bullets chewed the tarmac ahead of Pearce. He swerved onto the other side of the road, and wove between oncoming vehicles that were caught in the crossfire as the police car was hit by the thud and puck of bullets on the passenger side. Pearce glanced in his rear-view mirror to see the traffic behind him had stopped. He grabbed his MP7 from the passenger seat, and using his left hand, shot through the window. He hit one of the gunmen and the other dived for cover inside the van.

Pearce swerved around a double-decker bus, mounted the pavement, and raced on, until he was clear and had eyes on the van again. He was almost level with the vehicle and saw a gunman hanging out of the driver's window, targeting him.

Pearce opened fire and rained hell along the side of the van. Both tyres burst and the driver bucked like a wild bull as he was hit.

Pearce stepped on the accelerator, and, siren blaring, sped towards the remaining two vans. He had no idea which one contained Leila and Wollerton, or whether they'd been split between the two vehicles.

He straightened up and reloaded with one of the magazines pulled from his pocket, making the switch as quickly as possible to avoid veering off course.

With the gun loaded, Pearce switched to manual, and flipped into fourth gear as the X5 gathered speed. The engine roared and the car raced forward as the lead van dropped back. Traffic swerved everywhere, and pedestrians watched open-mouthed as the nature of the duel became clear. The van's rear doors opened and a masked man stepped forward holding an M60 machine gun. He opened fire and Pearce swerved as 7.62 mm M80 rounds shredded the street. Pearce hopped the pavement on the left, and used his right hand to shoot the MP7 at the gunman. He didn't hit his mark, but the big guy withdrew, and Pearce swerved onto the road and threw the X5 into third gear and accelerated towards the rear of the van.

As the big man stepped forward and raised the M60, Pearce shot him through the X5's windscreen. Everything went white for a moment as bullets shattered the glass. Then the windscreen crumbled away in giant flakes. As it cleared, Pearce felt a jarring thud. He'd collided with the back of the van, but his bullets had hit their mark. The big gunman lay motionless on the van's flatbed – and no one else looked to be in the load space. Pearce used the butt of the MP7 to smash more of the windscreen and create a bigger hole. Then he turned the gun around and shot out the rear tyres. He stepped on the brake as the van fishtailed and flipped into a tumbling roll. He swerved to avoid getting caught in the storm of metal, and veered across the road around a car that had pulled over.

Pearce straightened up as the van collided with a lorry and exploded.

The last van turned left onto Ashburn Gardens, and Pearce followed, tyres screeching, engine growling as he raced into the broad, quiet street that was flanked by a grand terrace on one side and a high-rise hotel on the other. He stepped on the accelerator and rocketed on towards the van, which was heading for a T-junction. A large lorry swung into the road, and Pearce saw the driver register what was heading his way. The startled man tried to find reverse, as the van bore down on him, but he only succeeded in stalling the lorry, so the van mounted the pavement on the right, trying to squeeze between the terrace railings and the parked cars, but it was too wide, and came to a grinding halt between a parked Mercedes M-Class and a white stone wall topped with black railings.

Pearce stopped twenty feet from the van, body charged, heart racing, breathing heavily, senses wired. He jumped out and leaned on the bonnet of the police car, and was ready before the back doors of the van opened and two ski-masked gunmen appeared holding Leila and Wollerton hostage. His friends looked groggy, as though in a stupor.

Pearce didn't hesitate. He shot Leila's captor first and caught him clean in the forehead. His comrade was too stunned to react.

There would be no negotiation.

No talk.

Wollerton punched his captor and Pearce opened fire as his friend moved clear. A man in black, wearing a matching ski mask, clambered out of the passenger window, gun in hand, and Pearce shot him in the neck the moment his feet touched the pavement.

Pearce sensed movement on the other side of the van and ran forward to bring himself level with the cab. Two masked figures had climbed out of the driver's window and were working their way along the white wall. One of them was unmistakeably a woman. Pearce raised his MP7 and shot the man, who fell over the railing into the basement well in front of the terrace. The execution had the desired effect and the woman froze.

'It's over, Alexis,' Pearce said. He kept his gun trained on her as he approached. 'You're coming with us.'

Chapter 80

There were sirens in every direction, and the carnage of Pearce's chase stretched for miles.

He grabbed Alexis and pulled off her mask. Her eyes blazed with defiance, but she didn't resist as he took the satchel she had slung over her shoulder. He pushed her towards the badly damaged police car and bundled her inside. Leila and Wollerton, who were groggy and disorientated, got in either side of Alexis, and Pearce slid behind the wheel and drove to the end of the road, past the lorry. The driver had finally managed to reverse and eyed Pearce in disbelief as the X5 made a left onto Courtfield Road.

'You OK?' Pearce asked.

Leila rubbed her neck and nodded. 'This messed-up play-pretend radical drugged us.'

'It's like a wicked hangover,' Wollerton added.

'Make a call,' Pearce said, handing Wollerton his phone. 'Get us off the street.'

Wollerton nodded and dialled.

'Who's on the other end of that phone?' Alexis asked. 'Who are you working for?'

Leila slapped her. 'Shut up. You know why you're a play-pretend radical? Because you've never suffered. Really suffered. You have no idea how far pain will make you go. But I'm going to help you find out.' She slapped her again. 'You speak when you're spoken to.'

Alexis glared at Leila and opened her mouth only to have it shut by another hard slap.

'Hello,' Wollerton said into the phone. 'We need a safe place. West London.'

'You got a knife?' Leila asked Pearce.

He looked at her in puzzlement, but knew better than to question her intentions, and pulled a six-inch blade from a pouch on his body armour.

'Got it,' Wollerton said into the phone, before hanging up. 'One-two-seven Conlan Street. Top of Ladbroke Grove,' he told Pearce, who nodded.

'Hold her,' Leila said to Wollerton.

'What are you doing?' Alexis demanded, squirming against her.

She punched the billionaire, dazing her.

'I said shut up,' Leila countered. 'Hold her, and give me that knife.'

Pearce passed her the blade, and Wollerton grabbed the dazed woman and held her arms. Leila took hold of Alexis's right hand and forced her thumb away from her clenched fist.

'No!' Alexis cried out, as she recovered her senses.

She struggled against Wollerton and Leila, but it was no good. Pearce glanced in the rear-view mirror to see Leila drive the blade into the cushioned pad of Alexis's thumb. She screamed and tried to break free, but Leila worked the knife deeper until she was able to prise something small from the wound. Pearce didn't need to see it to know what it was. The rear windows of the police car didn't open, so Leila handed him the small bloody metallic disc.

'Get rid of it,' she said.

Pearce dropped it out of the window as they approached Gloucester Road.

'No one can find you now,' Leila told Alexis.

'Left,' Wollerton said.

Pearce nodded as they approached a line of traffic waiting at the junction. He felt very exposed. The X5 had been badly shot up and given the number of sirens he could hear and his knowledge of procedure, he doubted they'd make it across London to the address Wollerton had given him. The police car's details would have been widely circulated and he had little doubt there would be a helicopter search for the car's rooftop markings.

He pulled up behind a Ford Mondeo estate, and came to a decision.

'Let's go,' he said, grabbing the MP7 and jumping out of the car.

He opened the back door and Wollerton followed him out, dragging Alexis with him. Leila came last.

Pearce ran to the Mondeo and pulled the driver's door open. A Capital Radio DJ blared from the speakers. The man behind the wheel registered the gun immediately, which was good. It made for sensible decisions.

'Police,' Pearce said. 'I need to commandeer this vehicle.'

The driver nodded hesitantly, fumbled with his seatbelt and got out. Pearce took his place at the wheel, turned down the radio, and Wollerton and Leila shoved Alexis onto the back seat. She cradled her hand and sucked her bloody thumb as she glowered at Pearce.

Wollerton and Leila got in beside their captive, and Pearce

put the car in gear and made a left onto Gloucester Road. As the car gathered speed, he saw Leila lean over to Alexis.

'You're ours now,' she said. 'And if you don't give us what we want, it will be my pleasure to cause you pain.'

Chapter 81

Conlan Street was a couple of blocks east of Ladbroke Grove, north of the Westway flyover. The south side of the street was filled with single-storey grey Victorian warehouses, and the north was lined with a terrace of yellow brick, two-storey warehouses. The address Wollerton had been given took them to a warehouse halfway along the north terrace. Blue cages covered the ground floor windows, and two rusting blue roll shutters secured the service entrances. Most of the surrounding warehouses had been converted into offices or studios, but this warehouse was dilapidated and looked as though it hadn't been occupied for a long time.

Pearce pulled up outside and Wollerton jumped out and went to a keypad beside one of the roll shutters. He tapped in a code, and as the shutter rose he ducked beneath it and hurried inside. Pearce steered the Mondeo into the warehouse as Wollerton found the lights.

Strip bulbs flickered on, overwhelming the golden afternoon sunshine that streamed through a row of dirty windows, and replacing it with a harsh artificial glare. Wollerton closed the shutter as Pearce drove into a giant space about the size of four tennis courts. There were three cars parked near the back; a silver Mercedes GLA, a black and yellow Ford Mustang, and a black Audi Q7. Pearce stopped in front of them and got out of the stolen Mondeo. Wollerton hurried over and helped him pull Alexis from the car, and Leila followed.

They took her to a door marked 'site office' behind the trio of cars, and Wollerton tapped a code into the keypad beside the door to access the locked room. Inside, there was an operations centre; workbenches with computers, a meeting table, and at the back of the room four large flight cases stacked two high. The room smelled of fresh plastic mixed with cheap leather that rose from chairs that dotted the space.

'See what we've got,' Pearce told Wollerton, nodding towards the flight cases.

They pushed Alexis into one of the chairs, and Wollerton went to the large, brushed-aluminium cases.

Pearce pulled up a chair and sat opposite Alexis, cradling his MP7. Leila walked behind her, brandishing the knife Pearce had given her.

'I have no interest in your games, Mr Pearce,' Alexis said. 'You can't win.'

He didn't reply.

'The world has lost its way,' she went on. 'People have forgotten themselves, created a new Sodom. They are out of control.'

Pearce was startled when Leila plunged the knife into Alexis's shoulder. She screamed and clutched at the handle. Leila pressed down, before removing it. The sight of the wound oozing blood reminded Pearce of his own injury. It had stopped bleeding and, whether a consequence of the adrenalin he'd been given or the rush of pursuit, it didn't seem to hurt. The same could not be said about Alexis's wound, and she cried and grabbed at it.

'Pain focuses the mind,' Leila said. 'At least that's my

experience. Do you know what the Alchemist's virus will do to this country?'

The colour had drained from Alexis's face, which made her look like a bone-china doll. She pressed a hand to the wound and tried to wipe her eyes with the other, but the movement caused her more pain and brought fresh tears.

'We'll send people to darkness.' Alexis grimaced. 'Every processor his virus touches will be destroyed. We'll shut down power stations, fuel refineries, trains, cars, planes.'

'Hospitals? Schools? Nursing homes?' Pearce added.

'Casualties of war,' Alexis remarked. 'Refrigeration, transportation, manufacturing, medicines, food supply. We're going to shut it all down.'

'Why?' Pearce asked.

'White Fire will claim responsibility. They will say they did it to end our energy consumption, and evidence will be found to show they were financed by China,' Alexis replied through gritted teeth.

'You discredit the environmental movement in one go,' Pearce remarked, and Alexis smiled insolently. 'And you sow the seeds of conflict.'

'This will be another step towards war with the East. America is still brooding over the Red Wolves attack. Conflict will bring chaos and from chaos comes order. Our order. You can't rebuild without first tearing down. And when people are exhausted and afraid, they will let you build whatever you want.'

Leila punched Alexis, who briefly drifted out of consciousness. When she came to, she glared defiantly.

'People will die,' Leila said. 'Innocent people. Good people.'

'Irrelevant people,' Alexis responded. 'A total loss of power would result in the deaths of one thousand people per day in London alone. And that's before food and medicine shortages kick in. And then comes civil unrest.'

Leila punched her again, and Alexis spat a glob of blood onto the floor.

'You can hit me all you want. It won't change anything.'

'You're going to tell us where the Alchemist is,' Pearce said. 'And we're going to stop him.'

Alexis smiled darkly, her lips swollen and edged with blood. 'You can't stop him.'

Leila raised the knife. 'You don't worry about that. Worry about this.'

'It makes no difference,' Alexis replied. 'And there's someone with him who wants to see you. Elroy Lang. He wants to give you the same send-off he gave Brigitte Attali.'

Pearce fumed, but managed to control his anger.

'They will be at One London Wall, the tower block near the Barbican, at midnight,' Alexis said. 'Top floor. I don't know where they'll be before then. They'll keep the Alchemist somewhere safe.'

Leila closed menacingly.

'Why would I lie? I've told you where they'll be. I don't know where they will keep him until then.'

Pearce took Leila aside.

'Tie her up and keep her here in case she's lying.'

'I want to come with—' Leila began, but Pearce cut her off.

'You can't. I'll take Kyle. You stay here. Take a look at the Alchemist's machine. See if you can figure out another way to stop him. In case we don't make it.'

Leila nodded, but Pearce could tell she didn't agree with him.

He went over to Wollerton, who was sorting through weapons and equipment he'd found in the flight cases.

'I wonder how many of these places are lying around?' Wollerton pondered. 'We've got enough gear to start a war.'

'Good,' Pearce said. 'We'll need it to stop one.'

Chapter 82

Pearce lay near the edge of the roof of Two London Wall, a twenty-storey glass office block with a white lattice-work shell that was across the street from the address Alexis had given them. Every inch of his body ached, and the wound in his shoulder, which had been bandaged, throbbed. His heart appeared to have settled for a while, but was beating erratically now his adrenalin was rising again. He couldn't think about the damage that might have been done to him; there would be time enough for treatment and recovery. He had to focus on the task at hand.

He stared down at One London Wall, a silver and glass building which, at seventeen storeys, was approximately thirty feet shorter. He could see half a dozen men patrolling the street below, covering the entrances and exits, and had no doubt they were heavily armed. There were some vehicles on the dual carriageway, but the city was quiet at this time of night. Even during the day, more people worked from home and fewer wanted to frequent the city's bars when they did come into the office – a legacy of the pandemic. The result was a financial district far more sedate than before the days of the virus.

He looked into the open-plan office on the top floor of the building and saw more men walking the perimeter of the space. He and Wollerton had been in position for almost two hours, and for a while he'd worried Alexis had lied, but then the exterior guards had emerged five minutes ago, and the top floor had filled with men. Pearce and Wollerton had been sweeping the building with the surveillance drone, but hadn't seen them arrive, which suggested underground access. Pearce was relieved; there was little doubt Alexis had sent him and Wollerton to the right place.

'What have we got?' he asked as he crawled away from the edge and joined Wollerton, who was crouched over the drone remote.

The video screen displayed footage as the tiny aircraft flew around the top floor of the building. Pearce saw a large number of armed men on all sides.

'I count twenty guards in the building,' Wollerton said. 'And I'm guessing this is the Alchemist.'

He pointed at a hooded figure on screen, partially obscured by an interior wall. The figure was hunched over a laptop. Pearce noticed the legs of a man leaning against the table next to the hooded figure.

'Lang?' Pearce suggested. The man's head and body were behind the interior wall.

'Maybe,' Wollerton conceded.

'What have you got?' Pearce asked Leila via a radio microphone in his cuff.

'*I'm working on shutting down Internet access to the building,*' she replied through his in-ear receiver. '*He has to upload his virus to Zyberian's network when their system update goes live at midnight. Any earlier than that and he risks their anti-virus and security protocols picking it up. He can't upload it if I cut the pipe to the building.*'

'Satellite data?' Pearce suggested.

'*That's where you come in,*' Leila said. '*We need human operators to do stupid things.*'

Pearce checked his watch. It was coming up to 11.40 p.m. He took a T-PLS Digital Force Technologies tactical line launcher from a holdall beside Wollerton, and crawled back to the edge of the roof. He was in black tactical gear with matching body armour and he and Wollerton had camouflaged their faces, so it would have been difficult to spot him, but he took no chances as he moved into a prone position behind the balustrade.

He aimed the muzzle of the launcher at a network of pipes on the roof of the building opposite, compensating for the gentle October breeze, and squeezed the trigger. A compressor in the barrel of the launcher sent the grappling hook flying over the street between the two buildings, and it took a length of 7 mm Kevlar line with it, uncoiling from a chamber beneath the barrel. The grappling hook landed in the network of pipes and the line went slack. Pearce took the line to an anchor point he'd attached to a girder that protruded from the roof. He looped the line into a ratchet and worked it taut.

By the time he'd returned to the edge, Wollerton was waiting with a couple of pulleys, and their gear bags, which were attached to a third pulley that had already been put on the line. Pearce looked at the top floor of the building opposite, and signalled they weren't being watched. Wollerton sent the bags across the line and they zipped down to the other rooftop. Pearce slung an MP7 that had been fitted with a suppressor over his shoulder, positioned his pulley on the line, clipped into the karabiner on his harness, and stepped off the roof. His heart raced and his breathing accelerated as he sped towards

One London Wall. When he'd cleared the building line, he hit the quick release on his harness and dropped onto the roof. Wollerton followed and hit the deck a few seconds later.

'We're across,' Pearce told Leila, as he and Wollerton hurried to grab their gear bags. 'Moving in.'

Chapter 83

'You know you'll lose,' Alexis remarked. 'You're ants. Nothing more than an irritation.'

'Do you want me to gag you?' Leila asked without turning around. 'Or maybe you want me to hit you again?'

The Syrian troublemaker was sitting at one of the computer terminals in the warehouse on Conlan Street, furiously trying to shut down the power and Internet access of One London Wall.

Did they think Lang was an amateur?

'Did it hurt?' Alexis asked. 'When you lost your child?'

That got the Syrian's attention. She looked round with hatred in her eyes.

'Did it hurt when you murdered your father?'

'Is that intended to wound me?' Alexis asked. 'We have to be prepared to make sacrifices. He knew that and he was willing to give his life for the cause.'

'You keep telling yourself that,' Leila said. 'If that's what it takes for you to sleep at night.'

Alexis smiled. This woman thought she knew her, but Leila Nahum was judging her by her own tiny perspective, her understanding of the world limited by her own narrow experiences. She couldn't possibly understand the world as Alexis saw it.

'I'm not as subtle or nuanced as Scott,' Leila said. 'I just know evil when I see it.'

'Evil?' Alexis scoffed. 'Far from it. We want a better world. One of order and tradition where people of different faiths and races remain separated, not intermingled. Look at the violence in your homeland. Muslim against Christian. Non-believer against the devout. Syria was destroyed by the disintegration that comes from the melting pot. Did that make the world better? Does it serve any of us to be mingled together without rules or guidance from God? To be forced to live with those whose ways and customs we don't agree with?'

'The men who murdered my family said similar things,' Leila responded. 'Like I said, I know evil when I see it, and I know when it needs to be stamped out.'

She returned her attention to the computer.

'Evil is a question of perspective,' Alexis said. She knew God or the universe or fate wouldn't have given them all this money and power if it didn't approve of their plans. Leila, Pearce and their associates, on the other hand, had to scrabble in the dirt for opportunity. Was any further evidence of Apostoli's righteousness needed?

Power favours the just, Alexis thought, recalling her stepfather's words as she worked the knot that bound her to the chair.

Chapter 84

Pearce used a shaped charge to blow the lock off the stairwell door, and the mayhem began the moment he moved in.

Staccato flashes of muzzle fire illuminated the dark space and bullets thudded into the wall by Pearce's cheek. He stepped back, took cover and lowered his night-vision scope, which was fitted to a head strap. Wollerton, who was on the other side of the doorway, did likewise. The rooftop immediately came alive in shades of green, and when Pearce looked into the stairwell he saw the shooter, a masked gunman with an infra-red scope, reloading his rifle. Pearce raised his MP7 and shot him in the face before he managed to insert the new magazine.

Pearce signalled to Wollerton and the two of them grabbed their gear bags, moved inside and went downstairs, past the body of the fallen gunman.

'Is the power out?' Pearce asked Leila.

'*Not yet,*' she replied.

'They've done this for us,' Pearce told Wollerton. 'The darkness is meant to make our lives difficult.'

'I love the dark,' Wollerton whispered.

They approached a door marked '17' and Pearce reached into his gear bag for a fibre-optic camera. He slid the fibre under the door and looked at the monitor, which displayed an infra-red image of the corridor beyond. There were three men to the right of the door, and, when he twisted the camera, he saw two to the left. They all wore infra-red scopes.

Pearce signalled two targets to the left and indicated they were Wollerton's. He signed three to the right and indicated he would take them. He pulled a flash-bang from his gear belt, unclipped the safety, and pulled the pin. He opened the door a crack and rolled the stun grenade through the gap, before slamming the door to the sound of gunfire and shouts. Then came a loud bang and a flash of light in the gap beneath the door, and he waited a moment before pulling it open. He crouched round the doorway, and behind him, Wollerton went high. Pearce's targets were struggling to see, blinded by the flash that had been amplified by their scopes. He shot them in rapid succession, and the rapid crack of Wollerton's suppressed MP7 indicated he was doing likewise.

Pearce glanced round to see two bodies further along the corridor. He nodded at Wollerton, and they hurried past the men he'd shot. They went left when they reached a T-junction and saw two men in a small lobby at the end of the corridor. Pearce shot them both before they could raise their weapons.

As the men fell, he and Wollerton split, moving either side of the double doors at the end of the lobby. Light framed the edges of the doors, so Pearce removed his night-vision scope and Wollerton did the same.

If their calculations were right, there would be a dozen men in the open-plan space, all heavily armed. Pearce reloaded his MP7, and looked at Wollerton, whose face was just visible in the faint light bleeding through the gap between door and frame.

His old mentor nodded. They were ready.

'Sitrep,' Pearce whispered into his mic.

'*Almost . . . there . . .*' Leila said, and as she uttered the final word, the frame of light edging the doors vanished. The power supply had been cut.

Pearce heard shouts on the other side of the door, and lowered his scope. Wollerton pulled his down, and gave him a thumbs up, so Pearce reached out a gloved hand and opened the door.

Chapter 85

Leila had succeeded in cutting the building's power and Internet by overloading the local supply, but she had little doubt the Alchemist would have a backup satellite connection. She needed to find some way to neutralize the Alchemist's virus. If he had another way to connect, it would spread through the Zyberian network once they'd launched their update. She'd analysed his code, looking for a way to use his design to neutralize it, but so far she'd failed to come up with anything . . . unless . . .

She'd designed the Ghostlink, an untraceable communicator, to piggyback satellite signals. Anonymous, the activist hacker collective, had once claimed it had developed an encrypted radio that used the old UHF ham packet frequencies, and Leila had applied the same principle to commercial satellite communications. There was a chance she could use the Ghostlink to overload any satellites serving the Alchemist's location, and block him from uploading his virus in case Pearce and Wollerton didn't get to him in time.

Leila got to work, coding a small programme that would make her Ghostlink perform the equivalent of a denial of service attack on the satellites over London. She pulled up the list of satellites in geosynchronous orbit and identified five serving the city.

'You're competent,' Alexis said.

Her plummy voice was enough to set Leila on edge. She'd been silent for a while, but now wasn't the time for distractions. If she spoke again, Leila would gag her.

'You should come and work for us,' Alexis suggested. 'We'd pay you very well.'

Leila turned and fixed her with a sneer.

'We could make sure you're reunited with your sister,' Alexis grinned. 'Hannan, isn't it?'

Leila's anger rose unbidden. *How dare this monster use her sister's name?*

'Better to be reunited than to find her dead somewhere,' Alexis said.

The threat hit home, and Leila went red with fury. She hauled herself out of her chair.

'I'll kill you if you ever—'

'We could help you find her,' Alexis said, cutting her off. 'You have no idea the resources we have at our disposal. We could find her much faster than you can on your own.'

Alexis fixed Leila with a smug grin, which was a provocation too far. Leila threw everything into a punch that almost knocked Alexis over.

'When I'm done here,' Leila said, shuffling back to her workstation, 'you and I are going to get to know each other better.'

Chapter 86

Pearce moved into the large office, which was illuminated by the ambient light of the city. His night-vision scope showed four men ahead of him, their guns sweeping the darkness as they searched for a target. He wondered why they weren't equipped with infra-red scopes like their associates in the lobby, and the moment the thought entered his mind, he got his answer.

There was a blinding flash and Pearce's scope went a painful, glaring white. The lights had come back on. They'd managed to restore power. Pearce lifted his scope and tried to adjust his eyes, but he knew it was too late when he felt strong hands on his arms.

'Scott Pearce.'

Pearce remembered the voice from Seattle. It was the man he'd been hunting, the man who'd killed Brigitte Attali: Elroy Lang.

Pearce's gun was snatched from him and he was marched further into the room.

'Easy,' Wollerton said.

Pearce heard his friend being manhandled and pushed through the room.

'Take a moment,' Lang said. 'Sometimes it can be a struggle to adjust to a new reality.'

The white-out that had overwhelmed Pearce's vision slowly turned to a grey haze, then a fog that blurred everything. He was able to pick out shapes. The Alchemist at a table. Lang standing beside him, armed men surrounding them.

'You've been interesting,' Lang said. 'But our journey together is nearing its end. It only remains for you to tell me who you're working for.'

Pearce's eyes came into focus and he saw Lang nod at one of his men, a squat guy in a tightly fitting suit, who pointed his pistol at Wollerton. The guy closed on Pearce's mentor until the muzzle of his gun was inches away from Wollerton's face.

'Kyle Wollerton, the man who recruited you into MI6,' Lang said. 'You must be old friends. How much does he mean to you?'

Wollerton's stern gaze told Pearce everything he needed to know. *Give him nothing.*

'In less than thirty seconds, the Zyberian system will be upgraded,' Lang said. 'And when the new upgrade goes live, our friend here will install a virus that will make every machine it touches go dark. In a few short moments, most of Britain will be back in the Dark Ages. Then we can really go to work.' He smiled. 'After that, your friend dies if you don't give me the name of who you're working for.'

'*Stay with me, Scott.*' Leila's voice came like a welcome breath in Pearce's ear. '*I'm working on something. Just give me a second.*'

'Why?' Pearce asked Lang.

'When good men do nothing,' he replied, 'you've seen what's become of the world. You've seen the chaos and disorder. The violence and hatred. We need to go back to a time when there was order and certainty, a time of purity. We need a world of simple tradition, of faith, not this decadent carnival that seduces people away from righteousness. Watch in wonder.'

Pearce saw the Alchemist look at Lang, who nodded. The young engineer hit a key on his machine.

'My code will propagate across London and in a few seconds be uploaded to Zyberian's server and spread to the whole country,' he said.

Outside, the first lights started to fail, as the Alchemist's virus travelled across the Zyberian network from node to node, making its way to the West London hub. Building after building went dark, and alarms briefly sounded before their power supplies failed.

Lang smiled, and Pearce felt the bitter sting of failure.

'Get ready,' Leila said via his in-ear receiver.

What for? Pearce wondered. *It's over.*

But it wasn't over. The darkness spreading across the city suddenly stopped a few hundred metres away, and beyond a ragged perimeter the lights stayed on and the city hummed with power and life.

Lang's smile fell. 'What happened?'

The Alchemist checked his machine, and his mood shifted from triumphalism to concern.

'Someone's isolated us,' he said. 'Cut off this part of London with a firewall.'

'*That was me,*' Leila said. '*No data in or out of the Square Mile. They'll move to satellite next, so we've got to stop them. On my count . . .*'

'I'm going to switch to satellite,' the Alchemist remarked.

'*Three . . .*' Leila continued.

Pearce moved his hand to the pouch on his gear belt that contained his knife.

'*Two . . .*'

He unclipped the fastener.

'One.'

'The satellite Internet has gone down too,' the Alchemist said. 'I can't connect to Zyberian.'

Lang looked at the Alchemist in puzzlement.

'Problem?' Pearce asked.

Lang's expression hardened, and he glared at Pearce.

'Kill them,' he said, as the lights went out.

Chapter 87

Leila's heart was racing. She'd managed to access the control unit for the emergency generator and shut it down. She hoped the darkness would give Pearce and Wollerton enough of an edge. Her improvised attack on the firewall followed by the denial of service on the satellites had taken out most of the communication traffic in London, but her attention now turned from stopping the Alchemist to saving Pearce and Wollerton. She only hoped she'd acted quicky enough.

'Scott?' she said into her microphone. 'Scott, are—'

The next word was knocked from her by a heavy blow to the head.

Leila slammed face first into the table and groaned as the world flashed white. Her heart, which had thundered with anxiety for the others, went into overdrive as she realized she was in a fight for survival. She rolled out of the chair a split-second before the butt of an MP7 slammed on the table where she'd been. She turned to see Alexis swing the gun at her, and cursed herself for underestimating the vile woman, as she ducked what would have been a crippling blow.

She shoved the chair into Alexis and followed it, barging her shoulder into the high back, forcing it into Alexis's gut. Alexis gasped as the wind was knocked from her, and the two of them tumbled over.

Leila was dimly aware her hair was wet and guessed she was bleeding from a cracked skull, but she had no time for wounds, and, as she landed on Alexis, the gun clattered across the floor. She set about Alexis with her fists, pummelling the woman furiously. Alexis became every wicked bully who had ever hurt her, and all the fury and resentment that had burned inside for so many years was poured into each blow.

Stunned by the violence, a dazed Alexis found strength from somewhere, and fought back. She caught Leila with a fist to the ear, and knocked her over. Leila rolled onto the floor beside the table, and saw the MP7 inches away. Alexis scrambled to her feet and ran over as Leila dragged herself to the gun. She kicked out, and caught Alexis in the groin. She staggered away, gasping, and Leila grabbed the MP7, but she knew instantly why Alexis hadn't shot her; the gun wouldn't fire because it wasn't loaded.

She heard footsteps and turned to see Alexis running to the Ford Mustang.

'Stop!' Leila yelled, getting to her feet.

Alexis smiled darkly as she jumped in the driver's seat. Leila hurried over to the flight cases, looking for ammunition, as the Mustang's engine growled. The internal sensor on the roll shutter activated as the car moved forward, and the blue metal barrier started to rise.

Leila reached the first flight case and saw a dozen magazines in the bottom. She reached for one, and slid it into the MP7 as she rose, but she was too late. The Mustang roared out of the warehouse and its tyres screeched as it hit the street.

Leila stood, breathless and dizzy, and it took her a moment to come to her senses. She took the gun, hurriedly put a workstation and other gear in a holdall and placed them all in the boot of the Audi Q7.

She eased herself into the driver's seat, wincing as she suddenly became aware of her head injury. She touched the back of her skull and was rewarded with sparks of pain and fingertips covered in blood.

There was nothing she could do about her injury now. She had to leave. With Alexis free, the warehouse was no longer safe, and Pearce and Wollerton needed her help. She pushed the ignition and the engine came to life. Moments later, she was on Conlan Street, racing east.

Chapter 88

Pearce drew his knife and drove it into the chest of the man standing to his right. As he pulled it out and plunged it into the neck of the man to his left, there was a gunshot a few feet away that lit up the darkness, and Pearce saw Wollerton's face, contorted in pain, illuminated by the flash. As Pearce's captors went down crying out in agony, he lowered his night-vision scope and the room came alive.

He saw Wollerton wrestle the gunman who'd had his pistol trained on him. Wollerton had hold of the gun, and the man was desperately trying to cling on to it, despite the bullet wound in his stomach. Pearce drove his blade into the man's back, and he instinctively tried to reach for the wound. Wollerton shot him twice, and lowered his scope as the man fell. He fired over Pearce's shoulder, and Pearce turned to see the man who'd taken the MP7 fall to the floor. Pearce ran over and grabbed his gun and sprayed Lang's men, who were backing away uncertainly in the darkness. He took out four of them, grabbed Wollerton's MP7 from the hands of a dying man, and tossed his partner the gun.

Partially obscured by an interior wall, Pearce saw Lang was hustling the Alchemist towards a window on the far side of the room. The Silicon Valley entrepreneur had his laptop in his hands, and was trying to stuff it into his satchel as he ran.

'Come on!' Lang said. 'We need to get to an Internet connection beyond the firewall.'

Pearce was about to follow when a volley of shots echoed around the room, and he saw muzzle flash beside a pillar on the other side of the office. He returned fire and tore the pillar to shreds. One of Lang's men staggered out from behind the wreckage, dropped his gun and fell to his knees.

Wollerton groaned, and Pearce saw his friend had been hit in the side, just by his kidneys, at a spot where their body armour was weakest. Blood showed up as a darker shade of green on his scope.

'How bad is it?' Pearce asked.

'I'll live. Come on, let's move.'

As they went towards the window, Pearce watched with horror as Lang pushed the Alchemist out. Pearce raised his MP7 as Lang moved to follow.

'Freeze! Don't move!'

Lang ignored him and stepped off the edge of the building.

Pearce ran over to see an evacuation chute, once-popular emergency measures pioneered after 9/11. Lateral pressure against the sides of a semi-flexible, collapsible tube enabled evacuees to execute a controlled descent to the ground.

Pearce slung his MP7, raised his scope, jumped into the chute, and pressed his hands and feet against the flexible polymer as he dropped seventeen storeys. He raced towards the ground, gathering tremendous speed, as he tried to close the distance between him and Lang. He fell out of the end of the tube, six feet above the pavement, and immediately rolled clear as he came under fire. He pressed himself to his knees and replied with a volley from his own gun. He saw

Lang on a walkway to his left, beyond a brick wall that separated them. As Pearce's bullets hit the wall, Lang ran for cover round the corner of the building, pistol in hand.

Pearce heard a loud thud behind him and turned to see Wollerton sprawled on the pavement. He was in bad shape and Pearce ran over and crouched at his side.

'Go on,' Wollerton said. 'I just need a moment to catch my breath.'

Blood was pooling from the wound in his side.

'Don't let him get away, Scott. Don't let this be for nothing.'

Wollerton fixed Pearce with an uncompromising stare.

'Go!'

Pearce nodded and set off at a sprint.

Chapter 89

Pearce raced across the service area along the side of the building. He reached the wall and jumped to grab the top of it. He hauled himself over it and came under fire the moment he hit the ground on the other side. The six men who'd been patrolling the building perimeter were shepherding Lang and the Alchemist into a tunnel to the east of the building, but a couple had stayed back to deal with Pearce.

He crouched and replied with his MP7, and shot his two assailants dead. The others urged Lang and the Alchemist further into the tunnel, and across the dual carriageway, towards an archway that would take them into the Barbican complex. Pearce pressed the stock of his MP7 to his shoulder and targeted the rearmost men, shooting first one, then the other, as the rest of the group made it into the archway.

As the men fell, Pearce got to his feet and sprinted into the dark tunnel, heart thundering unsteadily, breath shallow, senses alert. He reached the archway and sensed movement. One of Lang's men stepped out from behind a wall and brought a pistol round to Pearce's chest. Pearce sidestepped the shot, which echoed off the walls, and punched the man in the face. He stepped back and shot the man in the chest, then sprinted into the archway as the man dropped, pawing at his bullet wounds.

Pearce bounded up a flight of stairs, and saw movement above him as the last of Lang's men emerged from behind a wall and raised his gun. Pearce shot him in the leg and kept firing as he adjusted his aim along the man's body. The gunman cried out, fell forward and tumbled down the stairs.

Pearce ran past him and, when he reached the top of the stairs, he turned onto a raised walkway that led into the Barbican complex, a sprawling concrete estate that included high-rise apartment blocks, houses, theatres, cinemas and museums, all of which were shrouded in the darkness that had engulfed every building for blocks in all directions. Pearce saw Lang and the Alchemist twenty yards ahead, running towards an alleyway that led to a large courtyard. Lang looked round, and even at a distance Pearce sensed the man's fear. Pearce stopped running, raised his MP7, took aim, and opened fire.

The Alchemist went down, hit twice in the back. He wailed and tried to reach the wounds, but it was no use, and a moment later he fell onto his face. Pearce could not allow the escape of a man capable of inflicting such catastrophe on the world.

Lang tried to grab the Alchemist's satchel, but Pearce fired a volley into it, destroying whatever was inside. Lang moved quickly and vanished into an alleyway that led to the courtyard.

Pearce ran on. He'd taken nearly everything from Lang.

Now he would take the one thing he had left.

Chapter 90

Pearce sprinted along the concrete walkway, heading for the alley. When he rounded the corner, he was forced back by pistol fire. He replied with a volley from his MP7, but Lang had already gone, so Pearce raced on. He heard sirens coming from every direction, echoing around the dark, deserted streets.

Pearce ran through the alleyway and emerged into the large courtyard that connected many of the Barbican's buildings. He looked in every direction, but saw no sign of Lang, so he headed towards the nearest set of stairs, assuming Lang had prioritized escape. Pearce hadn't gone more than a couple of paces when Lang stepped out from behind a column and levelled his pistol at Pearce's head. Pearce responded instinctively and lashed out with his MP7, knocking the pistol from Lang's hand.

The gun clattered across the ground, but before Pearce could get a shot away, Lang grabbed the muzzle of the MP7 and twisted it out of Pearce's hands. Pearce pulled the magazine from the stock and Lang only managed to fire the chambered round, which cracked like thunder and echoed around the concrete maze of the Barbican, long after the bullet had flown wide, missing Pearce's head by inches.

Lang smiled, trying to appear confident, but Pearce saw

fear and bravado. He threw the empty MP7 over a railing that overlooked the street below, and Pearce heard it hit the pavement two floors down.

Lang squared up to Pearce. 'Let's see if you're as good as they say.'

Pearce took the measure of the man. Fast, strong and proficient, but arrogant and devoid of the thing that would give Pearce an edge: his hunger for revenge.

Pearce stepped to meet Lang and raised his hands in a Muay Thai boxing stance, more open than Lang's traditional boxer's positioning. They circled one another, throwing punches to gauge distance and feel each other out.

Lang startled Pearce with a vicious combination of kicks that caught him off guard. He blocked with his shins, knees and elbows, but two hit home, both to his right side, and when Lang backed off, Pearce was left feeling as though a couple of his ribs were broken.

Every breath he took was agony, but Lang didn't let him catch many. He sensed the advantage and unleashed a flurry of rapid punches, driving his fists at Pearce's head and body. Pearce blocked him and replied with a knuckle punch to Lang's temple that left him reeling. Pearce knew the best way to handle an adversary this dangerous was to get him on the ground, and he followed the debilitating blow with a finger jab to the windpipe, and when the man instinctively raised his hands to his throat, Pearce hit him with a lightning-fast flurry of punches to his solar plexus. He doubled over, and Pearce elbowed him in the neck, before stepping back to deliver a roundhouse kick to the side of Lang's head. Lang staggered, but didn't go down, so Pearce ran at him and barged his shoulder into him until his back hit the railings. Lang tried to fight back, but Pearce ignored the blows to his back, lifted the man up and over the railings, and threw him off the walkway.

Lang cried out as he fell, and Pearce watched him hit the pavement head first. There was a sickening crack and Lang fell silent. His body settled on the pavement beside Pearce's gun.

Elroy Lang was dead.

Chapter 91

Pearce staggered down the stairs, moving as quickly as his battered body would allow. Some people said there was no satisfaction in revenge, but he felt a sense of closure as he approached Lang's body. He couldn't bring Brigitte back, but the man who'd killed her had paid the ultimate price. He searched Lang's body and took his phone, wallet and a set of keys. Pearce grabbed his MP7 and ran along the street, retracing his steps through the tunnel, back to One London Wall. A police car sped directly towards him from the direction of Moorgate. It was followed by another, and yet another, sirens blaring, lights flashing, engines growling. Pearce ran to the wall that separated street level from the service area, climbed over and lowered himself down. His ribs stabbed him, and his body became a patchwork of agony as the adrenalin ebbed away.

There was no sign of Wollerton, and the police were getting close, so Pearce ran along the front of the buildings towards Wood Street. As he passed a doorway, he heard a weak cough. He stopped and raised his MP7 towards the shadows. Wollerton stepped out of the darkness, face pale, breathing fast and shallow, hand clutching the gunshot wound. He wore a thin smile.

'I don't look that bad, do I?'

Pearce shook his head, but he was scared for his friend.

'Job done?' Wollerton asked.

'Job done,' Pearce confirmed. 'Come on.'

He supported Wollerton and the two of them walked around the corner as the police cars screeched to a halt on the street behind them.

'Lyly,' Pearce said into his mic. 'We need a route out. Police are deploying to the location. They'll have a cordon soon.'

There was no reply.

'Kyle is wounded. We could really use a way out.'

'*I'm on my way,*' Leila replied, her voice so very welcome. '*Where are you?*'

'Wood Street, behind London Wall,' Pearce replied.

'*Meet me on the corner of Wood Street and Cheapside,*' she said. '*I'll be there in five.*'

'Copy that,' Pearce replied.

He dumped his gun in an industrial bin behind the office block, and helped Wollerton out of his body armour. He took his off too, and threw it all in the bin. Moments later, they were heading south on Wood Street, leaning on each other like a couple of matey drunks.

'How did he go?' Wollerton asked.

'Painfully,' Pearce replied.

Wollerton nodded approvingly. 'And the Alchemist?'

Pearce didn't reply, but his sombre expression spoke for him.

'You did well,' Wollerton said, but Pearce didn't feel that way.

Farida was dead. Mary and the members of White Fire had been manipulated into discrediting their own movement, and London was littered with the bodies of those Pearce had killed.

A few minutes later, they arrived at Cheapside, one of the principal routes through the City, and they loitered for a while, hugging a dark doorway, until Leila arrived in the Audi.

Pearce helped Wollerton into the back and staggered round to get in the passenger seat.

'Lang is dead,' he said, as Leila pulled away.

She nodded, but Pearce knew her well enough to sense something was wrong. When he looked more closely he saw her face was bruised.

'Alexis escaped,' she revealed. 'I'm sorry, Scott. I don't know how it happened.'

'It's OK,' Pearce replied, but even as the words left his mouth he knew they were a lie.

It was clear Alexis was a senior figure in Apostoli, and her escape was a setback. But that was tomorrow's worry. Pearce's work was done for today.

'I called our employer. He's arranged medical treatment on Harley Street. Somewhere discreet,' Leila revealed, and Pearce breathed a little easier.

Alexis and her toxic network would wait for another day. Tonight was a time for the three of them to heal, and as the car made its way west through London's quiet streets, Pearce found himself nodding off, and despite his best efforts to resist, he was soon asleep.

Chapter 92

The Harley Street doctor had told Pearce his ribs were fractured, but there wasn't much he could do for him. He'd removed the field bandage Pearce had applied to his shoulder and dressed the knife wound properly. Pearce had waited until he knew Wollerton was going to pull through before leaving for Pelcomb Cross in Wales. He'd bought a red CBR 600 and relished opening up the throttle on the curving country lanes as he put London and vengeance far behind him. He shouldn't have been thinking about Mary Knight, but he was. He wanted to explain himself and help her understand that he hadn't been using her. He wasn't sure whether that was true, but he felt he had to see her and try to put his thoughts into words. She was an idealist who'd been manipulated, and was perhaps less of a villain and more of a victim in all this. She deserved his sympathy and respect.

Pearce had learned a great deal from her and the other members of White Fire, and even though he disapproved of their methods, he supported their cause. He was troubled by where the world might go if governments didn't step up their measures to combat climate change. Would the people of White Fire be justified in their measures then? He smiled at his hypocrisy. A few hours ago, he'd killed a number of men without legal justification. He was in no position to judge others.

Pearce rode through Pelcomb Cross, past the petrol station and down the tree-lined road to the place Mary had called Sanctuary. When he arrived, the evening sun was shining through the trees and he turned onto the drive to find the gates open and the gate house seemingly deserted.

He cruised along the driveway, through the trees, tried not to look at the spot where Farida had died, and slowed when he reached the large parking area in front of the main house. The vans, campers and yurts had all gone, and the place was empty and still. The house had the air of a building that hadn't been inhabited for a long while, but it had only been a matter of days since Pearce had escaped. He stopped near the front door, dropped the kickstand, dismounted and removed his helmet. He looked around, trying to figure out what had happened. Had they been worried they'd be arrested? As far as Pearce was aware, the police hadn't tied White Fire to any of the more serious crimes.

Pearce was looking out over the paddock, remembering when he'd come down from his ibogaine trip, picturing an alternate life for himself away from all the violence, when he heard a noise. He turned to see Martin, the gatekeeper, emerge from the main house.

'What do you want?' he asked.

'I was looking for Mary,' Pearce replied.

'Hunter Grey has gone,' Martin said. 'She's gone. They're all gone.'

'Do you know where?'

The old man shrugged. 'They're just gone.'

'If you ever see her again, will you tell her I came to find her?' Pearce said.

Martin eyed Pearce for a moment and then said, 'Try the Prophet.'

Pearce nodded. 'Thanks.'

He got back on his bike, put his helmet on, started the engine, and left the White Fire Sanctuary behind him.

The bike chewed the miles to Wolf's Castle, and he reached the science park in under an hour. He rode through empty streets and felt the stillness of abandonment. The park was deserted, or so he thought until he approached the main building, where he saw Mary and Jacob emerge carrying boxes to a waiting campervan.

Mary was surprised to see Pearce, and hurried to deposit her box. He pulled to a halt, dropped his kickstand, and removed his helmet.

Jacob watched him uncertainly until Mary nodded at him. 'It's OK, Prophet. I'll be OK.'

'I'll be inside if you need me,' Jacob told her, placing his box next to hers in the back of the van.

'Thank you,' she replied, as he withdrew.

Pearce dismounted as she walked towards him. She took his hands.

'You're leaving,' he remarked.

She nodded. 'Our time here is done. We were used. Even if they were willing to keep funding us, I couldn't in good conscience take their money. Not after all this. Not knowing what I know.'

Pearce couldn't help but admire her. 'Where will you go?'

'Cursor has a farm on the Isle of Mull. The others have gone on ahead with him. Prophet and I are just gathering his research so he can continue his work,' she replied. 'You could come with us. We could live a quiet life away from the world.'

Pearce was tempted. A quiet life with this beautiful, intelligent woman would be more than most people could dream of.

'People like you and I aren't built for quiet lives,' he said.

She smiled, but welled up, and he wiped a tear from her eye. 'You're right, of course,' she responded. 'We know too much. We know the world needs saving.'

'Ready?' Jacob asked, emerging from the building with another box.

Mary nodded and kissed Pearce, before backing towards the van.

'If you ever change your mind,' she said as she climbed into the driver's seat.

Jacob deposited his box, closed the side door, and jumped in the passenger seat, as Mary started the van. She smiled at Pearce and drove away. He watched them until they were gone, and spent every moment regretting his decision.

Chapter 93

Alexis wasn't used to failure. Black Thirteen had been thwarted, but the failure had been her father's. She'd taken decisive action to stop the rot from spreading, and had drawn a line under the affair as far as Apostoli was concerned. Pearce had broken the Red Wolves, but the failure had fallen on Elroy Lang, who, it appeared, had overestimated his own abilities, while misjudging Pearce. Alexis had been tainted by his failure, and felt shame as she entered Kazan Cathedral in St Petersburg. Gold shone everywhere, and painted reliefs of saints greeted her wherever she looked. The magnificent building had been a place of worship for the righteous and worthy for more than two centuries, and Alexis didn't feel as though she fit either category as she walked to the golden gates that stood in front of the centrepiece. The cathedral was empty save for a lone, devout figure, who kneeled at an altar beside the centrepiece.

Markus Kral was praying, and Alexis knew better than to interrupt him. His faith was as real to him as his arm, and an attack on his faith was an attack on his person. His devotion was the reason he'd spent most of his adult life working to restore the primacy of God in the Christian nations who'd lost their way. While some in Apostoli were motivated by politics, ambition or money, Alexis shared Kral's purity of intention. The Bible foretold Rapture and the devout must do whatever possible to hasten it.

When Kral lifted his head and made it clear his devotions were at an end, Alexis approached. She adjusted her veil to make sure it covered her hair, and he smiled at the respect evidenced by the gesture.

'Alexis, my dear,' he said, rising from his knees.

'I'm sorry, Professor Kral,' she responded.

'There's no need.' He raised his hand and smiled. 'We try many things in life. Some succeed. Most don't.'

'Elroy is dead. The Alchemist too. His technology died with him.'

'I know,' Kral said.

Of course he knew. Few events of any importance happened anywhere in the world without Kral being made aware.

'Elroy's loss will be felt by us all. I have prayed for him.'

'He will be thankful for your devotion,' Alexis responded. 'May it help guide his journey in the afterlife.'

'It seems he suffered at the hands of the man who thwarted us in Hazelmere Darke and Seattle.'

'Scott Pearce,' Alexis replied.

'How do you think we should handle him?' Kral asked.

The question only had one answer.

'We should send him to join the Frenchwoman, Attali, in hell,' Alexis replied.

'Such a place should not be spoken of in such a place,' Kral said, gesturing at the cathedral. 'But you are right. Damnation awaits him and those who stand at his side.'

'Let me redeem myself,' Alexis said, desperate for the opportunity. 'Let me deal with him.'

'Of course, my dear,' Kral replied. 'I would have it no other way.'

Chapter 94

Two weeks later, after Wollerton had recovered from his injuries, he'd insisted on keeping an appointment with Leila. She'd tried to convince him to go home and spend time with his kids, but he wasn't in the mood to take her advice. Part of her thought he was looking forward to some action after a fortnight of enforced rest.

They travelled on the Eurostar, using false identities provided by Robert Clifton, and returned to the apartment block near the centre of Molenbeek-Saint-Jean. This time, when they rang the doorbell, a man answered and demanded to know who they were. Wollerton kicked the door so hard the lock smashed and the glass behind the ornate metalwork shattered. Tonsi Aboud tried to stop them, but Wollerton forced his way inside and knocked the man down. His family weren't home, so no one witnessed the cowering, pleading man being beaten until he revealed where he'd trafficked Leila's sister.

'Ebstorf,' he said at last. 'A pig farm near Ebstorf. North Germany.'

'If you're lying, we'll be back,' Leila told the bloodied, whimpering man.

He swore on his children's lives in Arabic, promising before God he was telling the truth.

His false piety and presumption with the children's lives infuriated Leila, and she hit him with her new cane so hard she knocked him cold.

'OK,' Wollerton remarked, and they left without saying another word.

She was a step closer to finding her sister.

Chapter 95

Pearce was standing in Huxley Blaine Carter's grand living room in his huge mountain home, admiring the view of the jagged peaks, the grass covering their lower slopes like an emerald stole. It had been three weeks since he'd said goodbye to Mary, and he still thought about her every day. He'd meant what he said, though; he wasn't built for a normal life, and she'd been right, neither of them could rest as long as they knew there was a world that needed to be saved.

'Brigitte would have been grateful for what you did,' Huxley said as he entered.

Pearce wasn't so sure, but he didn't correct the man.

'What can I do for you, Scott?' Huxley asked.

'You lost your right hand,' Pearce said, referring to Brigitte.

He'd hired her when she'd been dismissed by French Intelligence, and she'd run Huxley's operations.

'You offered me a job once. I want in. I want to help you avenge your father's death. I want to take the fight to these people. I want to dismantle their network piece by piece. I want to destroy them.'

'Where would you start?' Huxley asked.

'I analysed the location data from Elroy Lang's phone,' Pearce replied. 'Two months ago, he spent three days at Langley.'

He was gratified to see the billionaire's surprise. He was finally a step ahead of the man, which was a clear indication the nature of their relationship had changed.

'I want to find out what this man was doing at the head-quarters of the CIA, and who invited him there. I want to rip Apostoli apart and I'm going to start there.'

Huxley was nodding slowly, and Pearce held his gaze.

'I want to make them suffer.'

Acknowledgements

I'd like to thank my wife Amy and our three children, Maya, Elliot and Thomas, for their support.

I'd also like to thank my editor, Vicki Mellor, my literary agent, Hannah Sheppard, and my screen agent, Christine Glover. I'm extremely grateful for all the hard work and support from the whole team at Pan Macmillan. I'd also like to express my gratitude to Jot Davies for the wonderful work he did on the *Black 13* and *Red Wolves* audiobooks, and Fraser Crichton for his attention to detail and contribution copy-editing the Scott Pearce books.

I'm particularly grateful to Manda Scott for drawing my attention to the climate emergency, and to Professor Ken Rice for pointing me towards some useful research sources and helping me understand the prospect of runaway. I'd also like to thank reader and book champion extraordinaire Jules Swain for her advice on how paramedics bring a person back to life.

I'm also extremely grateful for all the kind words and support I've had from friends and family, and for the help I've had from so many writers who've generously shared their advice and experiences. I'd also like to thank all the reviewers, librarians, booksellers, journalists and readers who have helped spread the word about my books.

As always, I'd like to thank you, the reader, for giving Scott Pearce, Leila Nahum and the team your attention. I hope you enjoyed the book and that you'll join us for another thrilling adventure.

THE OTHER SIDE OF NIGHT

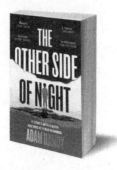

When disgraced former police officer Harriet Kealty
discovers a plea for help in the margins of a second-hand
book, she sets out to unravel a mystery that quickly leads
her to confront some uncomfortable ties to her own life,
including her ex-lover Ben.

Following the deaths of his close friends, Ben became
an adoptive father to their orphaned son Elliot. But Harriet
suspects that Ben knows more about these deaths
than he's willing to say . . .

What starts as a simple investigation becomes something
entirely different in this moving story that will open hearts
and minds as it answers the question: what would you
do for one more moment with someone you love?

'Wonderful' Stuart Turton
'Remarkable' Anthony Horowitz
'Incredible twists' James Patterson

Read on for an extract . . .

Chapter 1

Harriet Kealty had spent almost an hour sitting alone outside the Nantwich Bookshop, and was now nursing her third espresso. She watched the other customers and listened to their conversations as Steve and Denise, the friendly owners of the bookshop, and their staff shuttled in and out, ferrying orders of coffee and cakes. It was a Saturday, so the town centre was busy and the square opposite the crooked Tudor building was packed with shoppers buzzing from one market stall to another.

Harri checked her watch: 11.58. Two minutes off an hour. More than any reasonable person could be expected to wait. But she wasn't a reasonable person. She was desperate to reclaim a life she'd lost a few painful weeks ago. She'd been lured here by hope, and to leave would be admitting it had been extinguished.

But in the end, after another twenty minutes of sitting there with a gnawing sense of inevitability, Harri finally accepted defeat. John Marlowe, the man who'd emailed her, promising she would get her job back if she came to this meeting, had been yet another troll, a liar who felt entitled to waste her time and humiliate her because she'd been so successfully cast as the villain by the local papers.

Another dead end.

She asked Denise for the bill, paid in change, and drifted into the shop. There were tables and chairs arranged between bookshelves, and the hubbub of conversation filled the room. Friends and family bound together by shared experience. She had nothing to keep her company. Ever since that awful night, her life had been one misstep after another. She desperately wanted what all these people had: an ordinary life. She wanted to feel good. Overwhelmed by loneliness, her mind reached, as it had so many times, for Ben. He'd made her feel good for a while, and she was afraid she'd never meet anyone like him again. Self-pity brought tears to her eyes.

Great, she thought. A private humiliation and a public embarrassment. She hurried towards a flight of stairs and a sign that read 'Toilets'.

Her footsteps echoed around the narrow, crooked stairwell, and the sounds of the cafe faded as she emerged into an almost deserted second-hand books section. Cracked spines sliced long runs of other less damaged but clearly used books. Beyond the high shelves, almost directly opposite the top of the stairs, was a corridor that led to the toilets, where she might find a mirror in which she could check her make-up, and the privacy to compose herself. There was only one problem. The old man who stood between her and the corridor. He looked startled, as though her rushed arrival had caught him in some mischief.

'I'm sorry,' she said, fighting for composure.

'Please don't apologize,' he replied, obviously trying to recover his own.

'I didn't mean to startle you.'

He smiled indulgently and his face creased like an unmade bed. 'You didn't. I was just thinking.'

His eyes fell and for a moment Harri forgot her own worries. The man's sadness hit her like a wave. His craggy face was downcast and his eyes were heavy and shining with the prospect of a storm. His mop of grey hair was neatly combed, and he looked as though he was dressed for a date. His tweed jacket, black trousers, and white shirt were well pressed, and his red woven silk tie was bright and clean. If he was on a date, then like her, he had been stood up, because there was no one else around. He was tall, and might once have been handsome, but whatever gifts youth had conferred were long gone. Only a brightness in his eyes hinted at the charisma that might have drawn people to him and the energy he might have had long ago. His slight frame was angled against a supportive ebony walking stick. Harri took a generous guess he was the right side of ninety. She wanted to get past him, but felt awkward as it seemed as though he was expecting a conversation.

'My wife and I fell in love the instant we met. She's gone now, but she's always with me, you know, in all the moments we shared,' he said, and Harri feared he might cry. He took a couple of breaths, and she prayed he would hold it together, because she didn't think she'd be able to stop herself if she saw someone else weeping. 'She loved to read,' he added at last.

He managed a false smile. The world was full of people like him, their best days gone, their glories forgotten. All they loved, everything they'd done, nothing more than memories fading like writing in sand, washed away by the tide of time.

'I'm sorry. It's not long since I lost her and . . .' he trailed off, and they stood in awkward silence for a moment.

'It's all so overwhelming,' he added sadly. 'You take a journey together, and you know everything that starts will have an end, but you can never quite bring yourself to believe it.

Somewhere there's a secret tribe of quiet immortals, right? Some race of souls who never perish. You come to believe you'll find a way to join them, and you push the end from your mind.'

He took a step forward, and for a moment Harri thought he'd reach out and touch her, but he stopped a pace away and settled on his cane.

'It was sudden. Heart attack. We never had the chance to say goodbye,' his voice was cracked with age, but as he spoke of his loss, emotion fractured it further. 'I couldn't save her. It was one of those things. I'm so sorry . . .'

His words drifted to nothing, but his eyes stayed on Harri, before shifting away.

'She was very beautiful, you know? Like you.'

Harri didn't feel at all beautiful. She'd gained six pounds since her dismissal, and even though she wasn't overweight, she felt the extra baggage on her normally slight five-foot six-inch frame. She hadn't been to the salon for months and had her light-brown hair tied in a tail to conceal the tangles and split ends. Her usual wardrobe of suits had been replaced by scruffy trainers, jeans, and T-shirts, and whereas she'd once taken time over her make-up, she could barely muster the enthusiasm for lipstick. She might be many things, but right now beautiful wasn't one of them.

She thought he was just being polite, so she didn't thank him for his dishonesty, and grew increasingly uncomfortable in the beat that followed. She could hear the hubbub rising up the stairs, and longed to be part of the crowd. Fate had thrown her in the path of this broken old man, but she didn't have what it took to fix him. She was just as damaged. Her discomfort must have shown, because his demeanour changed.

'Listen to me.' His voice brightened, but his eyes told her the levity was forced. 'I'm a blathering old fool.'

'Not at all,' Harri said automatically. Her mother had raised her to be polite. 'Death is difficult.'

'If you could know the moment of your end, would you want to?' the old man mused.

She thought about all the bad things that had ever happened to her. Would it have helped to know about them in advance?

'No. No, I don't think I would,' she replied. 'It would hang over me like a cloud.'

'True.' He nodded. 'I promised myself I wouldn't get carried away, that I'd be strong, but it's so hard. I'm so alone, you see. Almost everyone I've ever known is gone. She was my love. She still is. Just being here is so difficult.'

'It's OK. That's normal. In the police we call it survivor's guilt.'

The man bit his lip and cast around the room, as though something in the old books might support him in his grief. He found strength from somewhere.

'You're good and kind. You have a big heart,' he said, and Harri almost broke down in tears. He was a soul in torment and he was trying to be nice to her. 'We all face the same end. Whatever our road, we finish the journey pleading with the void. Begging for just one more moment. But there's never enough time. The relentless turn of the seconds. The ticking clock. That is our enemy. I loved her so much.'

His eyes met Harri's and they shimmered.

'What would you give for just one more moment with someone who meant everything?'

Harri found herself wanting to take the old widower's hand and soothe the pain, but he moved back a half-step and eyed her with the sudden alertness of someone waking from a dream.

'Listen to me casting a shadow over your day. That's not who I am. I'm a bringer of smiles. You know what my wife used to say? "You are my star. You light up the darkest day." Don't you think that's beautiful?'

'Very,' Harri replied.

'That's what I should be doing; lighting up days, not darkening them. I'm sorry I've upset you.'

'Not at all,' she assured him.

'I've wasted your time at the very least. It's most selfish of me. Clinging to moments. Hoarding memories. I'm old. My day is done. Yours is ahead of you and I have no right to waste another second. It's been my absolute pleasure. Thank you for your kindness. Goodbye.'

Harri couldn't suppress a surprised smile when the old man abruptly pivoted around his walking stick and hurried past her. Within moments, he was clanking down the stairs.

She was about to head to the toilet when she noticed a book on the floor. It had been concealed by the man, and lay cover wide, spine broken, like a dead bird. Had he been looking at it when she'd startled him?

Happiness: A New Way of Life.

A woman smiled up from the cover. She looked annoyingly contented. Harri preferred thrillers and would never normally have been interested in such a book, but she was desperate, and if the smiling author, Isabella Tosetti, had just one useful nugget of advice, she'd take it. Harri picked up the book and checked the inner leaf. Fifty pence for a whole new way of life.

Bargain, she thought, and she took the book with her.

Chapter 2

There was a knock at the door, and she put down the book and crossed the small bedroom of the little flat she'd bought when she first moved to Stoke-on-Trent. It was on the sixth floor of a modern building on a quiet back street, not far from the old pot banks that stood to the south of Hanley. Harri's one-bedroom home might have been small, but the big windows in the living room gave her a panoramic view of the city and the emerald countryside beyond. It used to inspire her, but she didn't even glance at it now.

'Who is it?' she asked, pressing her eye to the spyhole.

'Me,' Sabih Khan said.

He was in a tailored suit which clung to his wiry frame, and his hair was as immaculately coiffed as ever, the black waves shining with product.

Harri opened the door for her old partner.

'All right?' he said, lingering on the threshold. 'I thought I'd stop by to see how you're doing.'

'Did Powell send you?' Harri asked, sensing Sabih's reticence.

'No,' he replied indignantly. 'I'm here because—'

She cut him off. 'Because you care?'

'You know, people ask if I miss you, but right now I can't say that I do.'

'Well, you know the way out.'

'I will come in, thank you,' he said, pushing his way past Harri.

She shut the door and followed him through the open-plan kitchen diner to the living room, and she flushed as she suddenly saw her home through a newcomer's eyes. It was a battlefield of misery and the casualties of her war with depression were scattered everywhere: clothes, magazines, unopened post, half-consumed cups of coffee, crumb-covered plates – some relatively recent, others relics from weeks ago. She hadn't felt this low since her relationship with Ben had ended. Harri registered the look on Sabih's face.

'I know what it looks like,' she said. 'But these aren't telltale signs. I've just been busy.'

'Empty bottles, discarded food, unkempt appearance,' Sabih responded, and Harri's hand rose instinctively to straighten her hair. 'None of these are signs of depression. Is that what you're telling me?'

He held her gaze, and they stood in silence as she eyed him defiantly.

'I was just passing,' he said at last. 'I'm not here to intrude on your business. If you say you're fine . . .' he trailed off. 'But if you need help—'

'Listen,' she interrupted. 'You can tell Powell, or anyone else who wants to know, that I'm doing brilliantly and winning at life.'

'I'm sorry, Harri,' Sabih said. 'I let you down. I never thought Powell would go for you like that. I don't know what to say. I wish I could take it back. Do better. Be stronger.'

And just like that he took the angry wind of indignation out of her sails. Harri couldn't cope with kindness. Not today.

She nodded, not trusting herself to reply. She'd thought about that night so many times, and wondered what she could have done differently. Her partner, her friend, was being beaten to death. If she hadn't stepped in to save him, well, he wouldn't be here. In her self-righteous self-pity she'd forgotten his suffering.

'How are you?' she asked. 'The ribs?'

'OK. Still hurts to breathe, and I don't think I'll be setting any track and field records for a while. The body heals. It's the mind that's harder, right? Do I still have what it takes? Will I be the first in next time, or a step behind everyone else?'

She could only imagine how his confidence had been knocked. Her own was shot.

'You'll be the classic fool rushing in,' she remarked.

He didn't look reassured. 'What about you?' he asked. 'How are you doing? Really?'

'I've been better. Some guy wasted an hour of my life today. Emailed me claiming he knew something about the footage of that night. Said I'd get it if I came to meet him in Nantwich. Never showed. I emailed him, giving a few choice thoughts on him wasting my time, but it's probably some troll with a fake account.'

'*Harami*,' Sabih said. 'Powell should have done more to keep your name out of the papers.'

Harri nodded. She'd devoted her life to the police, but none of that had mattered and her boss had hung her out for the vultures.

Sabih's phone rang and he pulled it from his pocket.

'Sorry, it's the guv'nor,' he said. He answered the call. 'Go ahead, guv.' There was a brief pause and Harri imagined Powell rattling off an instruction. 'I'm on my way.'

He hung up and gave Harri an apologetic puppy-dog shrug. 'Sorry. Duty calls.'

Harri felt a pang of envy. A few weeks ago, she would have been going with him.

'Ah, that was insensitive of me. Great body, sharp mind, not so hot on all these complicated human things,' he said, his index finger shuttling back and forth through the air between them.

Harri suddenly felt sorry for him. He'd been beaten and battered physically and psychologically, and he was grieving too. He'd lost a partner.

'Complicated human things?' Harri replied. 'What are you, a robot? Just say, "Let's grab a beer sometime", and leave with a smile on your face.'

'Let's grab a beer sometime,' Sabih said as he backed towards the door. 'You're the best, Harri. A top girl.'

She couldn't resist a smile at his awkwardness.

After he was gone, Harri stood in the little flat for a moment, listening to the distant sounds of the city, where thousands of lives far more productive than hers were being played out. She glanced around the messy room and thought about tidying up, but the brief surge of energy that had risen in Sabih's presence soon dissipated. The mess could wait. She left everything as it was, and returned to her book.

Extract from *Happiness: A New Way of Life*
By Isabella Tosetti

Printed with permission of Vitalife Press

Happiness as Love

Romeo and Juliet. Star-crossed lovers, ill-fated to suffer. A picture of love that's endured to this day. One of pain and sacrifice. Love as tragedy. Alongside this runs a steady stream of novels, television, film and song that tell us love is the most powerful source of happiness.

Death cannot stop true love.

You had me at hello.

You complete me.

And so on.

The world's libraries could be filled with nothing but books on love, and still the poets would think more needed to be said.

Dr Martha McClintock demonstrated what we perceive as falling in love is actually a sense of attraction manufactured by our brain because it has used a combination of visual and olfactory stimuli to gauge that union with the man or woman in question would produce offspring with optimized immune systems. Less star-crossed love, more evolutionary biology. This is true even of same-sex relationships, because the matching of immune systems is blind to prejudice and untroubled by concepts of gender.

We've all heard friends say, 'I don't know what she sees in him,' or, 'He loses his mind when he's around her.'

The obsessive, infatuated lover is a staple of romantic poetry. In addition to manufacturing a powerful sense of attraction to help with evolutionary optimization, our brains increase the chances of mating by shutting down the regions of our brain associated with critical reasoning. Semir Zeki and his colleague John Paul Romaya found that people deeply in love experience temporary and specific loss of brain function whenever they think about their lover. Using brain-imaging techniques, Zeki and Romaya measured a significant deactivation of the frontal cortex. If we could see a person's faults, we'd be less likely to mate with them, so our brains quite literally blind us with love.

Eventually the hormone rush wears off and the brain stops its tricks. Some people wake up one day and wonder what they ever saw in the person lying next to them. Others stay together, and blind love, that evolutionary trap, turns into something else, something profoundly real.

Love can make you blind. It can give you fleeting brain damage, it can cause pain, anguish, and suffering. But when all that is gone, you're left with someone whose life you share. You hope you make each other better. You share experiences. You sacrifice, but each sacrifice must be repaid, or else there is imbalance and exploitation. The most powerful relationship (and always remember why I use the word powerful) is the one that is harmonious. A healthy relationship strikes a note of truth and brings equilibrium to the lives of the lovers. It is through that truth and balance that we find happiness, because without being true to ourselves and those around us, we manufacture an illusory self, and a gap is created between who we really are and who we're pretending to be. If there is no harmony in the relationship, that gap is likely to grow, and it is this gap between the true self and the projection we manifest into the world that is the source of so much unhappiness.

Love should create no gap. It should not force you to manifest any illusion about who you really are. Love that is worthy of the word will be real and true. It will provide fuel for your generator. In ordinary times, love should heal you. It should bring you happiness. If you find yourself in extraordinary circumstances and your world requires sacrifice, make sure it brings you harmony, and through whatever it is you do for the one you love, you must ultimately find balance and that all-important power. A love that helps you be true to who you really are is the most powerful love of all.